TONKO HOUSE
AND
FIRST SECOND

PRESENT

the
DAM KEEPER
BOOK TWO

by
ROBERT KONDO
DAISUKE "DICE" TSUTSUMI

producer / agent
KANE LEE

art lead
YOSHIHIRO NAGASUNA

art
YOHEI HASHIZUME
JJ JAEHEE SONG
KITIKHUN PAN VONGSAYAN

additional art
TOSHIHIRO NAKAMURA   YOHEI TAKAMATSU
ERI ANDO   YOICHI NISHIKAWA   YUI KURITA

graphics
TIM PALMER

production
COURTNEY LOCKWOOD
DAISUKE "ZEN" MIYAKE
KAZUYUKI SHIMADA

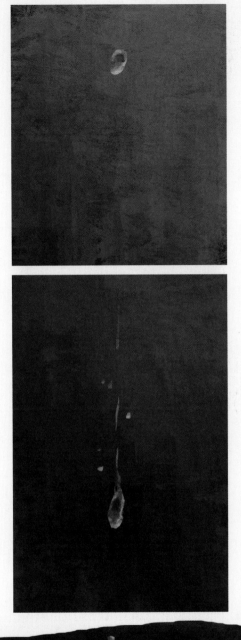

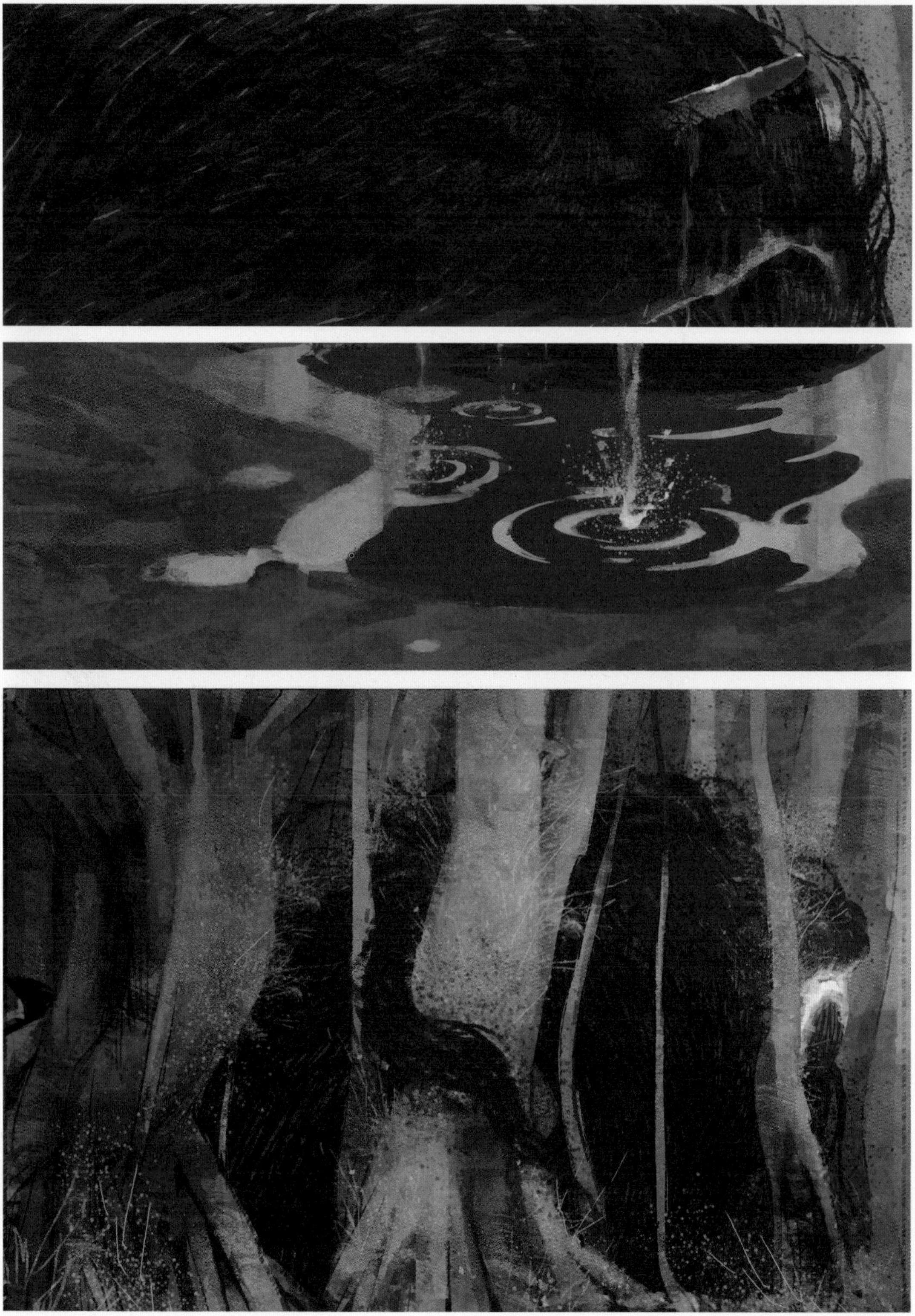

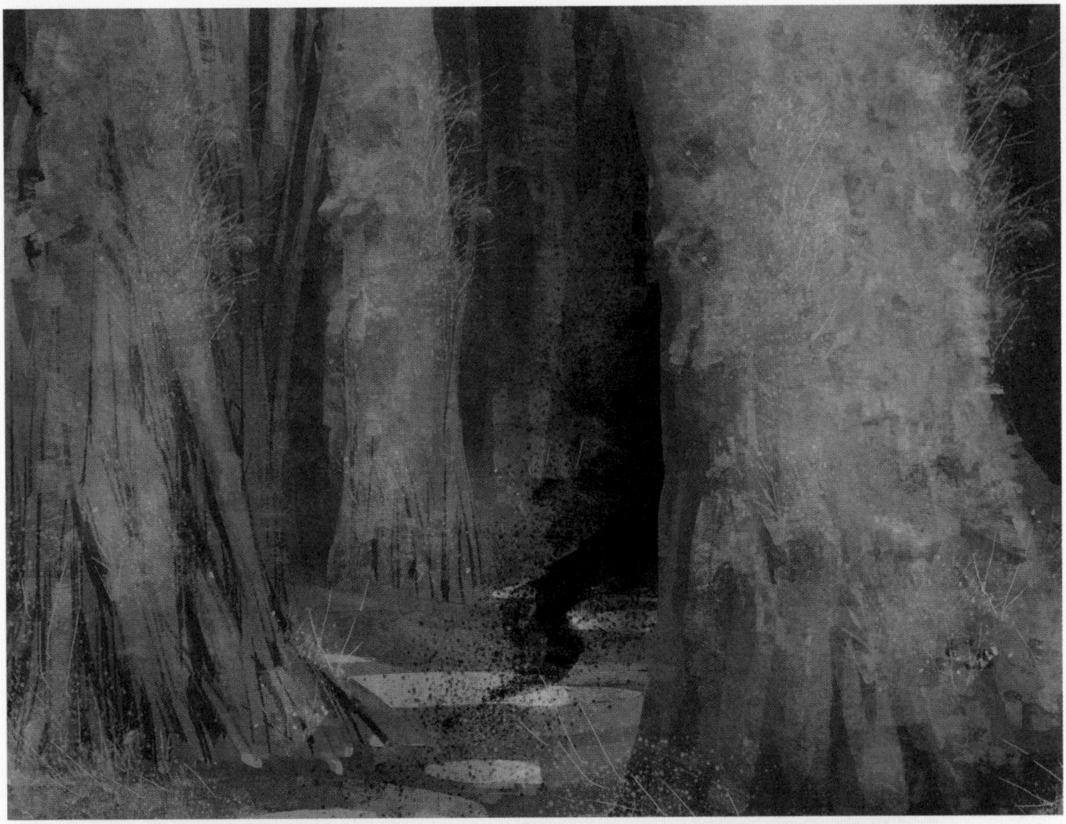

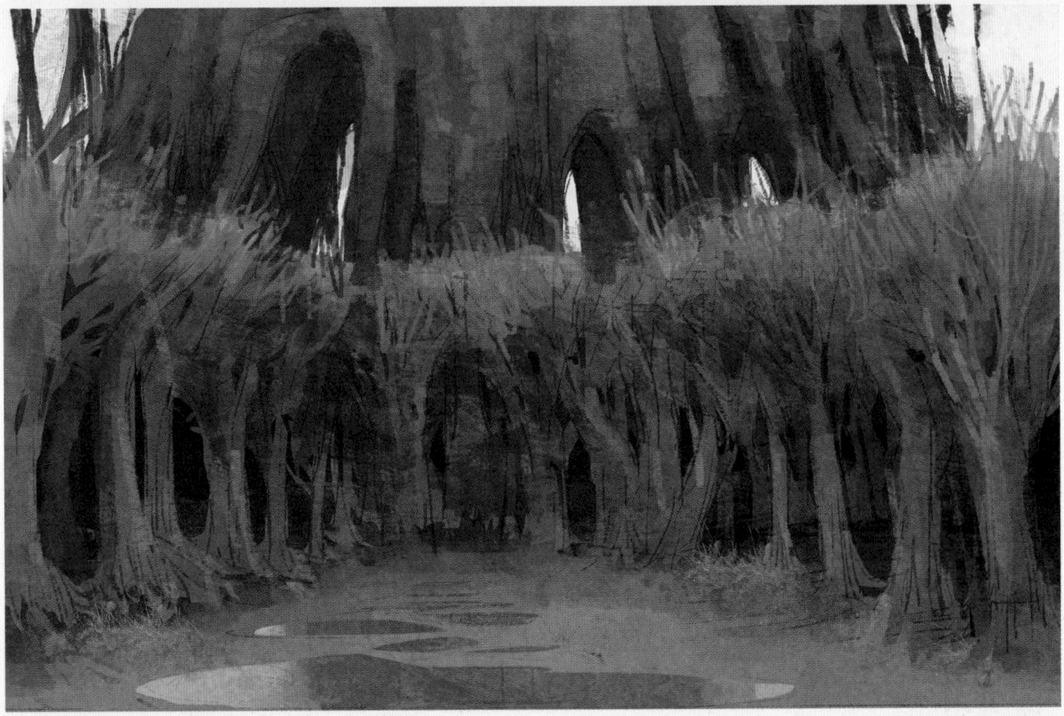

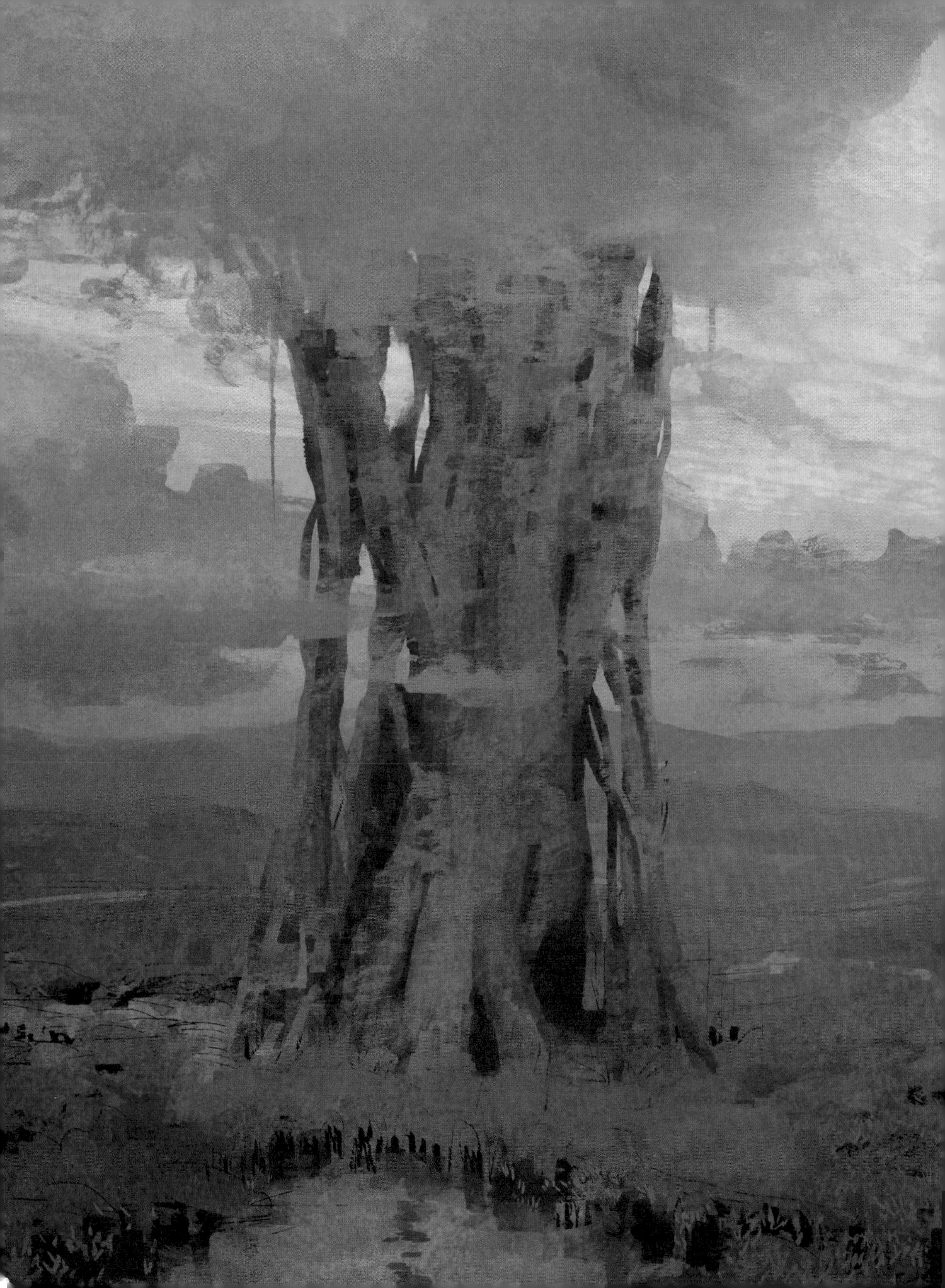

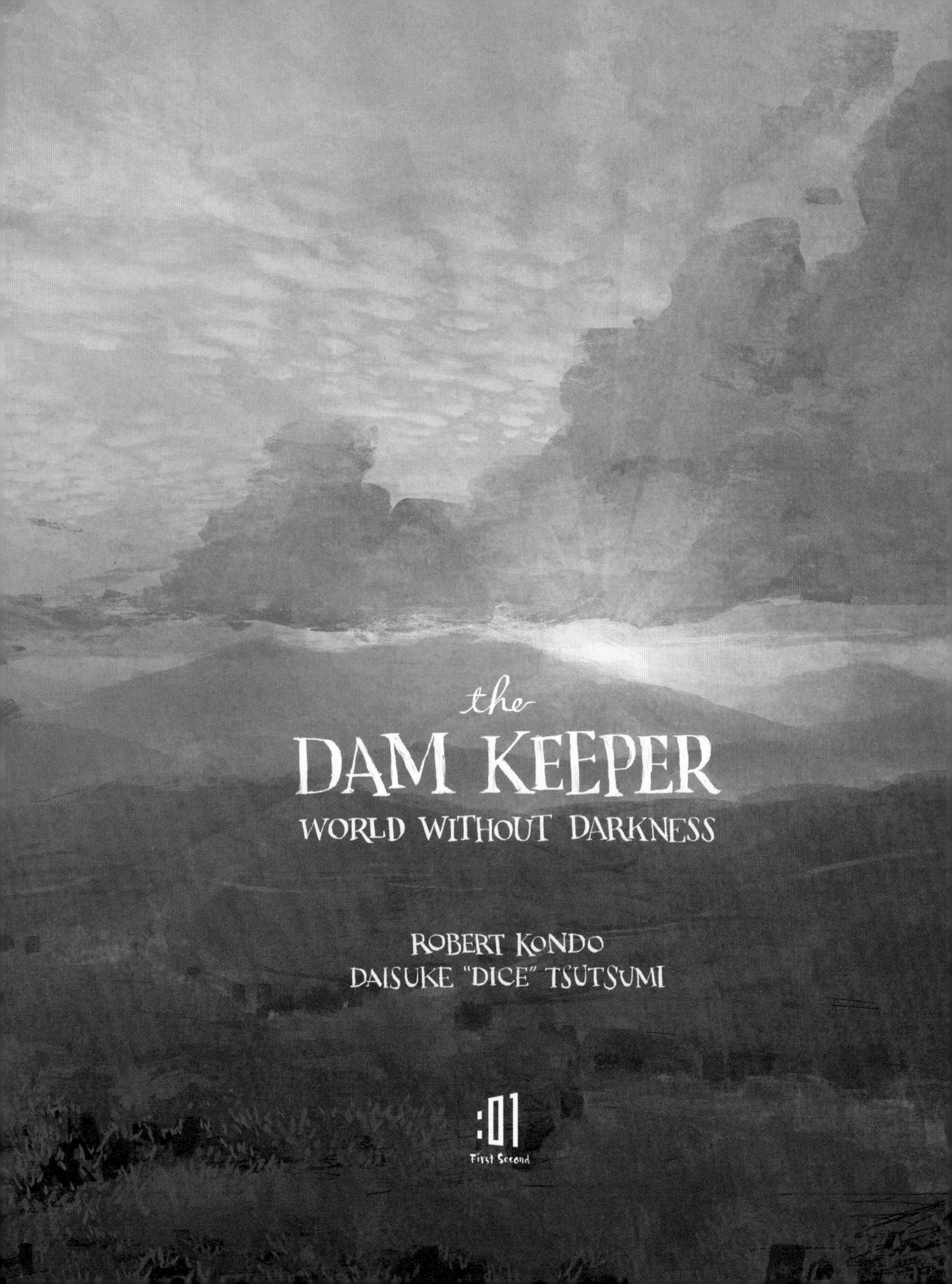

the

DAM KEEPER

WORLD WITHOUT DARKNESS

ROBERT KONDO
DAISUKE "DICE" TSUTSUMI

:01
First Second

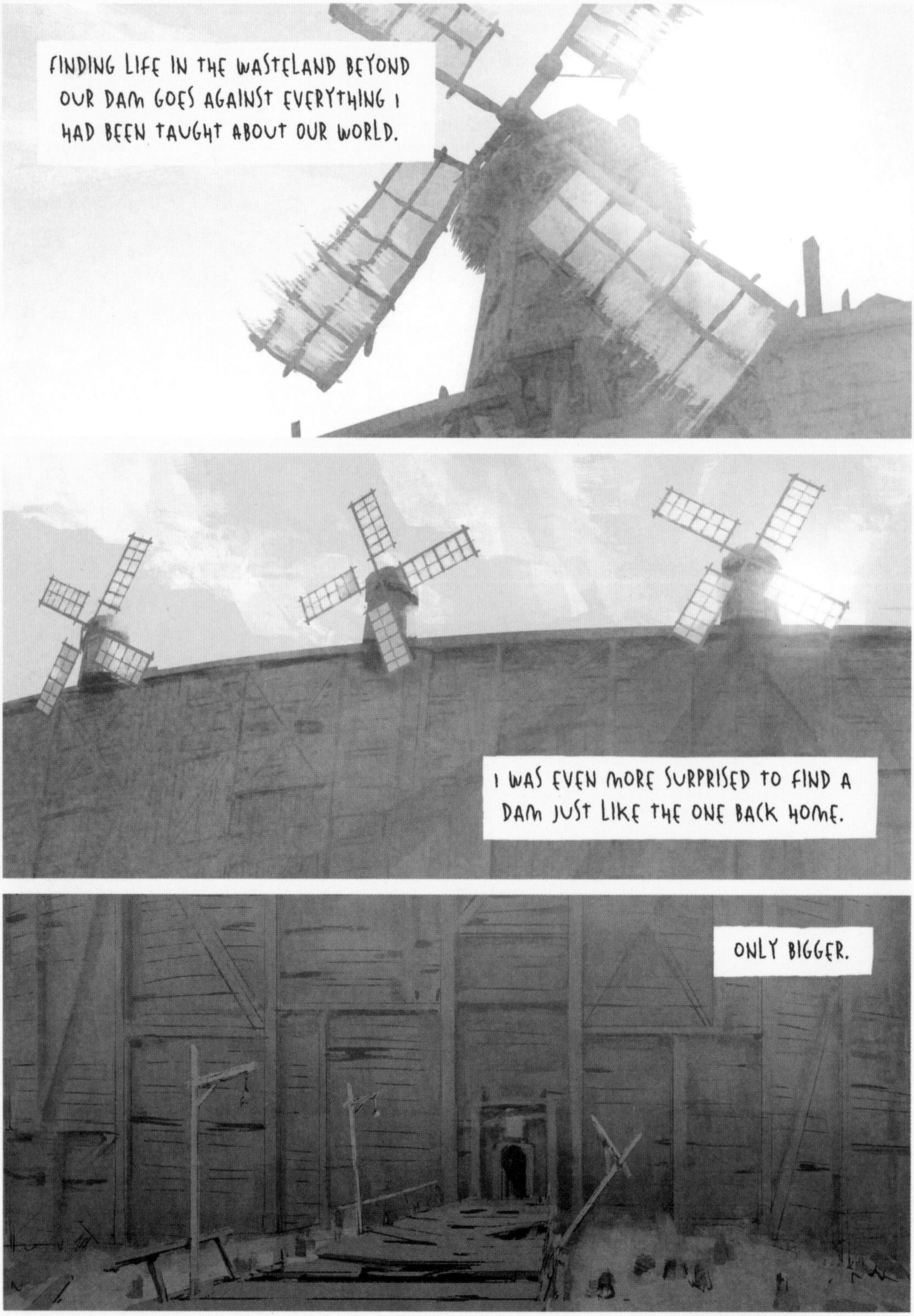
FINDING LIFE IN THE WASTELAND BEYOND OUR DAM GOES AGAINST EVERYTHING I HAD BEEN TAUGHT ABOUT OUR WORLD.
I WAS EVEN MORE SURPRISED TO FIND A DAM JUST LIKE THE ONE BACK HOME.
ONLY BIGGER.

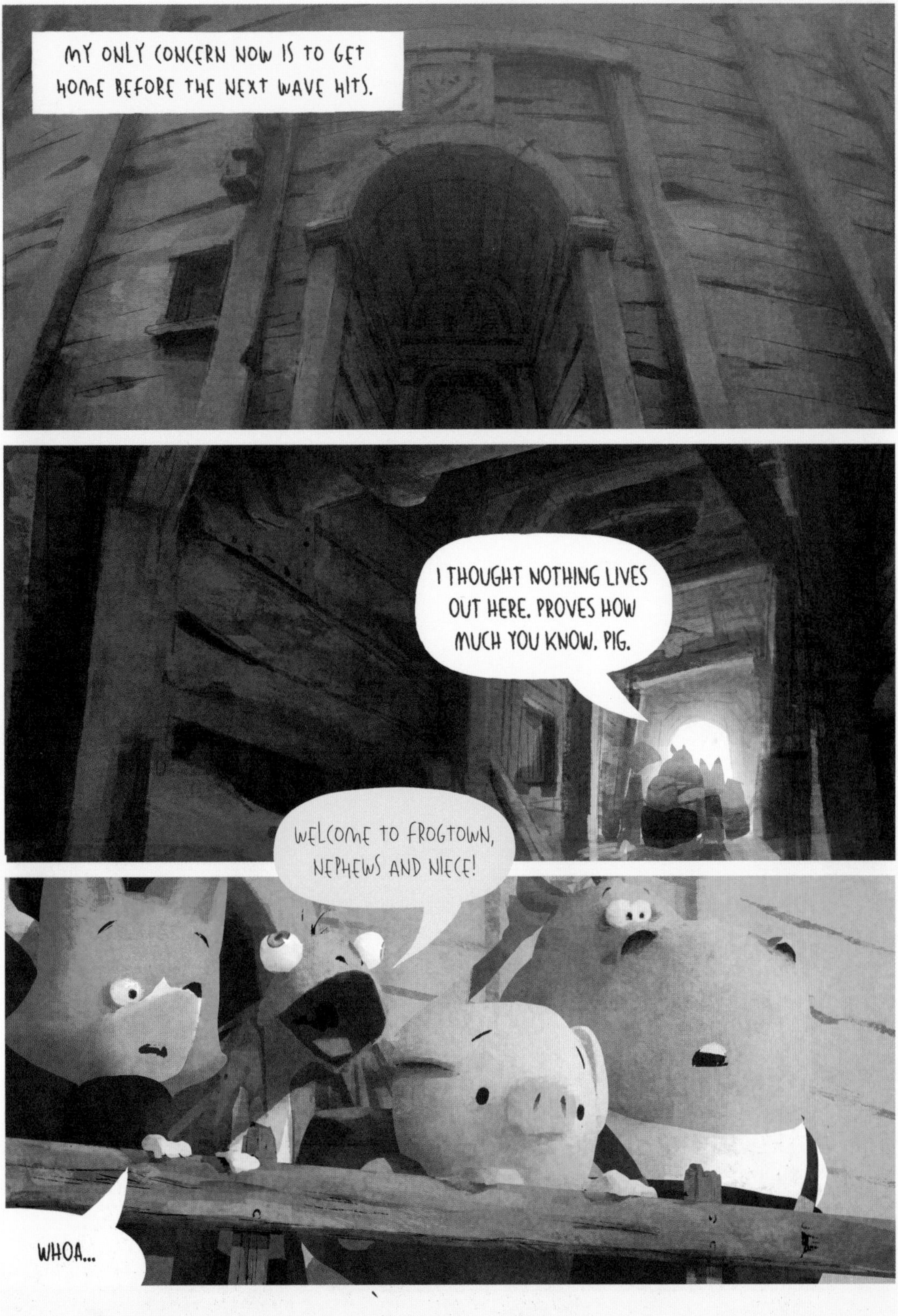
MY ONLY CONCERN NOW IS TO GET HOME BEFORE THE NEXT WAVE HITS.
I THOUGHT NOTHING LIVES OUT HERE. PROVES HOW MUCH YOU KNOW, PIG.
WELCOME TO FROGTOWN, NEPHEWS AND NIECE!
WHOA...

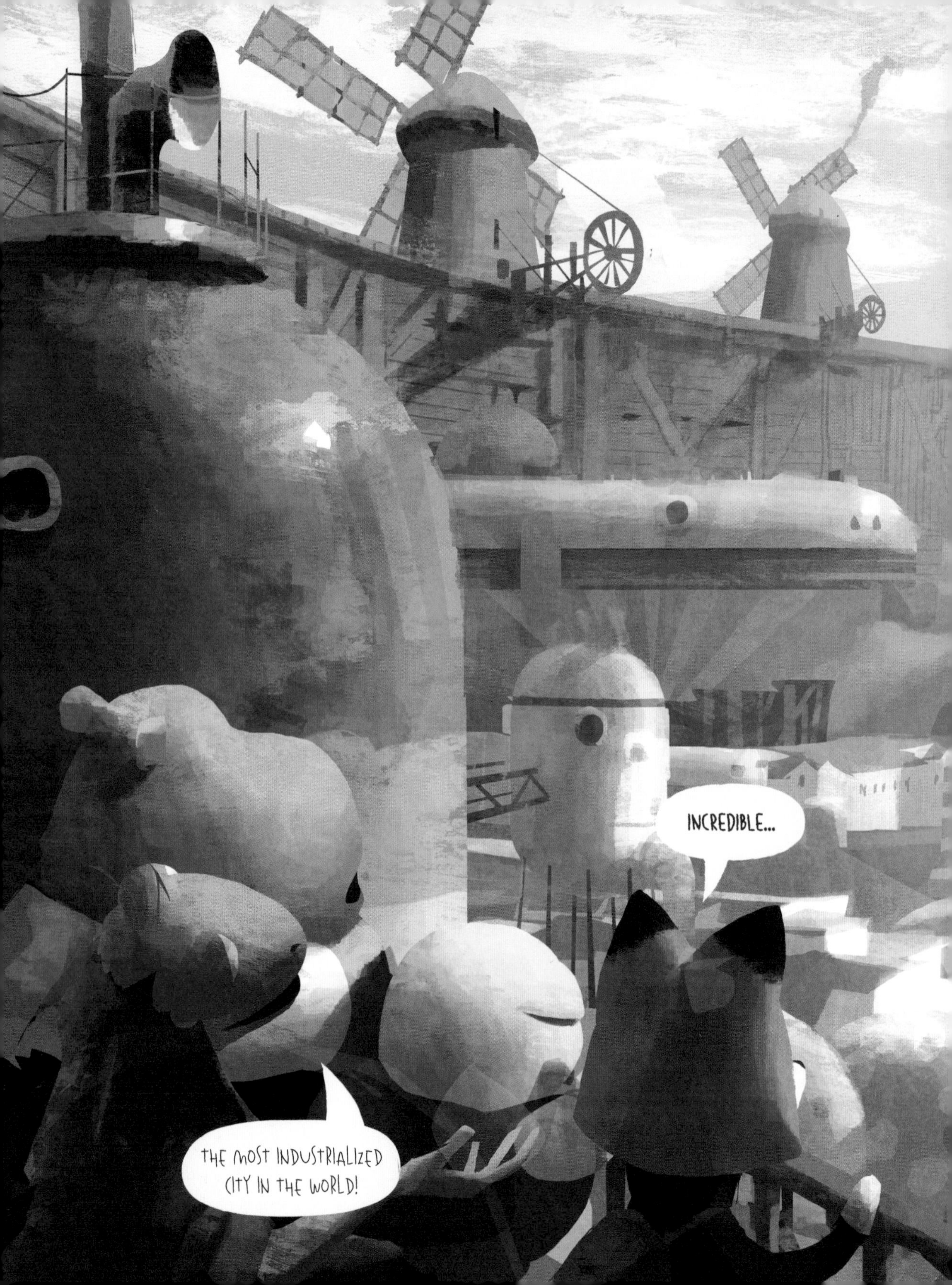
INCREDIBLE...
THE MOST INDUSTRIALIZED CITY IN THE WORLD!

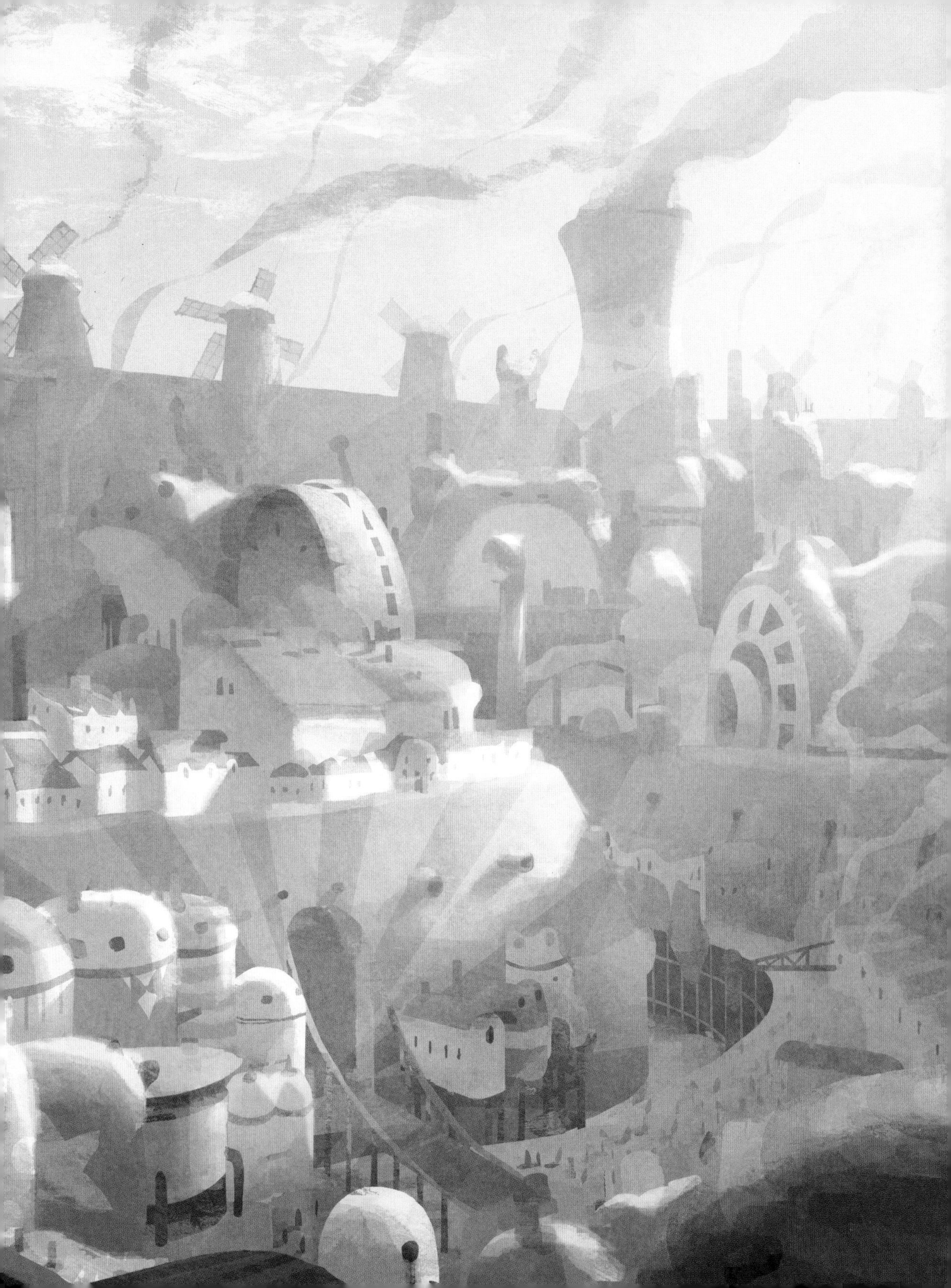

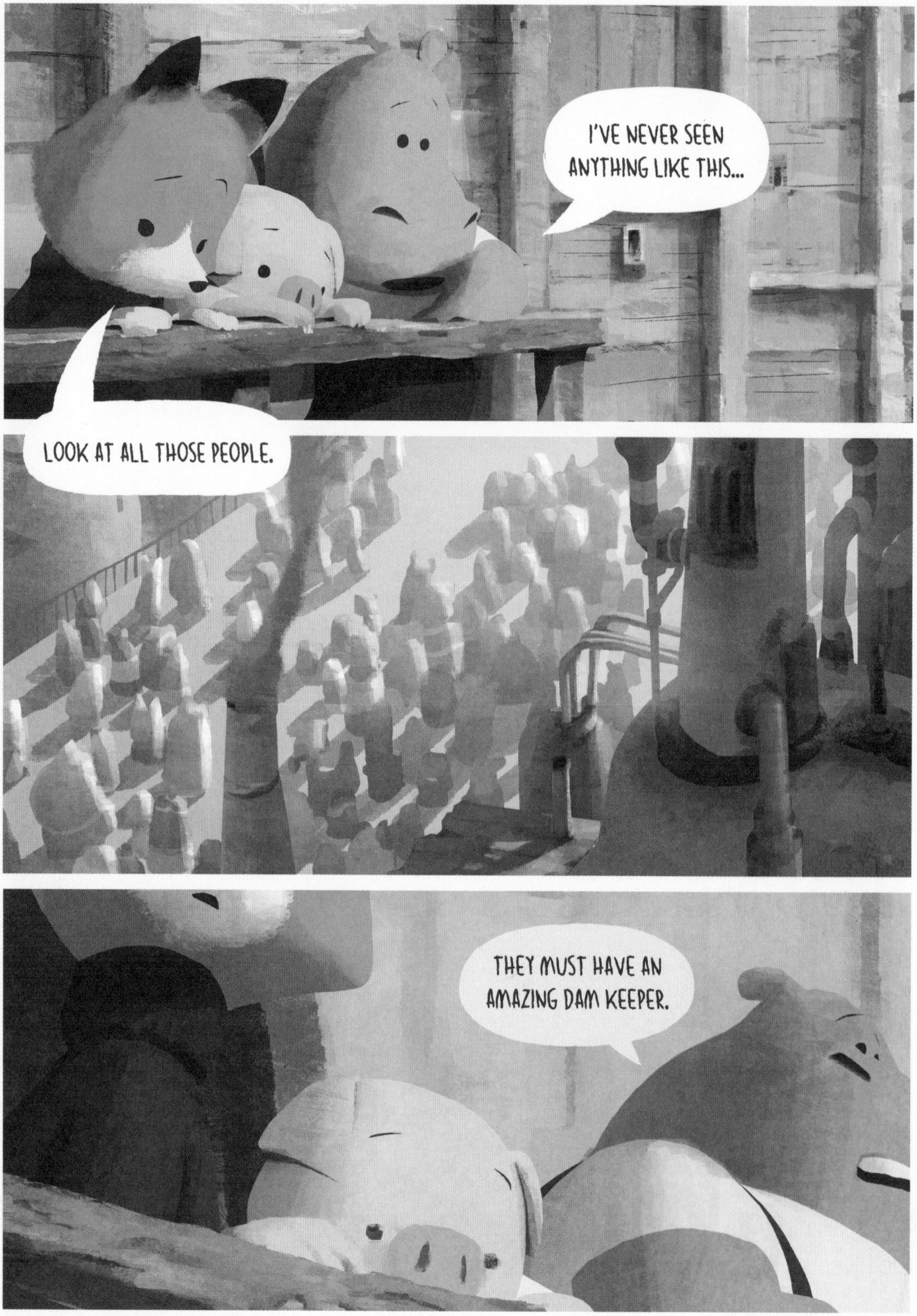
I'VE NEVER SEEN ANYTHING LIKE THIS...
LOOK AT ALL THOSE PEOPLE.
THEY MUST HAVE AN AMAZING DAM KEEPER.

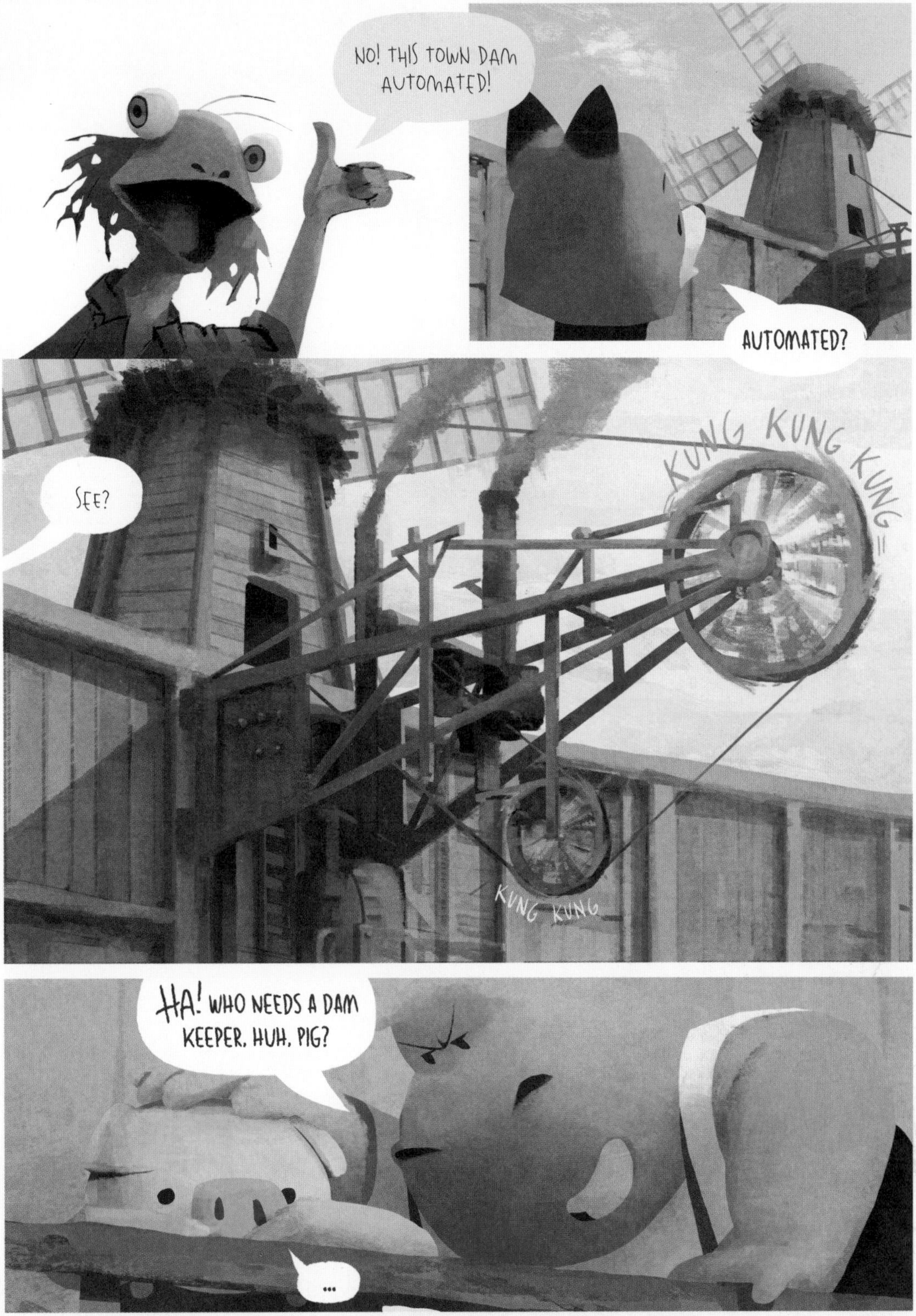
NO! THIS TOWN DAM AUTOMATED!
AUTOMATED?
SEE?
KUNG KUNG KUNG KUNG
KUNG KUNG
HA! WHO NEEDS A DAM KEEPER. HUH, PIG?
...

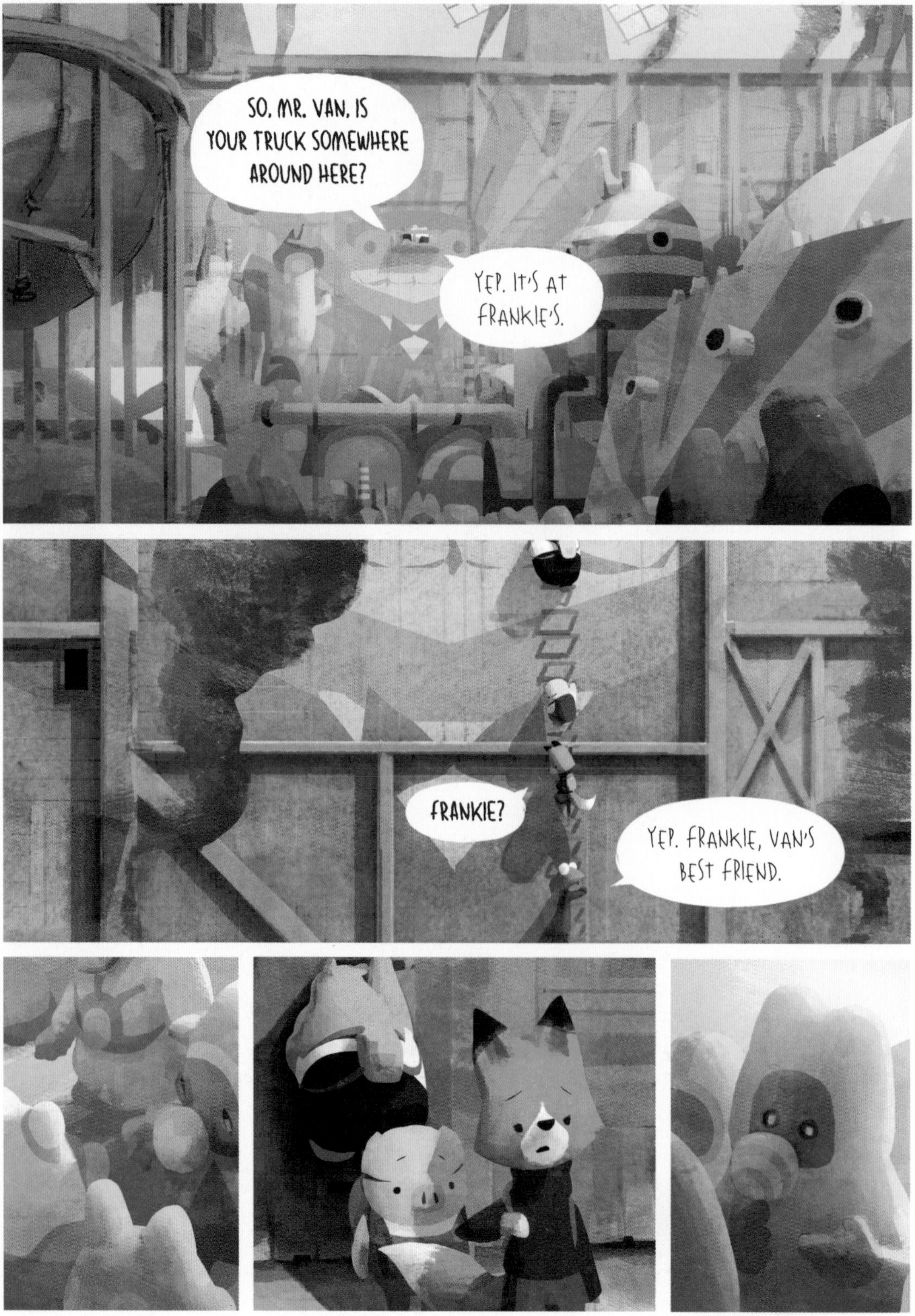
SO, MR. VAN, IS YOUR TRUCK SOMEWHERE AROUND HERE?
YEP. IT'S AT FRANKIE'S.
FRANKIE?
YEP. FRANKIE, VAN'S BEST FRIEND.

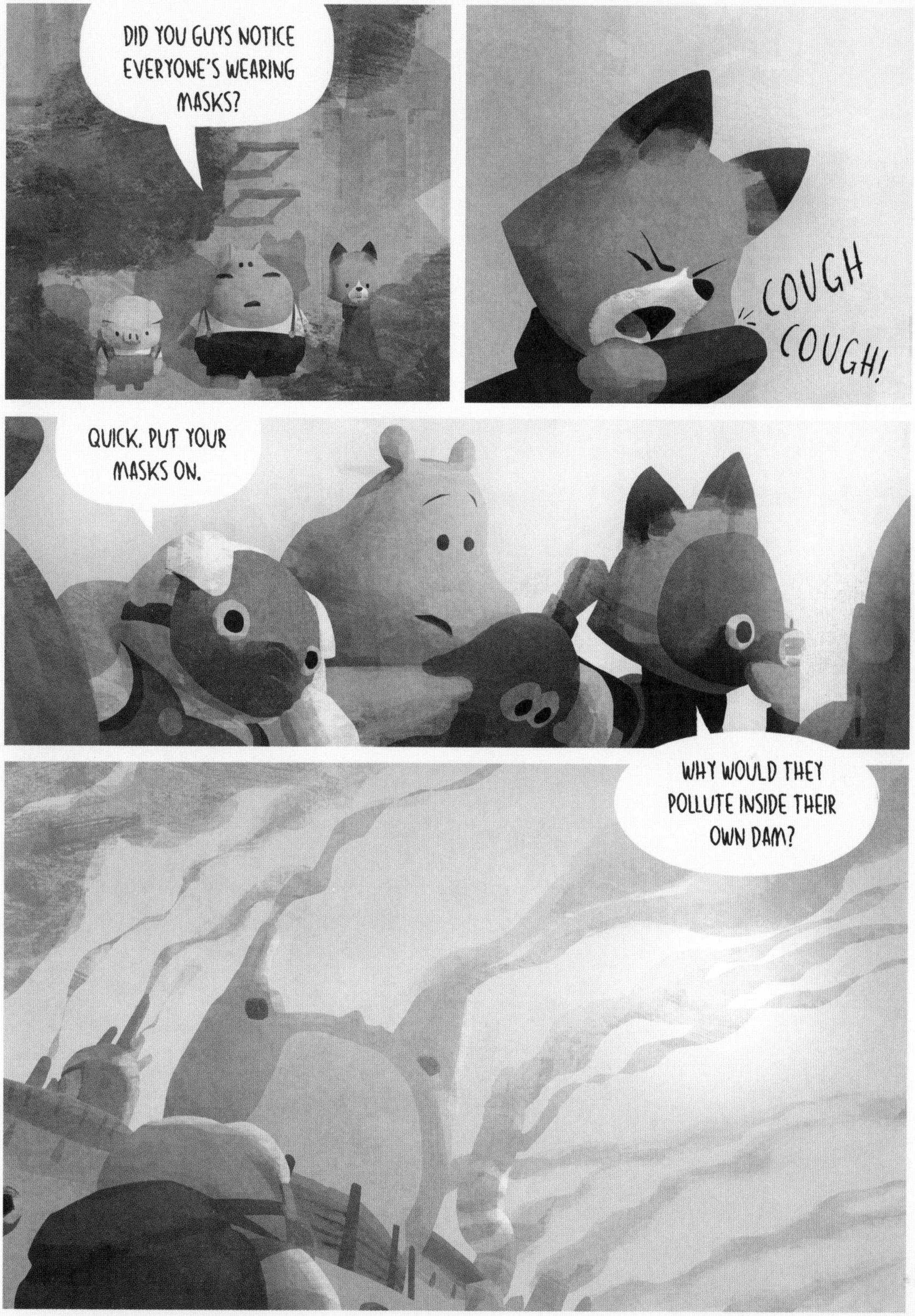
DID YOU GUYS NOTICE EVERYONE'S WEARING MASKS?
COUGH COUGH!
QUICK. PUT YOUR MASKS ON.
WHY WOULD THEY POLLUTE INSIDE THEIR OWN DAM?

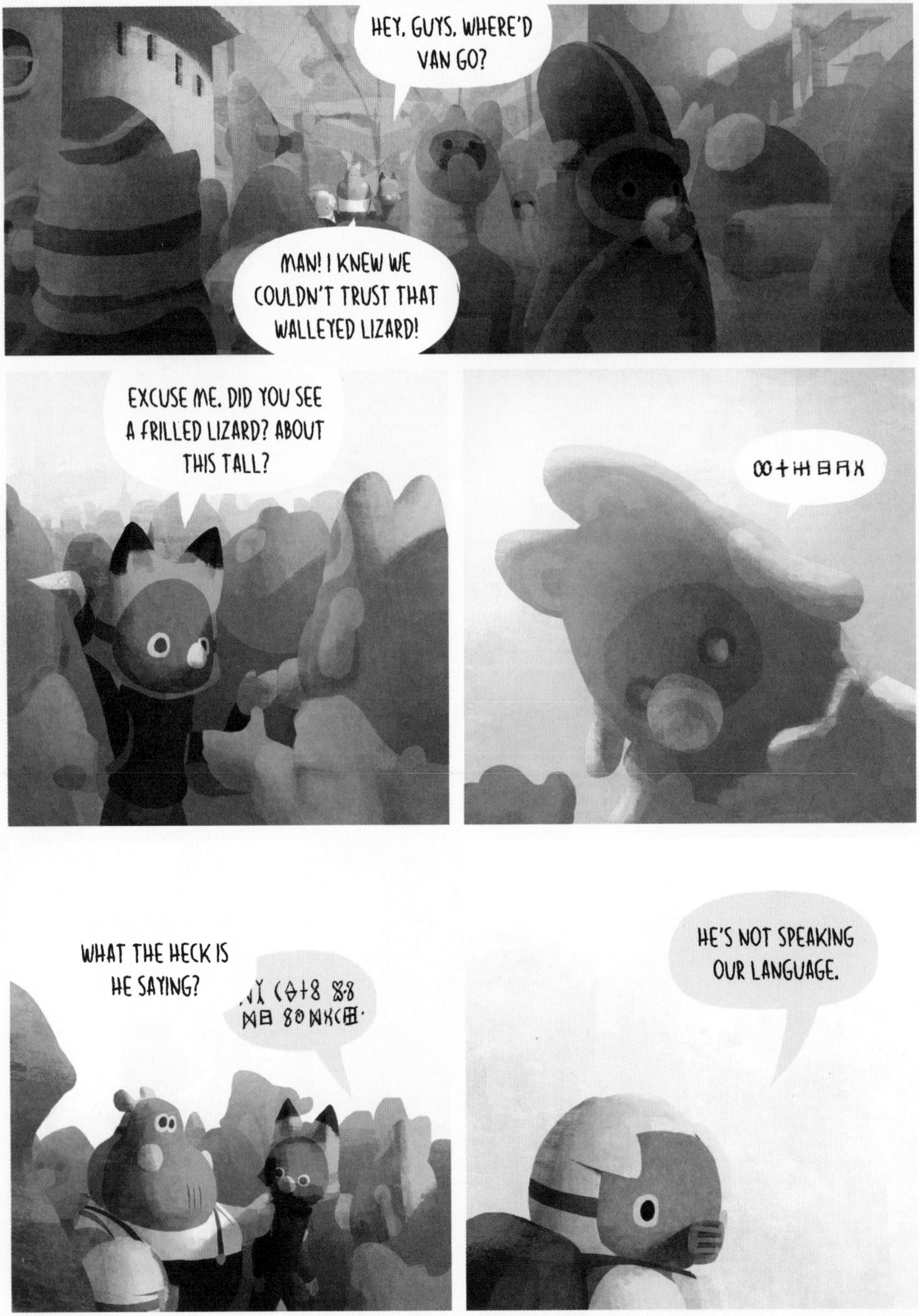
HEY, GUYS, WHERE'D VAN GO?
MAN! I KNEW WE COULDN'T TRUST THAT WALLEYED LIZARD!
EXCUSE ME. DID YOU SEE A FRILLED LIZARD? ABOUT THIS TALL?
WHAT THE HECK IS HE SAYING?
HE'S NOT SPEAKING OUR LANGUAGE.

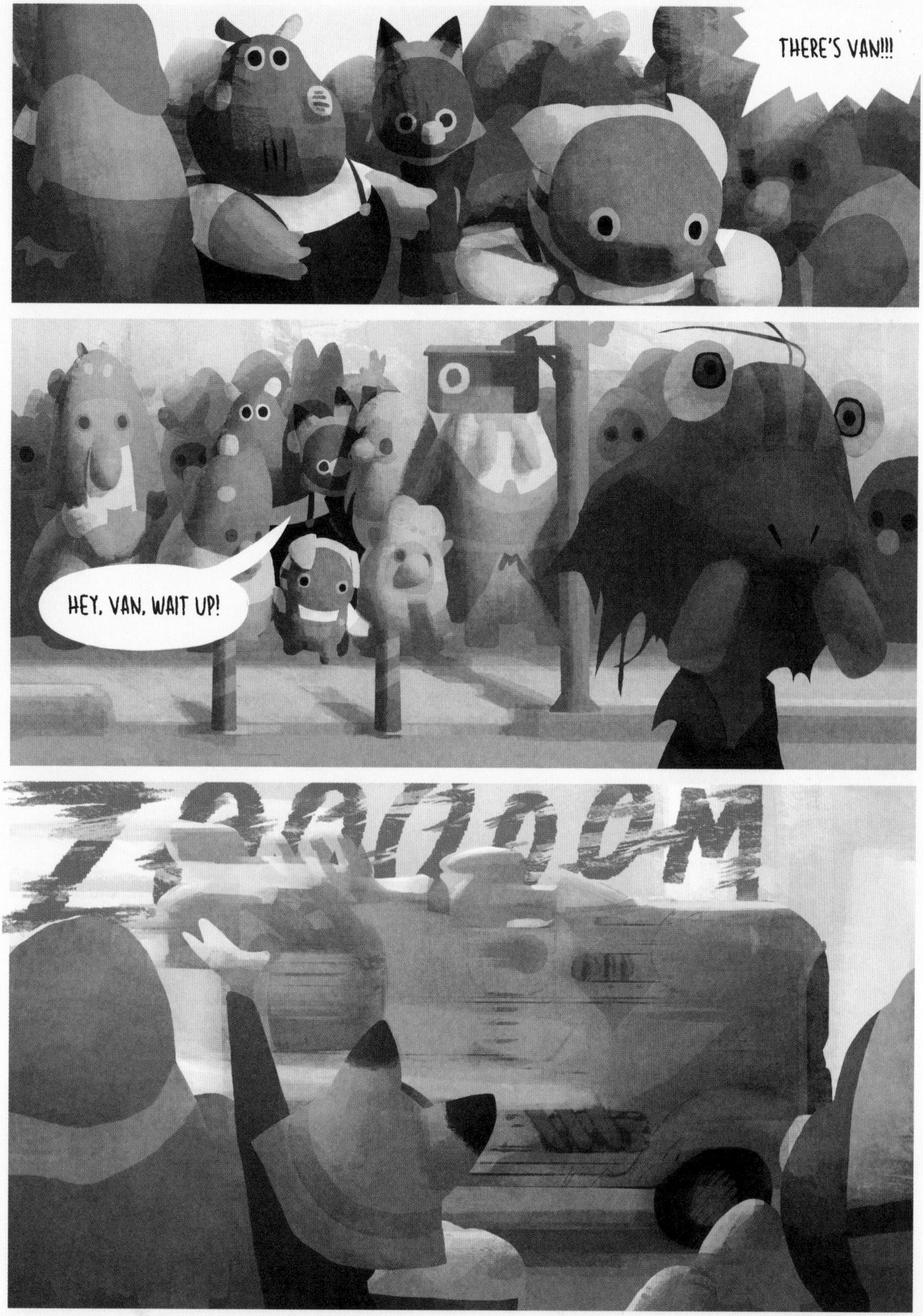
THERE'S VAN!!!
HEY, VAN, WAIT UP!
ZOOOOOM

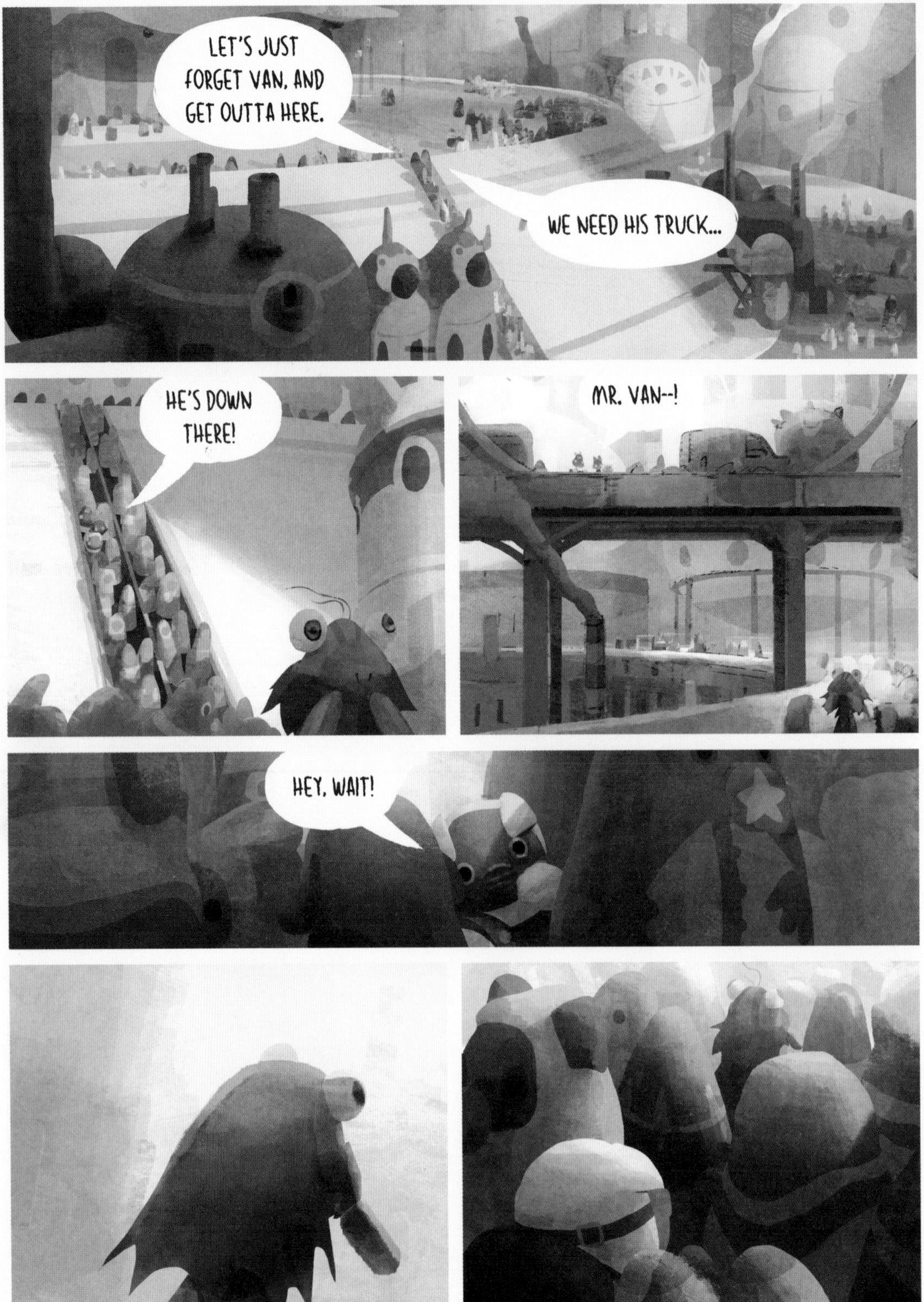
LET'S JUST FORGET VAN, AND GET OUTTA HERE.
WE NEED HIS TRUCK...
HE'S DOWN THERE!
MR. VAN--!
HEY, WAIT!

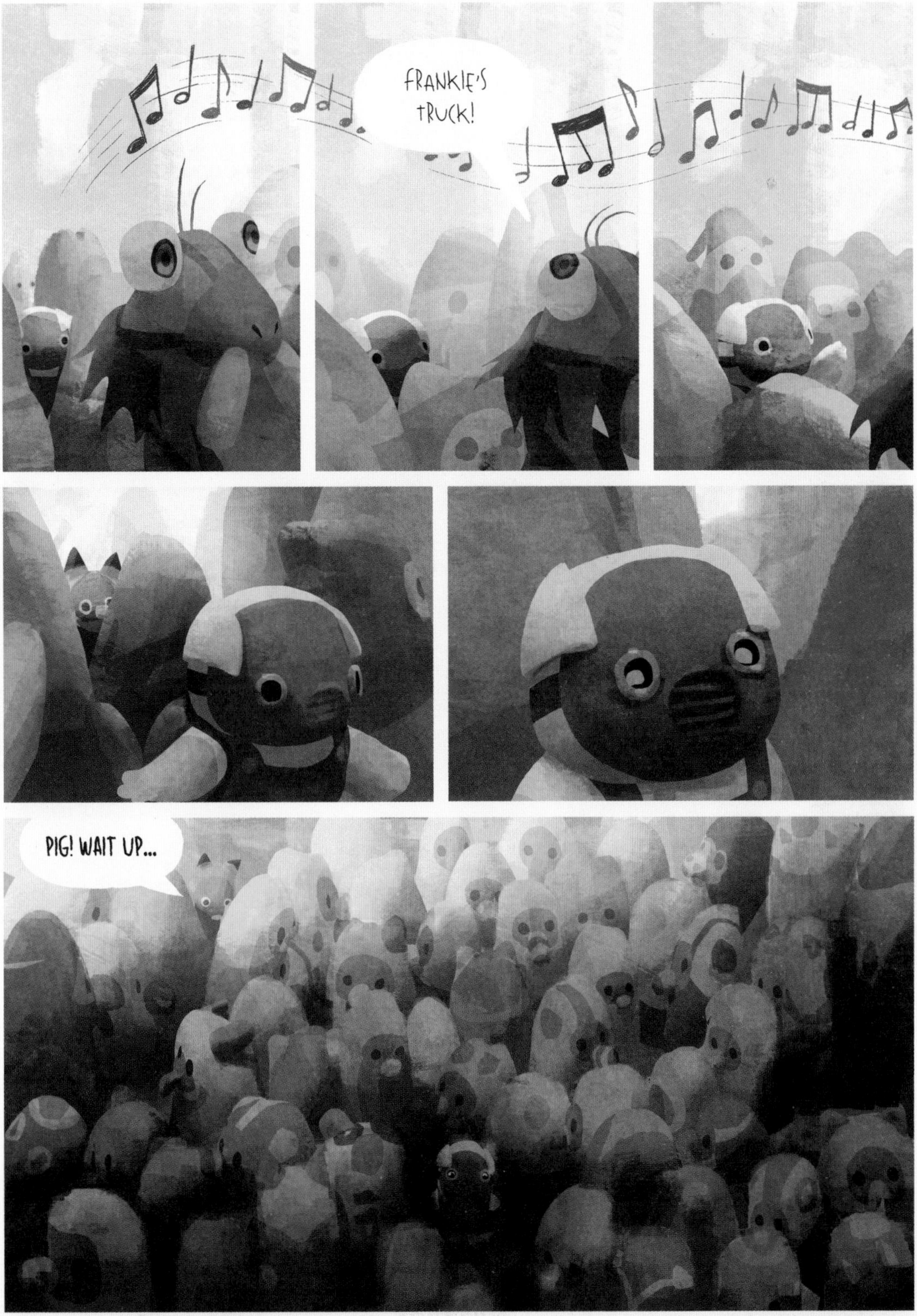
FRANKIE'S TRUCK!
PIG! WAIT UP...

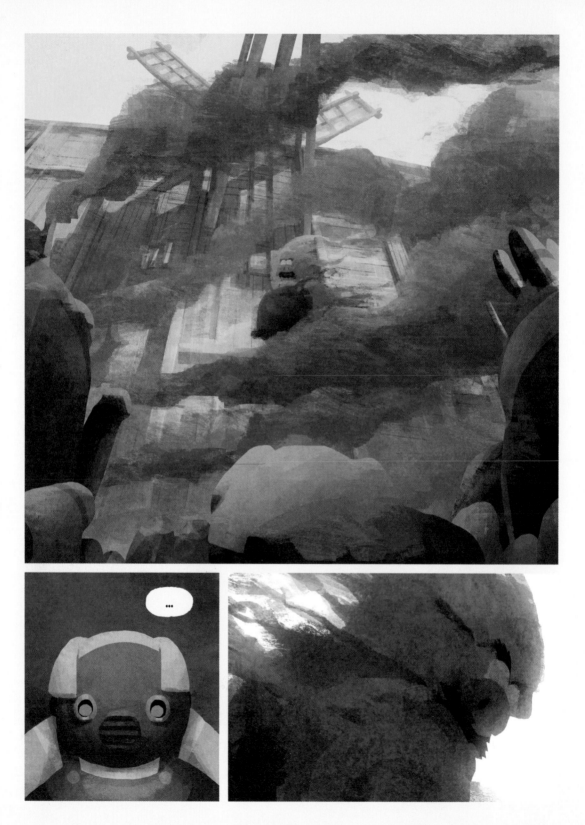

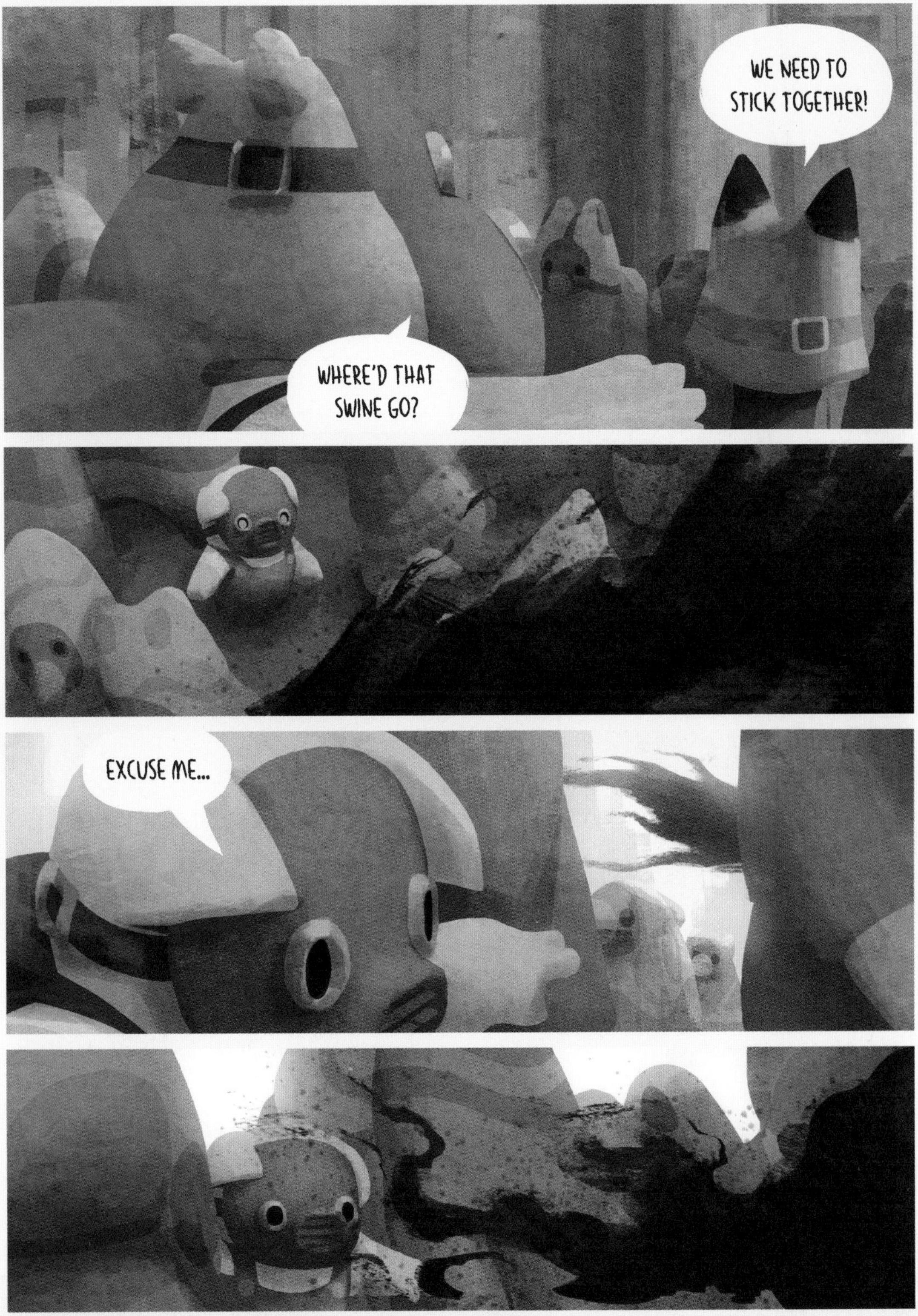
WE NEED TO STICK TOGETHER!
WHERE'D THAT SWINE GO?
EXCUSE ME...

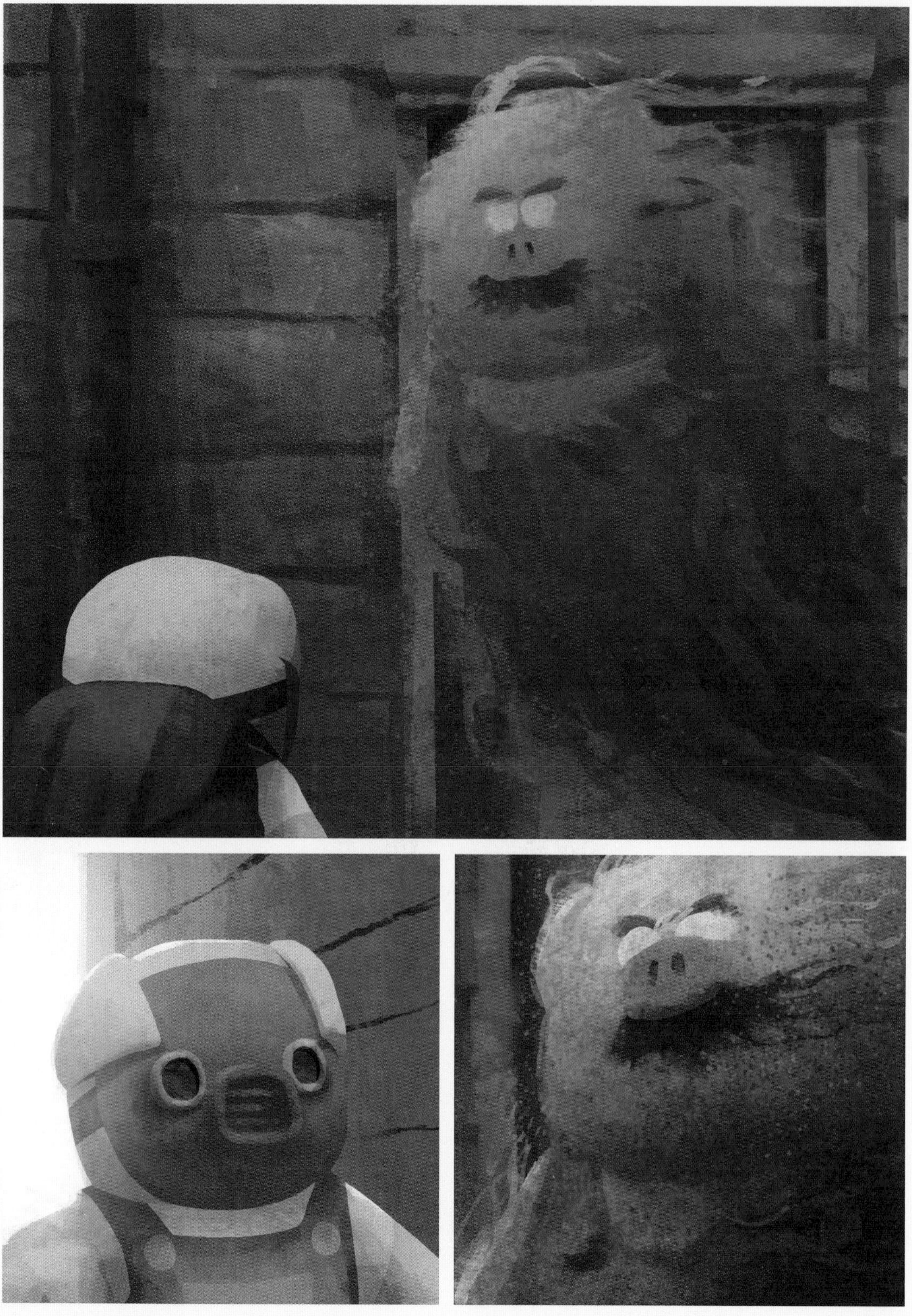

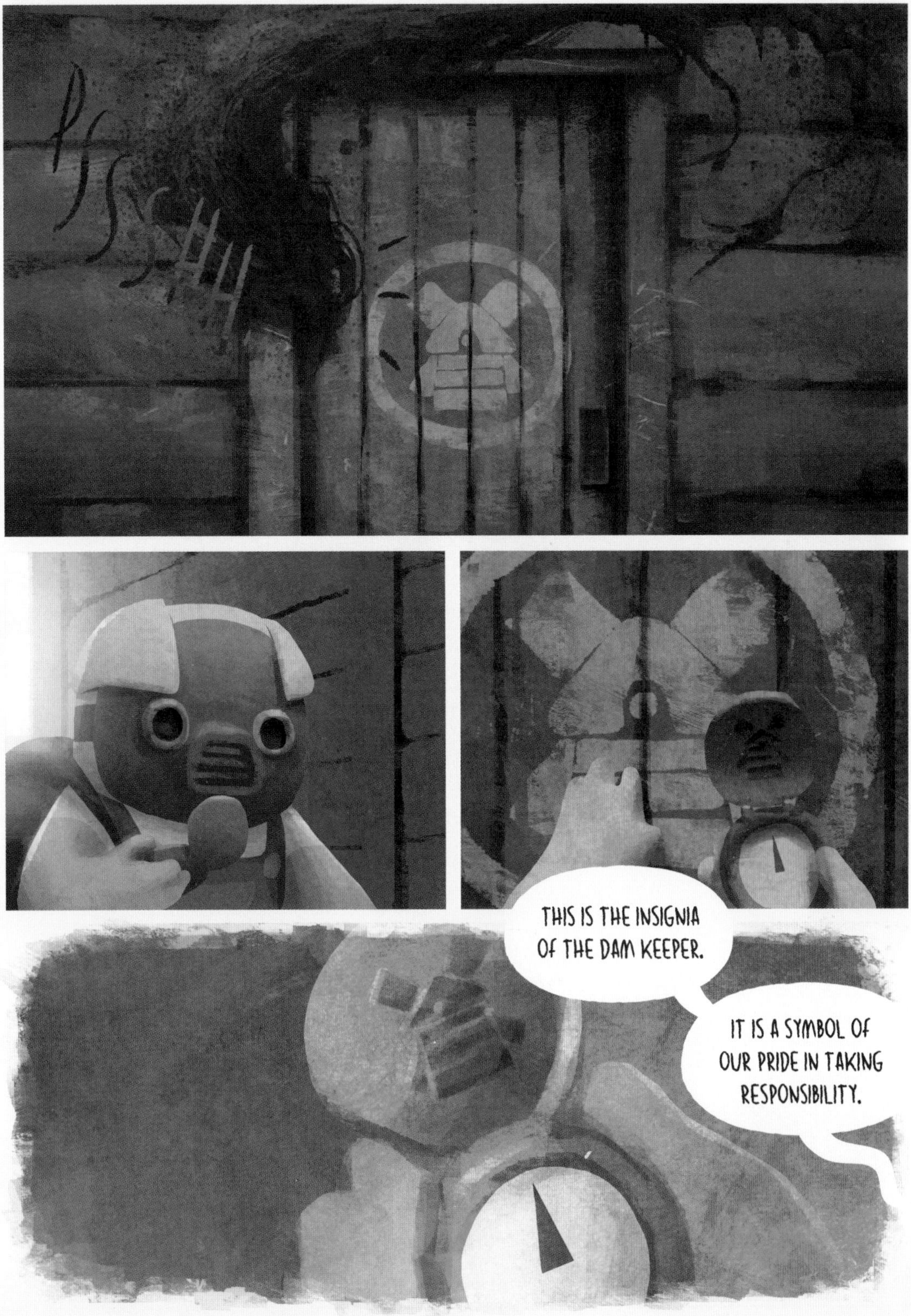
THIS IS THE INSIGNIA OF THE DAM KEEPER.
IT IS A SYMBOL OF OUR PRIDE IN TAKING RESPONSIBILITY.

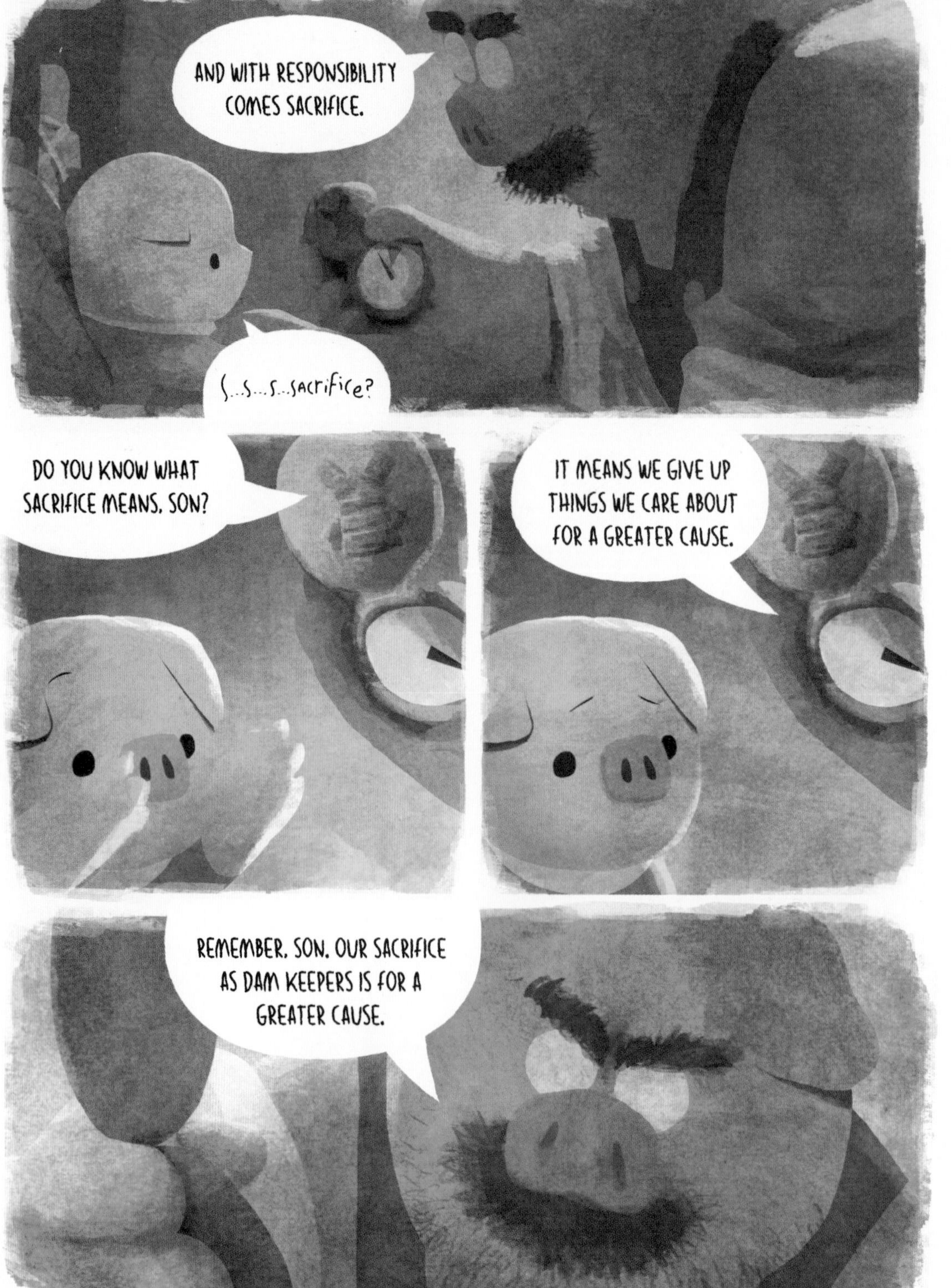
AND WITH RESPONSIBILITY COMES SACRIFICE.
S...S...S...SACRIFICE?
DO YOU KNOW WHAT SACRIFICE MEANS, SON?
IT MEANS WE GIVE UP THINGS WE CARE ABOUT FOR A GREATER CAUSE.
REMEMBER, SON, OUR SACRIFICE AS DAM KEEPERS IS FOR A GREATER CAUSE.

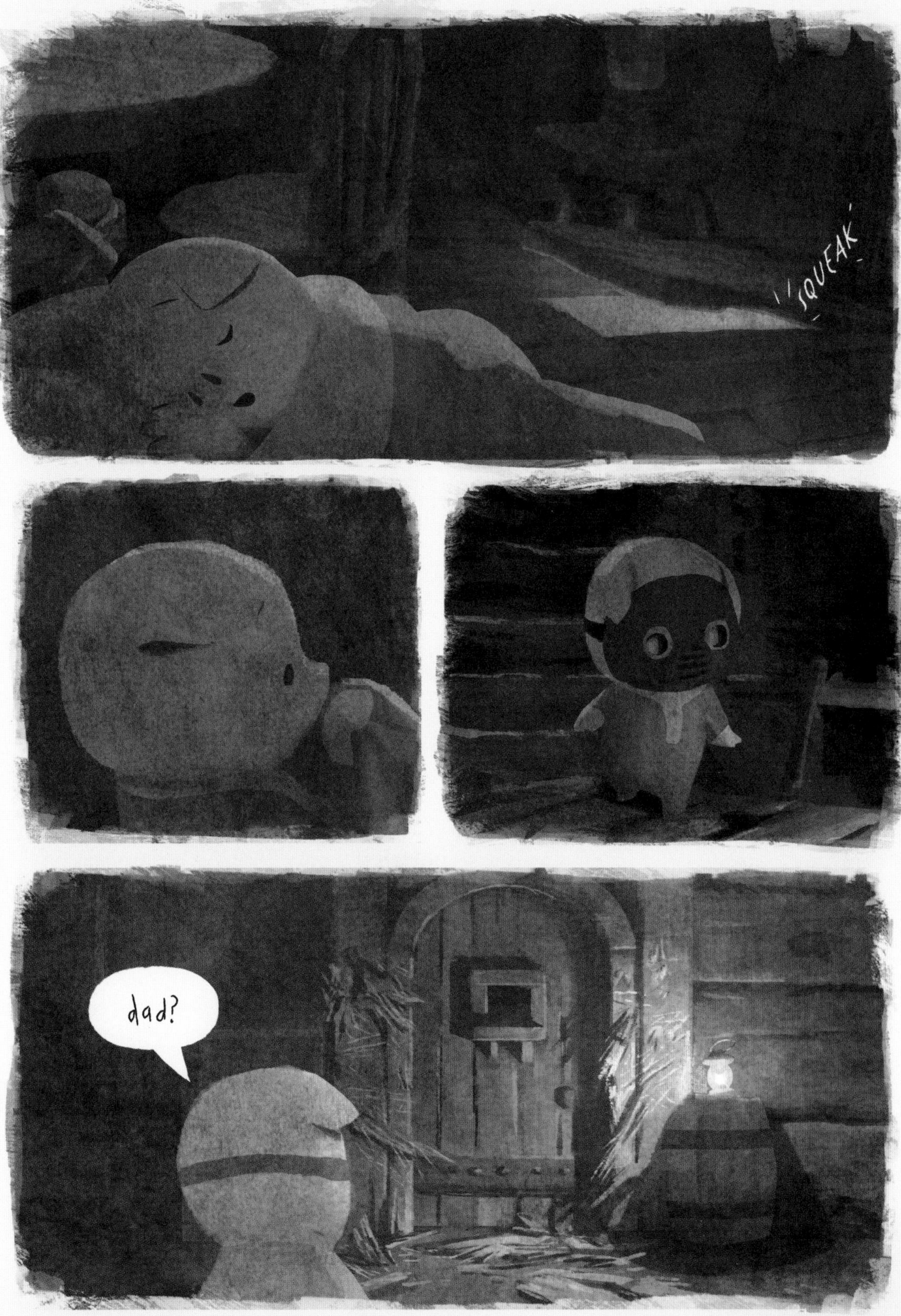
SQUEAK
dad?

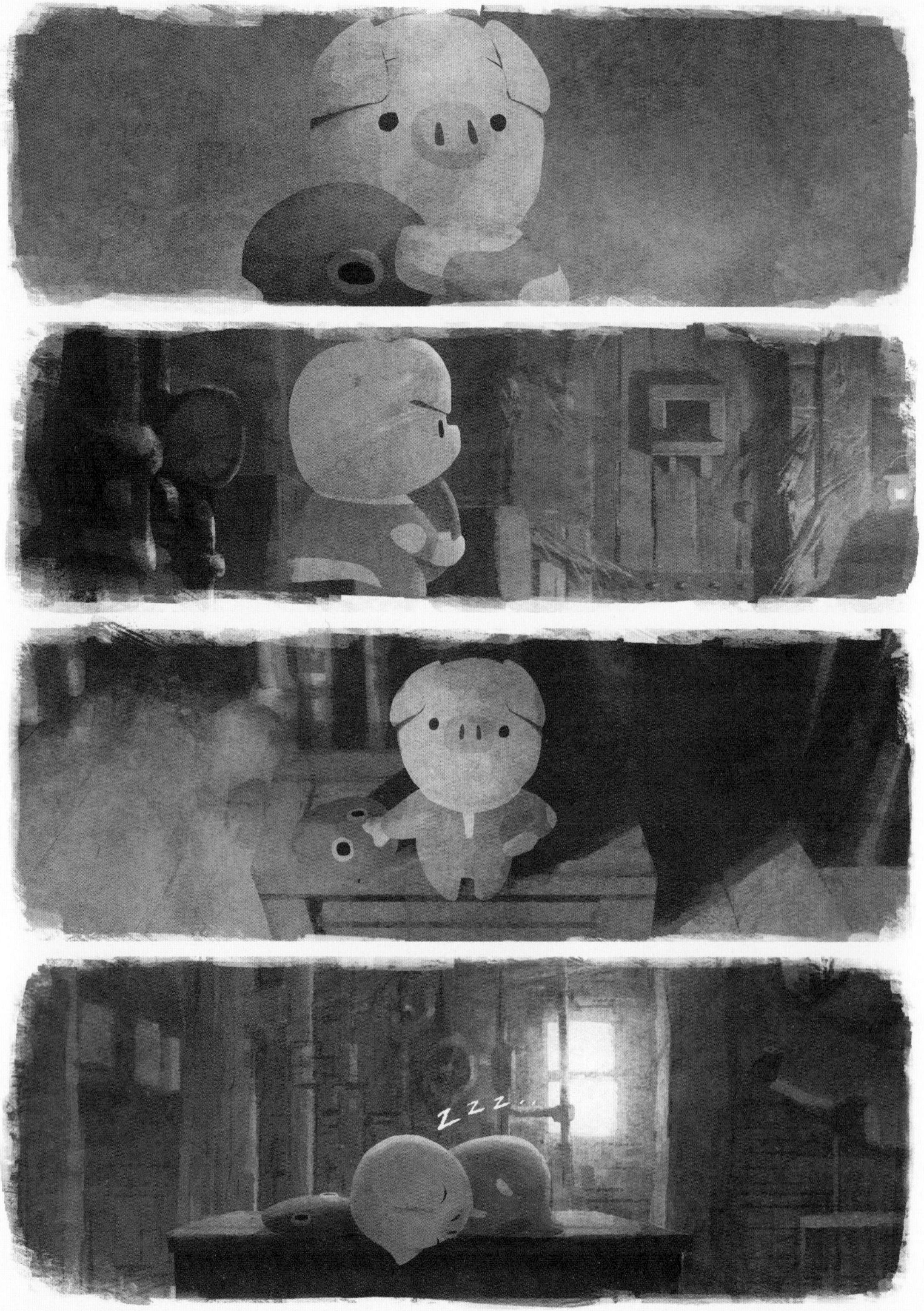
Z Z Z . .

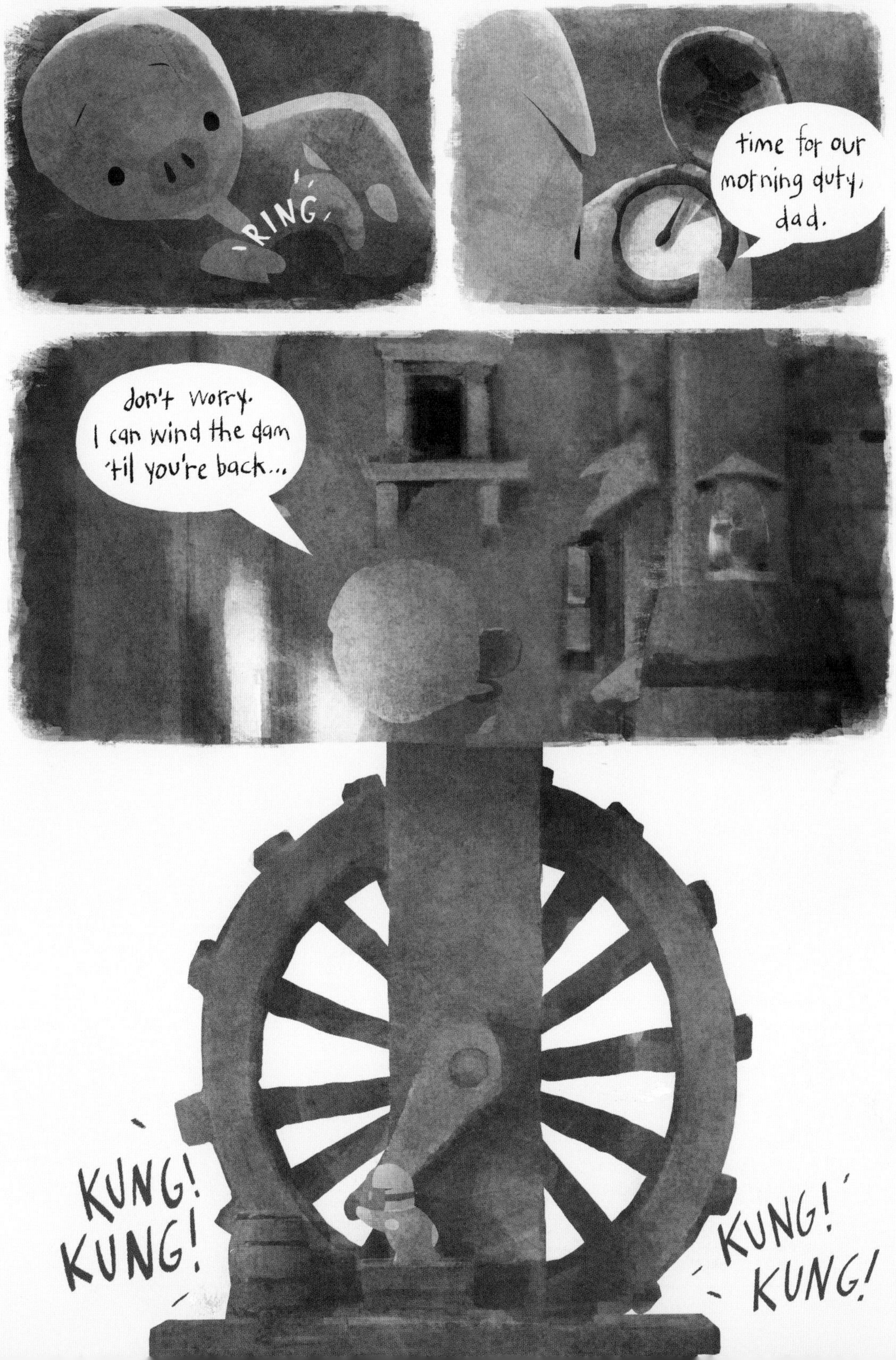
RING
time for our morning duty, dad.
don't worry. I can wind the dam 'til you're back...
KUNG! KUNG!
KUNG! KUNG!

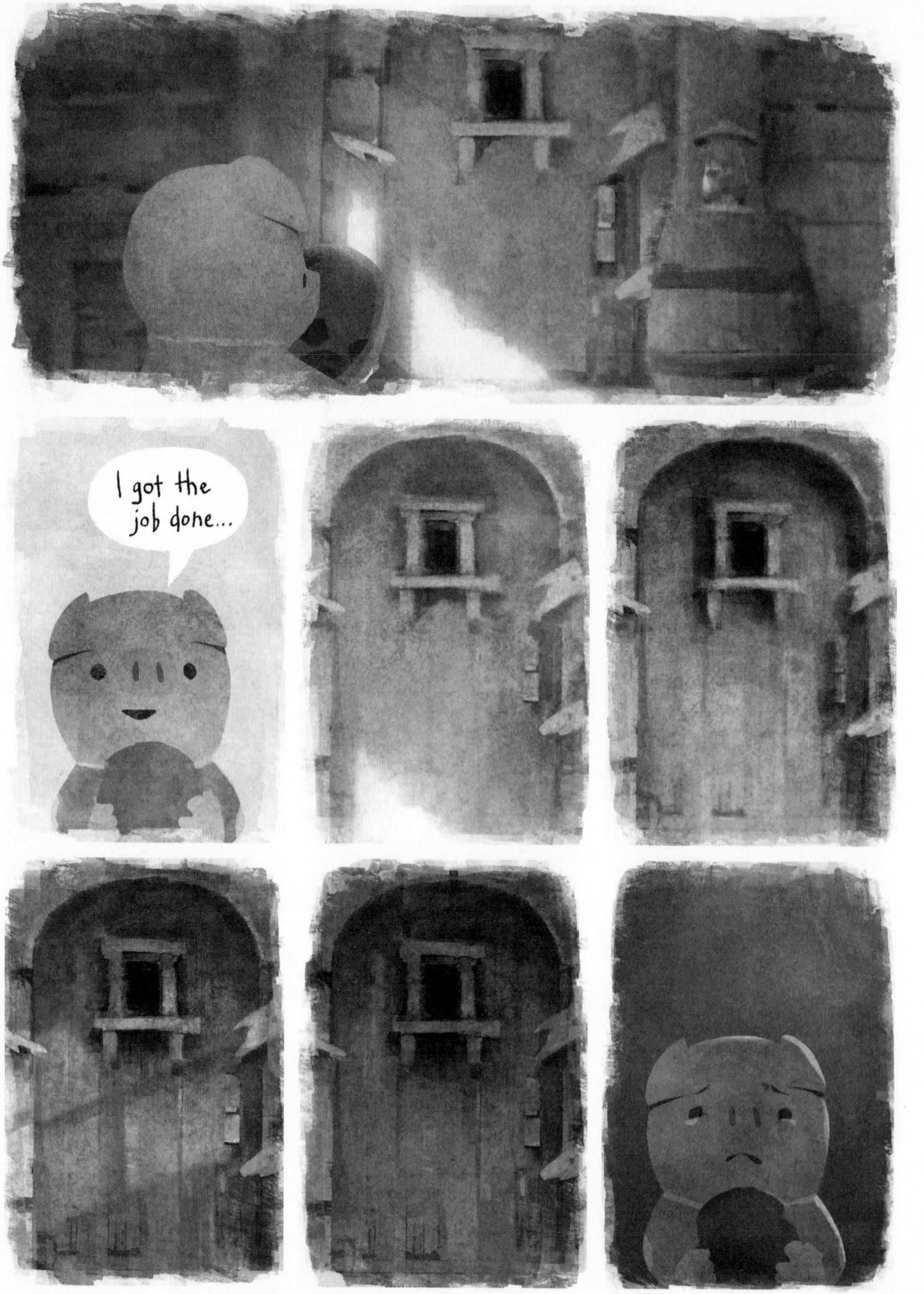
I got the job done...

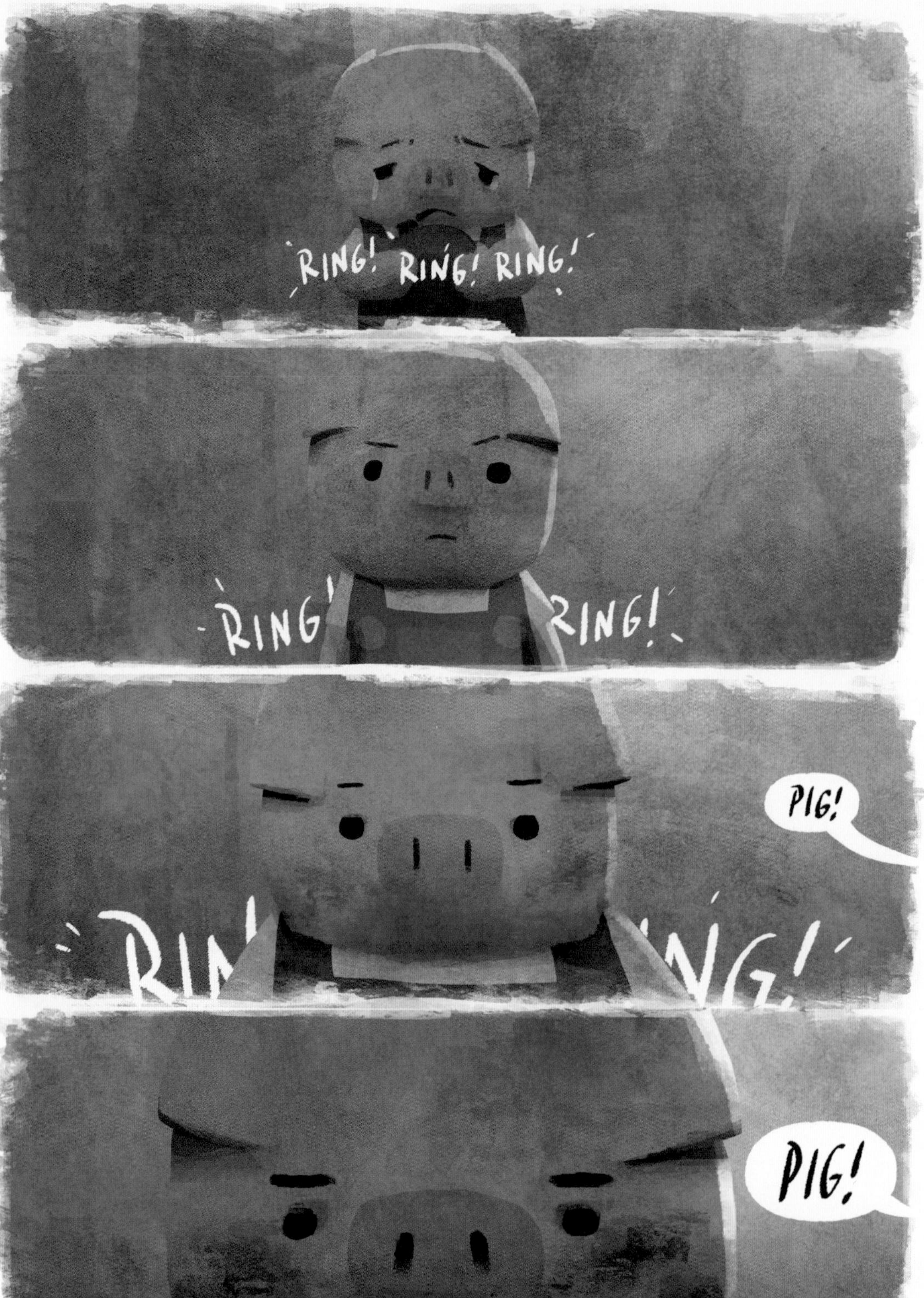
RING! RING! RING!
RING
ING!
RIN
NG!
PIG!
PIG!

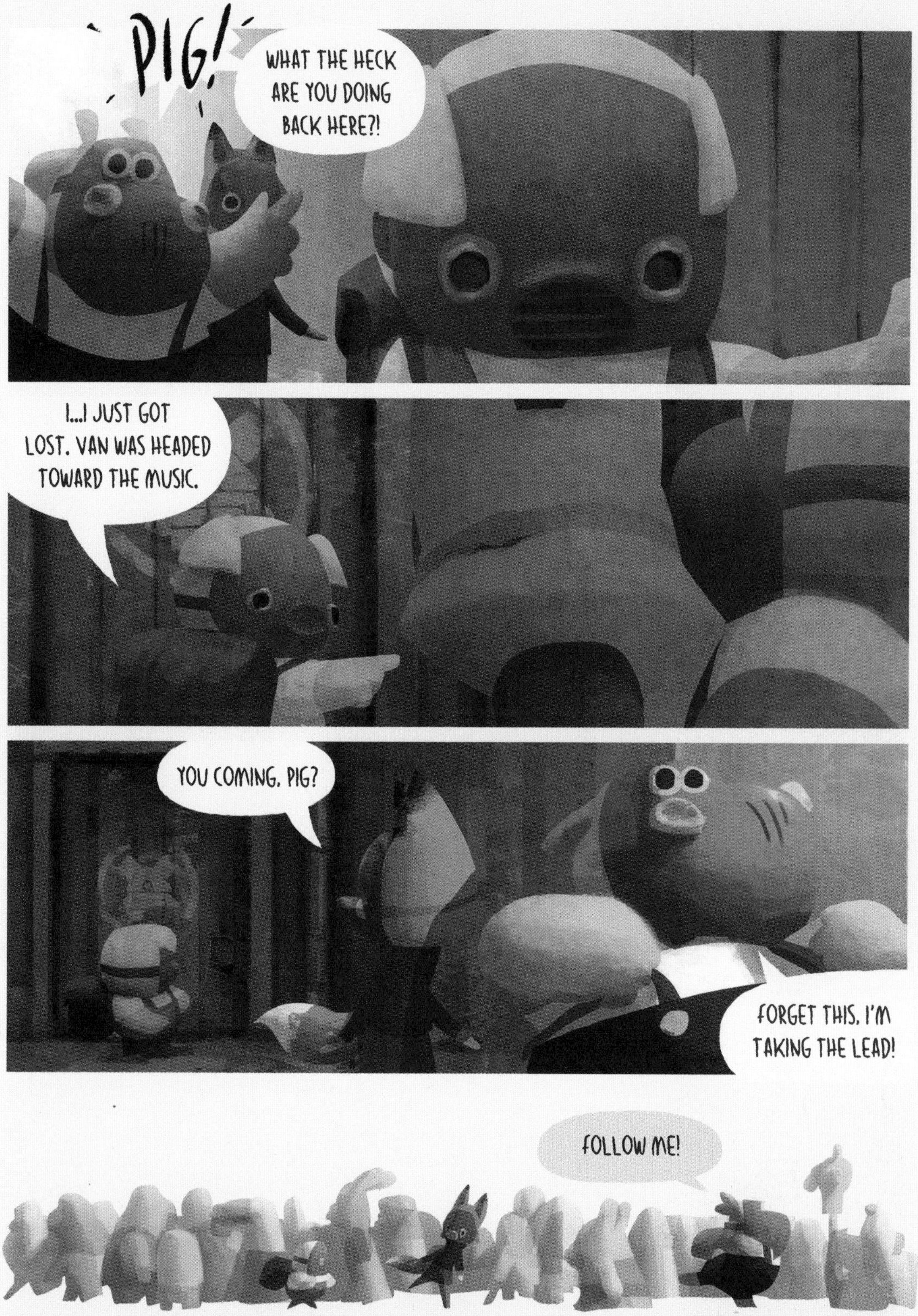
PIG!
WHAT THE HECK ARE YOU DOING BACK HERE?!
I...I JUST GOT LOST. VAN WAS HEADED TOWARD THE MUSIC.
YOU COMING, PIG?
FORGET THIS, I'M TAKING THE LEAD!
FOLLOW ME!

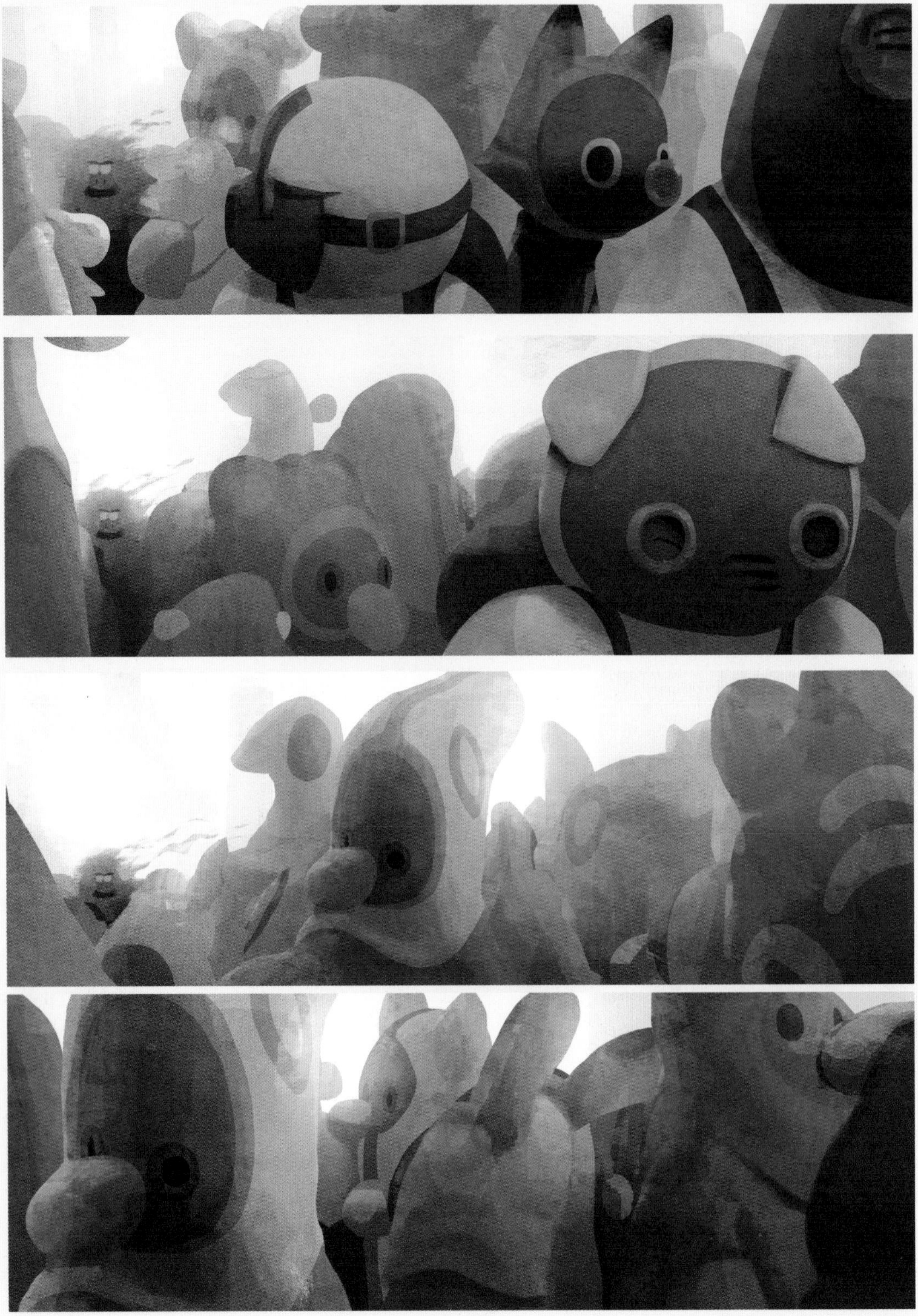

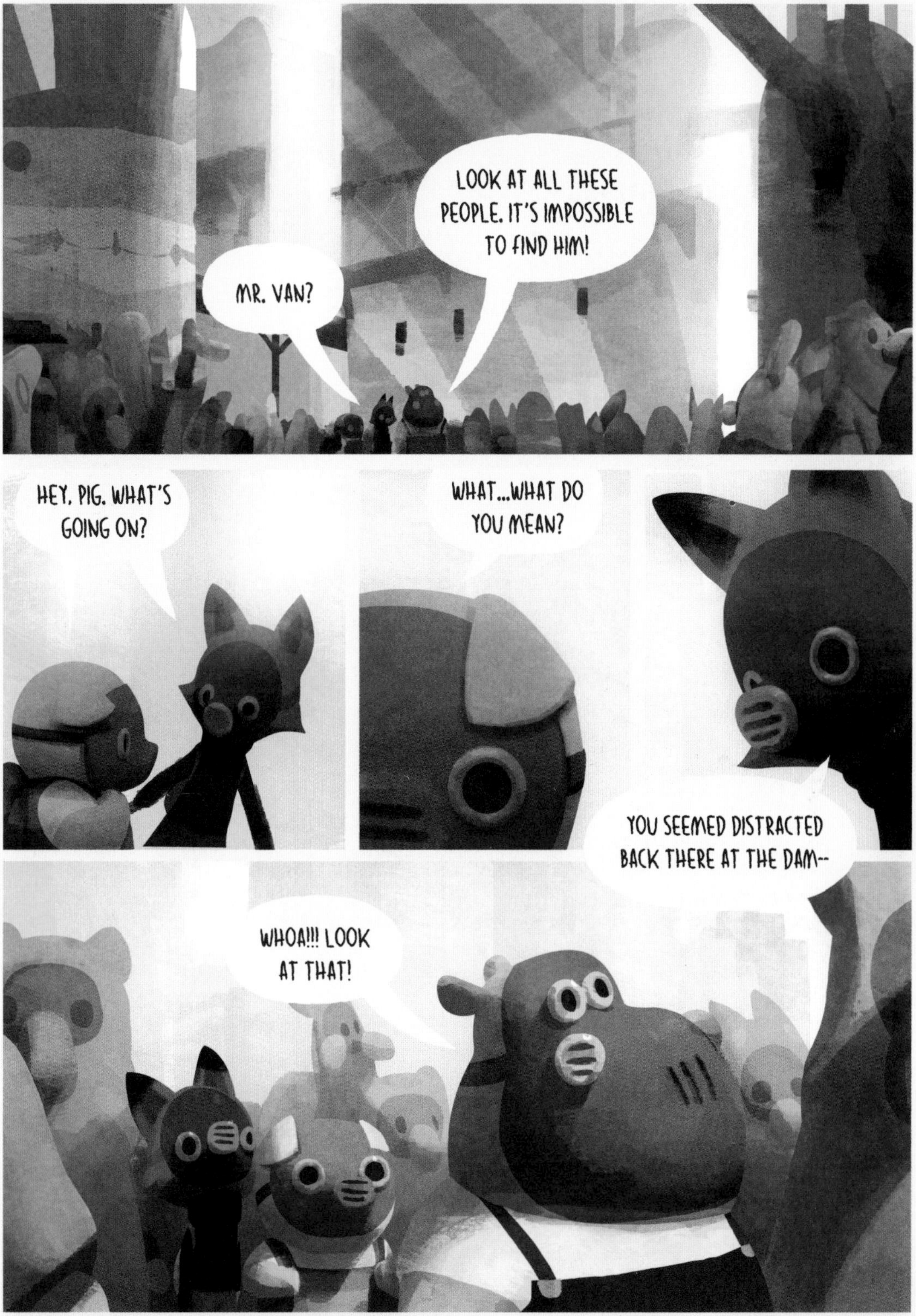
MR. VAN?
LOOK AT ALL THESE PEOPLE. IT'S IMPOSSIBLE TO FIND HIM!
HEY, PIG. WHAT'S GOING ON?
WHAT...WHAT DO YOU MEAN?
YOU SEEMED DISTRACTED BACK THERE AT THE DAM--
WHOA!!! LOOK AT THAT!

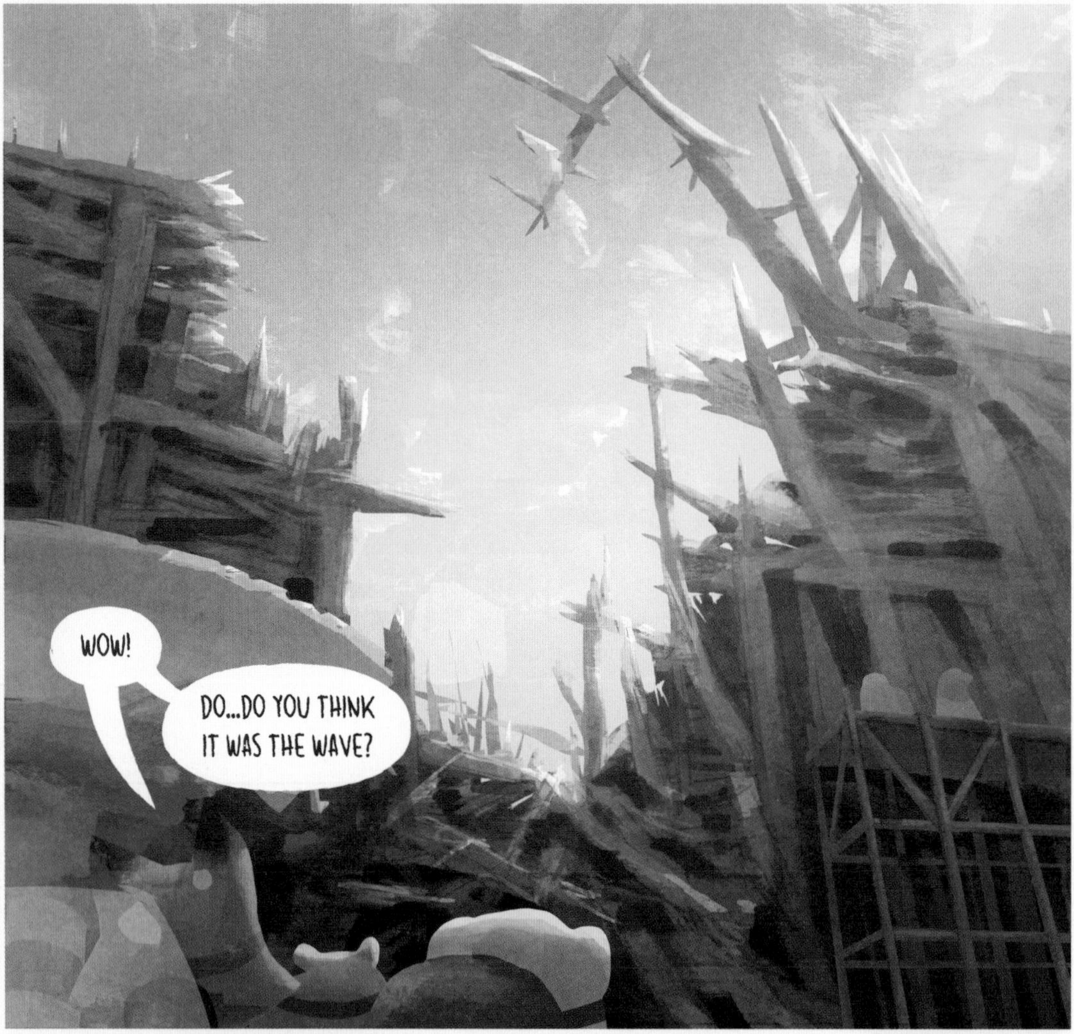
WOW!
DO...DO YOU THINK IT WAS THE WAVE?

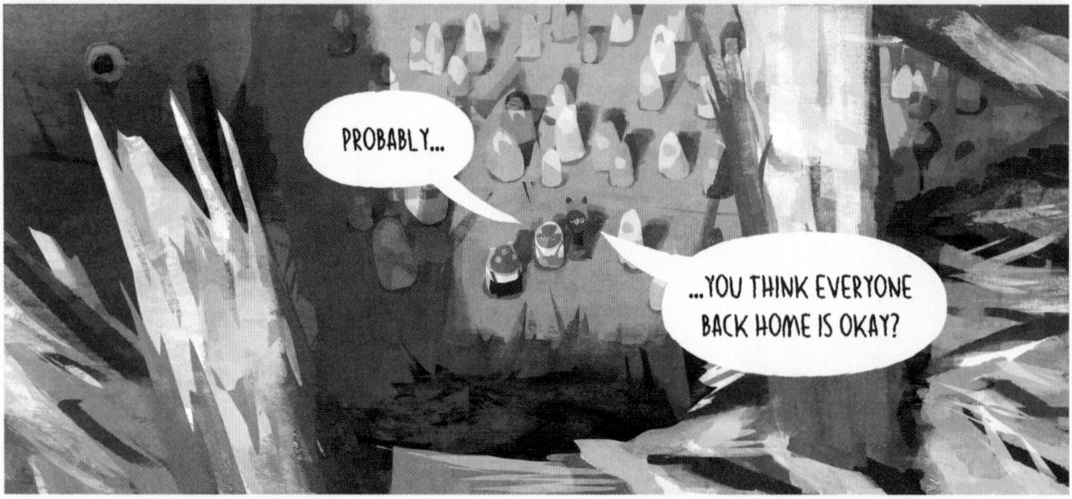
PROBABLY...
...YOU THINK EVERYONE BACK HOME IS OKAY?

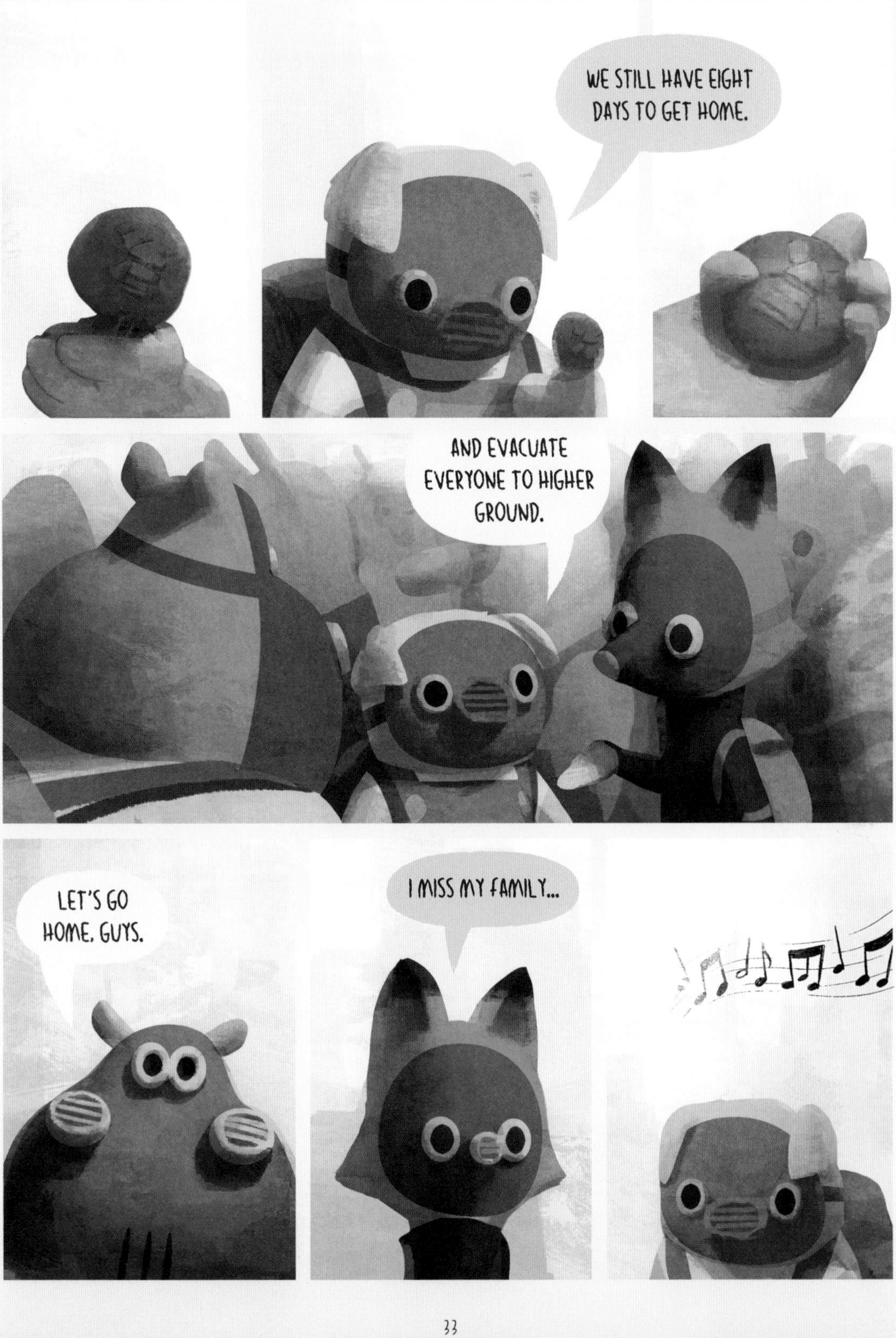
WE STILL HAVE EIGHT DAYS TO GET HOME.
AND EVACUATE EVERYONE TO HIGHER GROUND.
LET'S GO HOME, GUYS.
I MISS MY FAMILY...

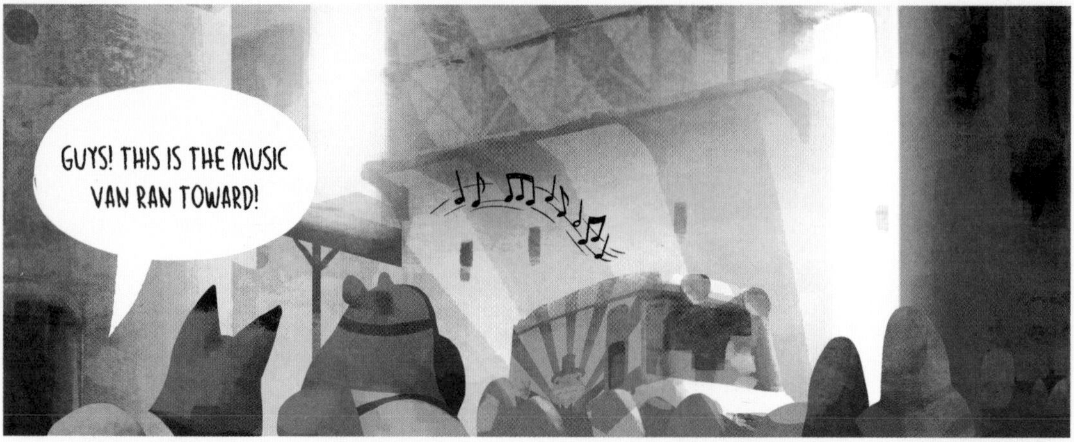
GUYS! THIS IS THE MUSIC VAN RAN TOWARD!

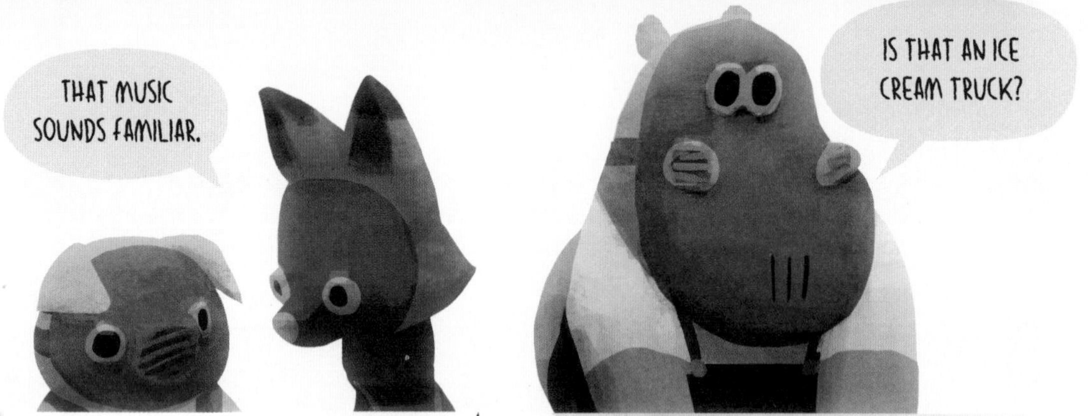
THAT MUSIC SOUNDS FAMILIAR.
IS THAT AN ICE CREAM TRUCK?

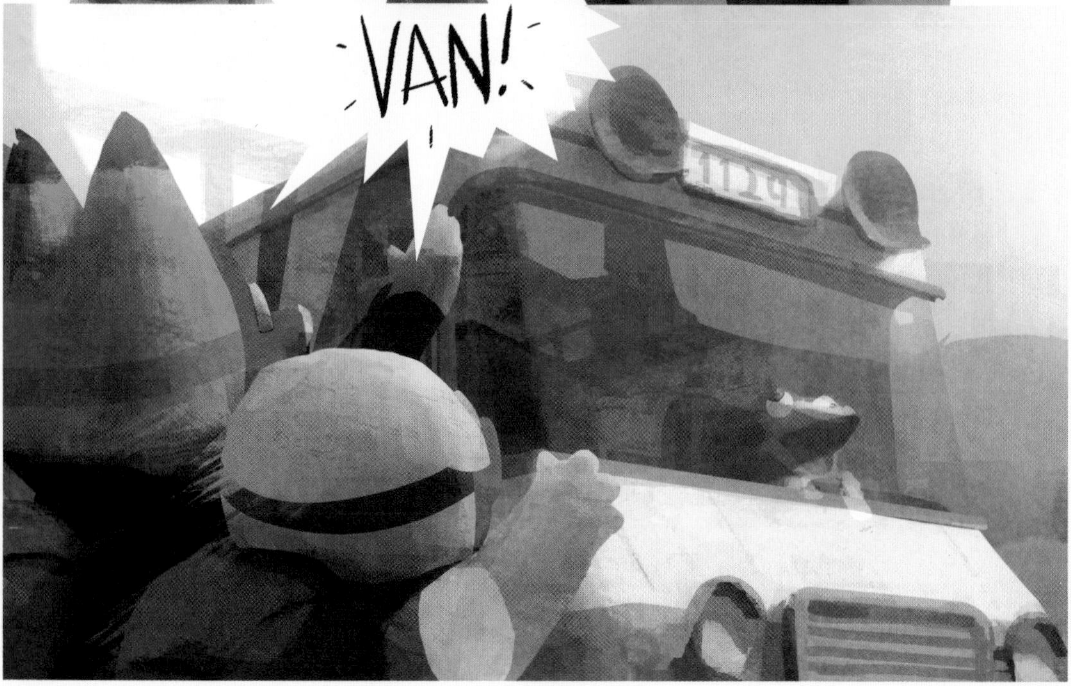
VAN!

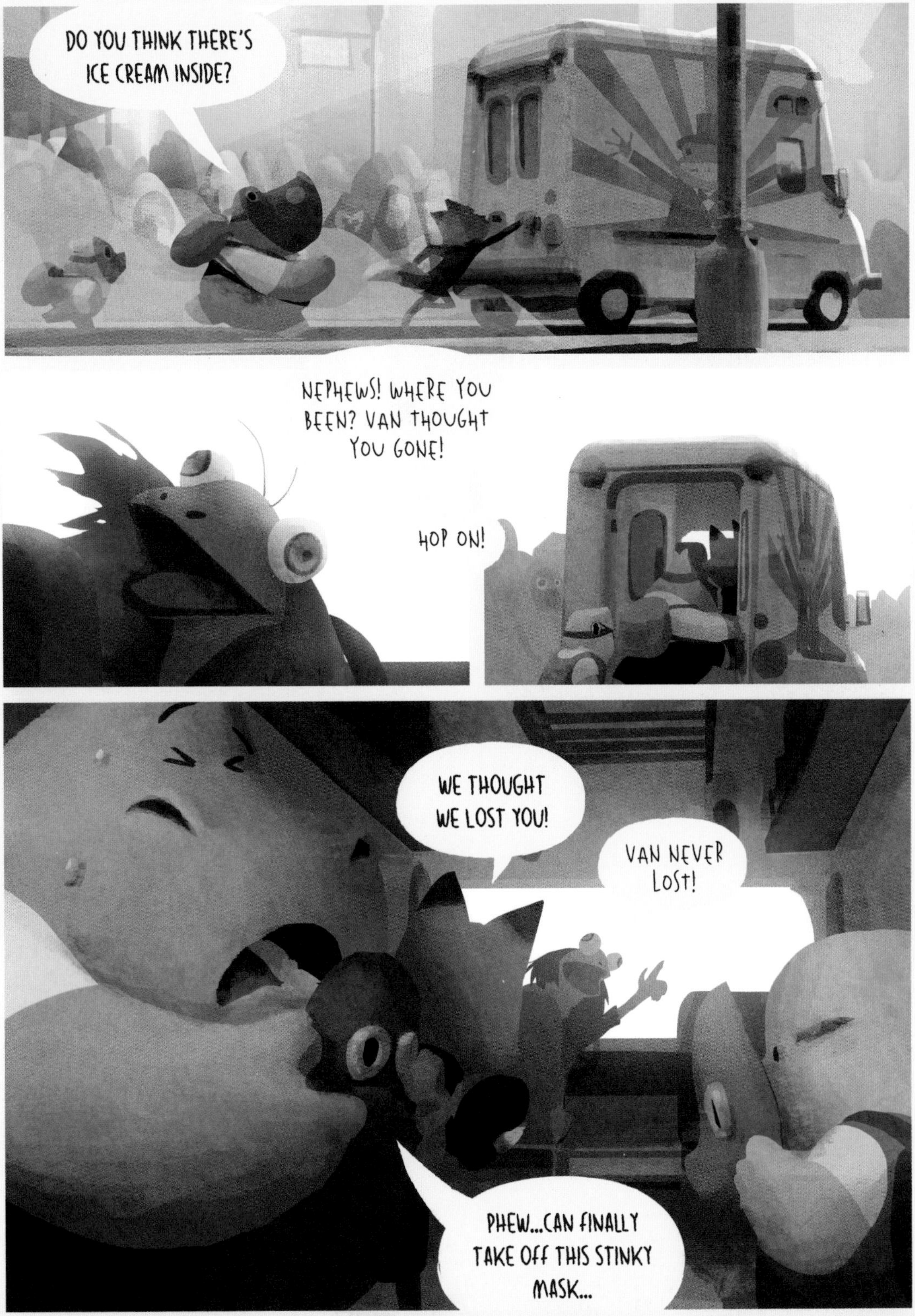
DO YOU THINK THERE'S ICE CREAM INSIDE?
NEPHEWS! WHERE YOU BEEN? VAN THOUGHT YOU GONE!
HOP ON!
WE THOUGHT WE LOST YOU!
VAN NEVER LOST!
PHEW...CAN FINALLY TAKE OFF THIS STINKY MASK...

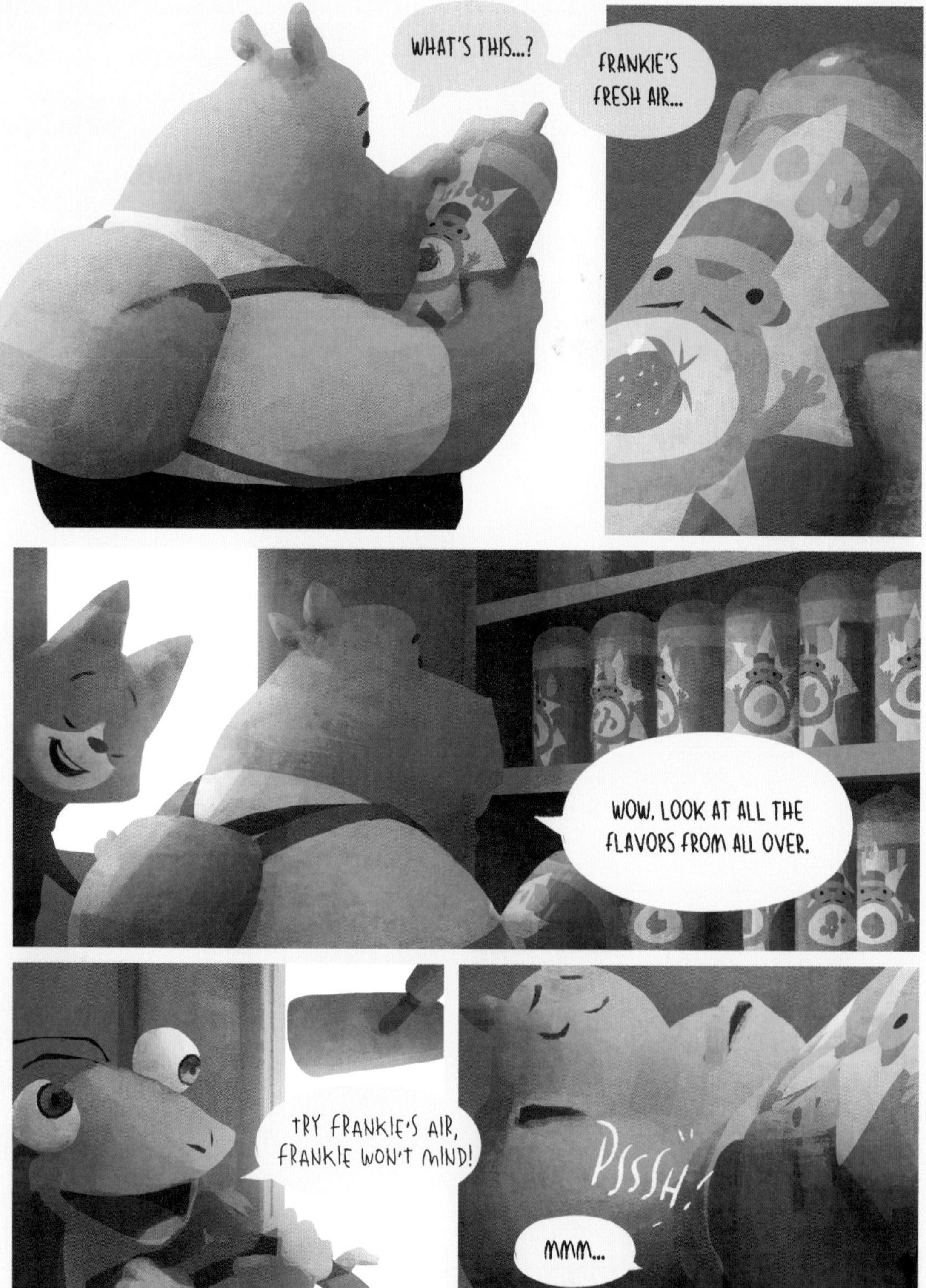
WHAT'S THIS...?
FRANKIE'S FRESH AIR...
WOW. LOOK AT ALL THE FLAVORS FROM ALL OVER.
TRY FRANKIE'S AIR, FRANKIE WON'T MIND!
PSSSH!
MMM...

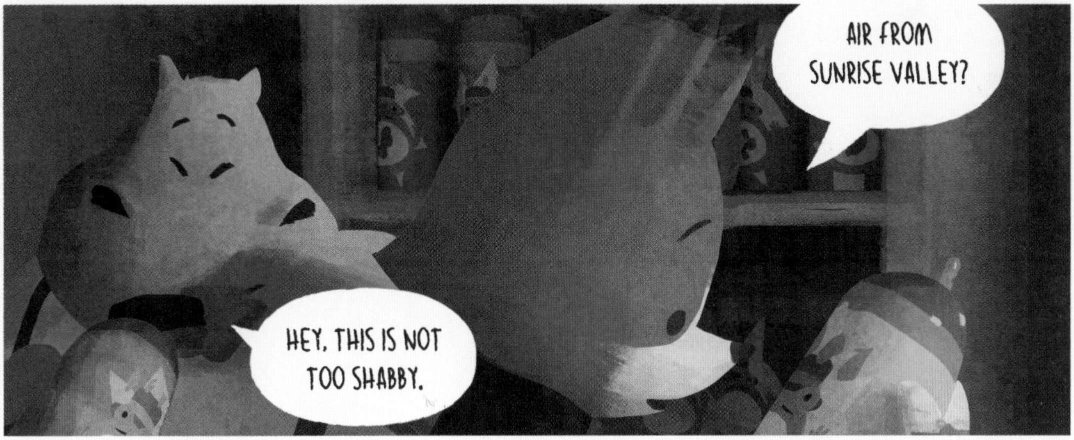
AIR FROM SUNRISE VALLEY?
HEY. THIS IS NOT TOO SHABBY.

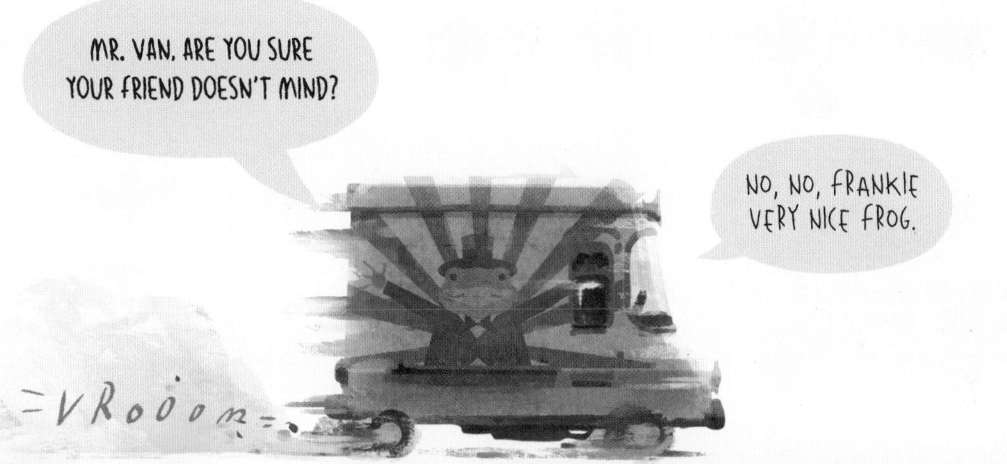
MR. VAN. ARE YOU SURE YOUR FRIEND DOESN'T MIND?
NO, NO, FRANKIE VERY NICE FROG.
VROOOM

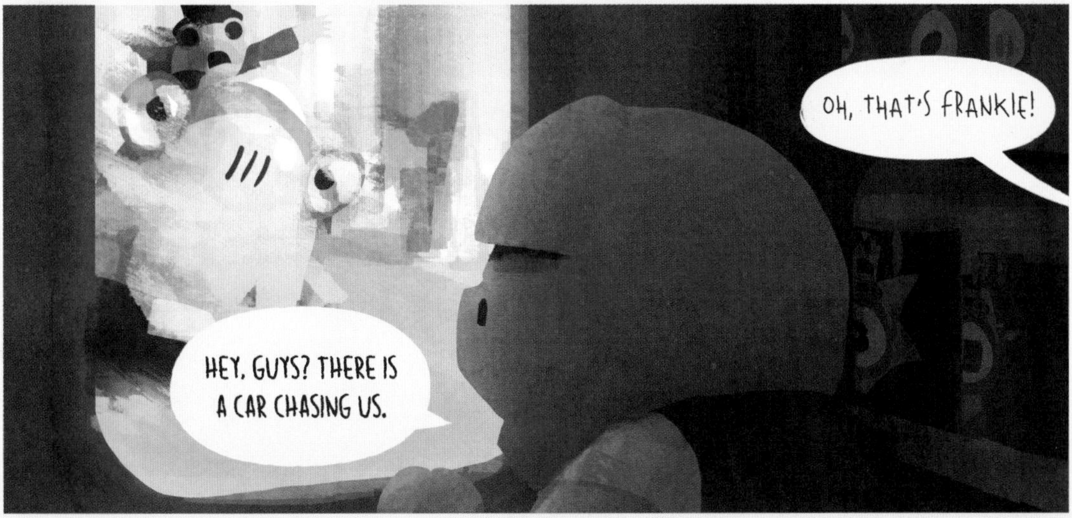
OH, THAT'S FRANKIE!
HEY. GUYS? THERE IS A CAR CHASING US.

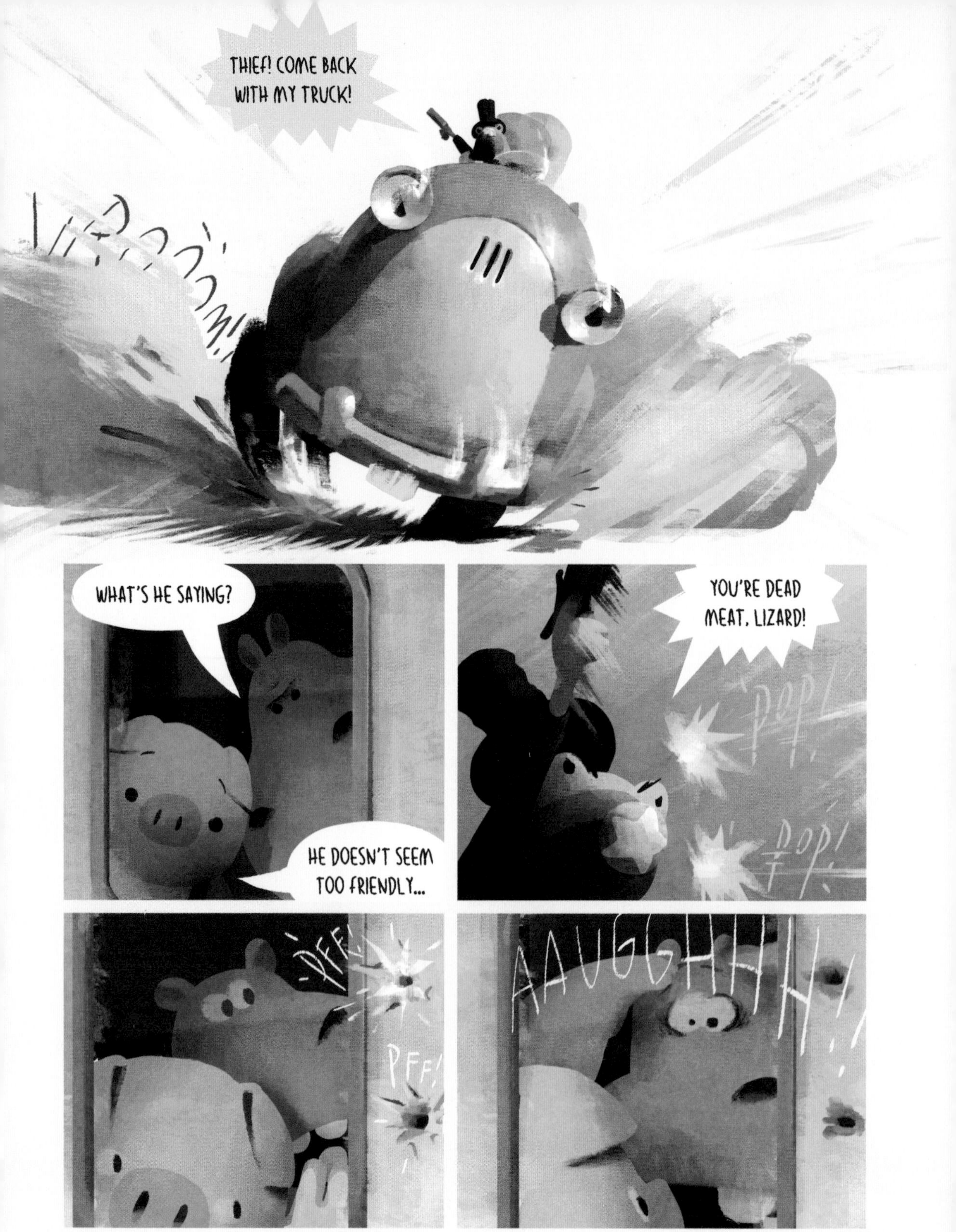
THIEF! COME BACK WITH MY TRUCK!
VROOOM!!
WHAT'S HE SAYING?
HE DOESN'T SEEM TOO FRIENDLY...
YOU'RE DEAD MEAT, LIZARD!
POP!
POP!
PFF!
PFF!
AAUGGHHH!!

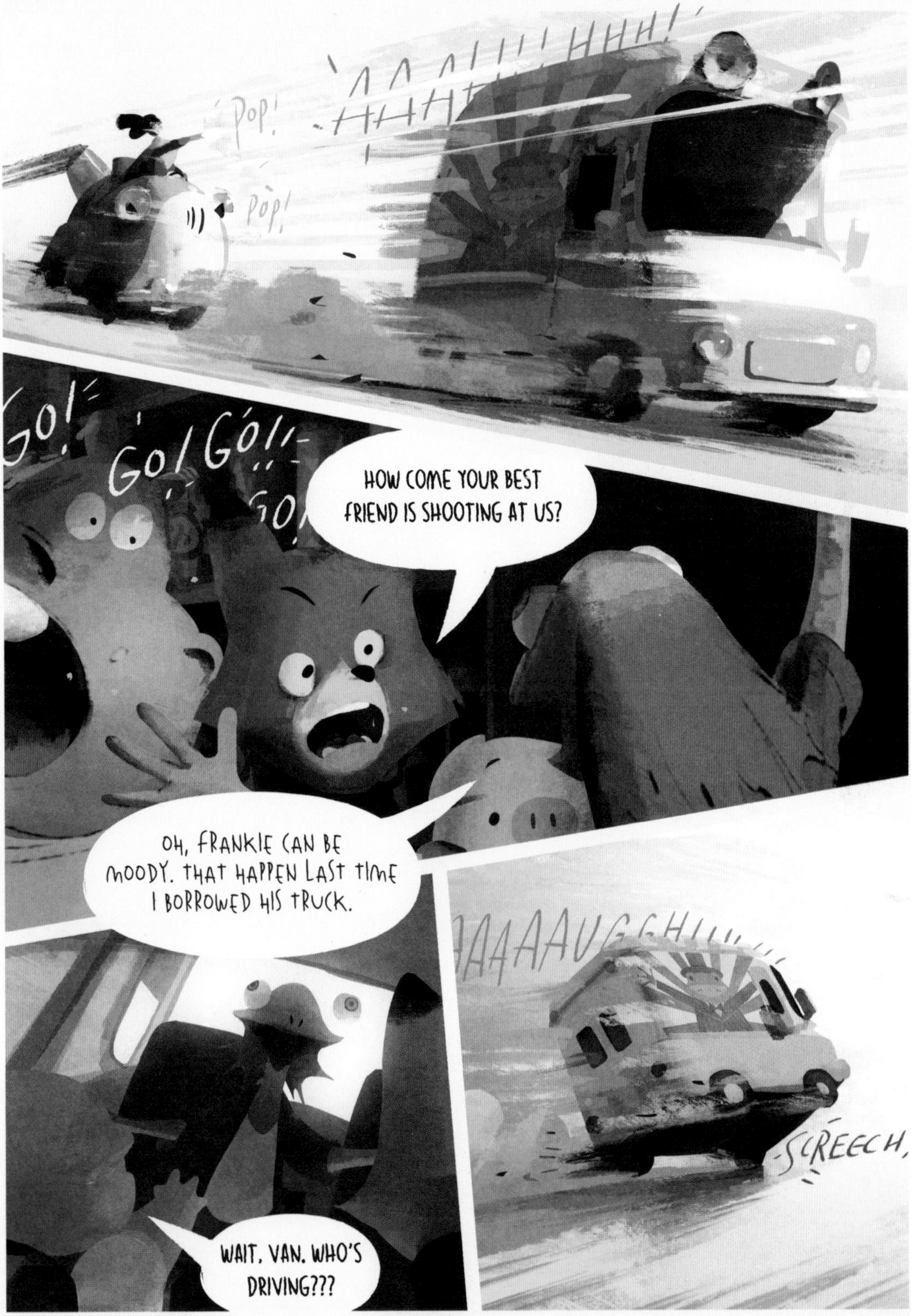
POP!
POP!
AAAAHHHHH!
GO!
GO! GO!
GO!
HOW COME YOUR BEST FRIEND IS SHOOTING AT US?
OH, FRANKIE CAN BE MOODY. THAT HAPPEN LAST TIME I BORROWED HIS TRUCK.
WAIT. VAN. WHO'S DRIVING???
AAAAAAUGGHH
SCREECH

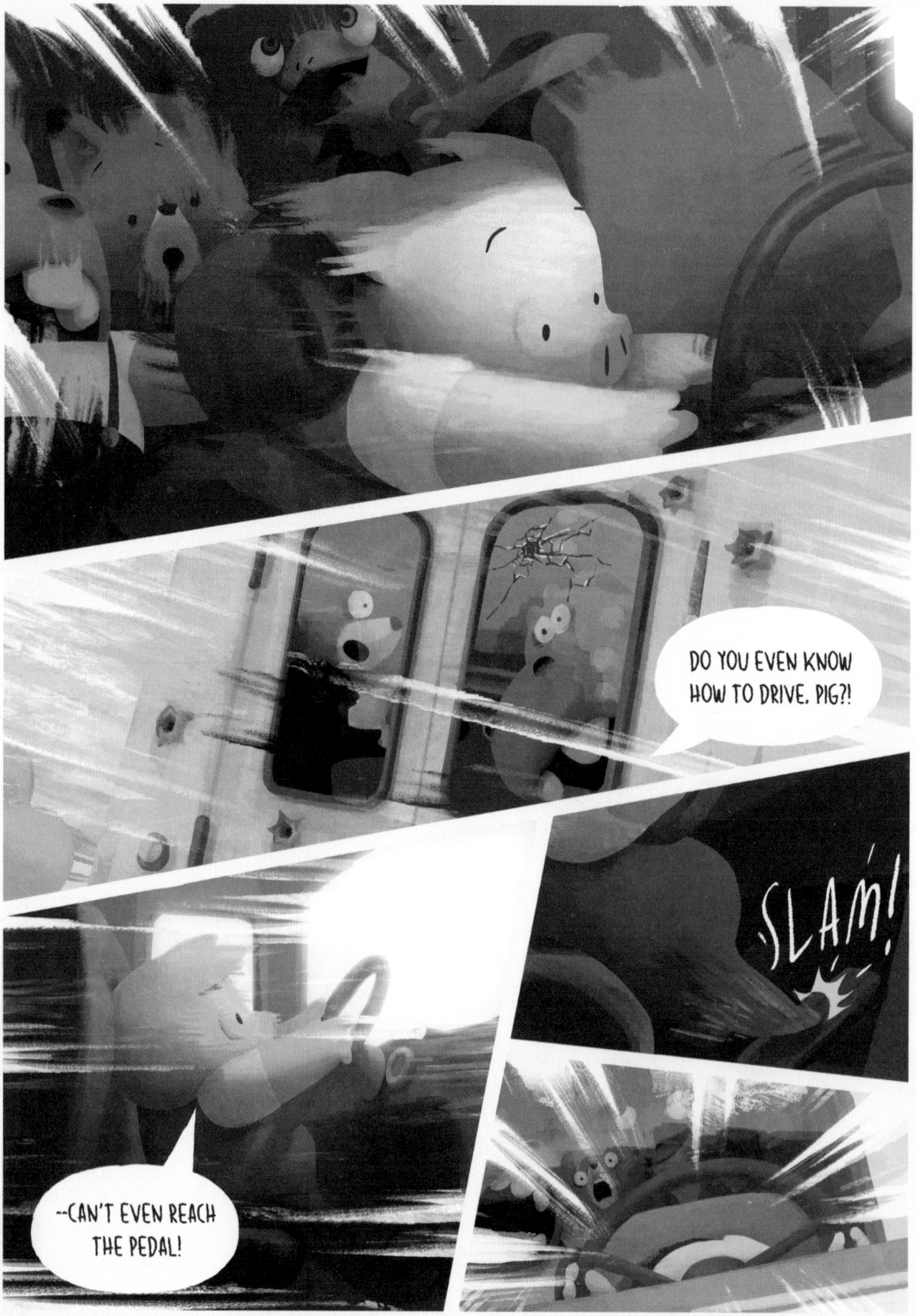
DO YOU EVEN KNOW HOW TO DRIVE, PIG?!
SLAM!
--CAN'T EVEN REACH THE PEDAL!

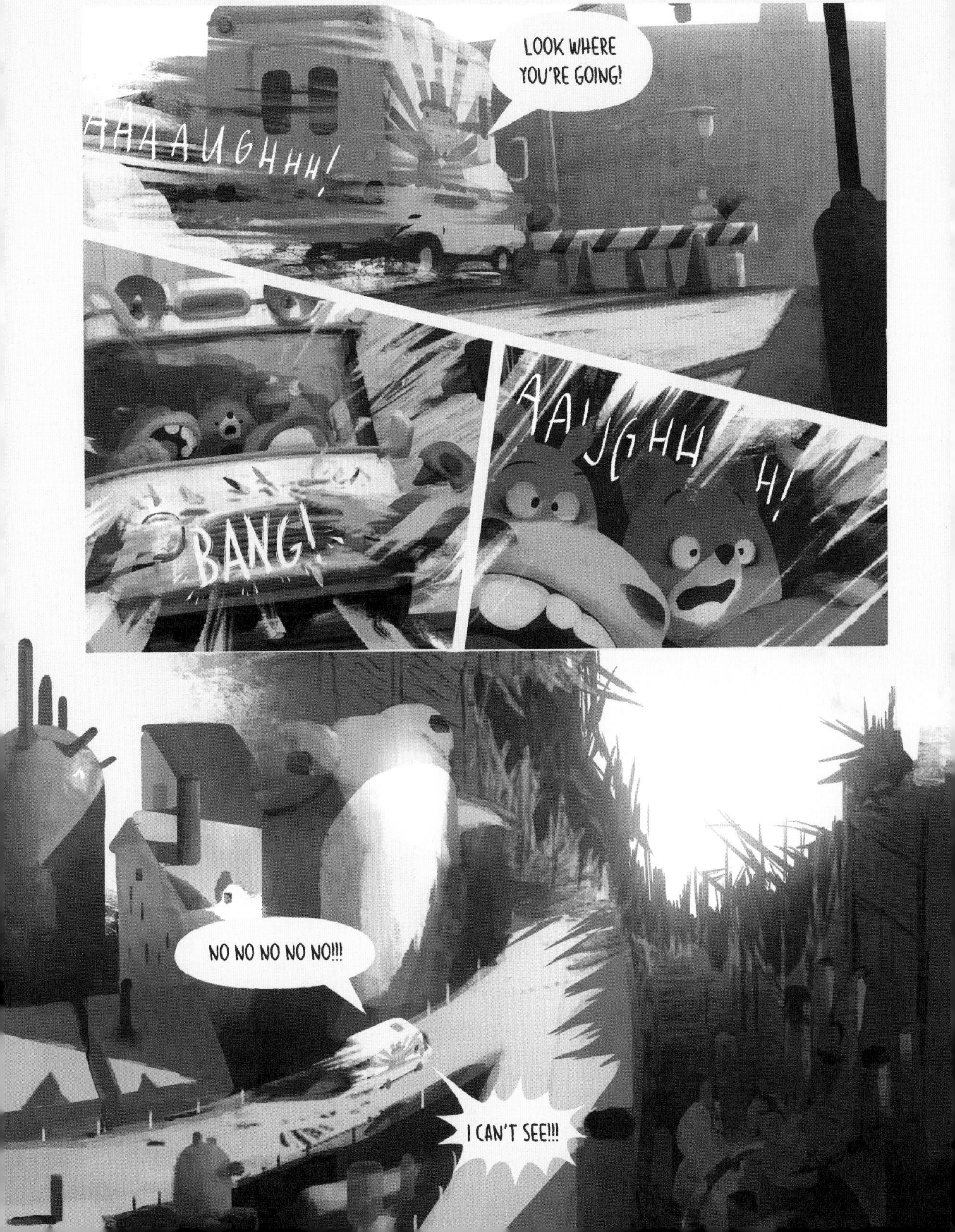
AAAAAUGHHH!
LOOK WHERE YOU'RE GOING!
BANG!
AAUGHHH!
NO NO NO NO NO!!!
I CAN'T SEE!!!

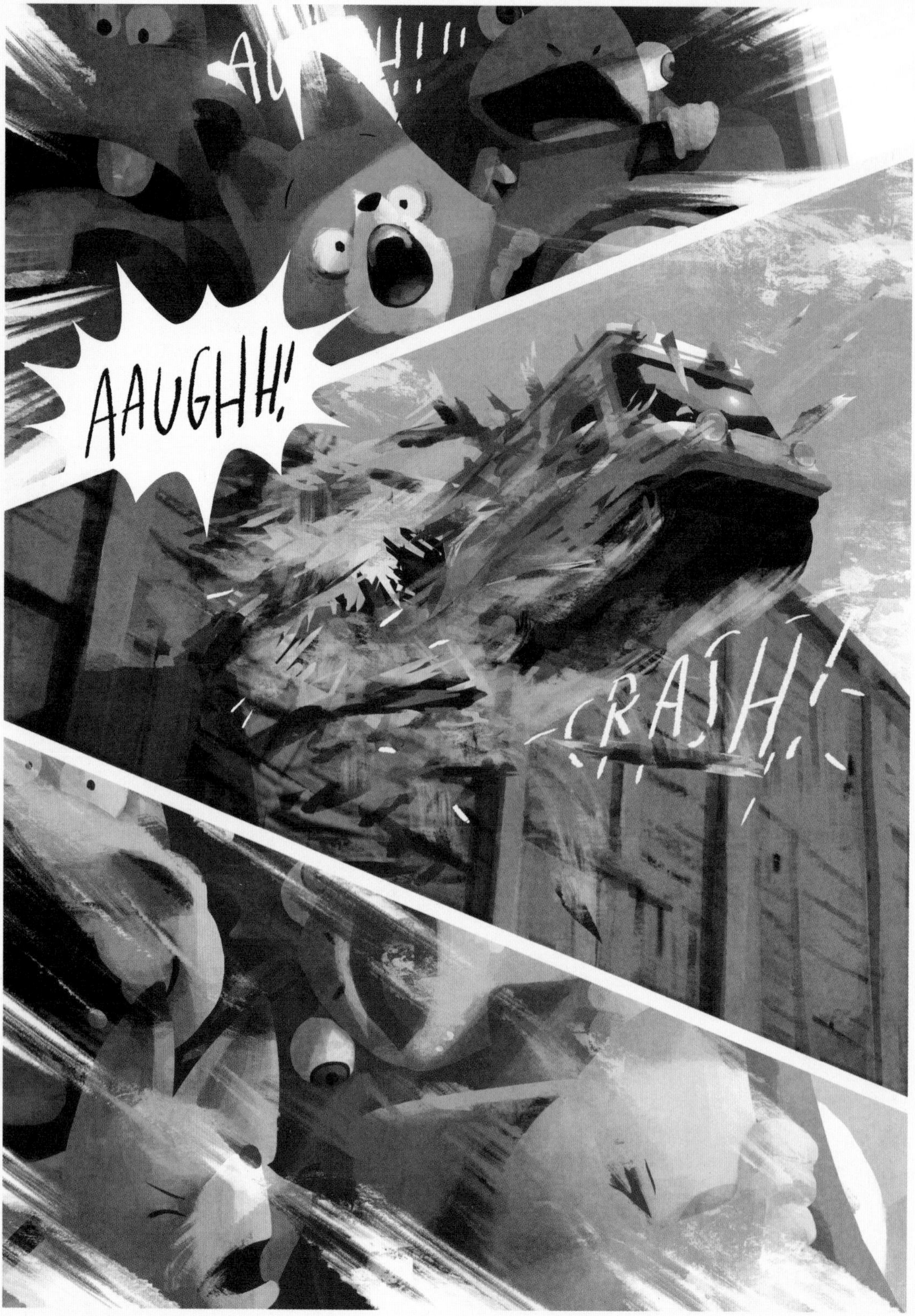
AAUGHH!
CRASH!

CRASH!

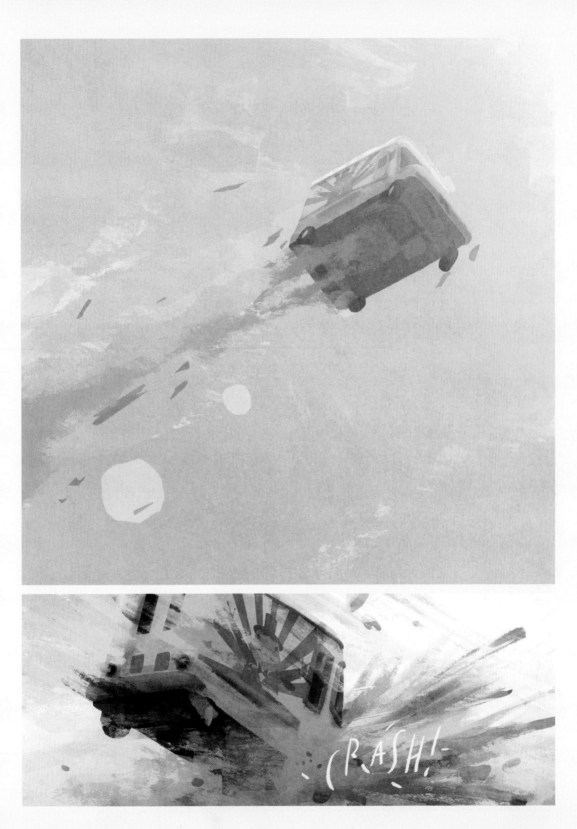

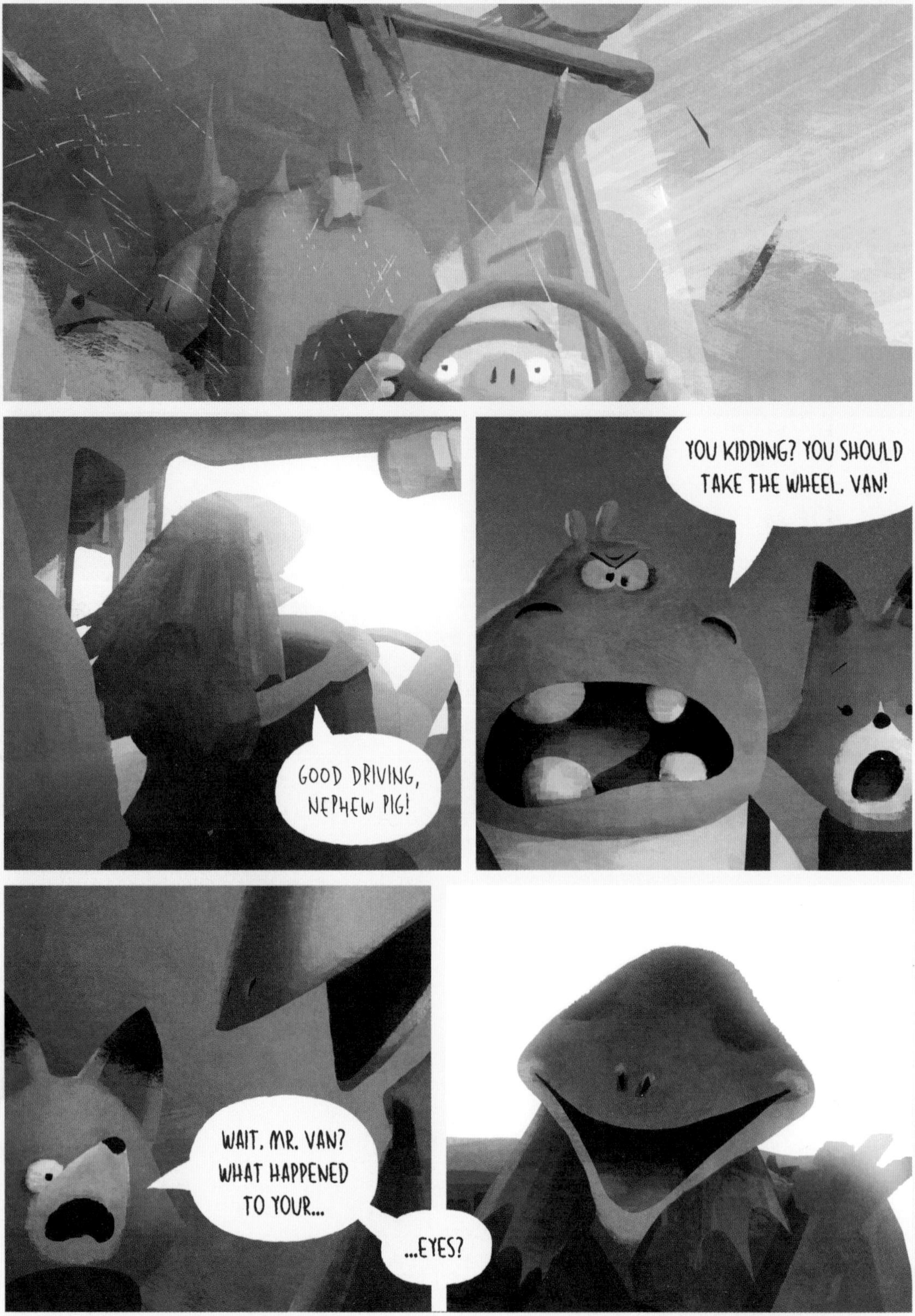
GOOD DRIVING, NEPHEW PIG!
YOU KIDDING? YOU SHOULD TAKE THE WHEEL, VAN!
WAIT, MR. VAN? WHAT HAPPENED TO YOUR...
...EYES?

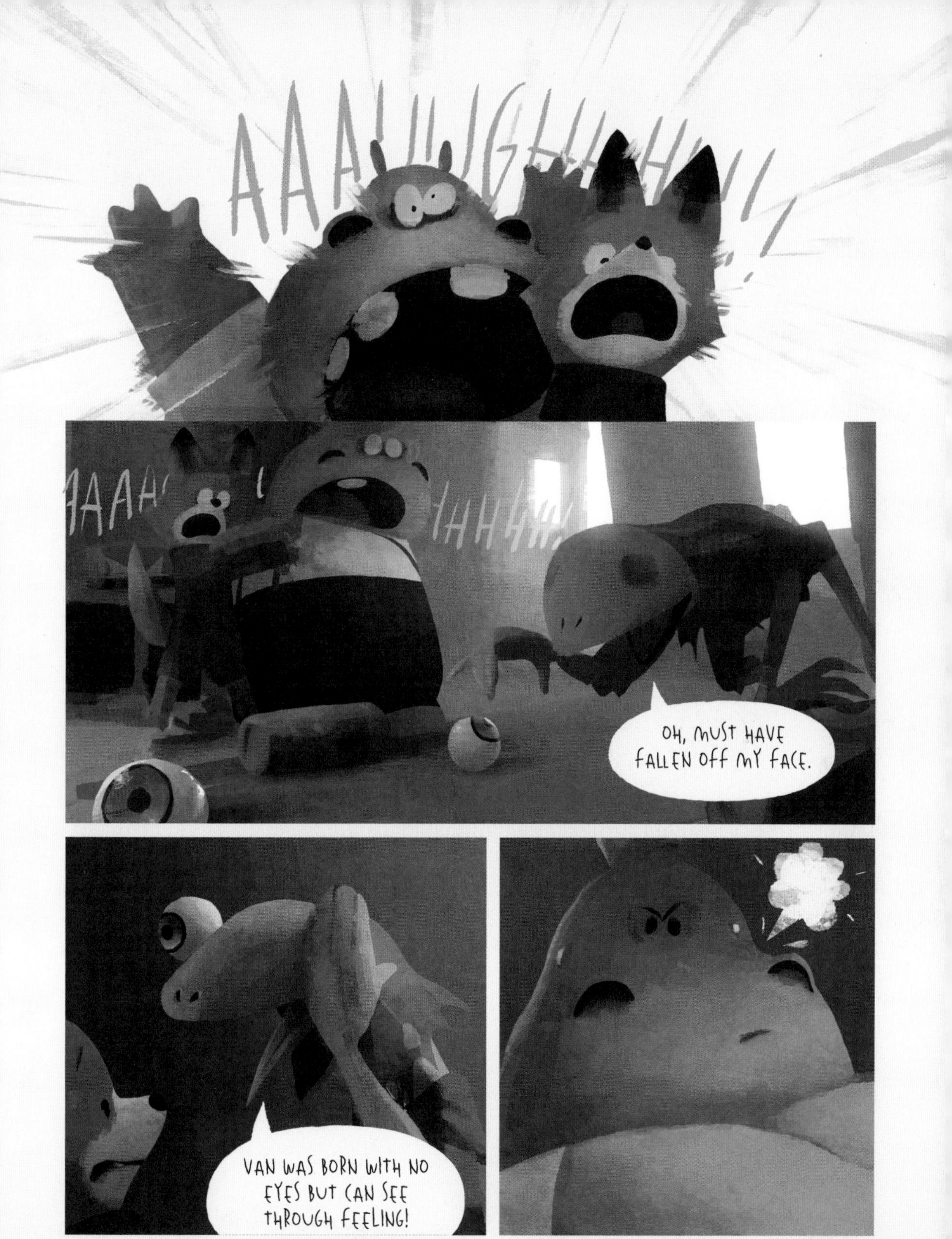
OH, MUST HAVE FALLEN OFF MY FACE.
VAN WAS BORN WITH NO EYES BUT CAN SEE THROUGH FEELING!

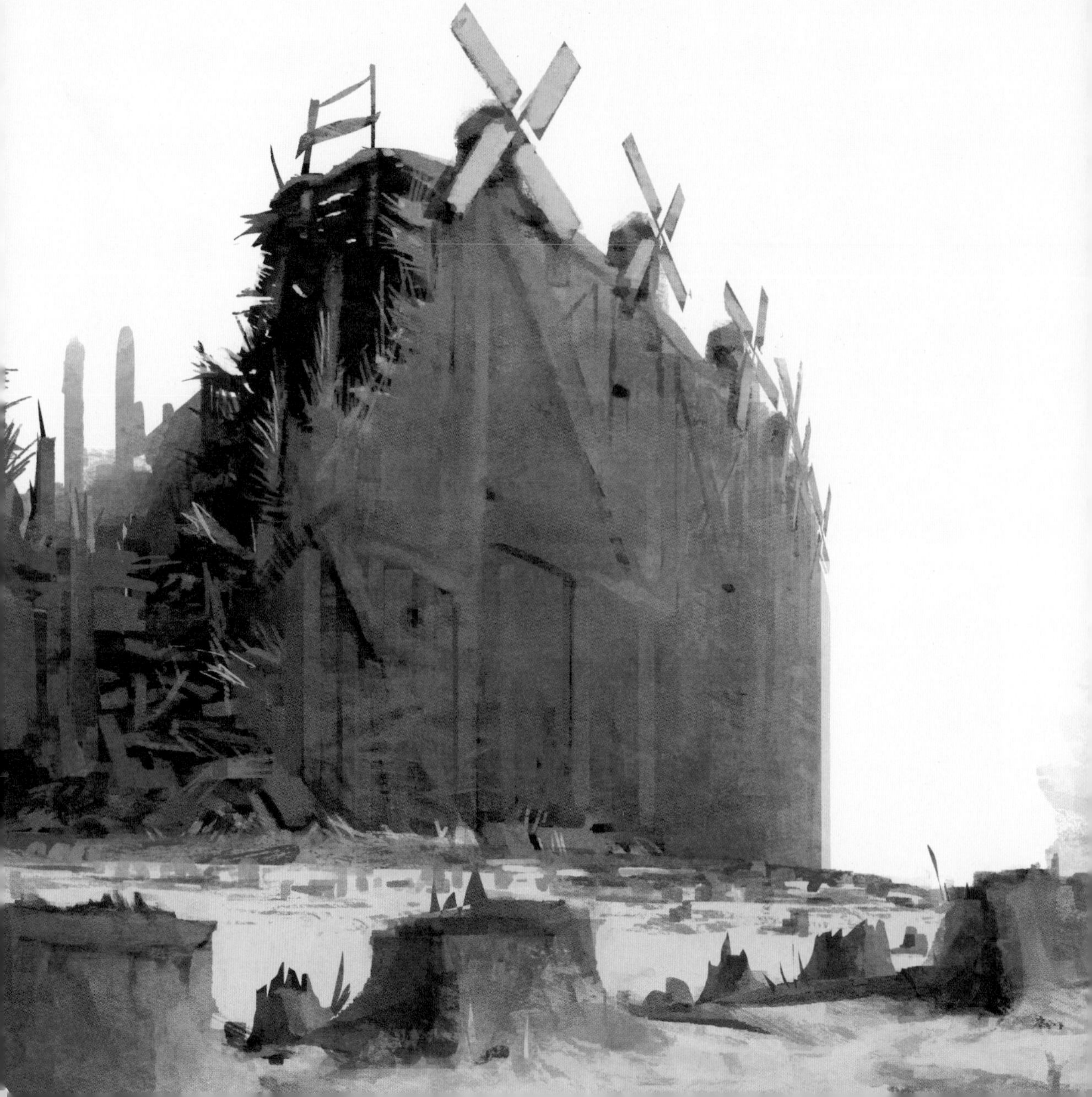

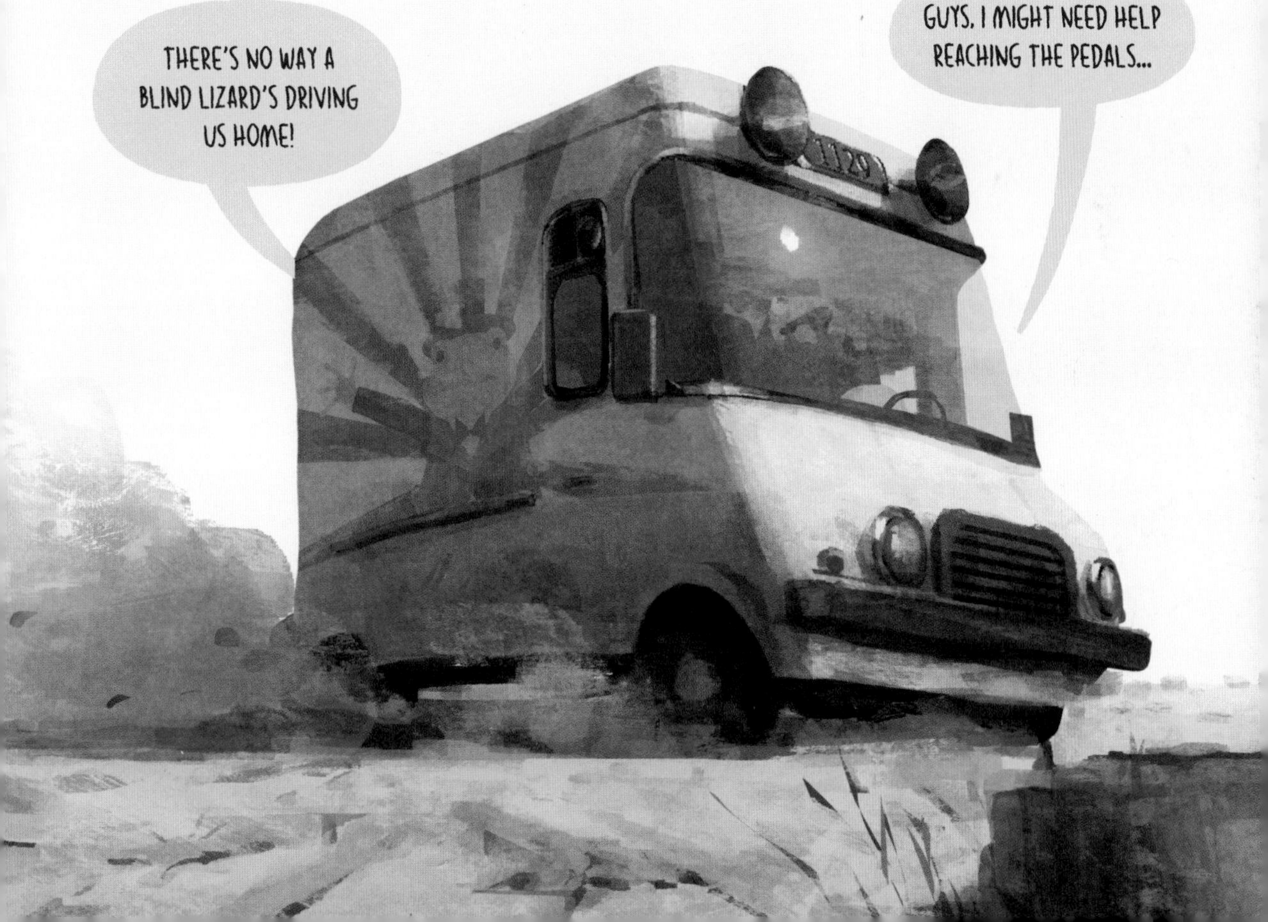
THERE'S NO WAY A BLIND LIZARD'S DRIVING US HOME!
GUYS, I MIGHT NEED HELP REACHING THE PEDALS...

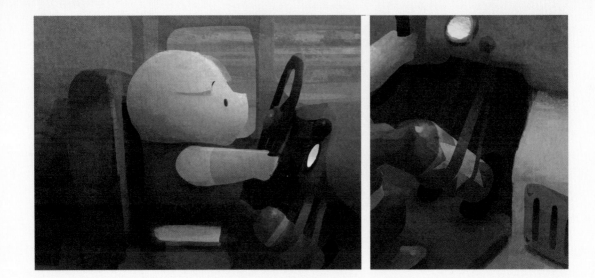

..ZzZ...

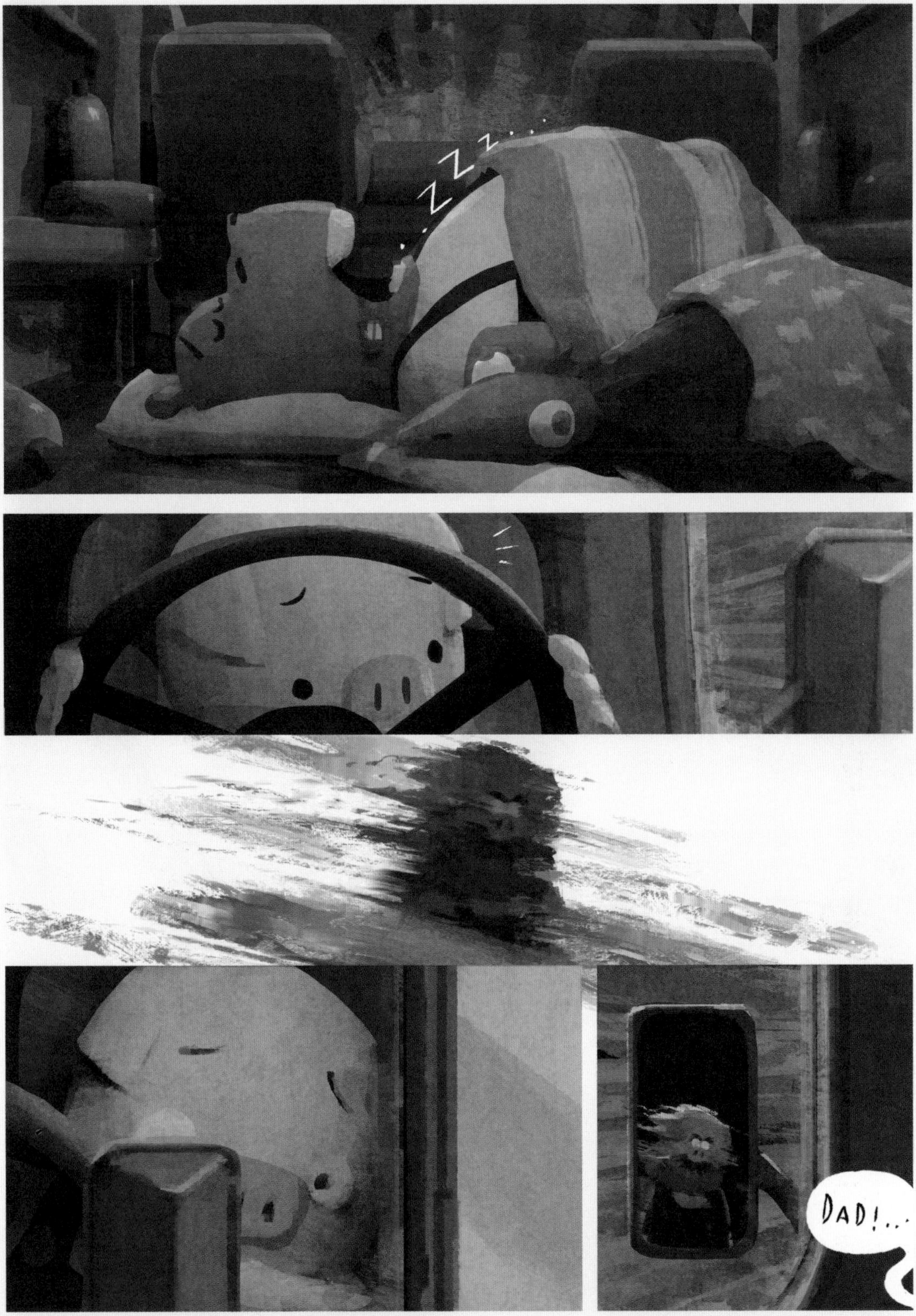
ZZZ...
DAD!...

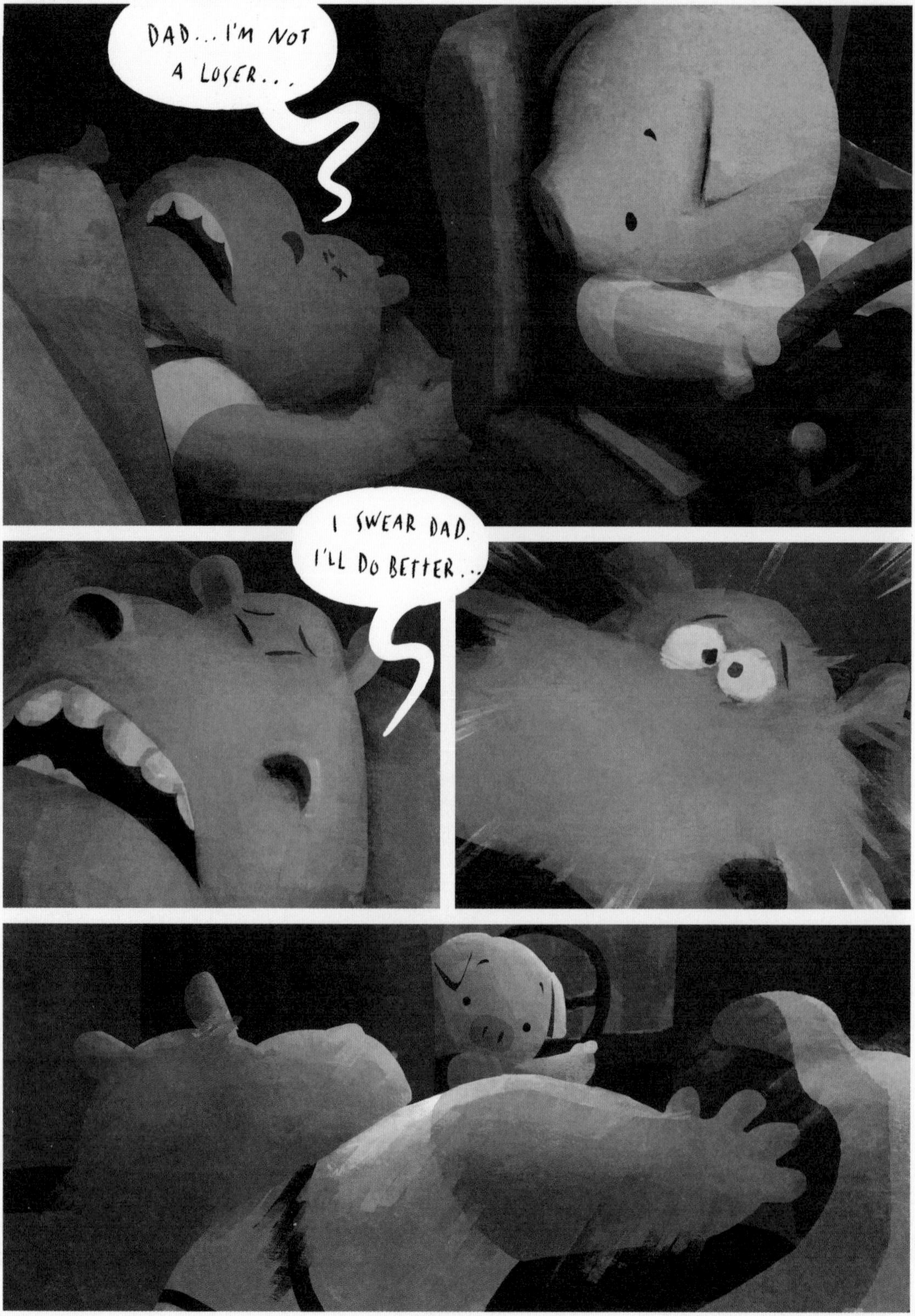
DAD... I'M NOT A LOSER...
I SWEAR DAD. I'LL DO BETTER...

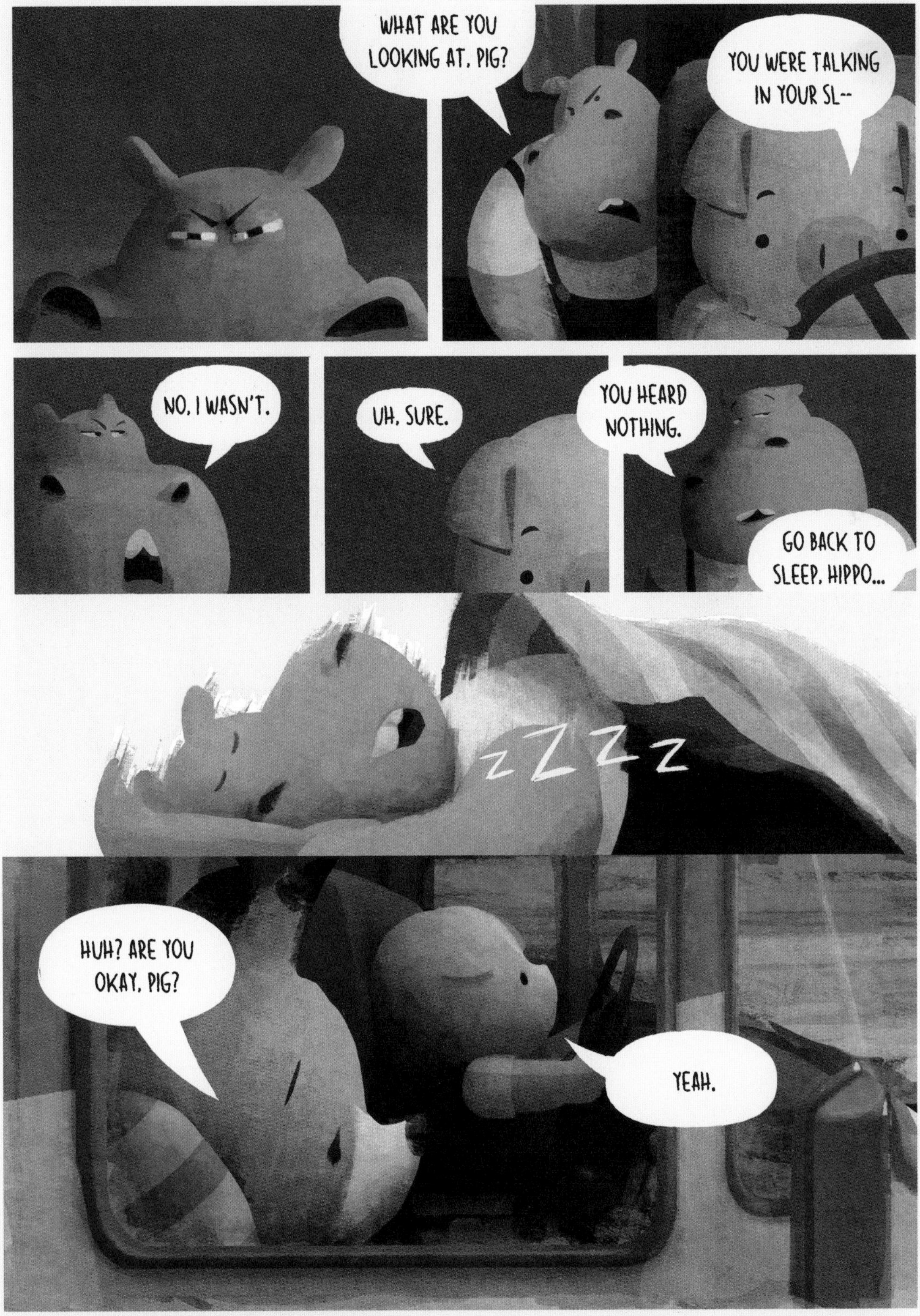
WHAT ARE YOU LOOKING AT, PIG?
YOU WERE TALKING IN YOUR SL--
NO, I WASN'T.
UH, SURE.
YOU HEARD NOTHING.
GO BACK TO SLEEP, HIPPO...
ZZZZZ
HUH? ARE YOU OKAY, PIG?
YEAH.

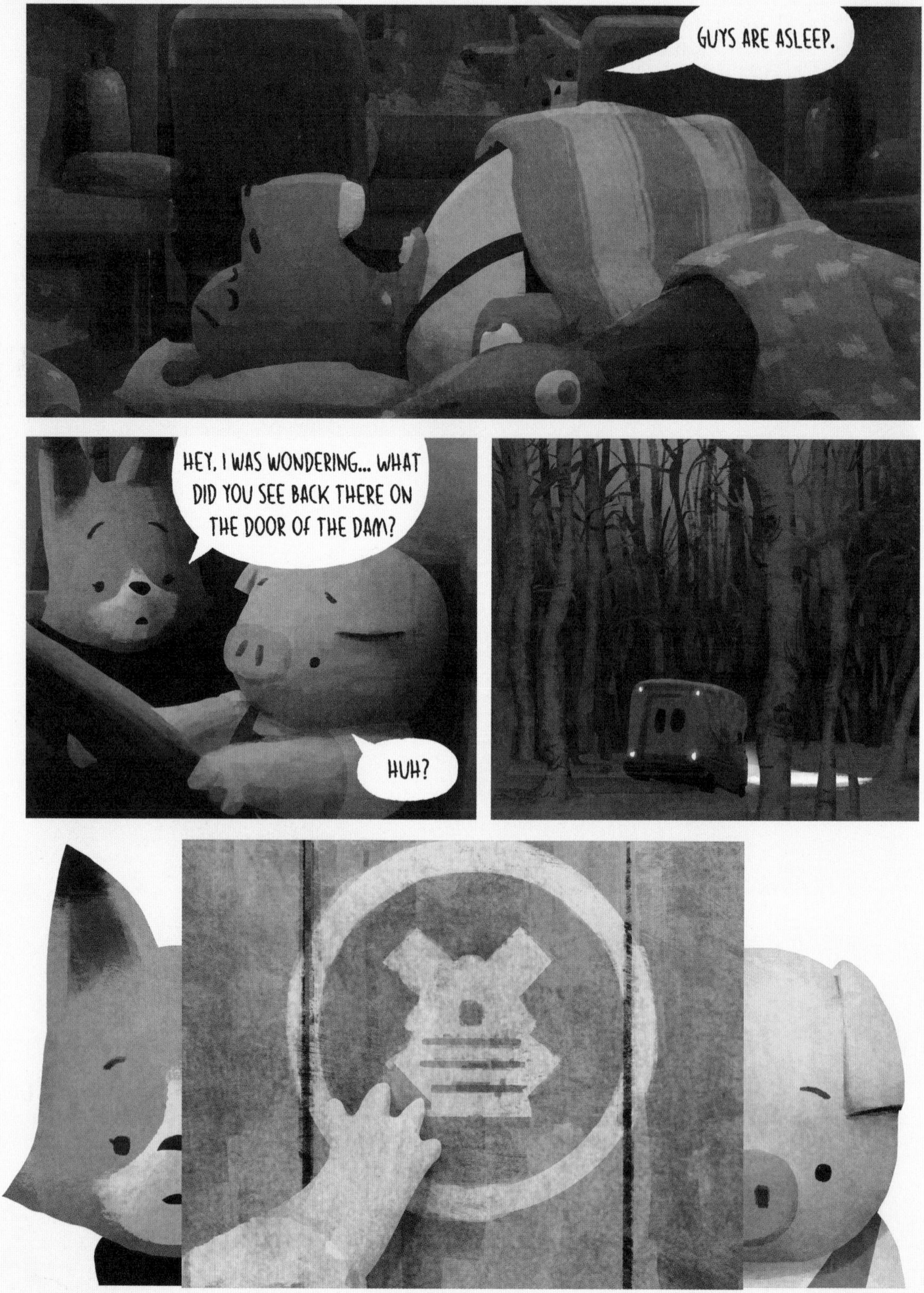
GUYS ARE ASLEEP.
HEY, I WAS WONDERING... WHAT DID YOU SEE BACK THERE ON THE DOOR OF THE DAM?
HUH?

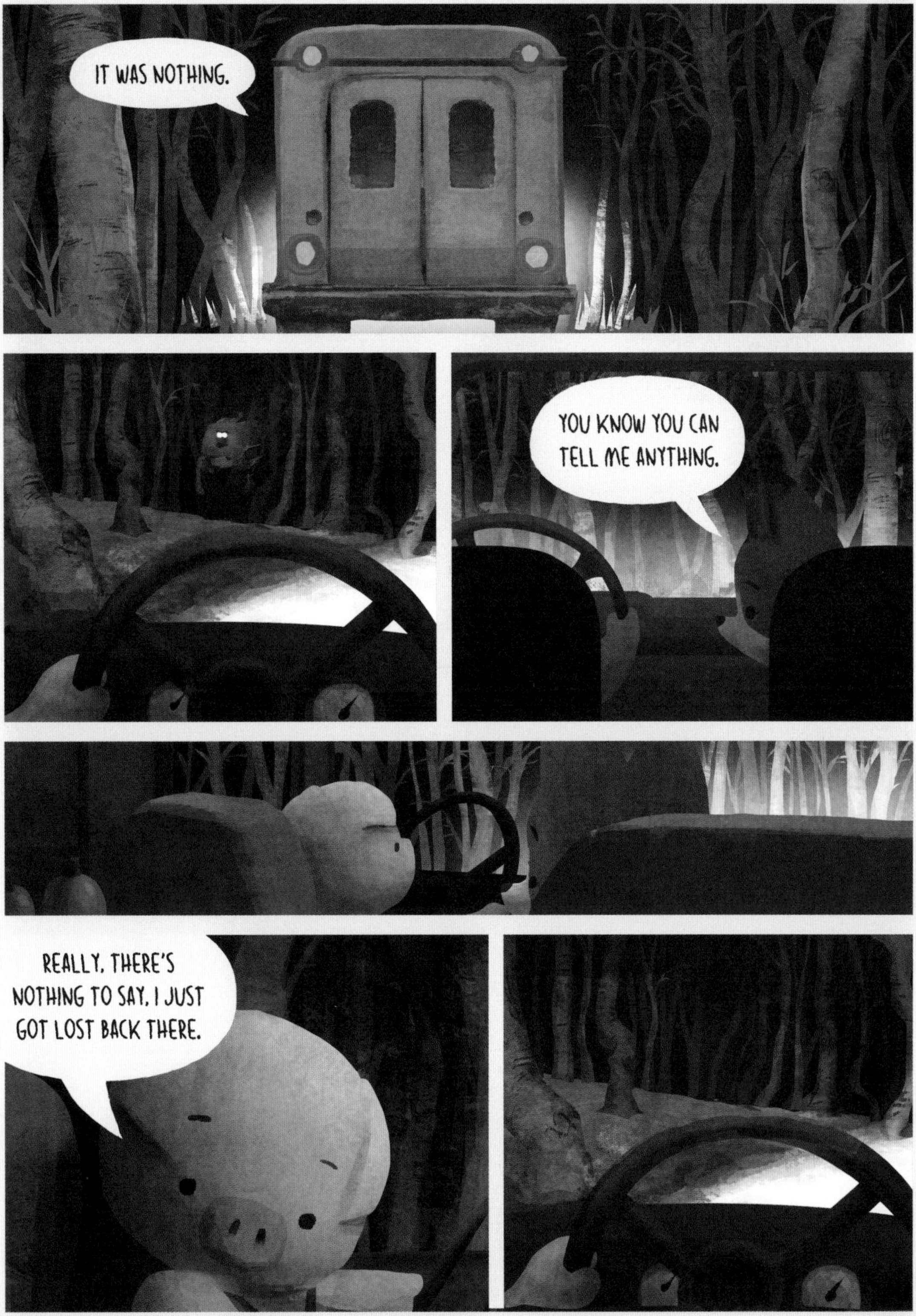
IT WAS NOTHING.
YOU KNOW YOU CAN TELL ME ANYTHING.
REALLY, THERE'S NOTHING TO SAY, I JUST GOT LOST BACK THERE.

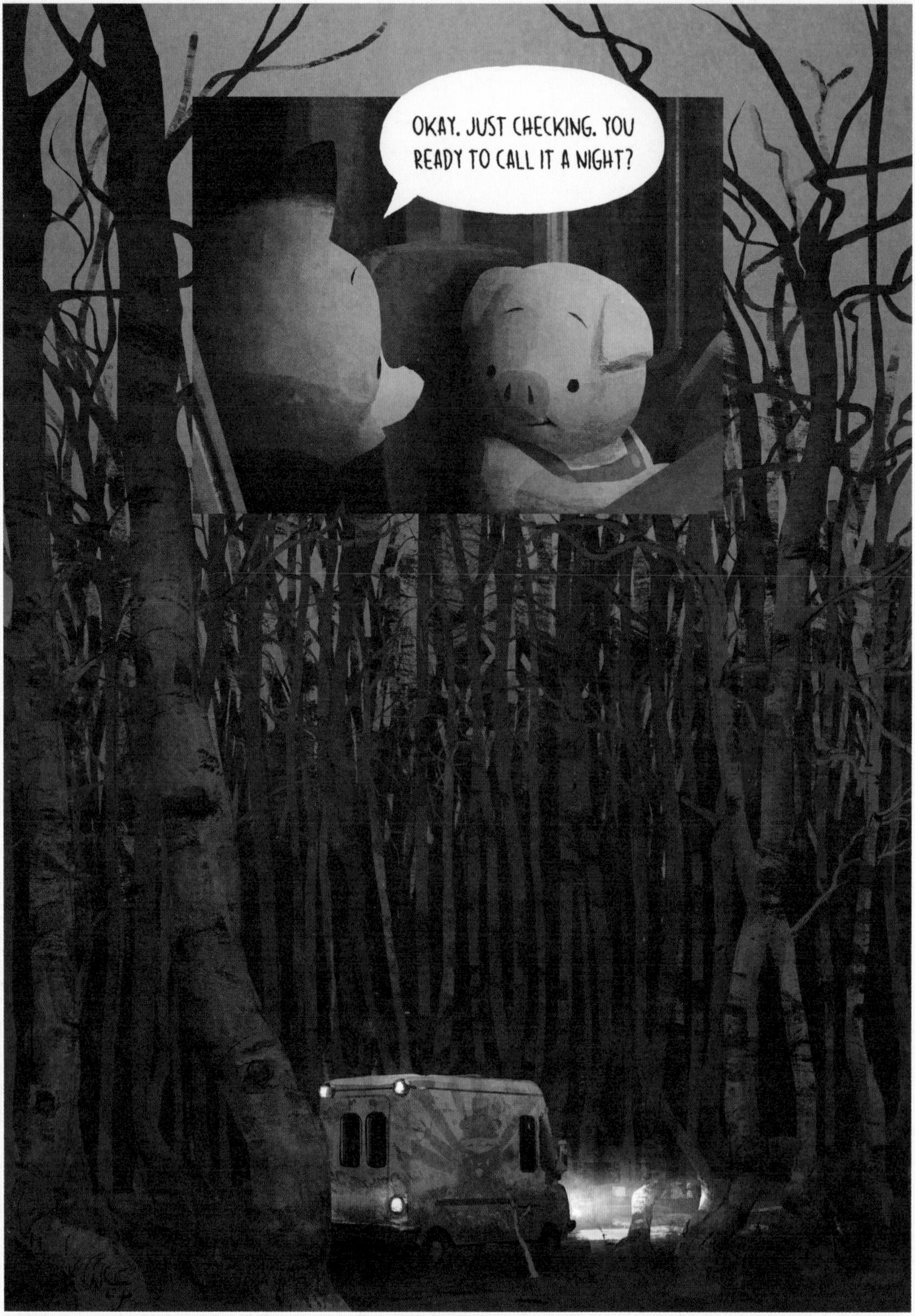
OKAY. JUST CHECKING. YOU READY TO CALL IT A NIGHT?

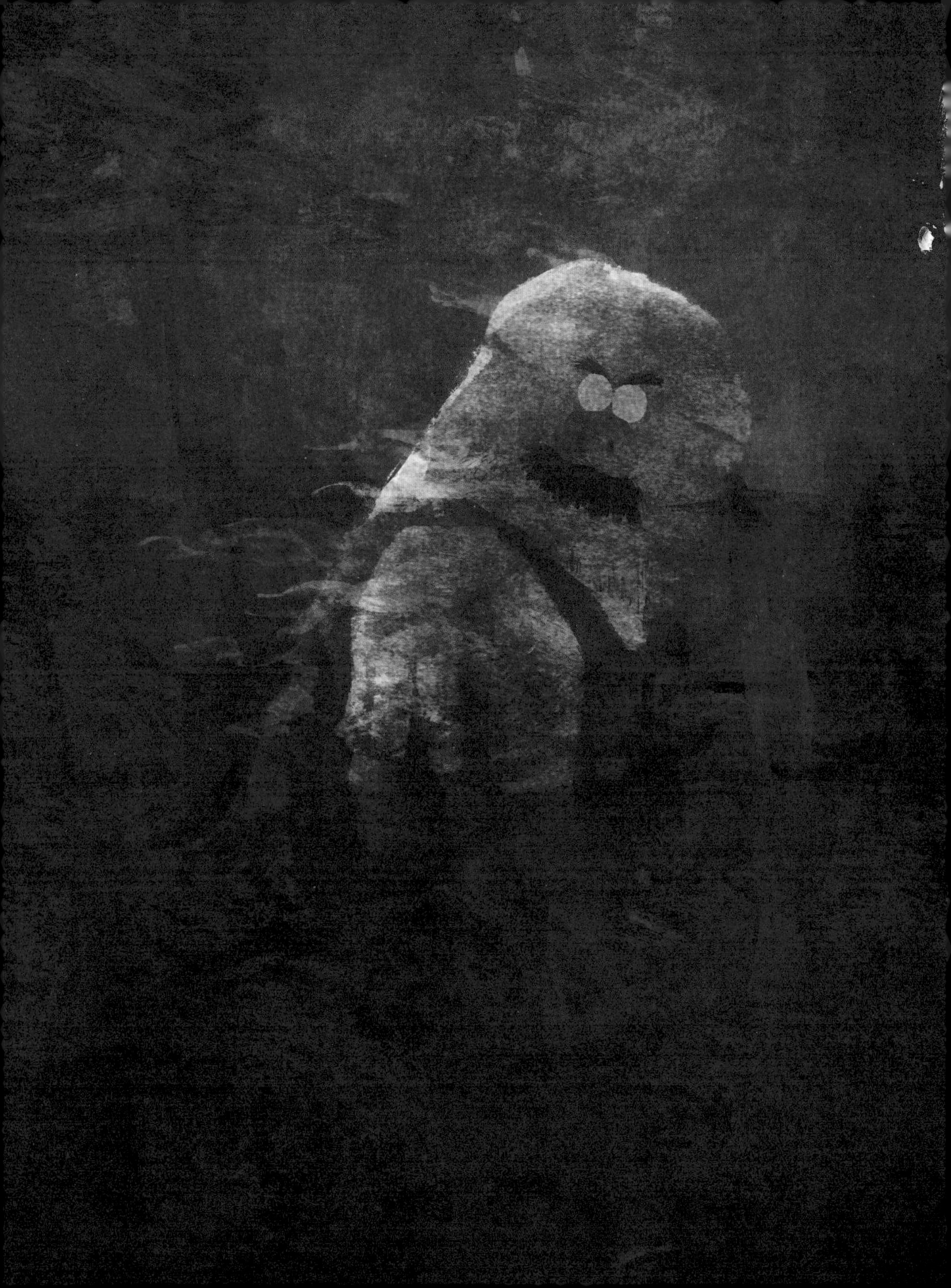

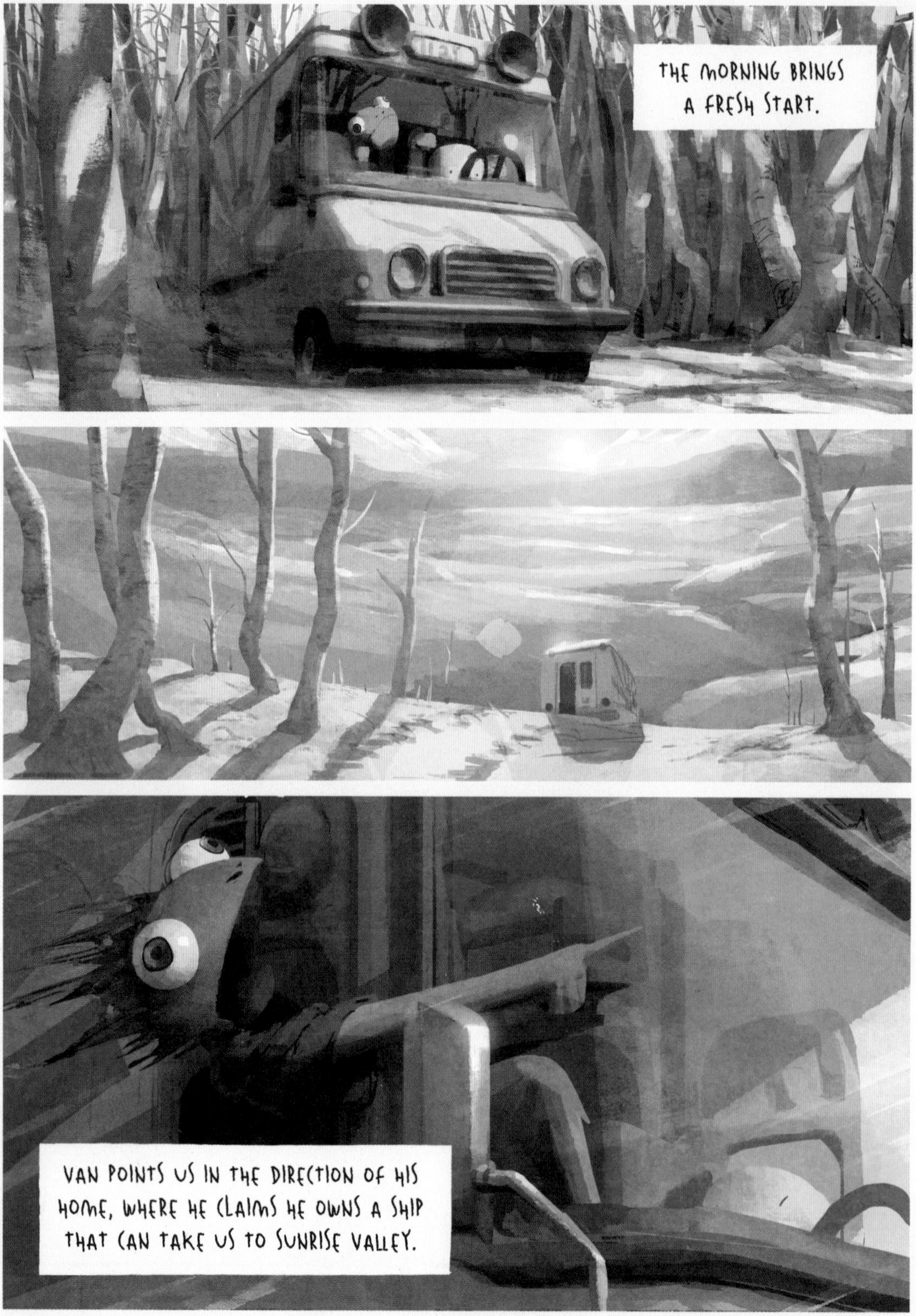
THE MORNING BRINGS A FRESH START.
VAN POINTS US IN THE DIRECTION OF HIS HOME, WHERE HE CLAIMS HE OWNS A SHIP THAT CAN TAKE US TO SUNRISE VALLEY.

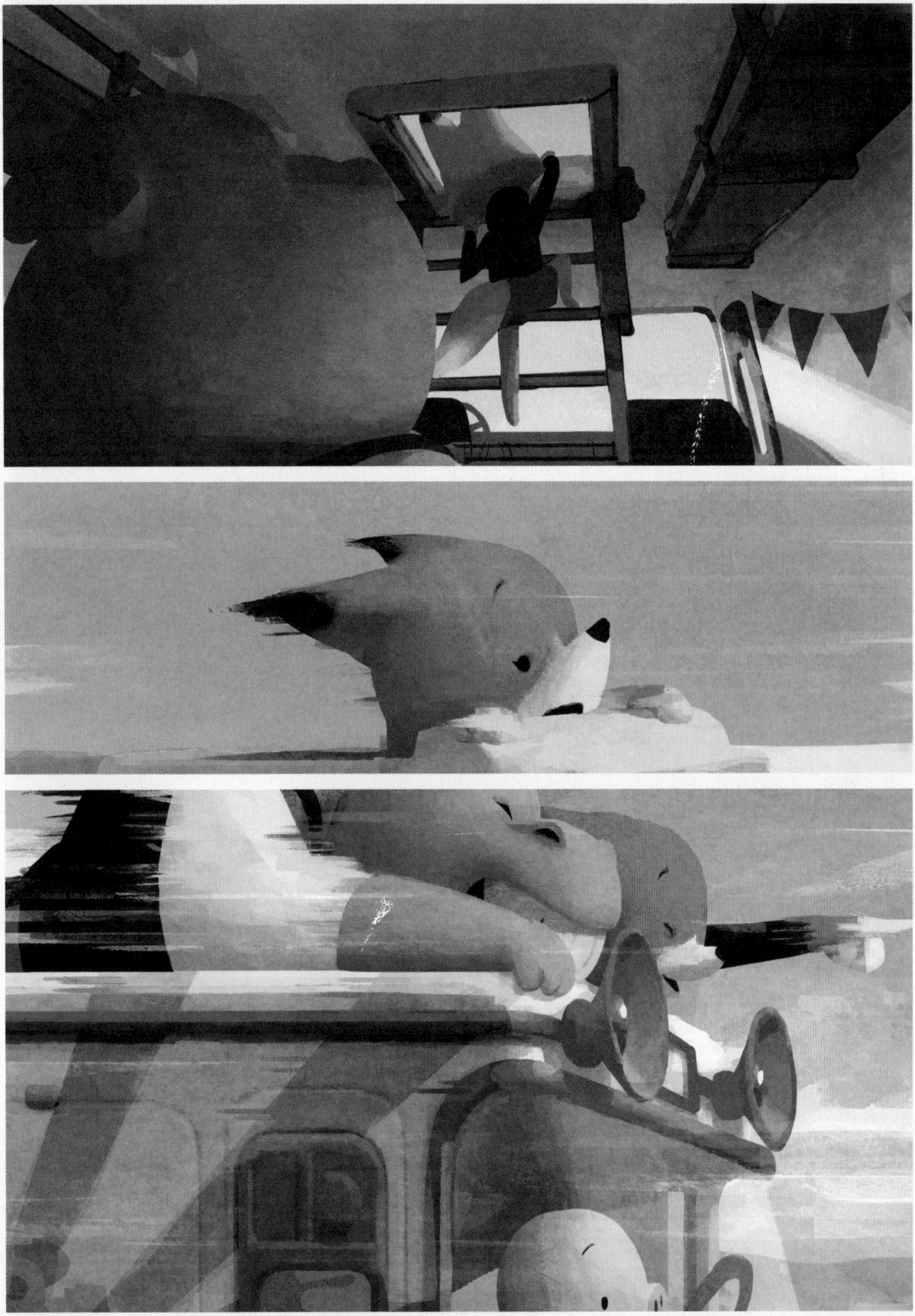

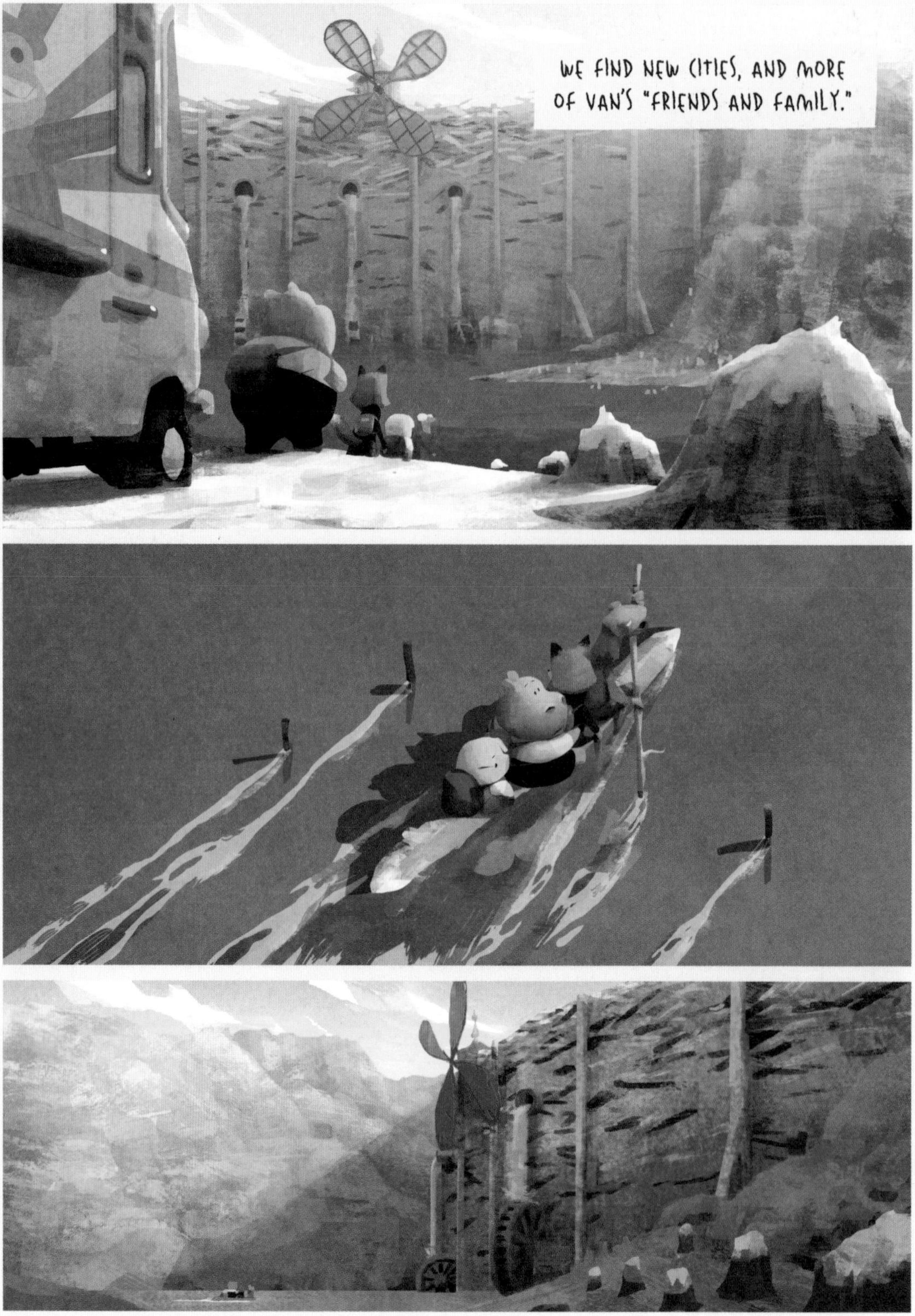
WE FIND NEW CITIES, AND MORE
OF VAN'S "FRIENDS AND FAMILY."

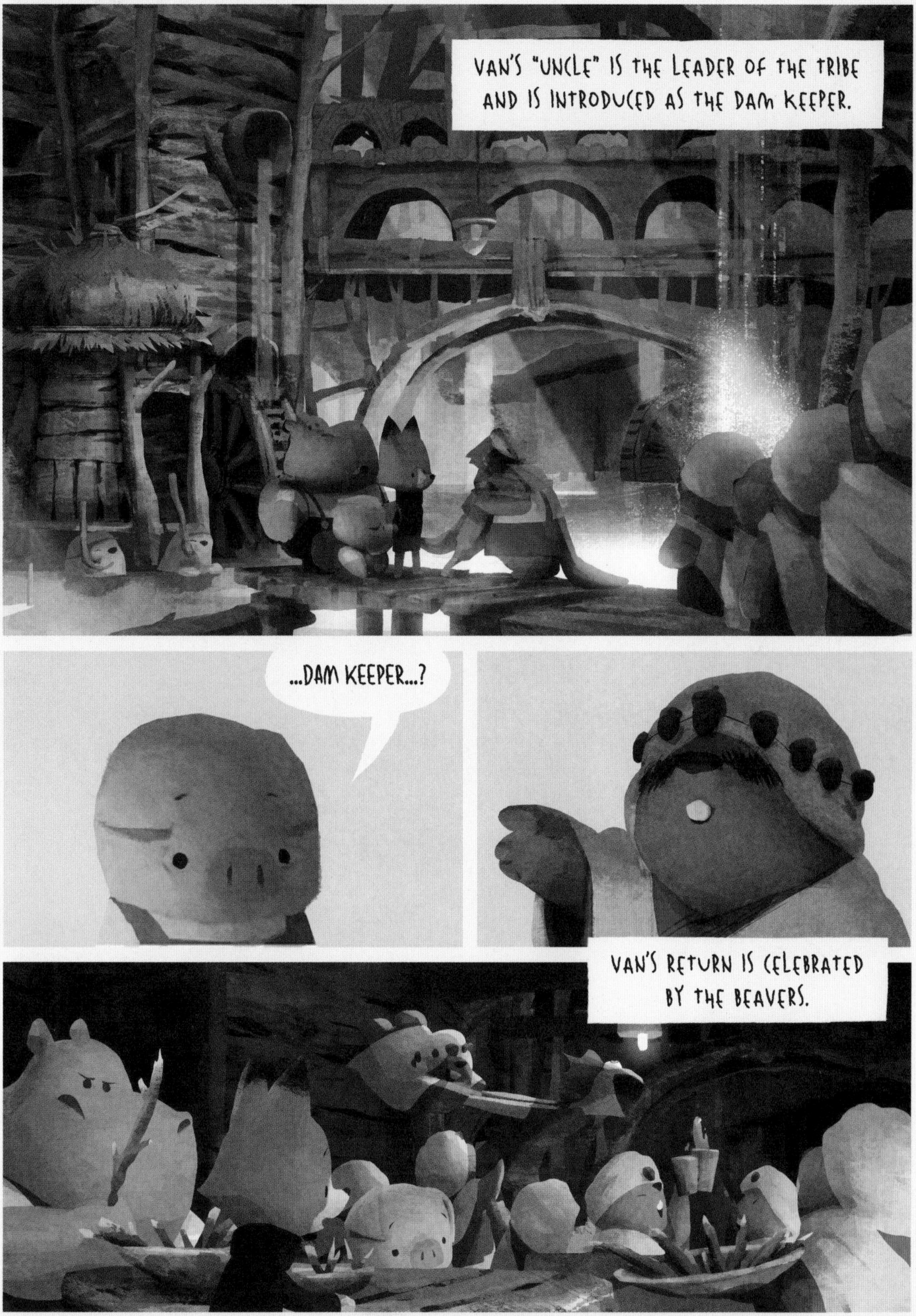
VAN'S "UNCLE" IS THE LEADER OF THE TRIBE AND IS INTRODUCED AS THE DAM KEEPER.
...DAM KEEPER...?
VAN'S RETURN IS CELEBRATED BY THE BEAVERS.

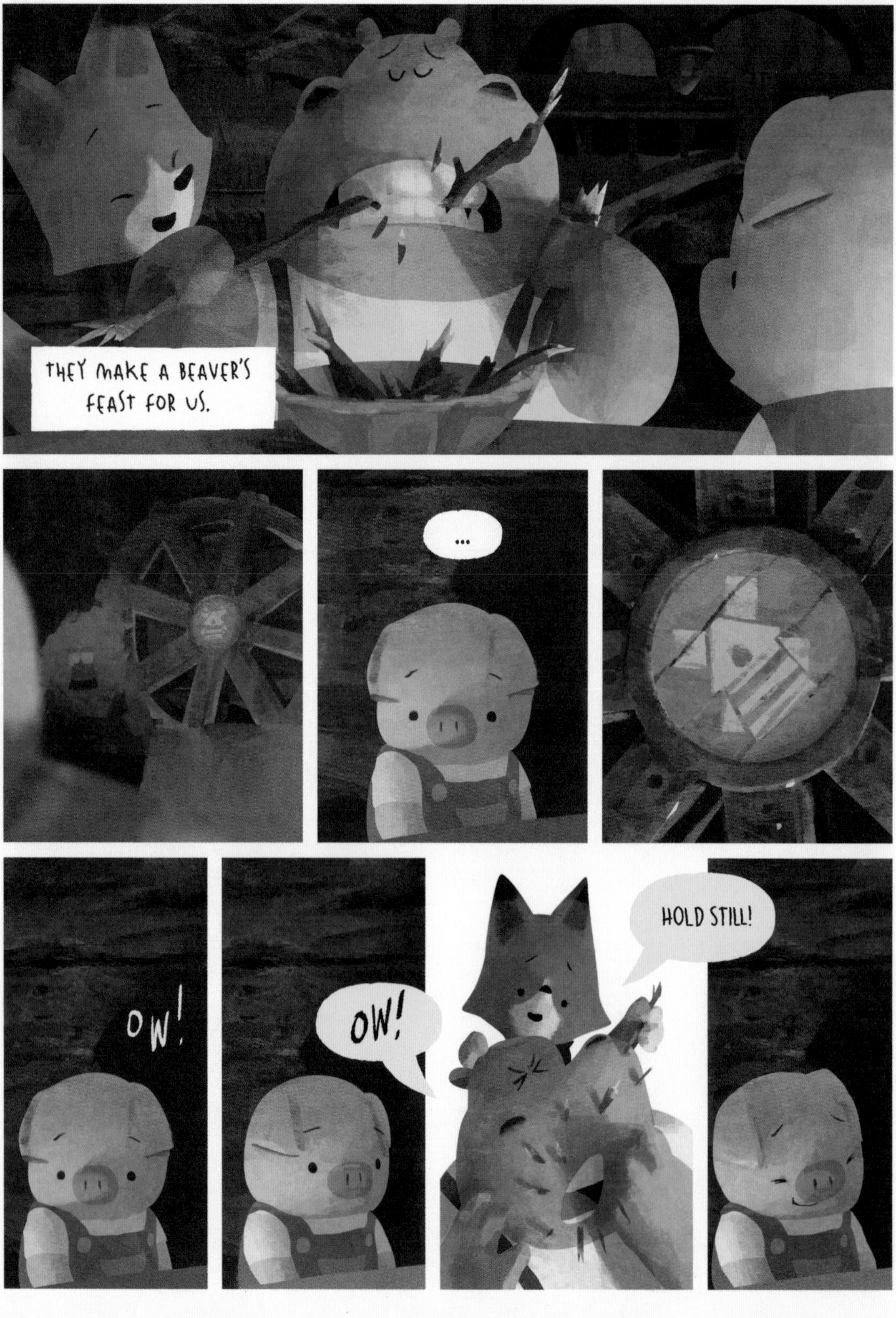
THEY MAKE A BEAVER'S FEAST FOR US.
...
OW!
OW!
HOLD STILL!

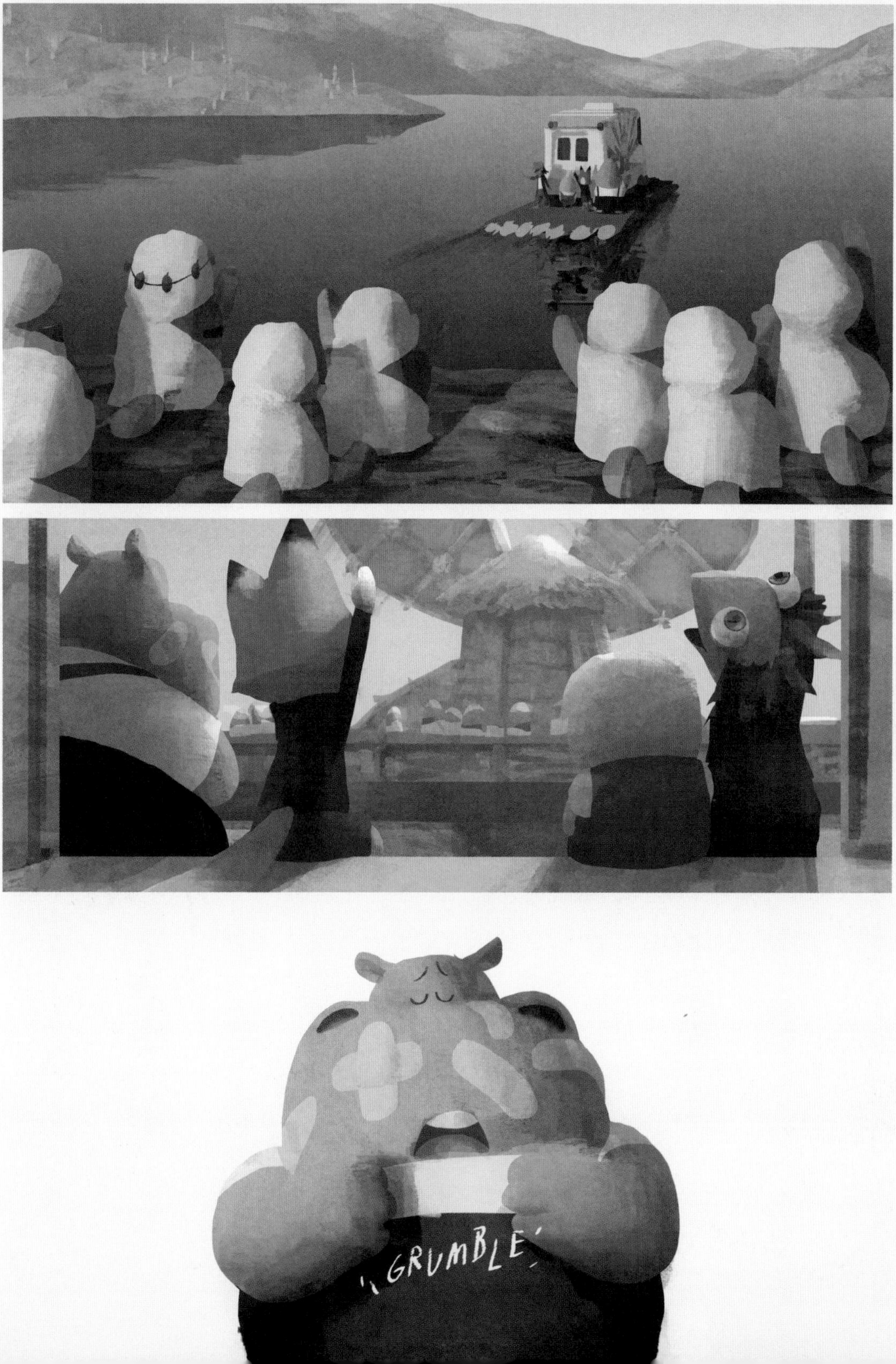
GRUMBLE

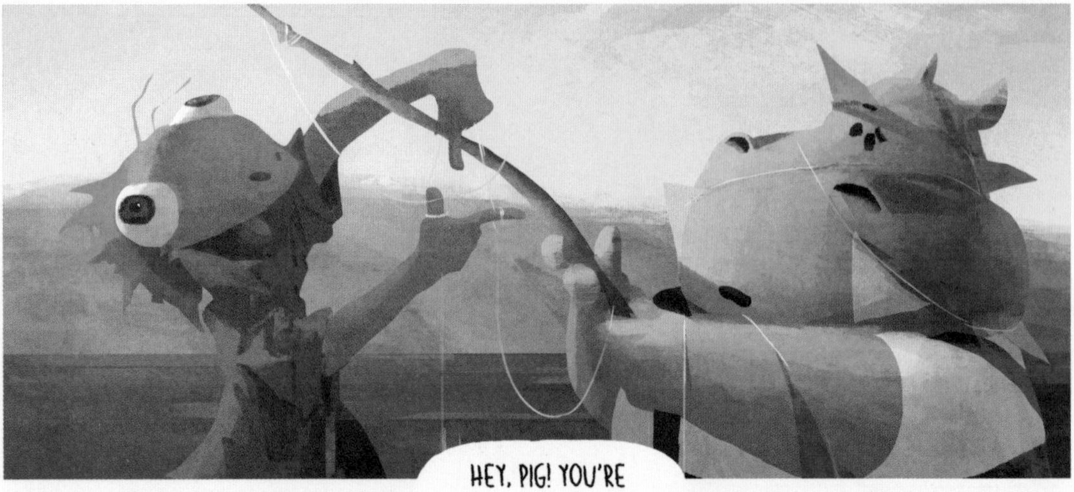

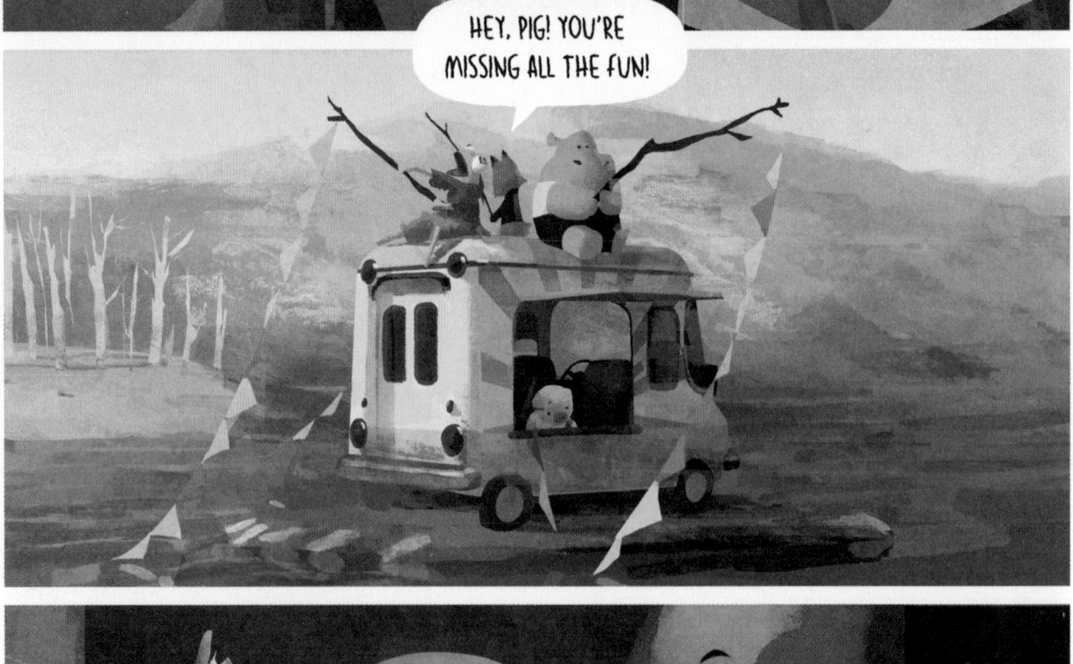
HEY, PIG! YOU'RE MISSING ALL THE FUN!

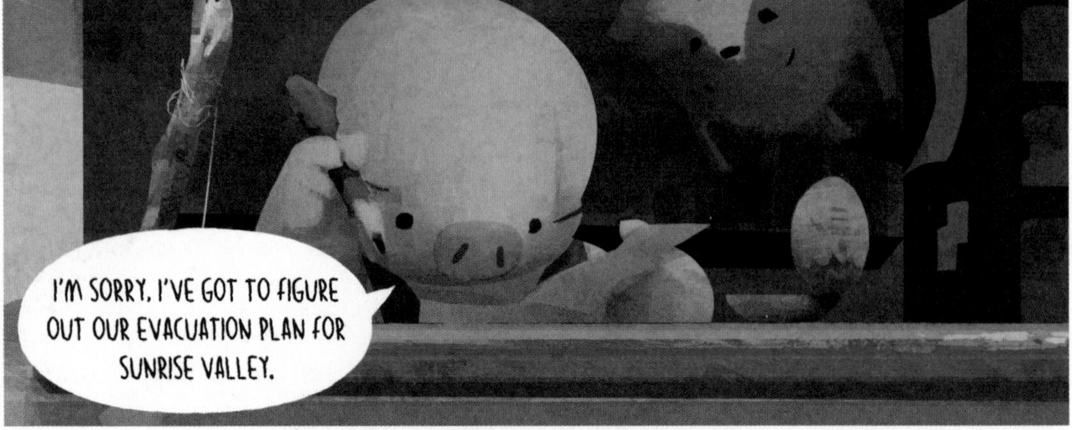
I'M SORRY, I'VE GOT TO FIGURE OUT OUR EVACUATION PLAN FOR SUNRISE VALLEY.

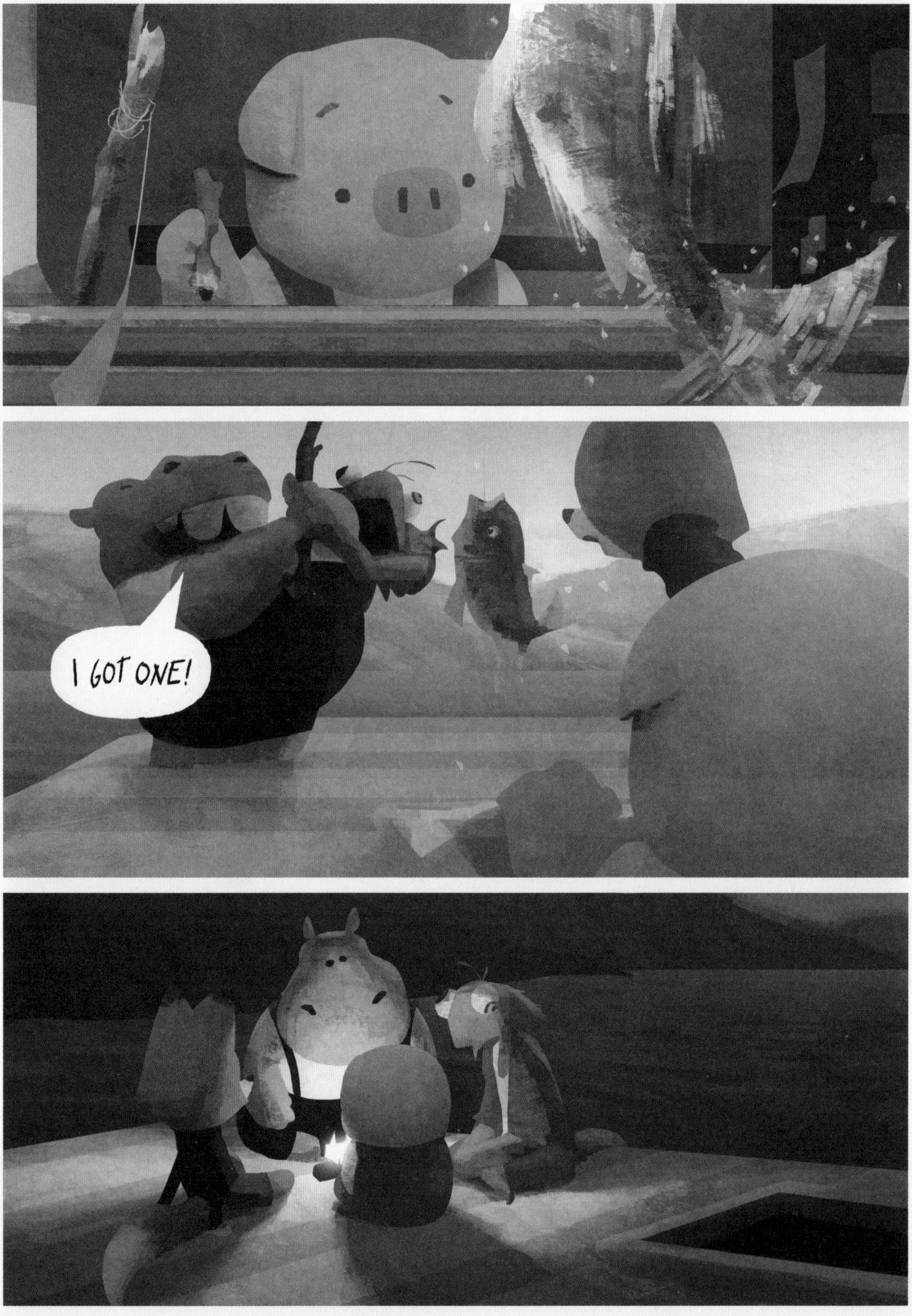
I GOT ONE!

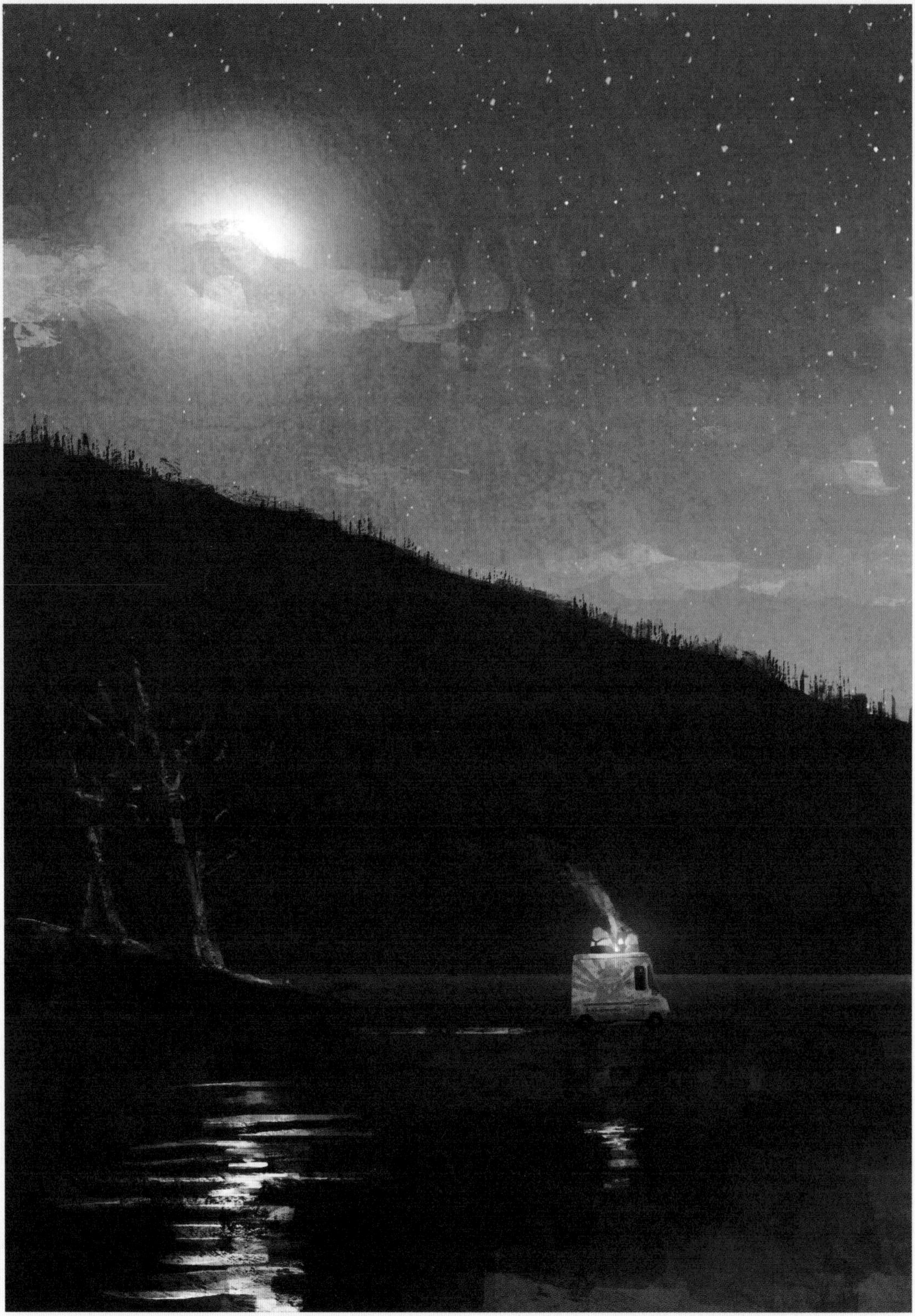

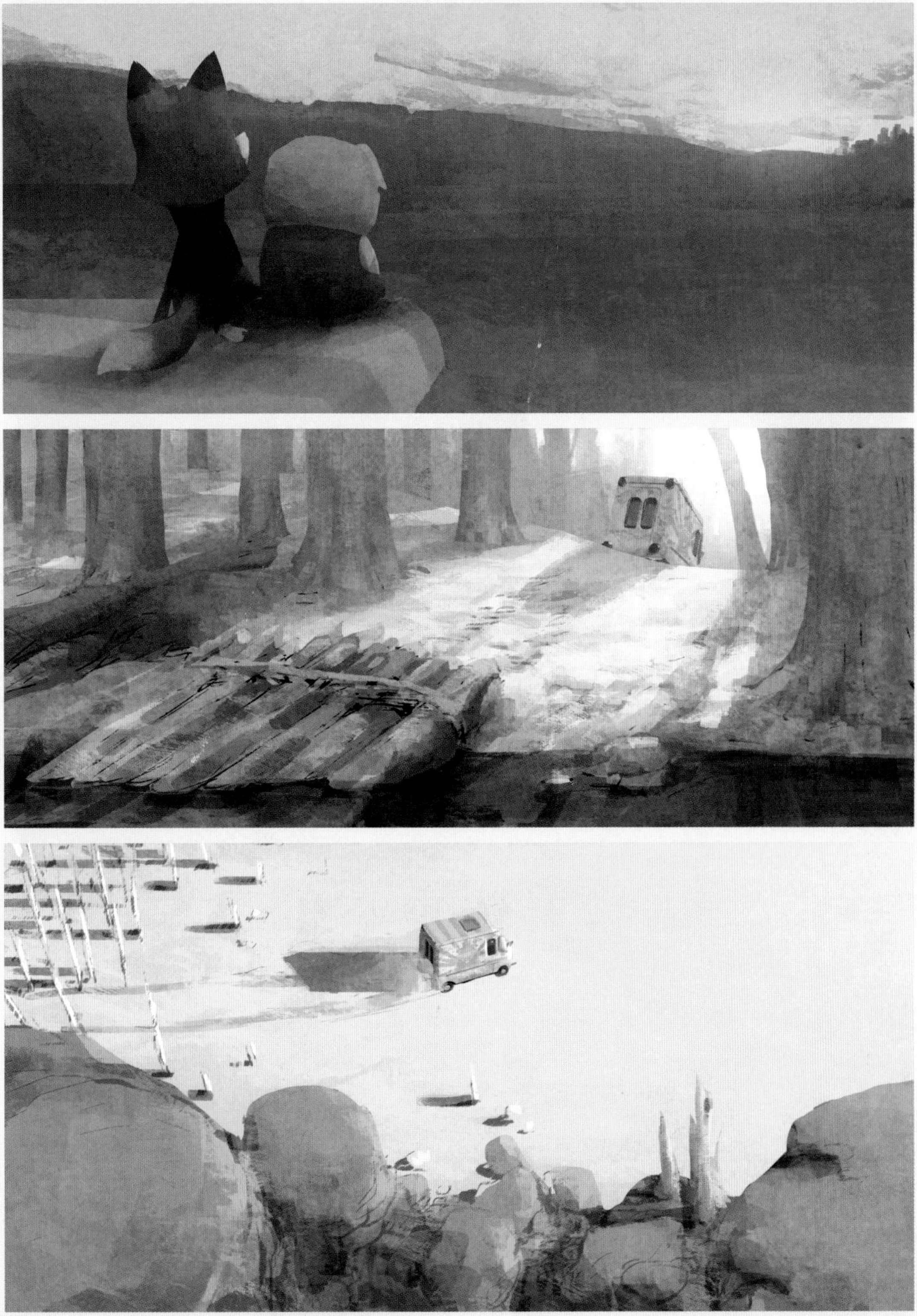

VAN'S TRUCK OVERHEATS,
AND SO DO WE.

THE HEAT CAN MAKE
YOU SEE THINGS.

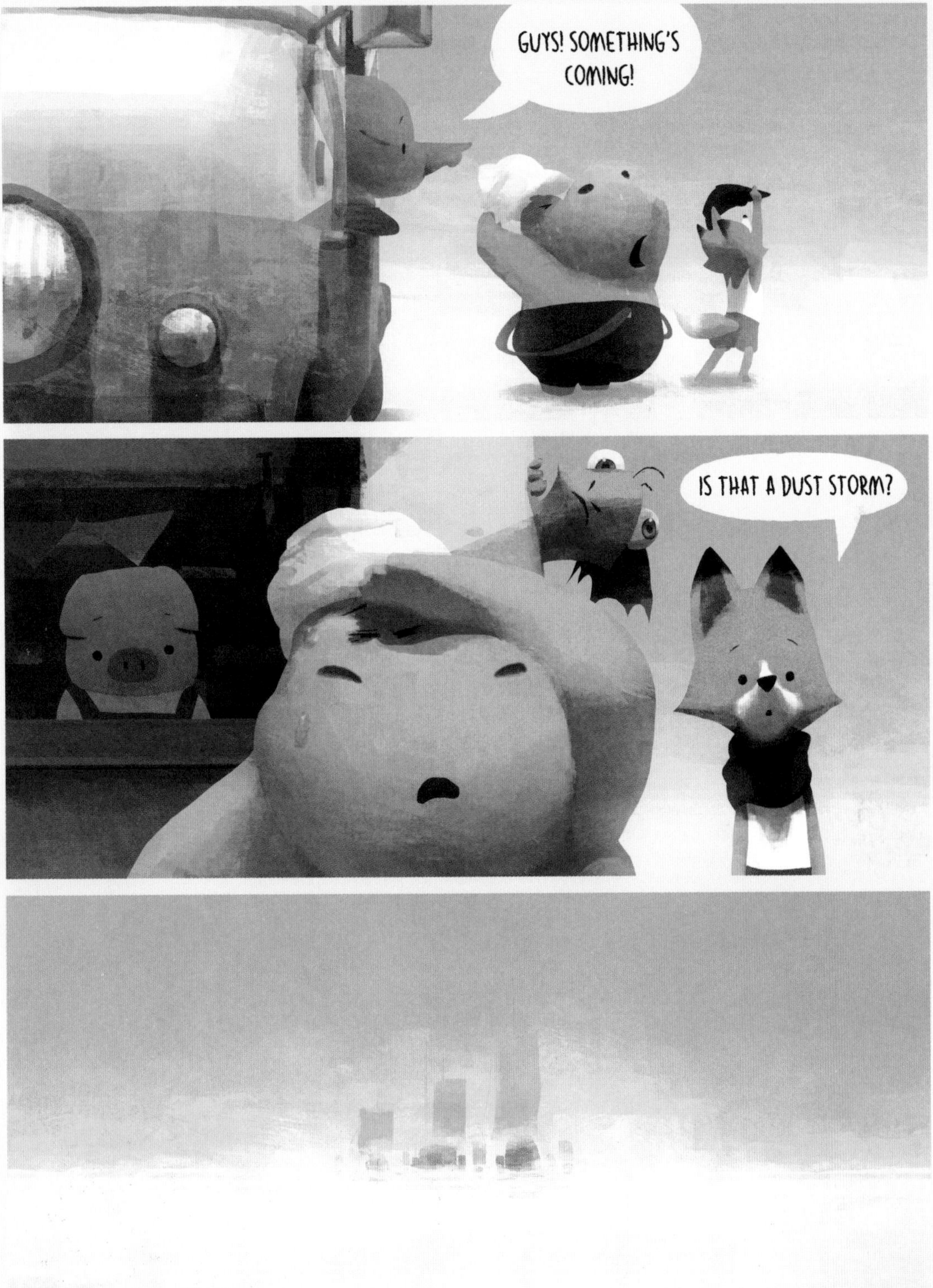
GUYS! SOMETHING'S COMING!
IS THAT A DUST STORM?

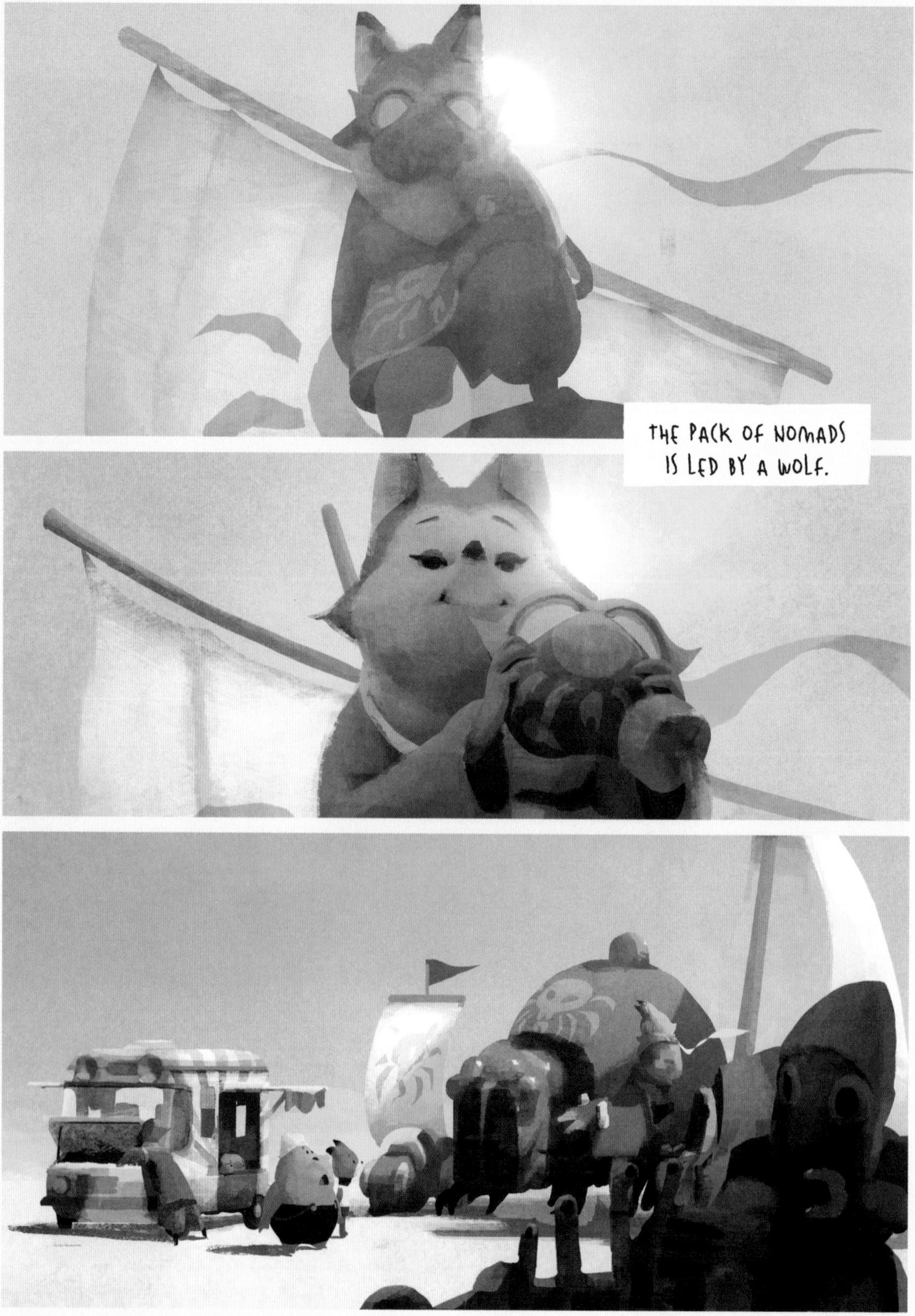
THE PACK OF NOMADS IS LED BY A WOLF.

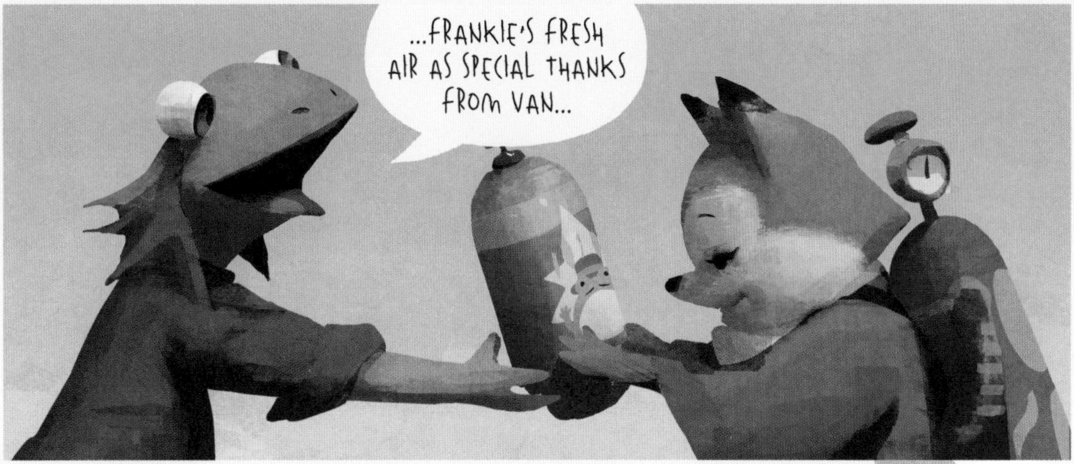
...FRANKIE'S FRESH AIR AS SPECIAL THANKS FROM VAN...

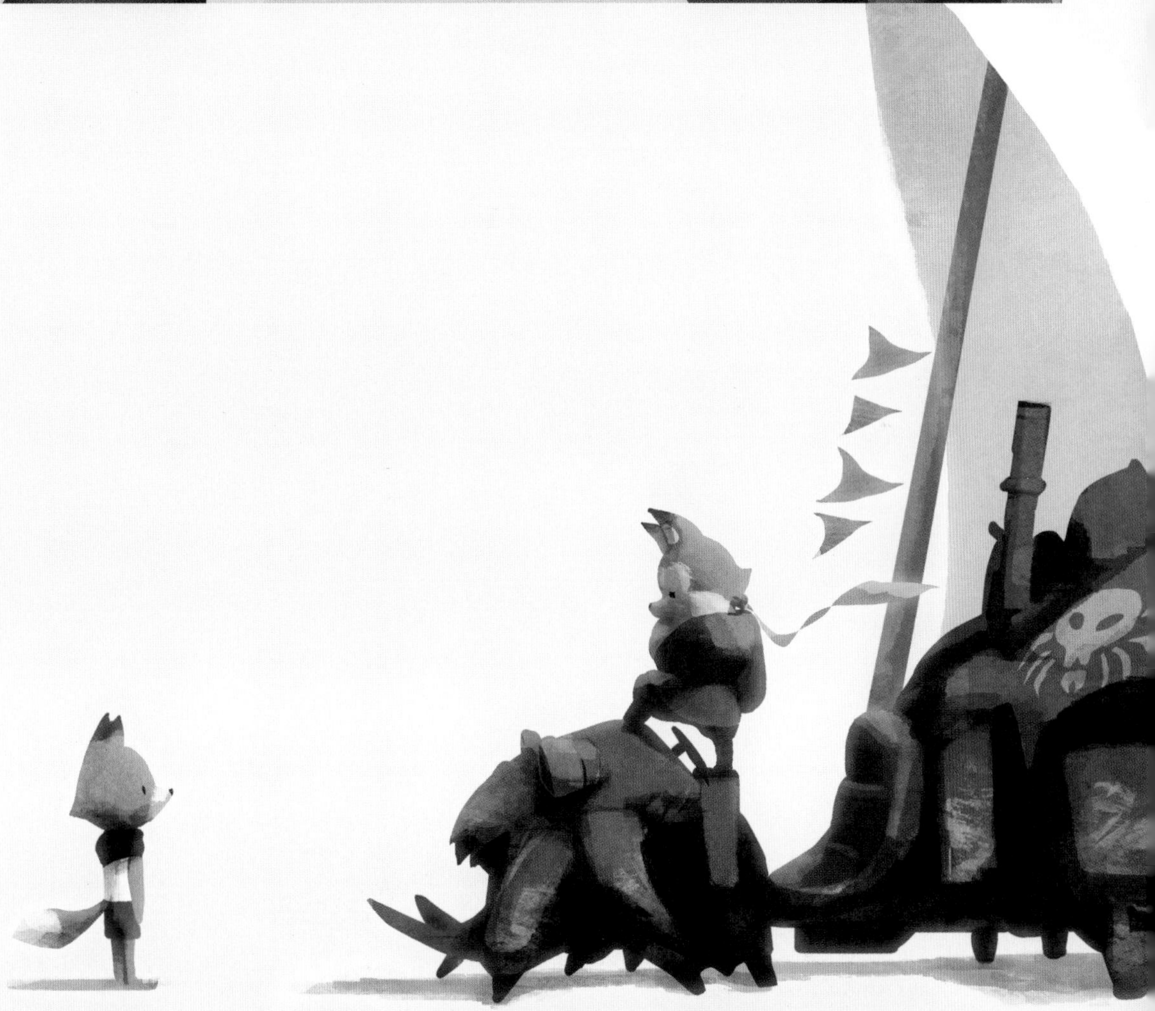

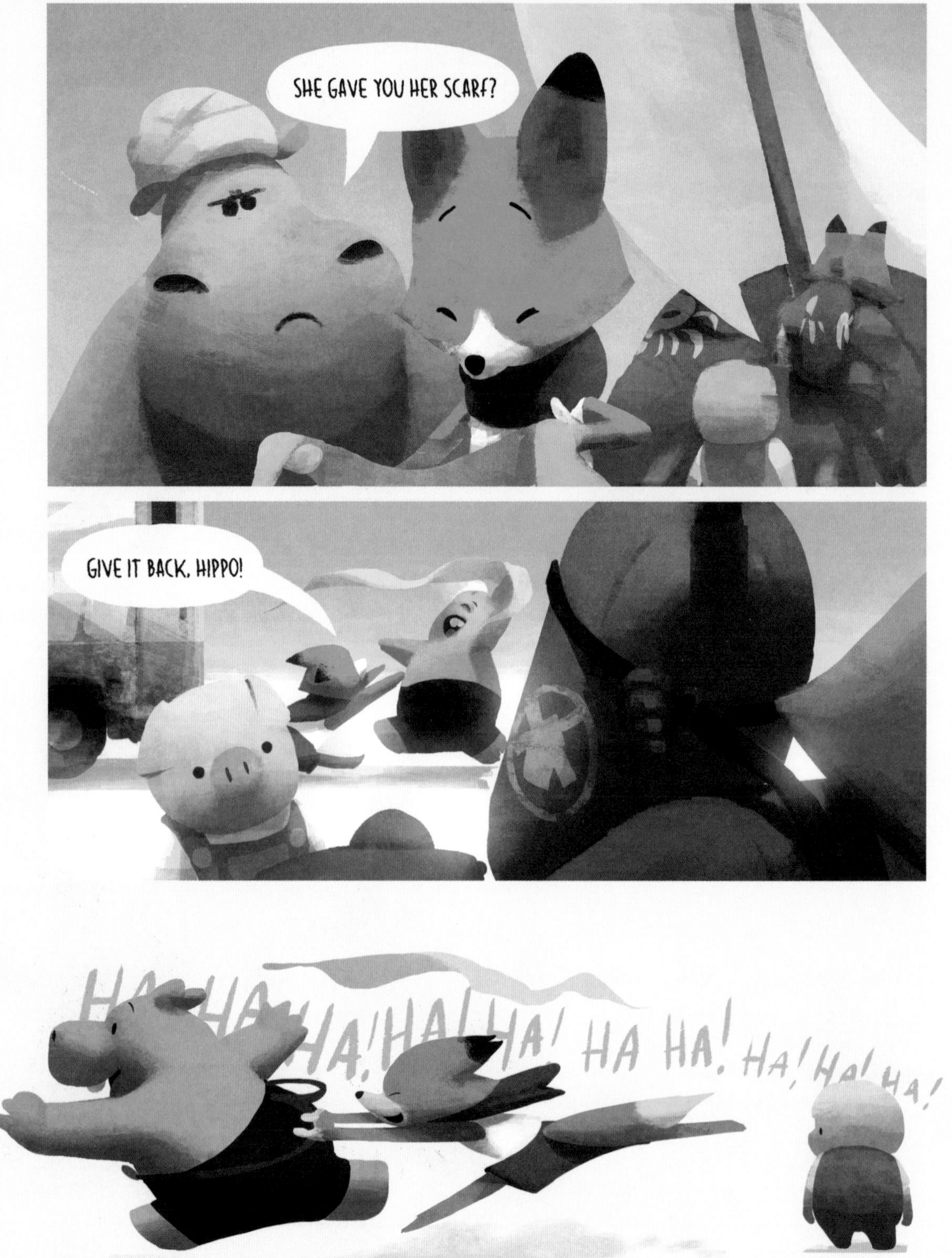
SHE GAVE YOU HER SCARF?
GIVE IT BACK, HIPPO!
HA HA HA! HA! HA! HA HA! HA! HA! HA!

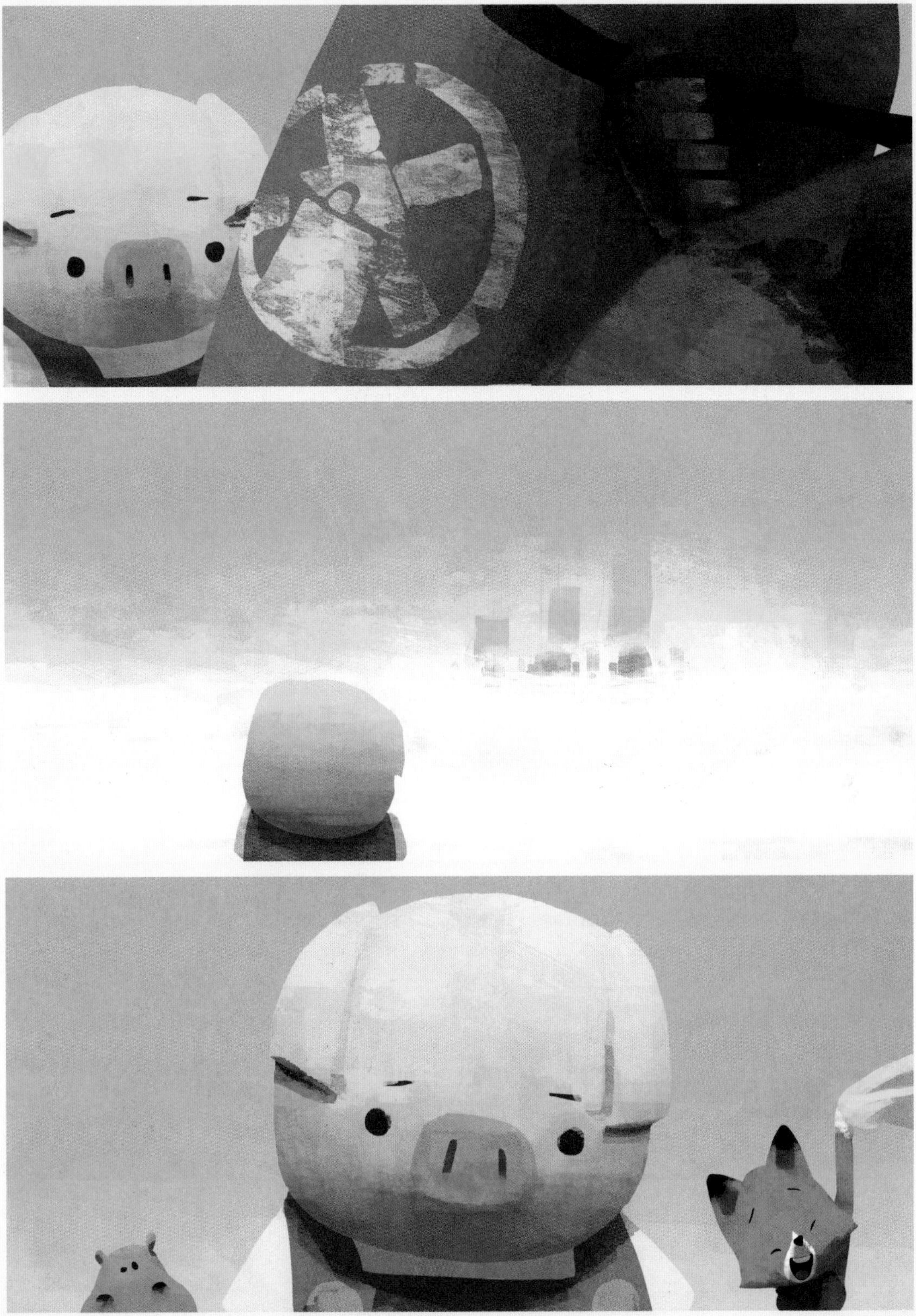

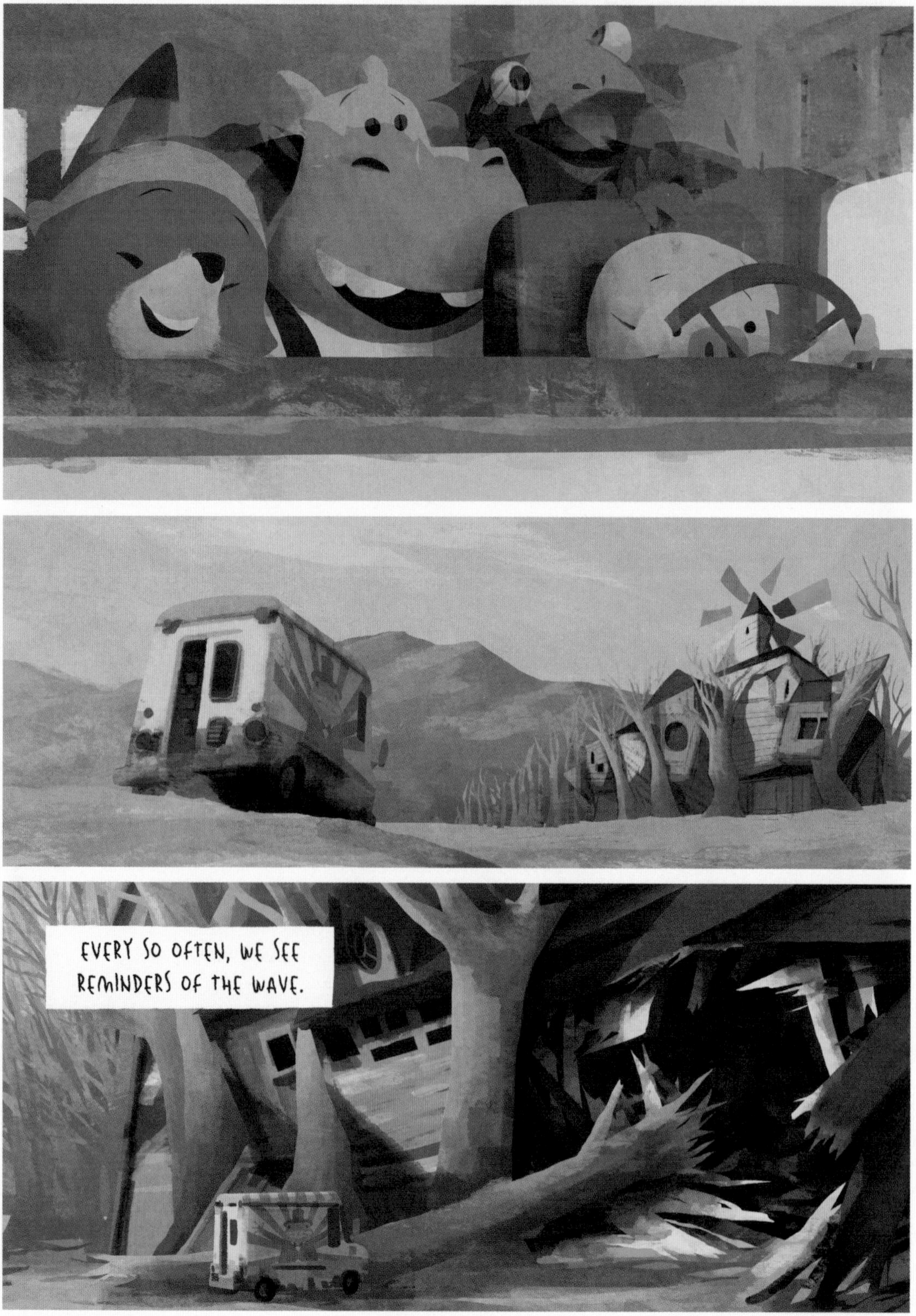
EVERY SO OFTEN, WE SEE REMINDERS OF THE WAVE.

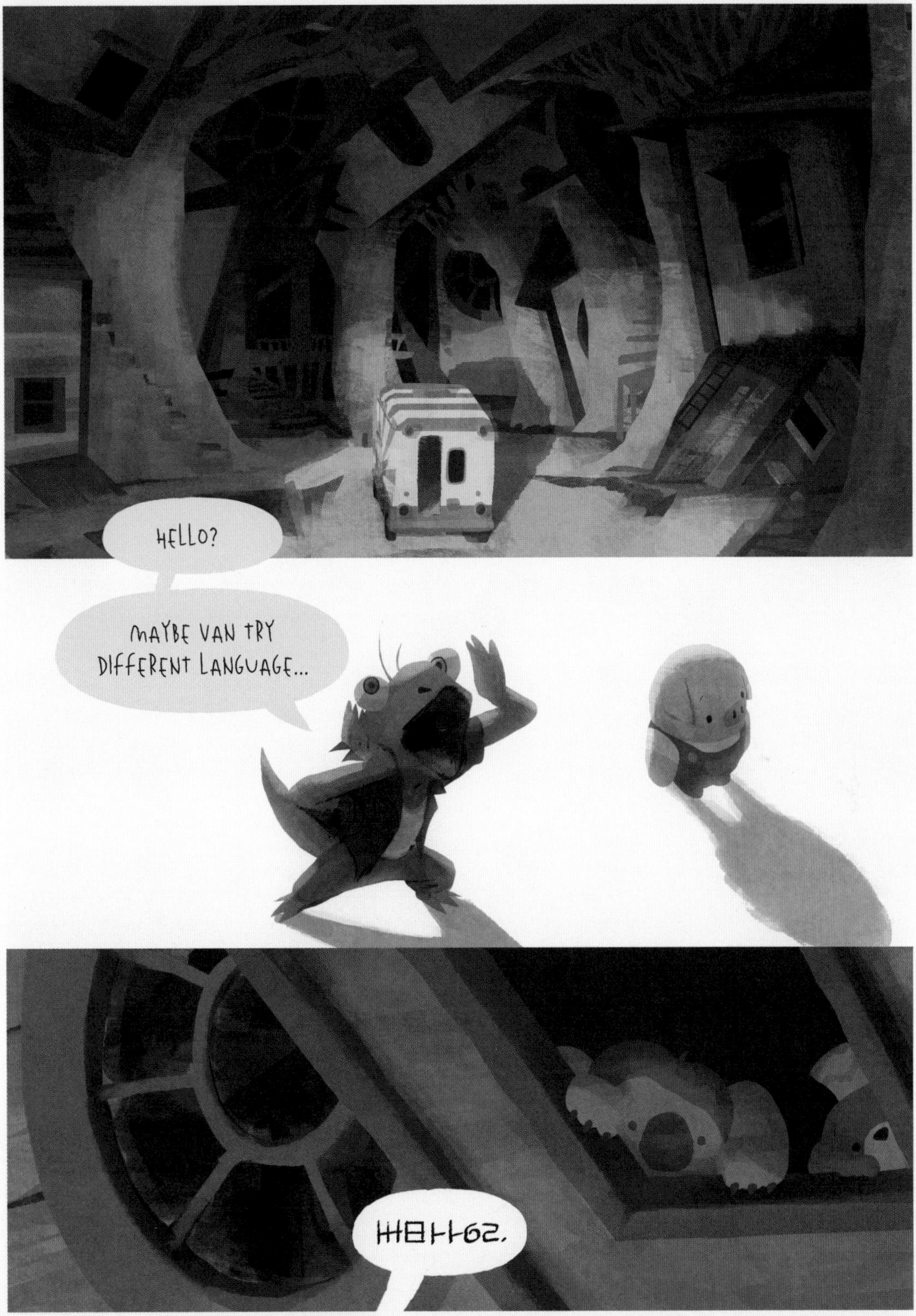
HELLO?
MAYBE VAN TRY DIFFERENT LANGUAGE...

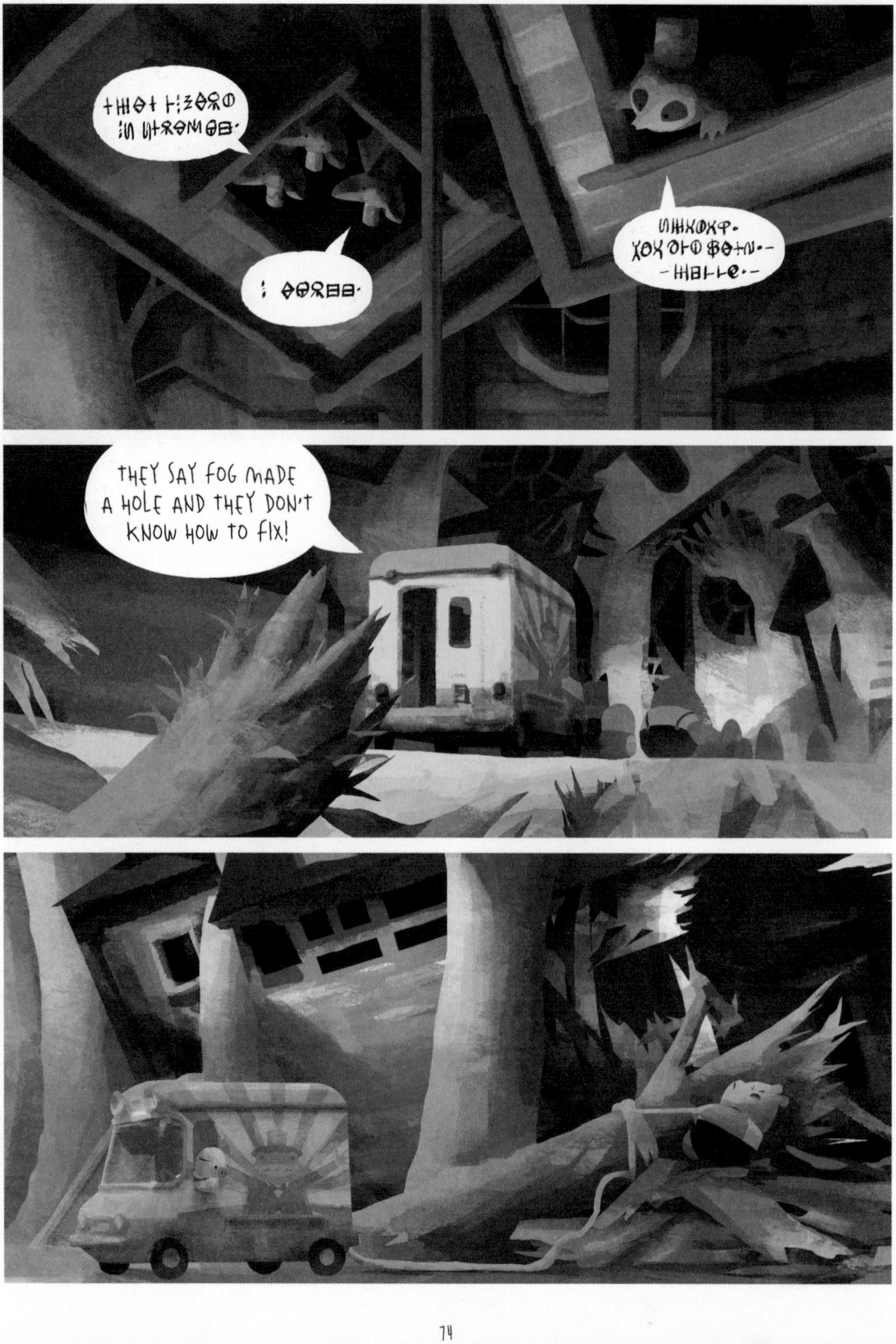
THEY SAY FOG MADE A HOLE AND THEY DON'T KNOW HOW TO FIX!

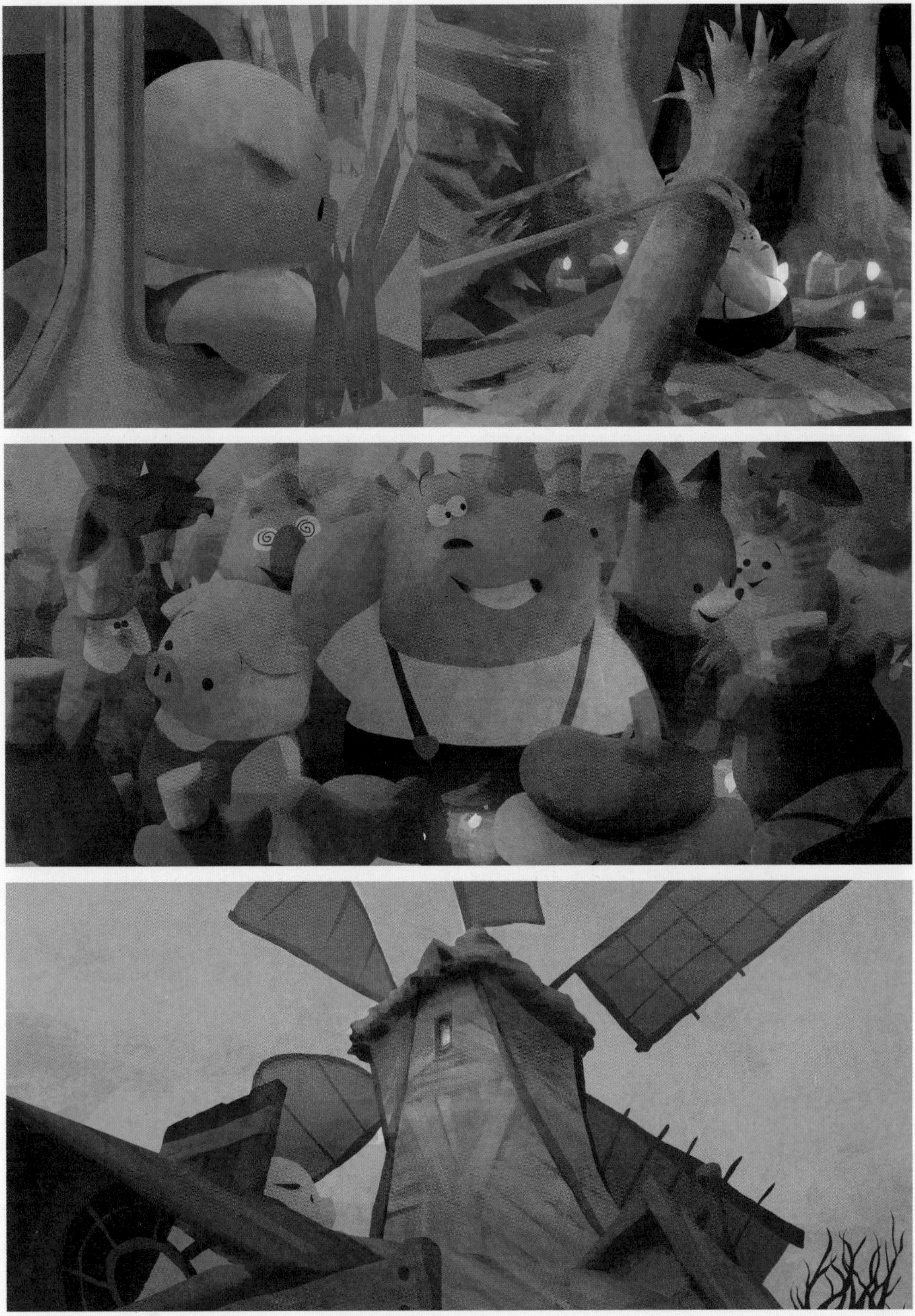

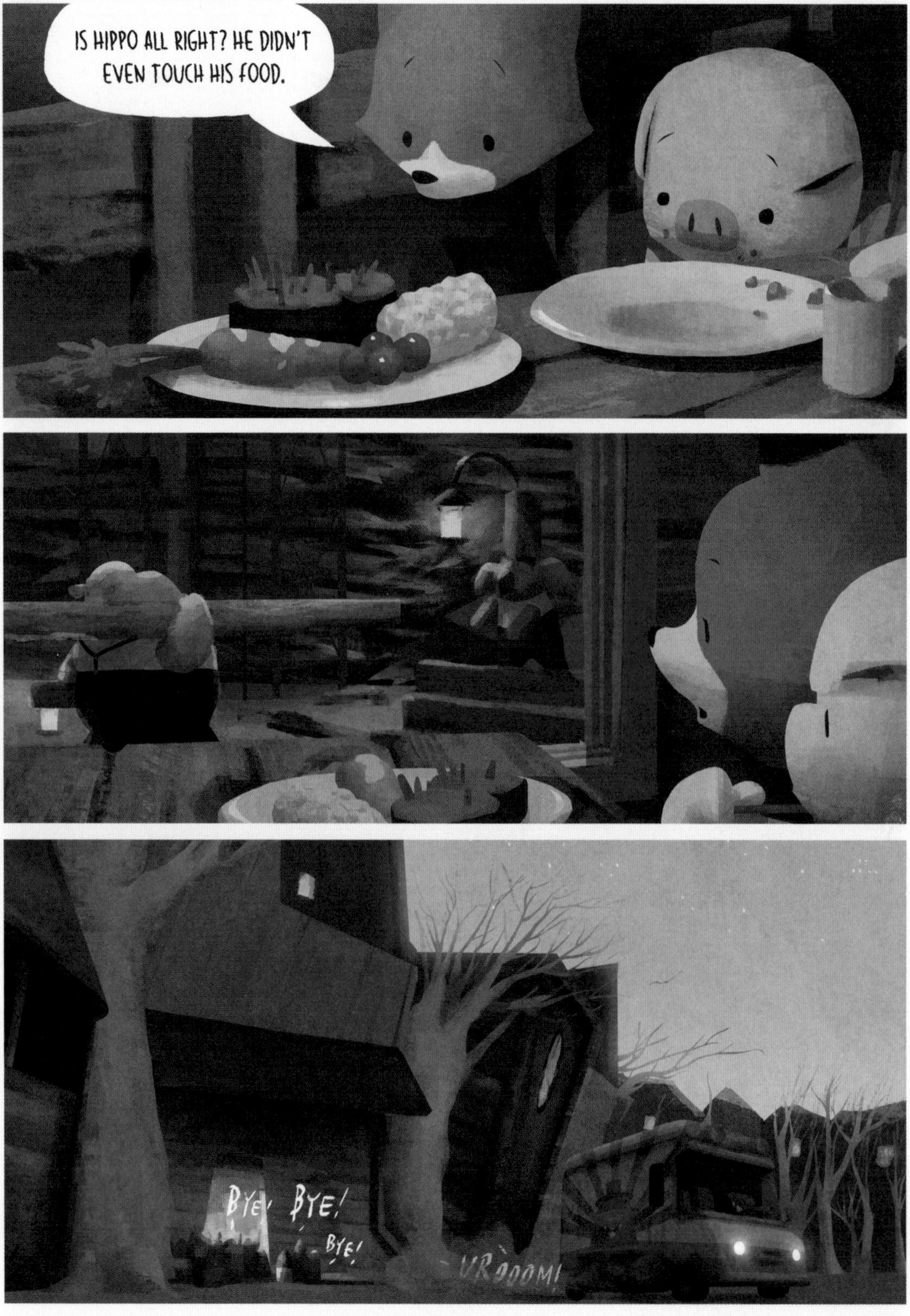
IS HIPPO ALL RIGHT? HE DIDN'T EVEN TOUCH HIS FOOD.
BYE, BYE!
BYE!
VROOOM!

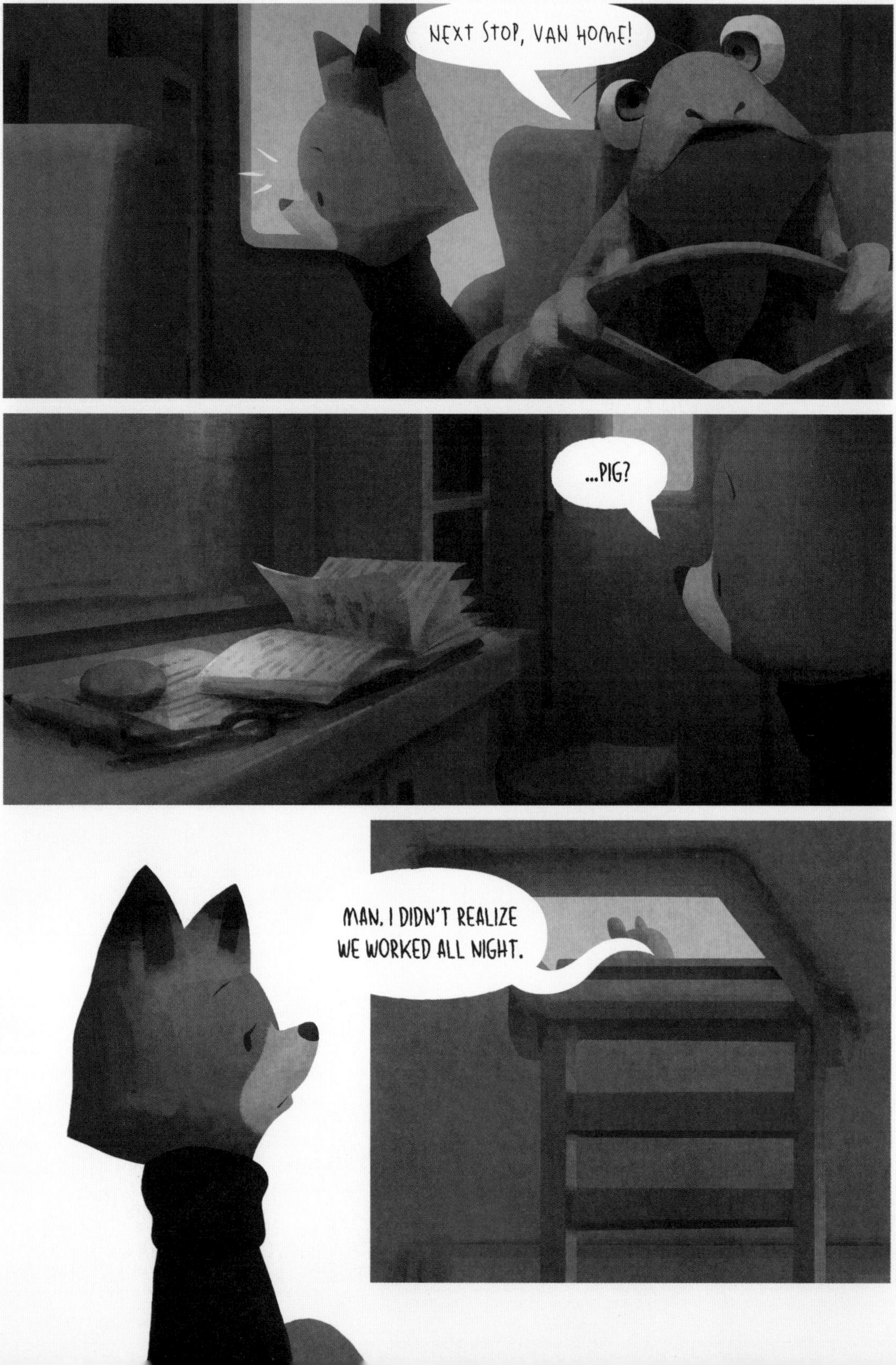
NEXT STOP, VAN HOME!
...PIG?
MAN. I DIDN'T REALIZE WE WORKED ALL NIGHT.

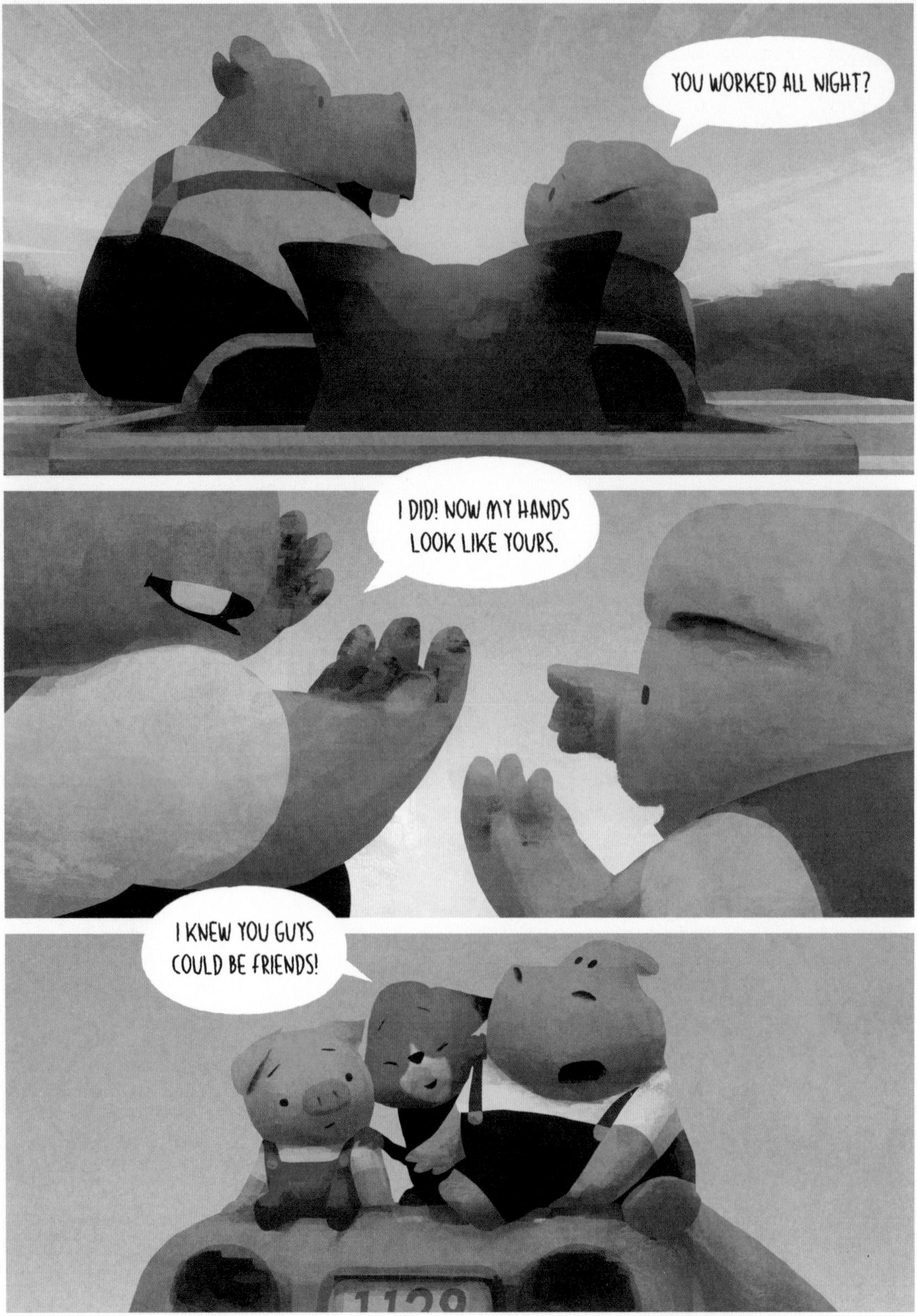
YOU WORKED ALL NIGHT?
I DID! NOW MY HANDS LOOK LIKE YOURS.
I KNEW YOU GUYS COULD BE FRIENDS!

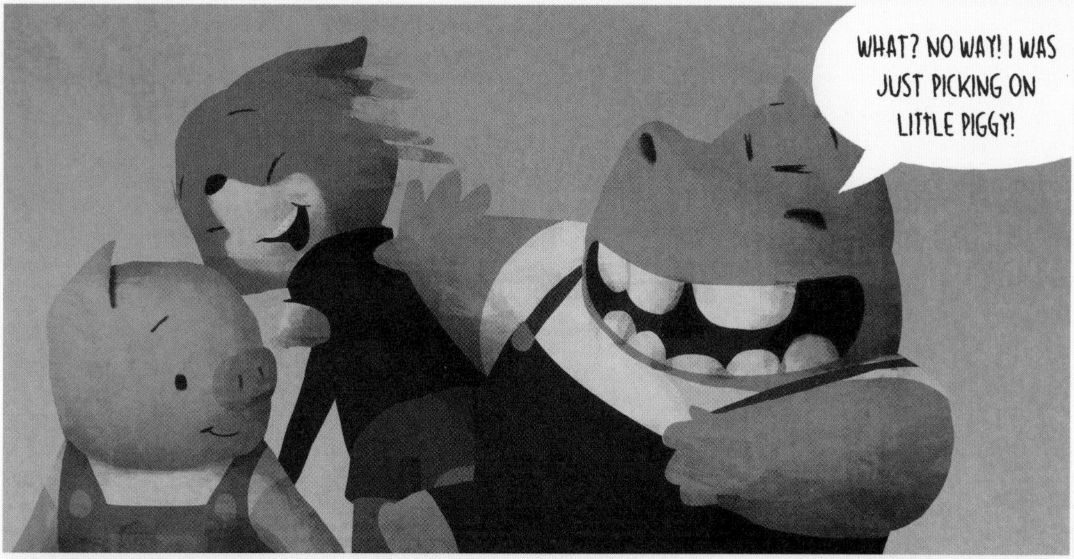
WHAT? NO WAY! I WAS JUST PICKING ON LITTLE PIGGY!

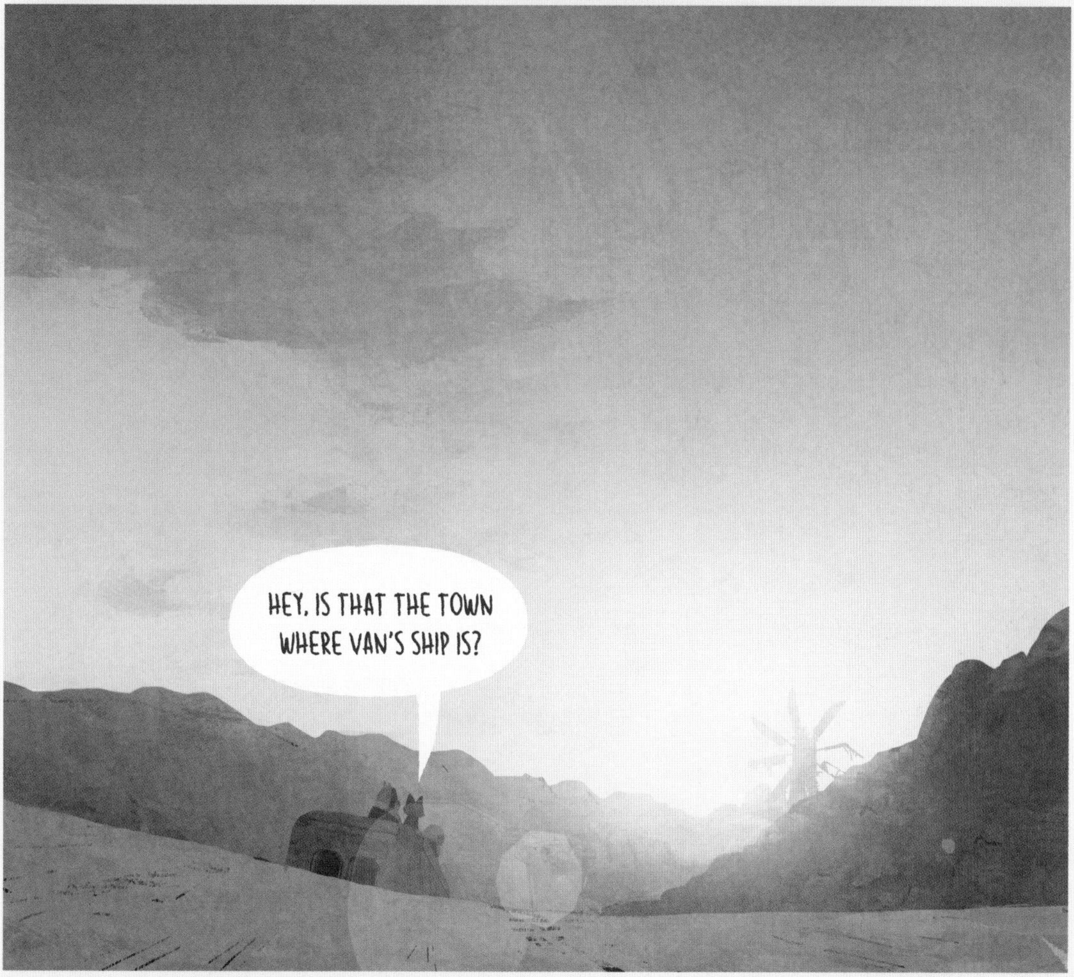
HEY. IS THAT THE TOWN WHERE VAN'S SHIP IS?

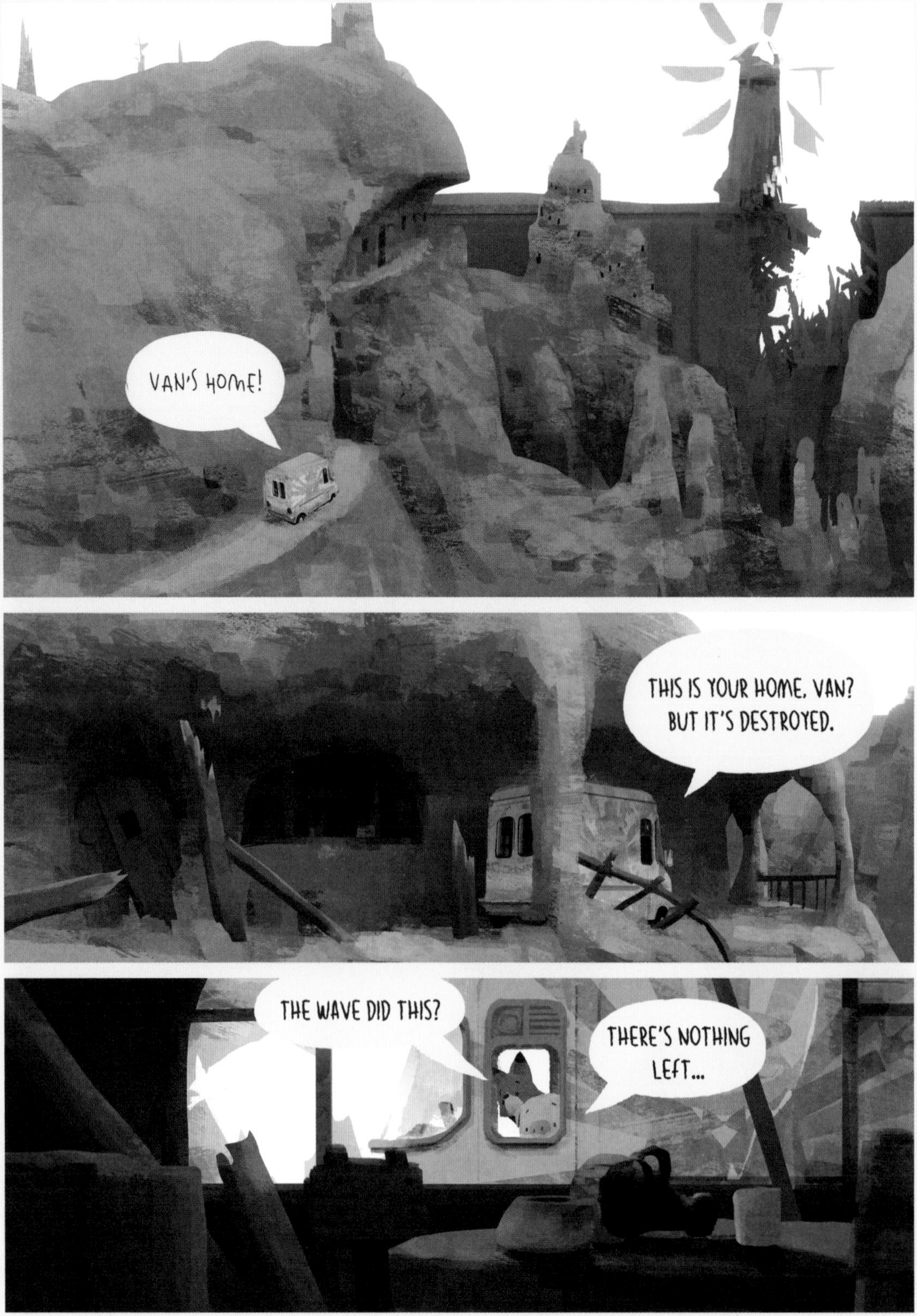
VAN'S HOME!
THIS IS YOUR HOME, VAN? BUT IT'S DESTROYED.
THE WAVE DID THIS?
THERE'S NOTHING LEFT...

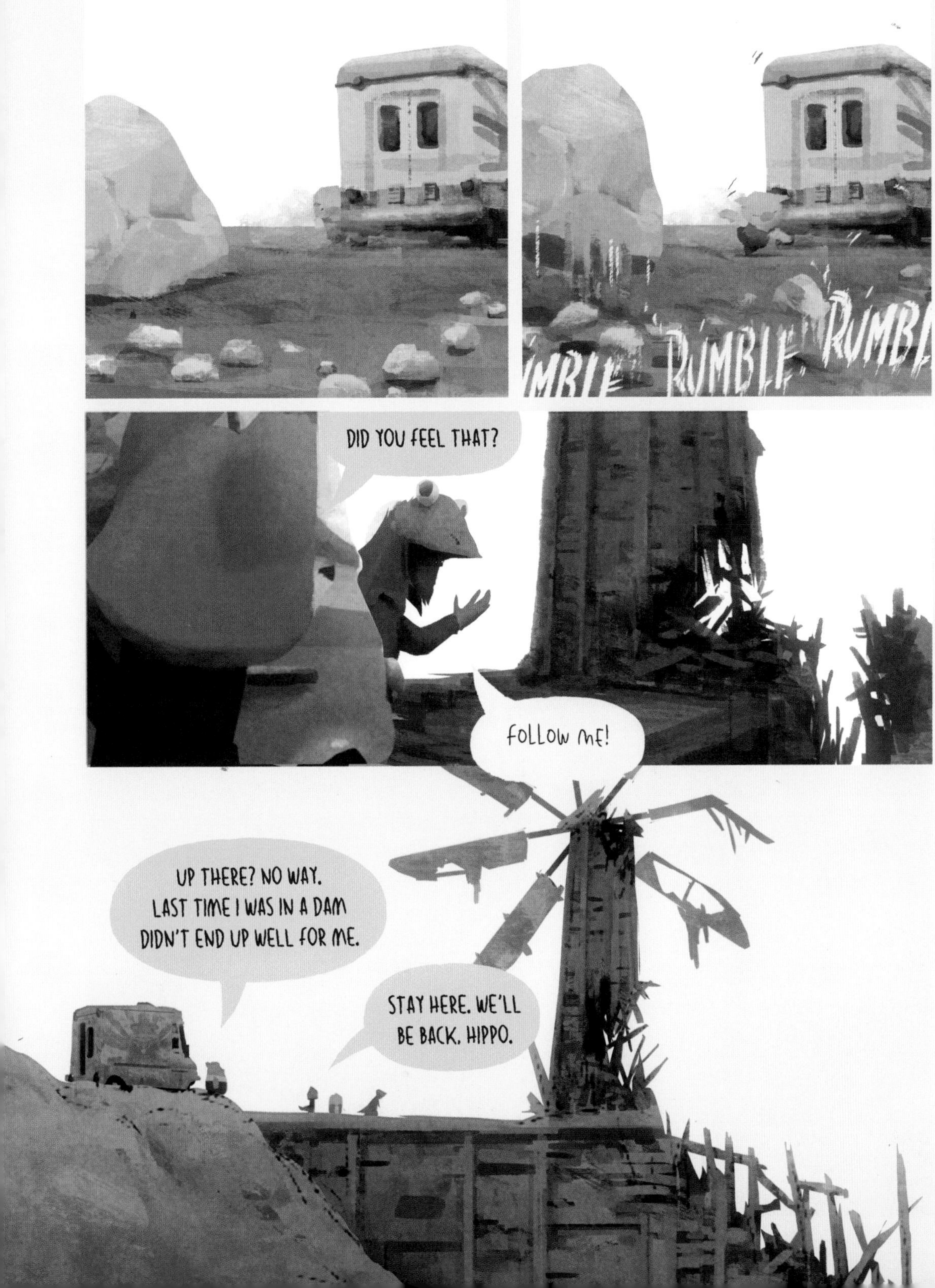
RUMBLE
RUMBLE
RUMBL
DID YOU FEEL THAT?
FOLLOW ME!
UP THERE? NO WAY.
LAST TIME I WAS IN A DAM
DIDN'T END UP WELL FOR ME.
STAY HERE. WE'LL
BE BACK, HIPPO.

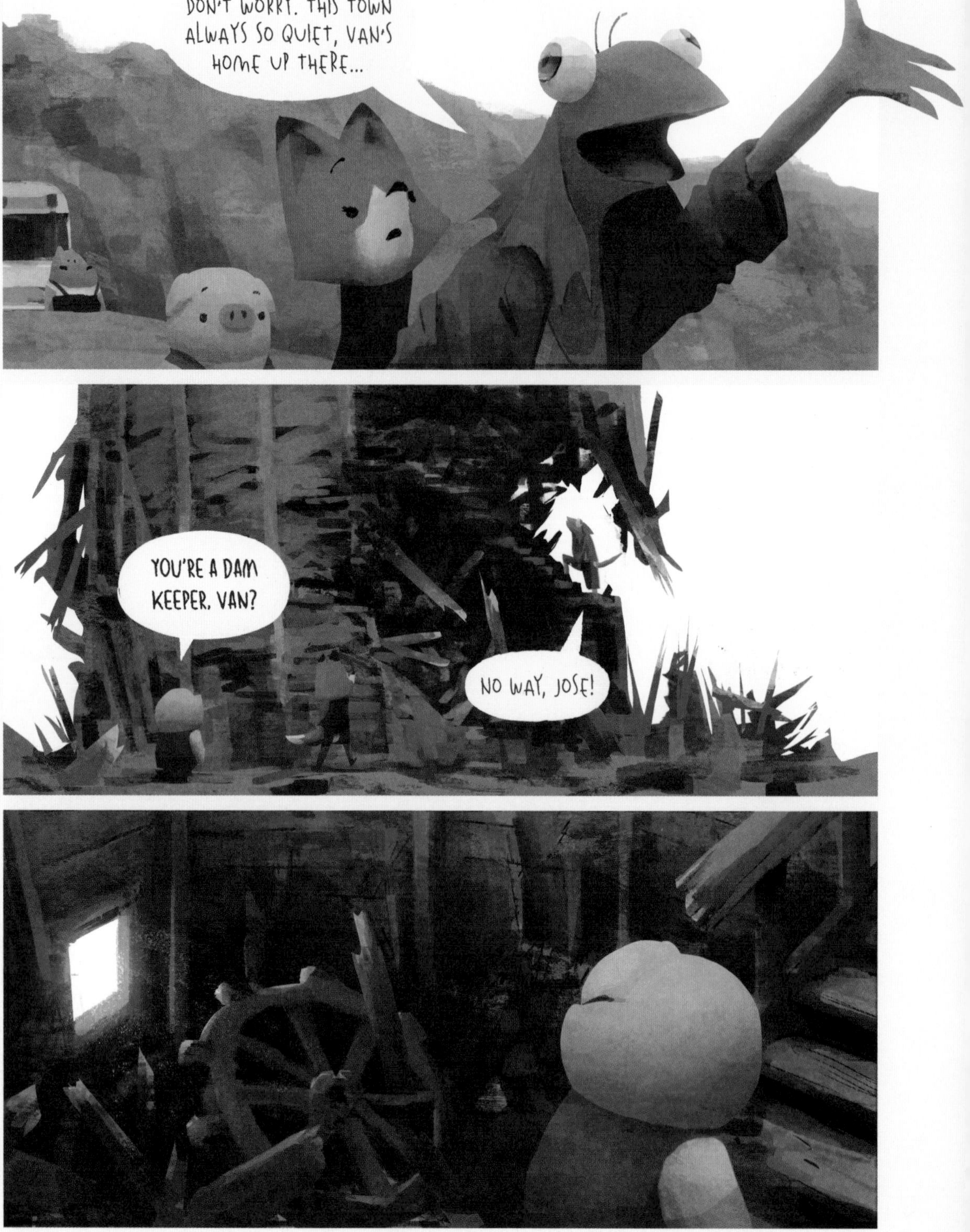
DON'T WORRY. THIS TOWN ALWAYS SO QUIET, VAN'S HOME UP THERE...
YOU'RE A DAM KEEPER, VAN?
NO WAY, JOSE!

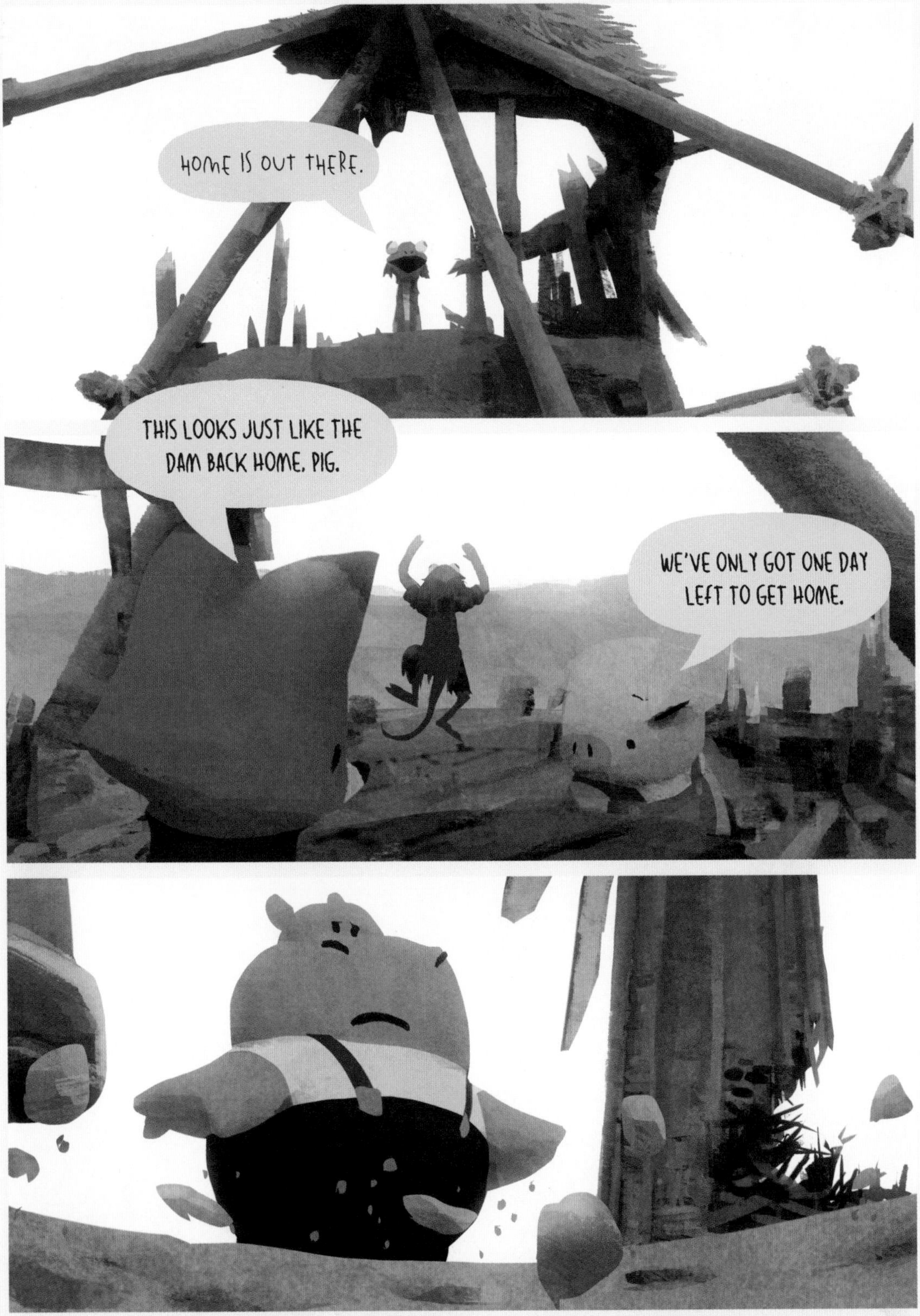
HOME IS OUT THERE.
THIS LOOKS JUST LIKE THE DAM BACK HOME, PIG.
WE'VE ONLY GOT ONE DAY LEFT TO GET HOME.

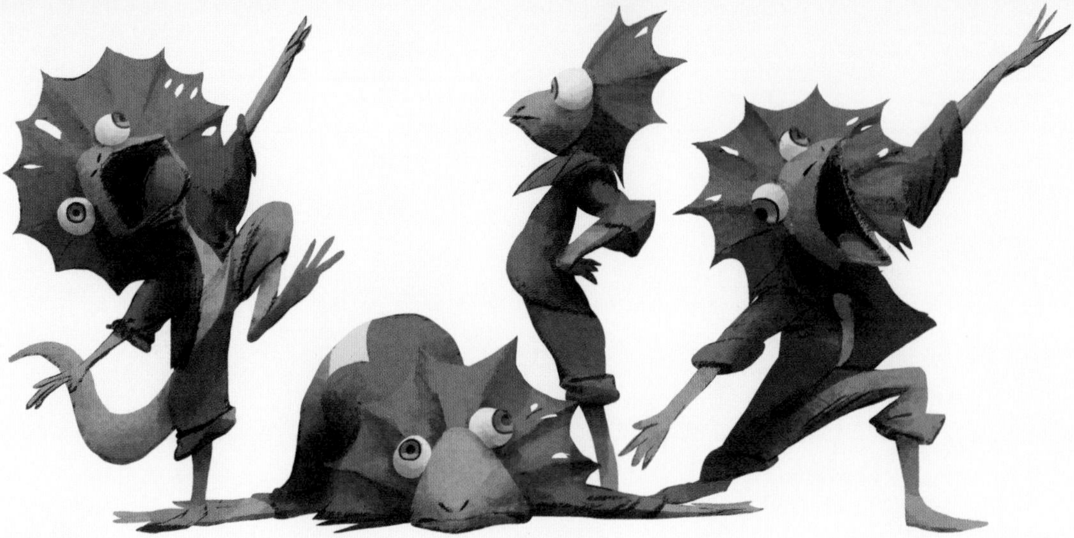

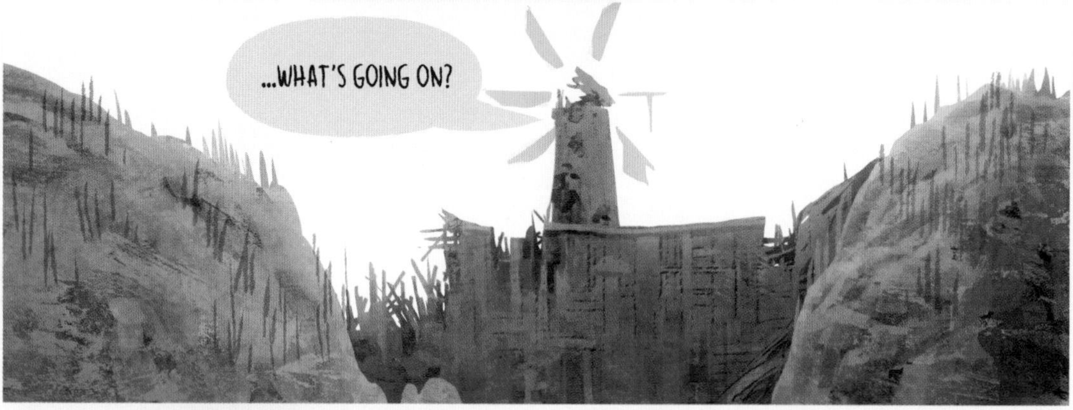
...WHAT'S GOING ON?

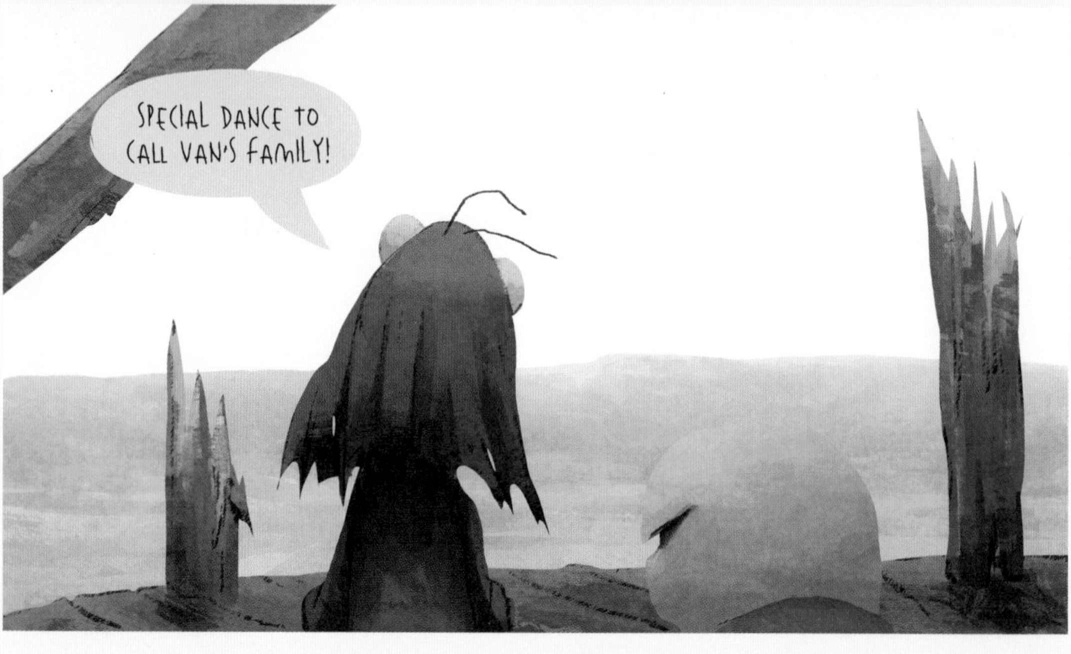
SPECIAL DANCE TO
CALL VAN'S FAMILY!

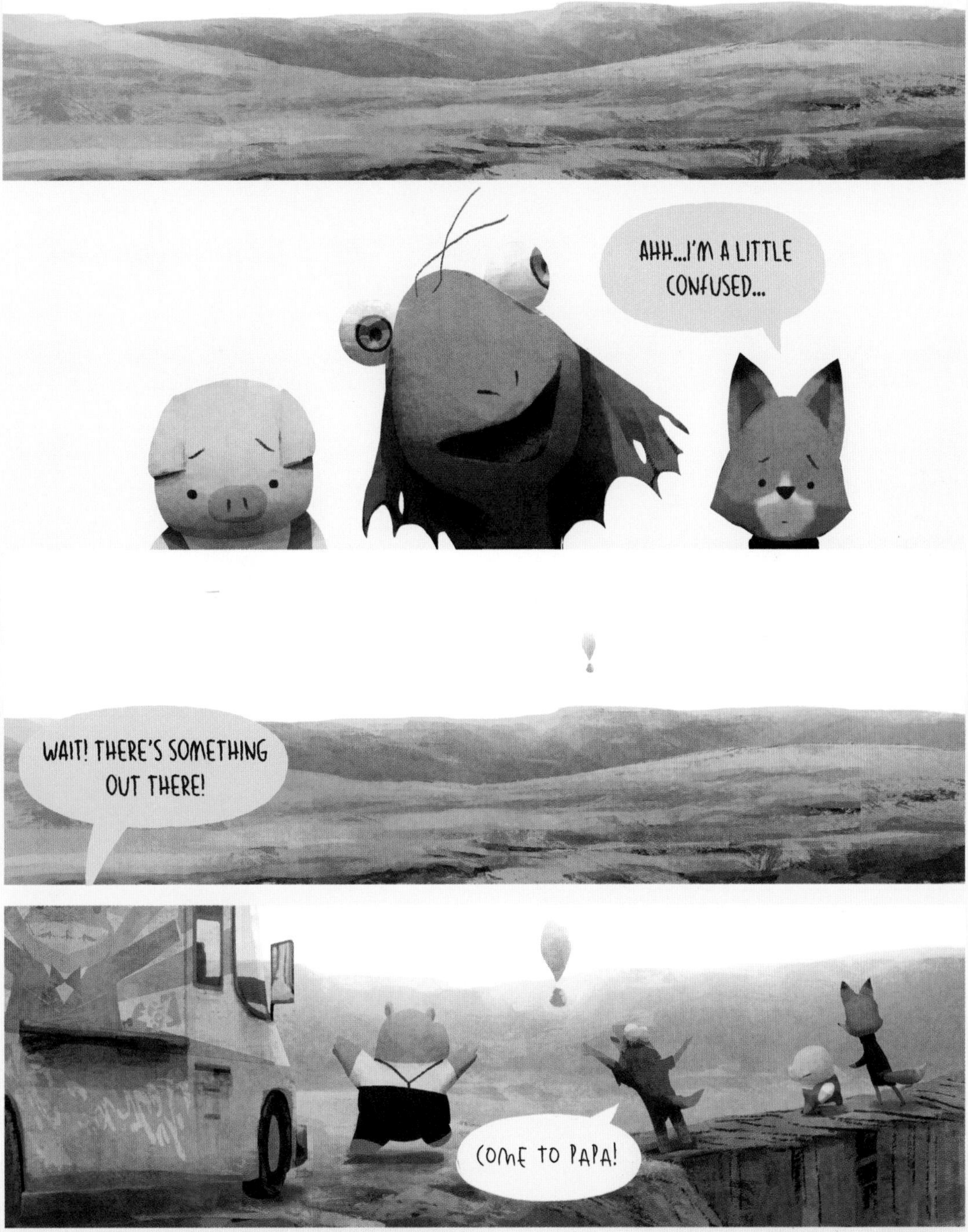
AHH...I'M A LITTLE CONFUSED...
WAIT! THERE'S SOMETHING OUT THERE!
COME TO PAPA!

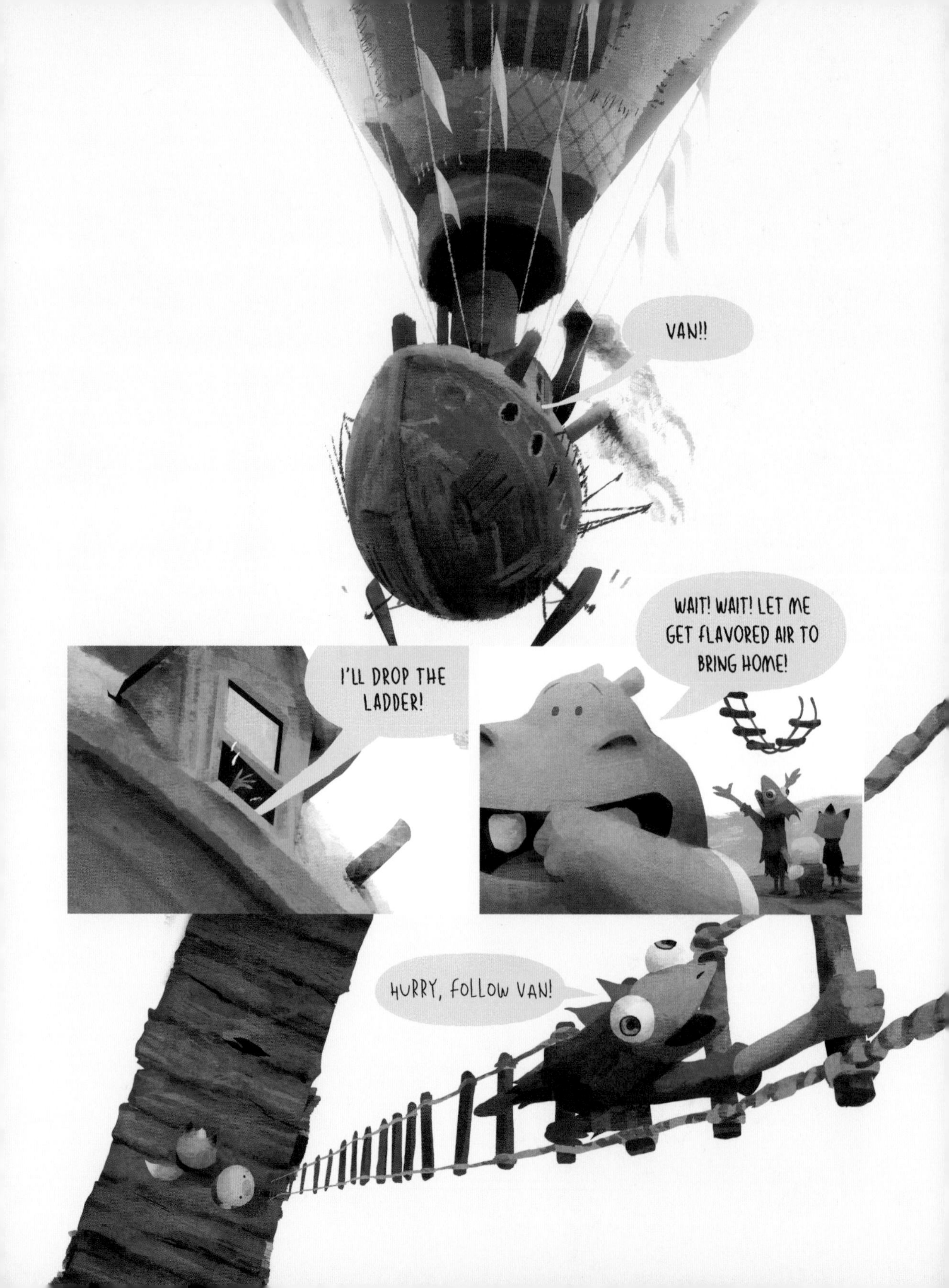
VAN!!
I'LL DROP THE LADDER!
WAIT! WAIT! LET ME GET FLAVORED AIR TO BRING HOME!
HURRY, FOLLOW VAN!

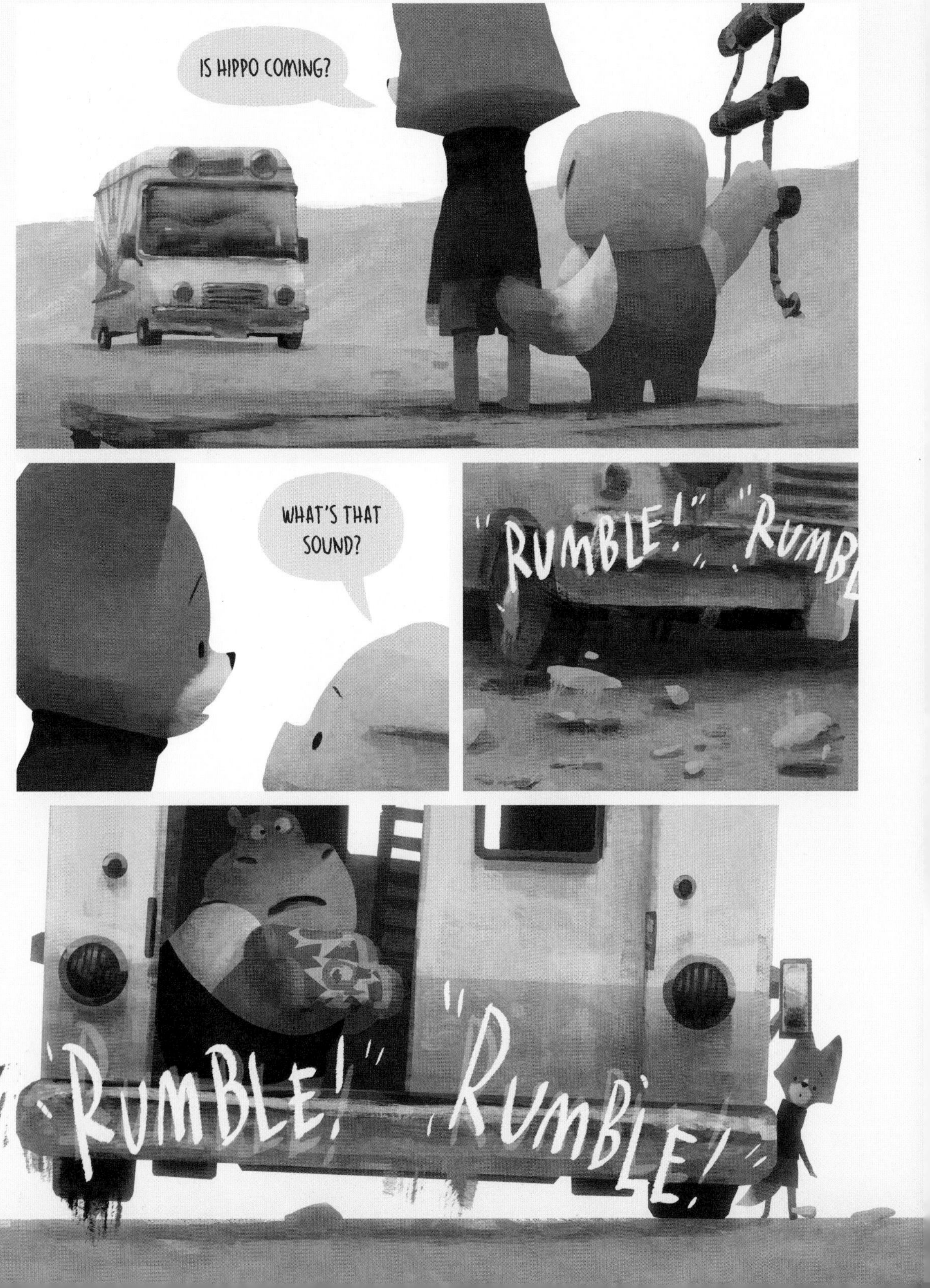
IS HIPPO COMING?
WHAT'S THAT SOUND?
"RUMBLE!" "RUMBLE
"RUMBLE!" "RUMBLE!"

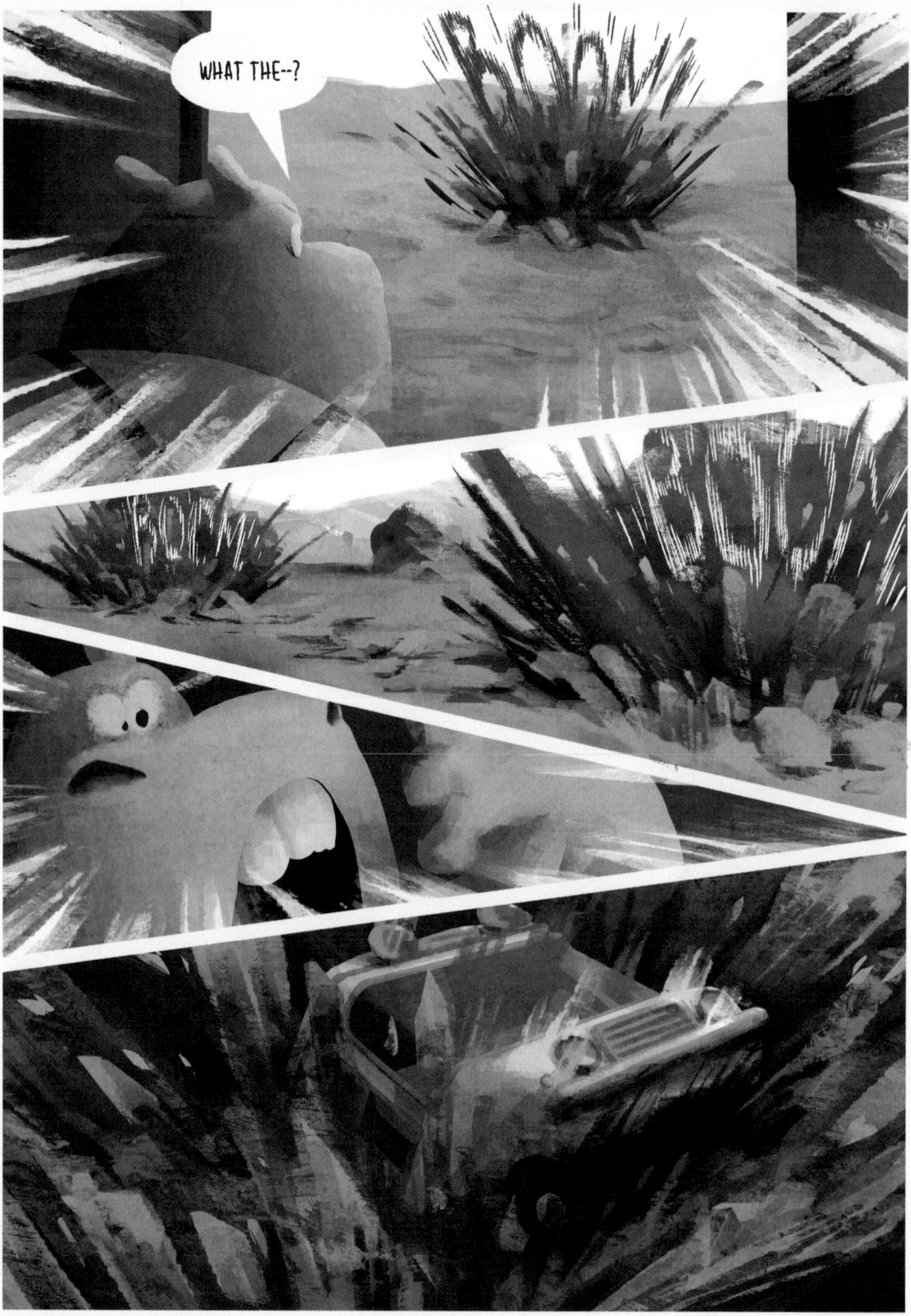

WHAT THE--?
BOOM
BOOM
BOOM

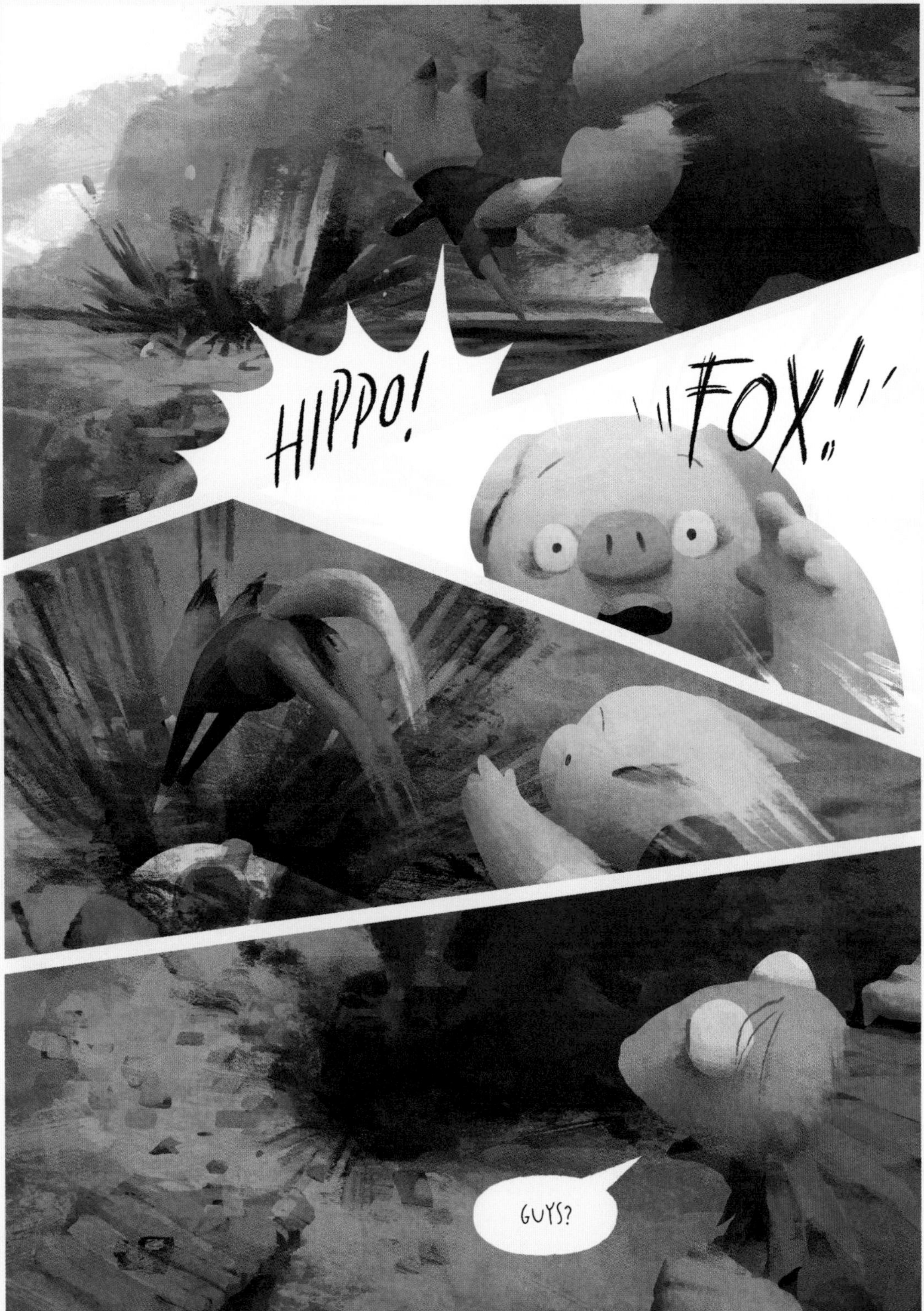
HIPPO!
FOX!
GUYS?

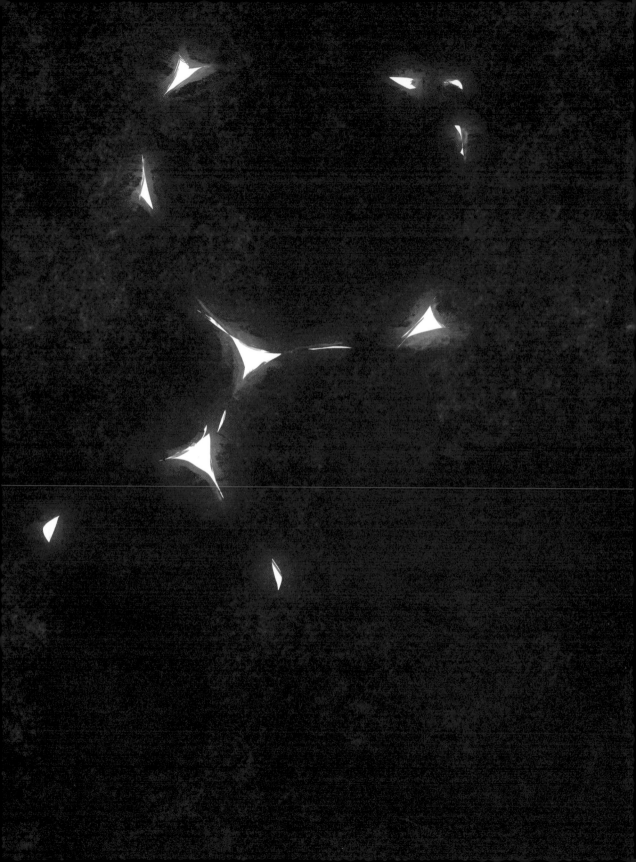

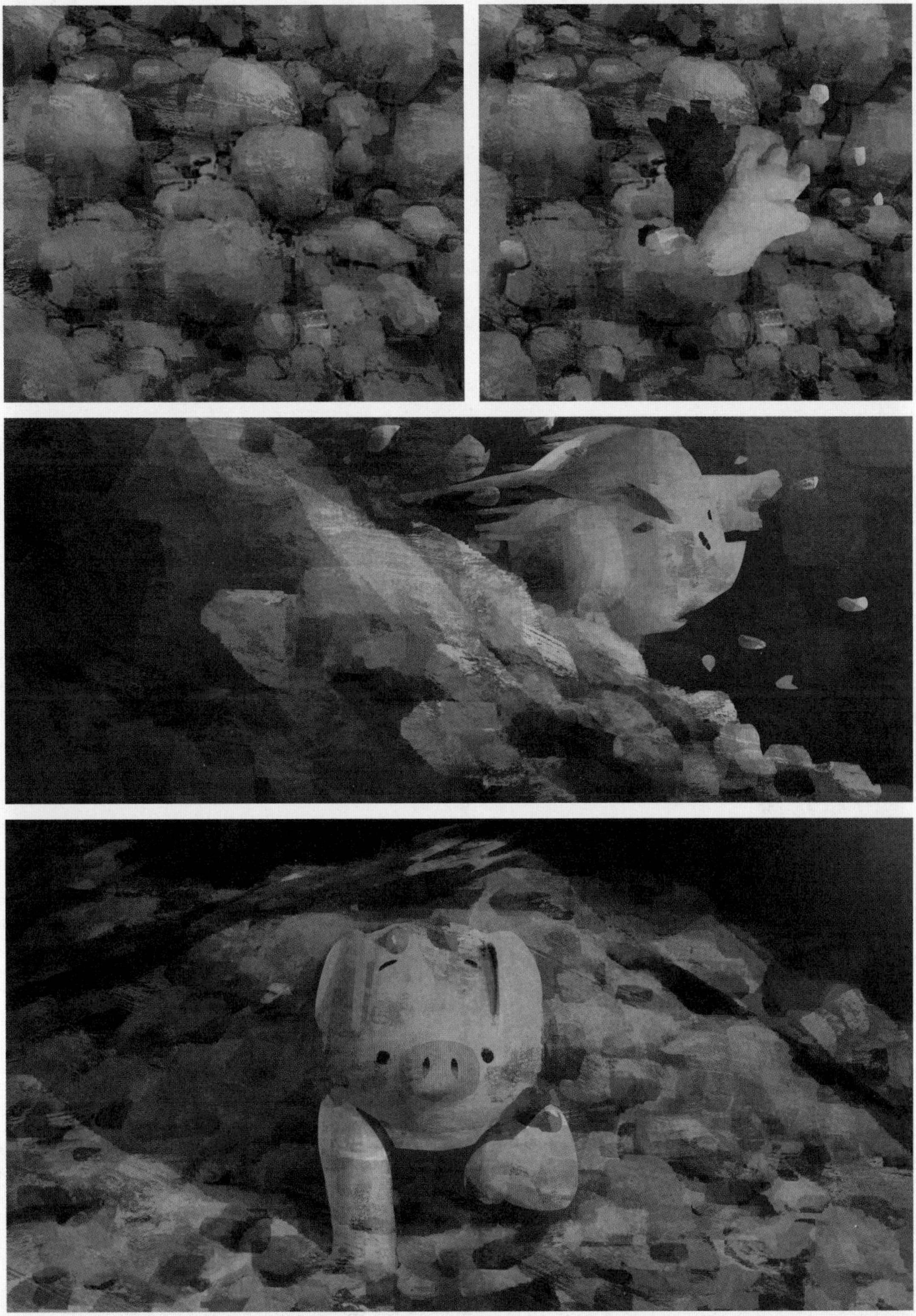

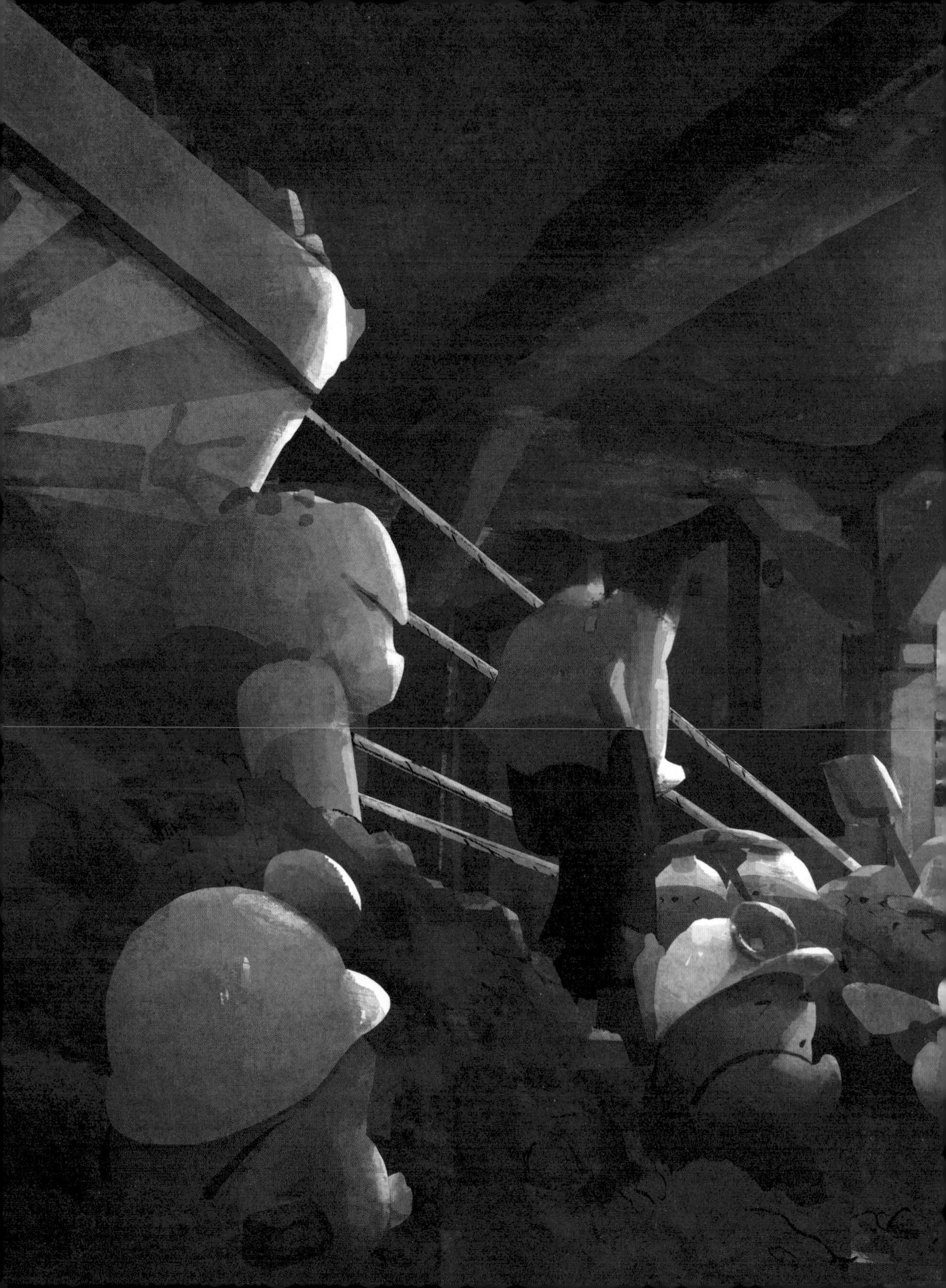

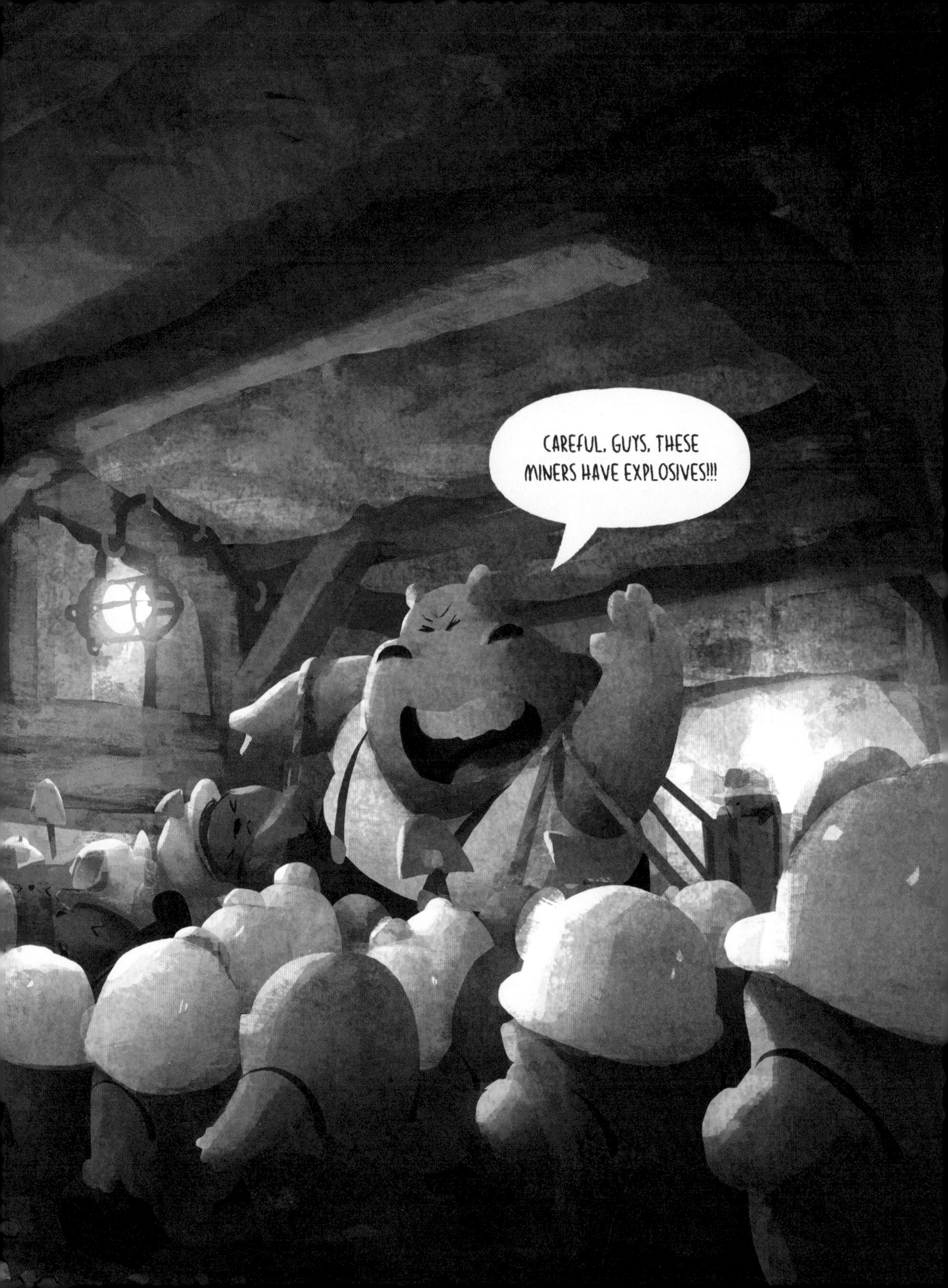
CAREFUL, GUYS, THESE MINERS HAVE EXPLOSIVES!!!

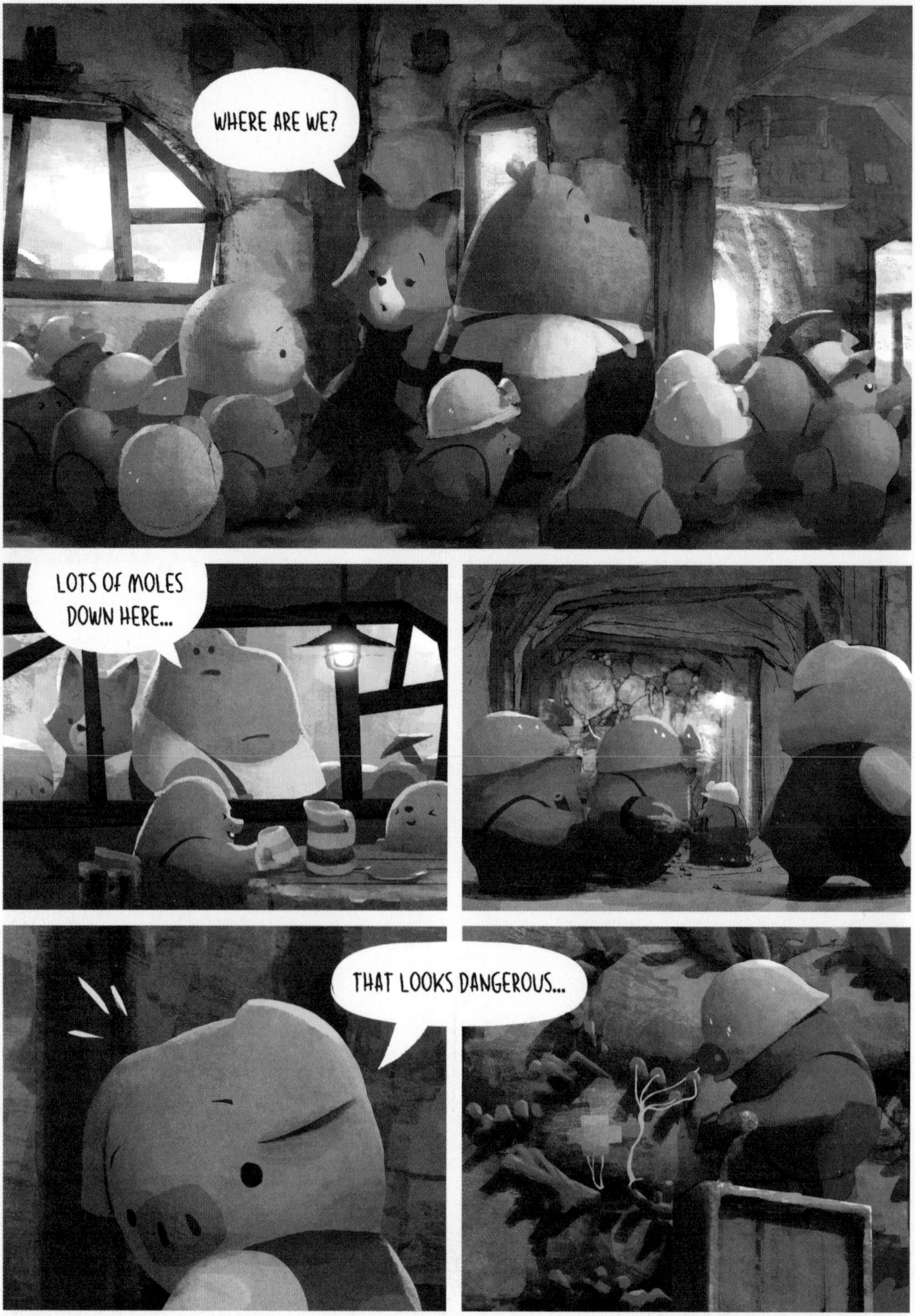
WHERE ARE WE?
LOTS OF MOLES DOWN HERE...
THAT LOOKS DANGEROUS...

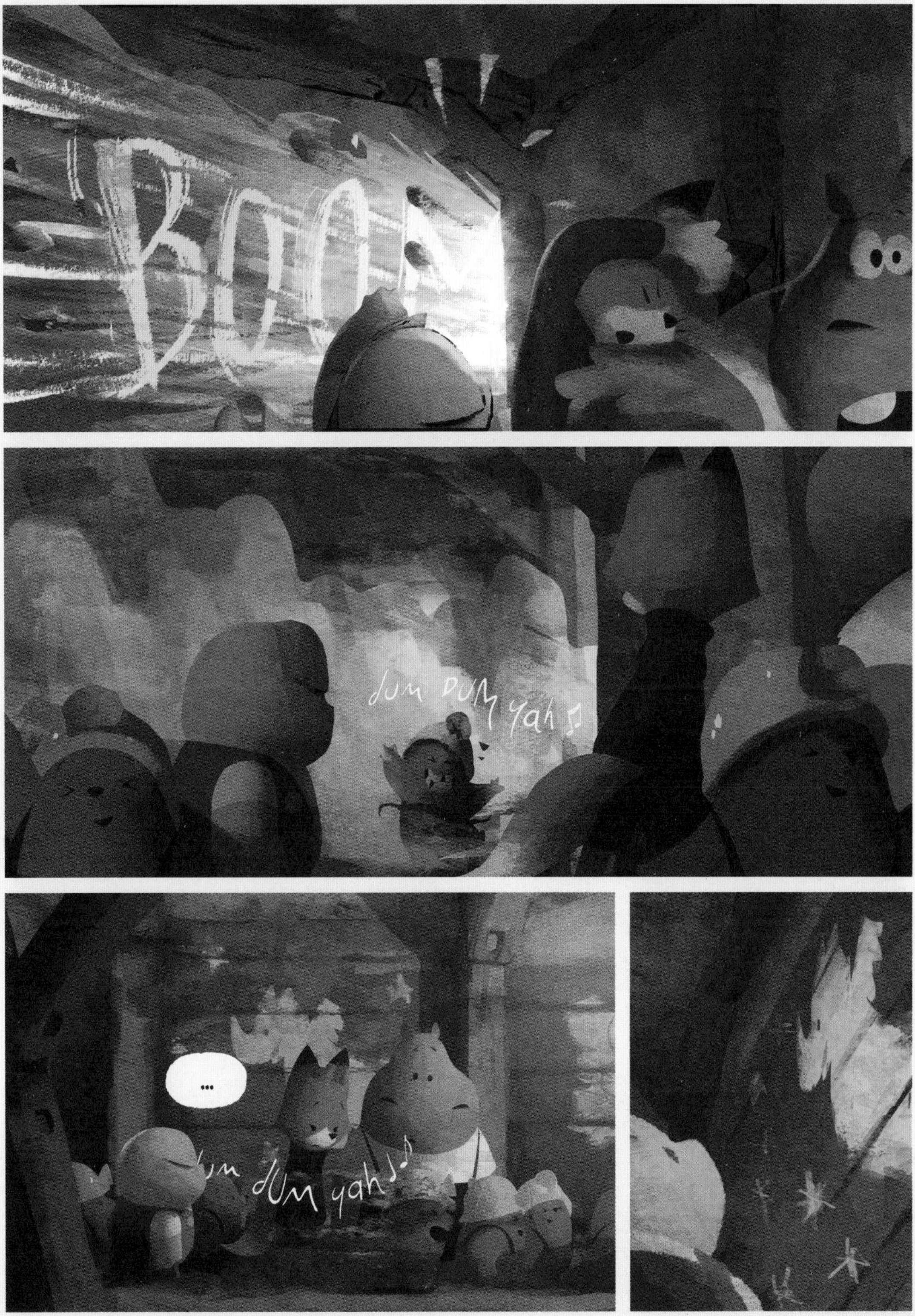
BOOM
dum DUM yah ♫
...
um dUM yah ♪

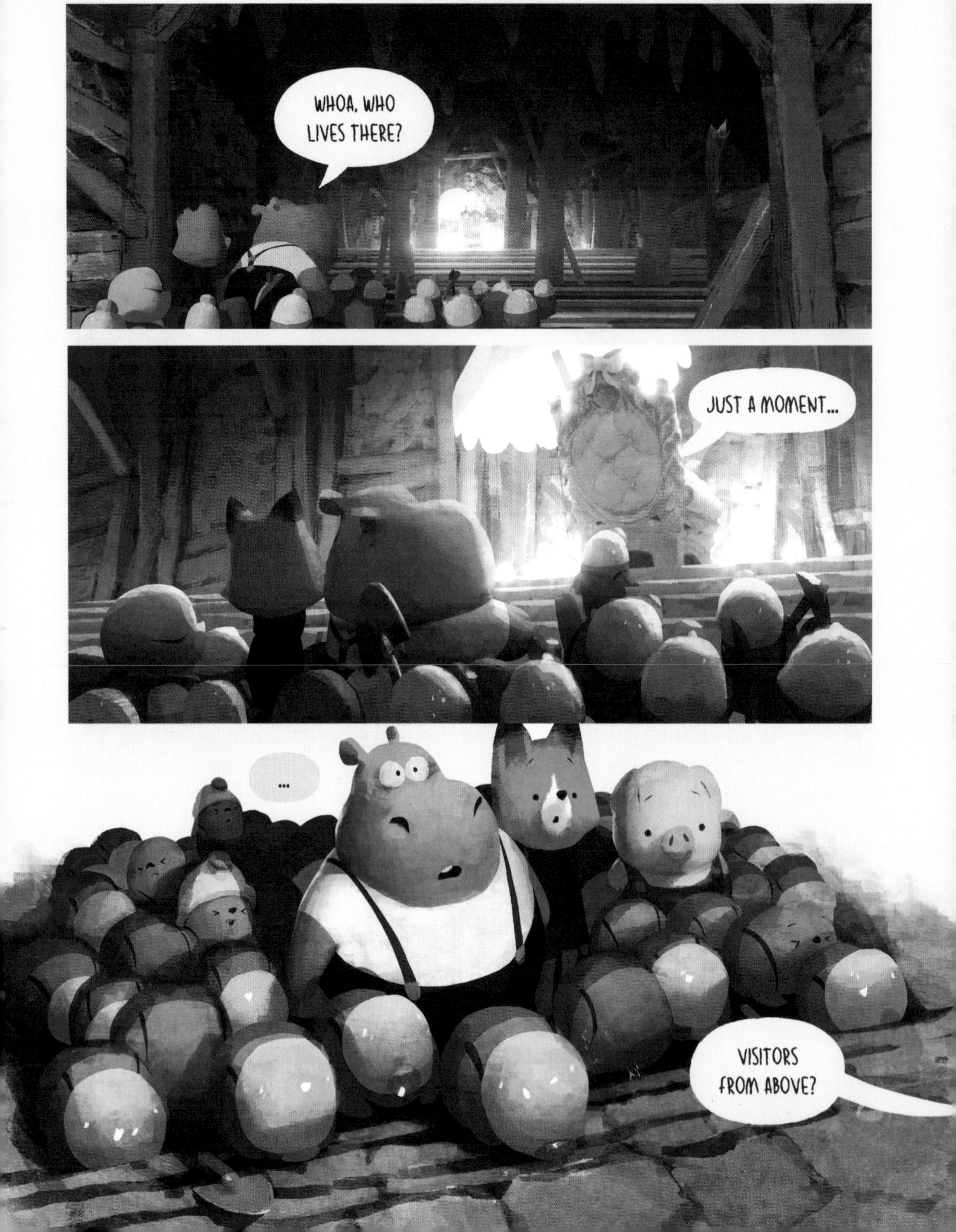
WHOA, WHO LIVES THERE?
JUST A MOMENT...
...
VISITORS FROM ABOVE?

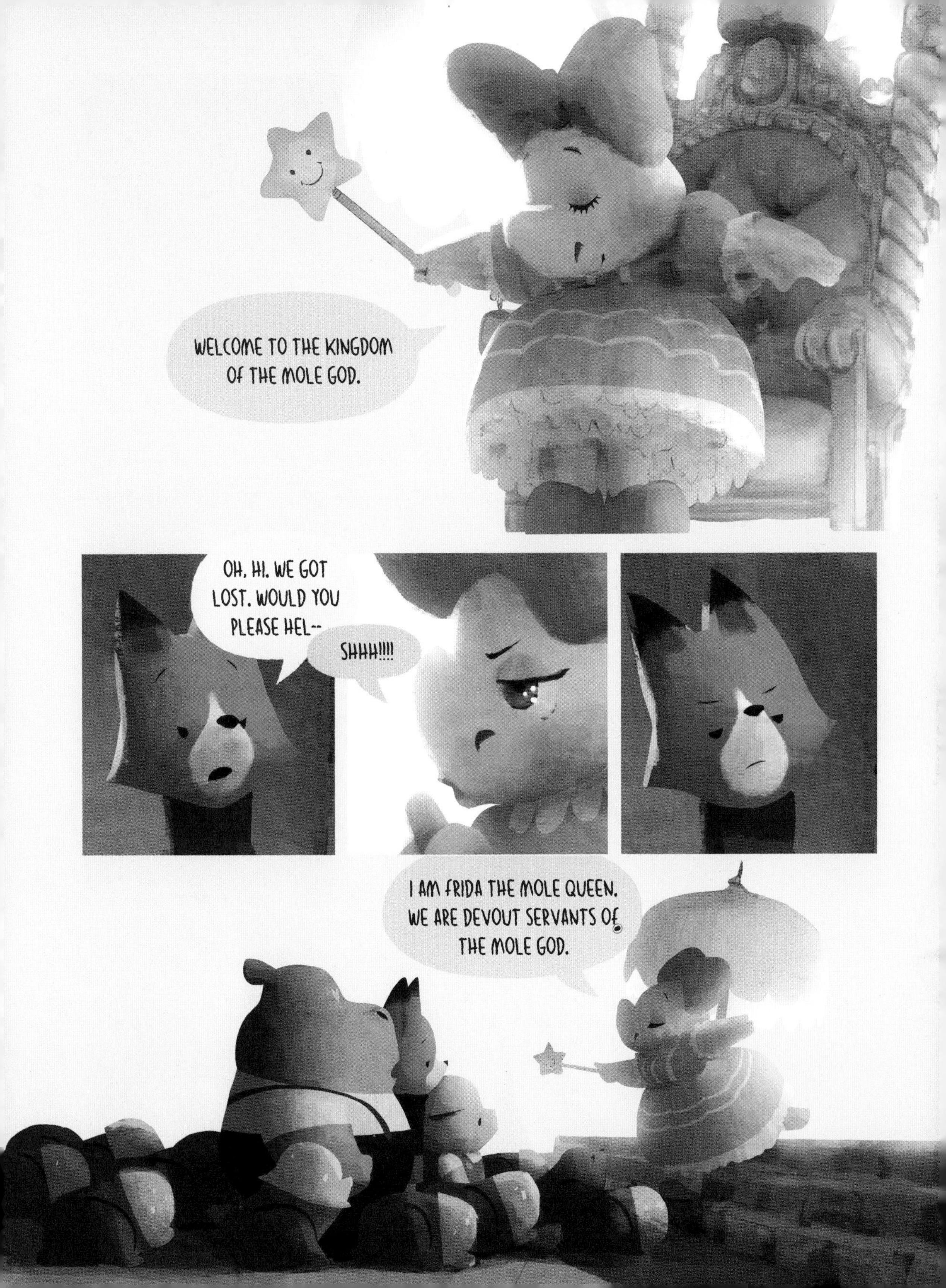
WELCOME TO THE KINGDOM OF THE MOLE GOD.
OH, HI. WE GOT LOST. WOULD YOU PLEASE HEL--
SHHH!!!!
I AM FRIDA THE MOLE QUEEN. WE ARE DEVOUT SERVANTS OF THE MOLE GOD.

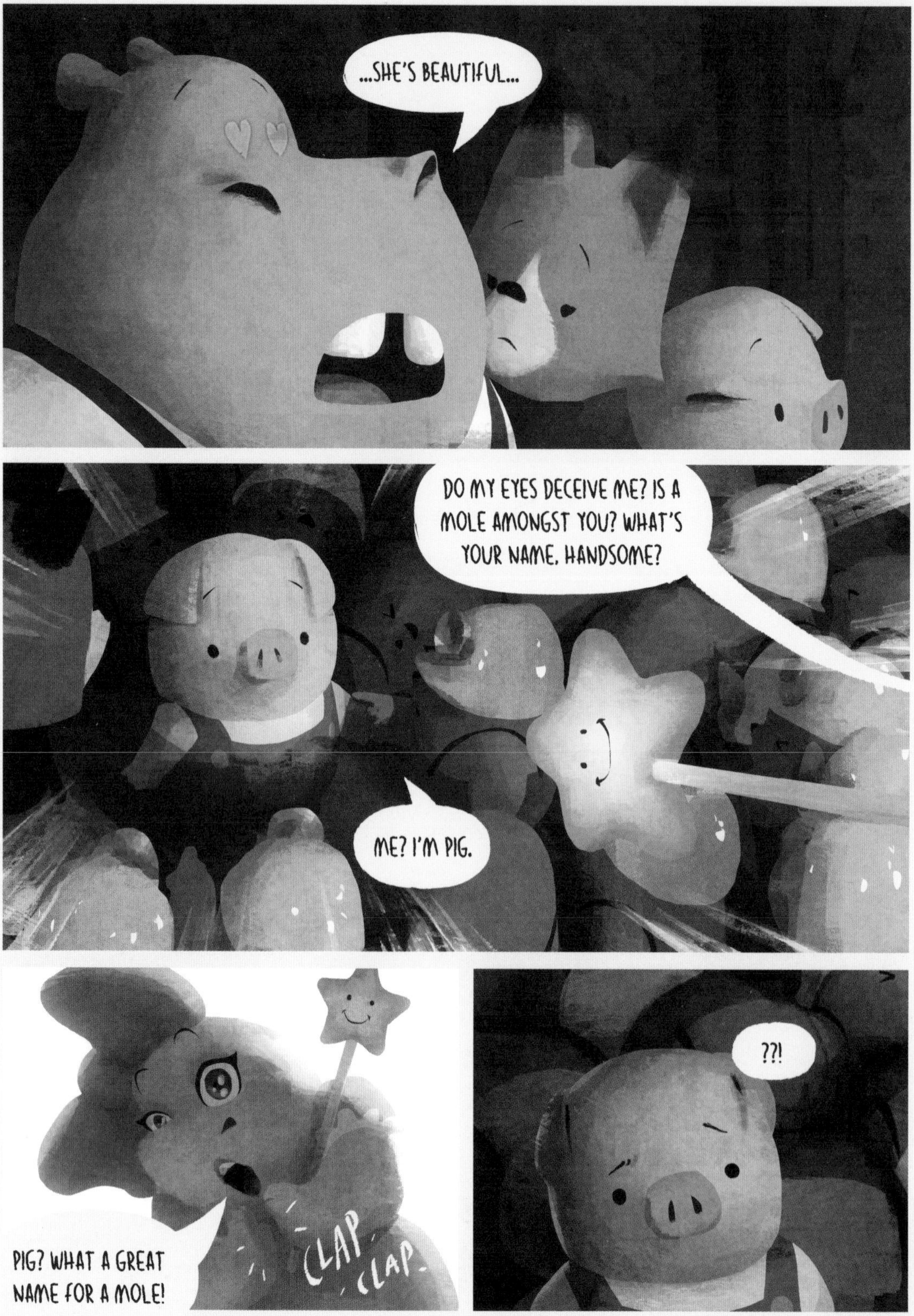
...SHE'S BEAUTIFUL...
DO MY EYES DECEIVE ME? IS A MOLE AMONGST YOU? WHAT'S YOUR NAME, HANDSOME?
ME? I'M PIG.
PIG? WHAT A GREAT NAME FOR A MOLE!
CLAP
CLAP
??!

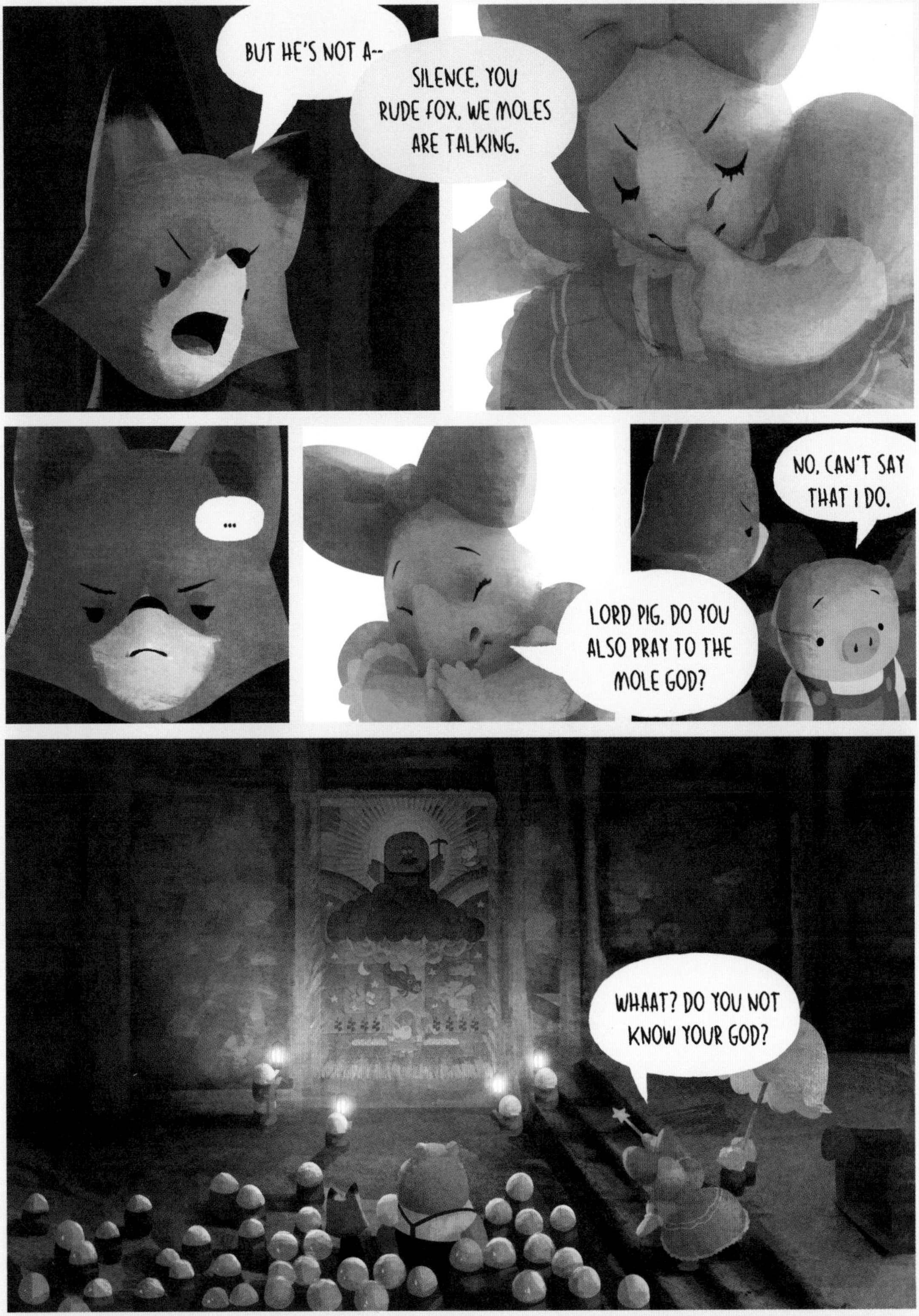
BUT HE'S NOT A--
SILENCE. YOU RUDE FOX. WE MOLES ARE TALKING.
...
LORD PIG. DO YOU ALSO PRAY TO THE MOLE GOD?
NO. CAN'T SAY THAT I DO.
WHAAT? DO YOU NOT KNOW YOUR GOD?

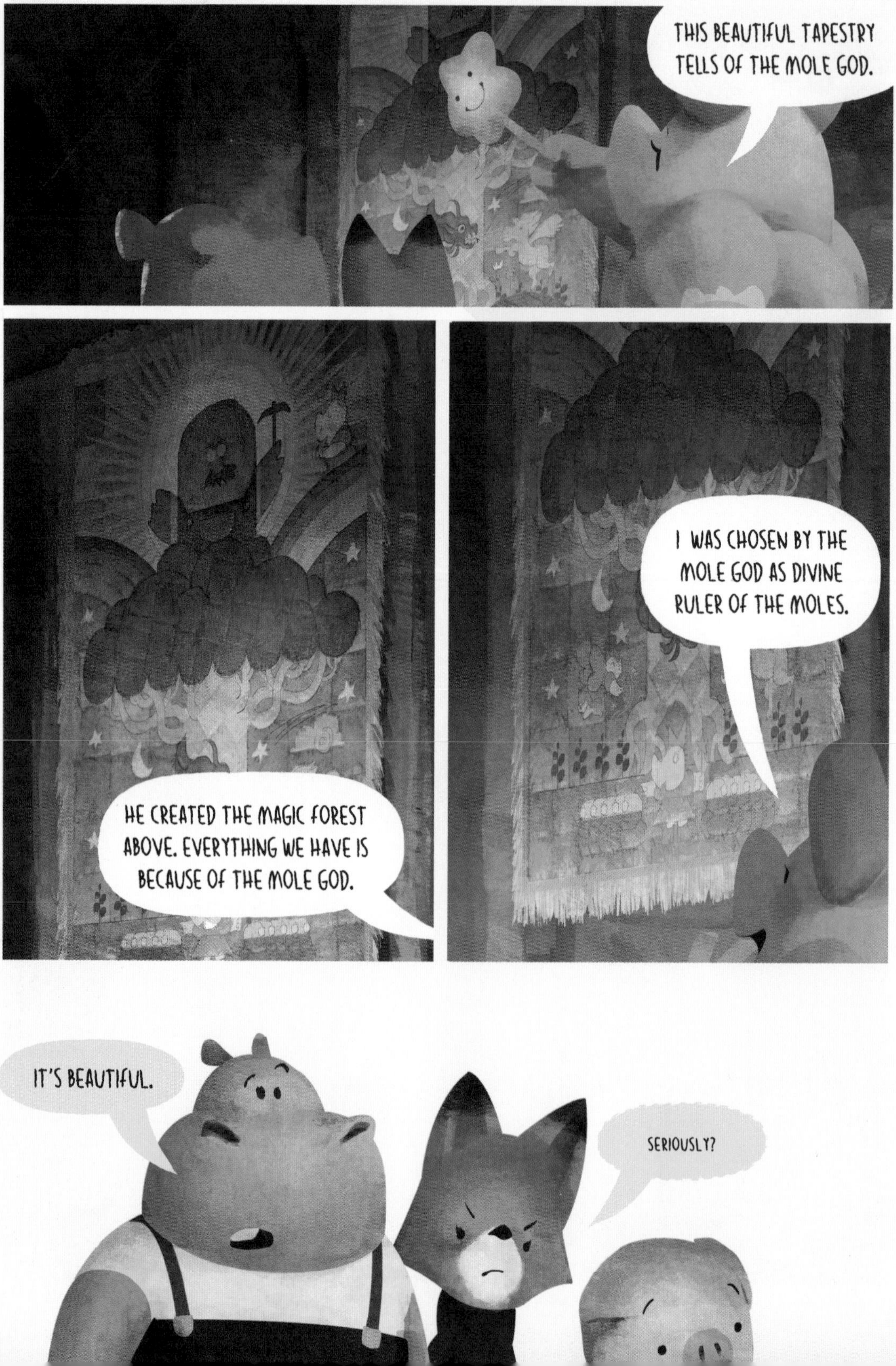
THIS BEAUTIFUL TAPESTRY TELLS OF THE MOLE GOD.
HE CREATED THE MAGIC FOREST ABOVE. EVERYTHING WE HAVE IS BECAUSE OF THE MOLE GOD.
I WAS CHOSEN BY THE MOLE GOD AS DIVINE RULER OF THE MOLES.
IT'S BEAUTIFUL.
SERIOUSLY?

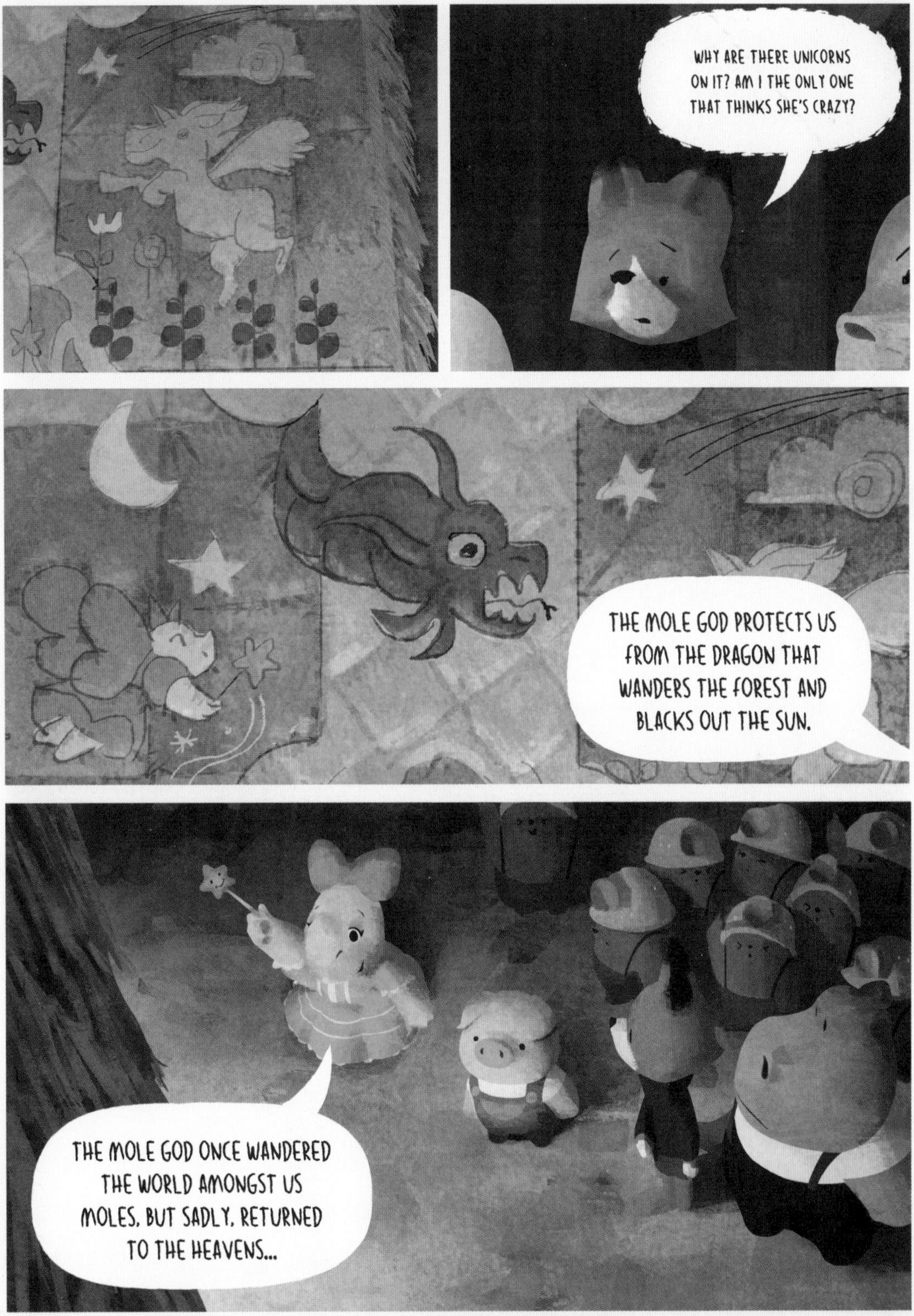
WHY ARE THERE UNICORNS ON IT? AM I THE ONLY ONE THAT THINKS SHE'S CRAZY?
THE MOLE GOD PROTECTS US FROM THE DRAGON THAT WANDERS THE FOREST AND BLACKS OUT THE SUN.
THE MOLE GOD ONCE WANDERED THE WORLD AMONGST US MOLES, BUT SADLY, RETURNED TO THE HEAVENS...

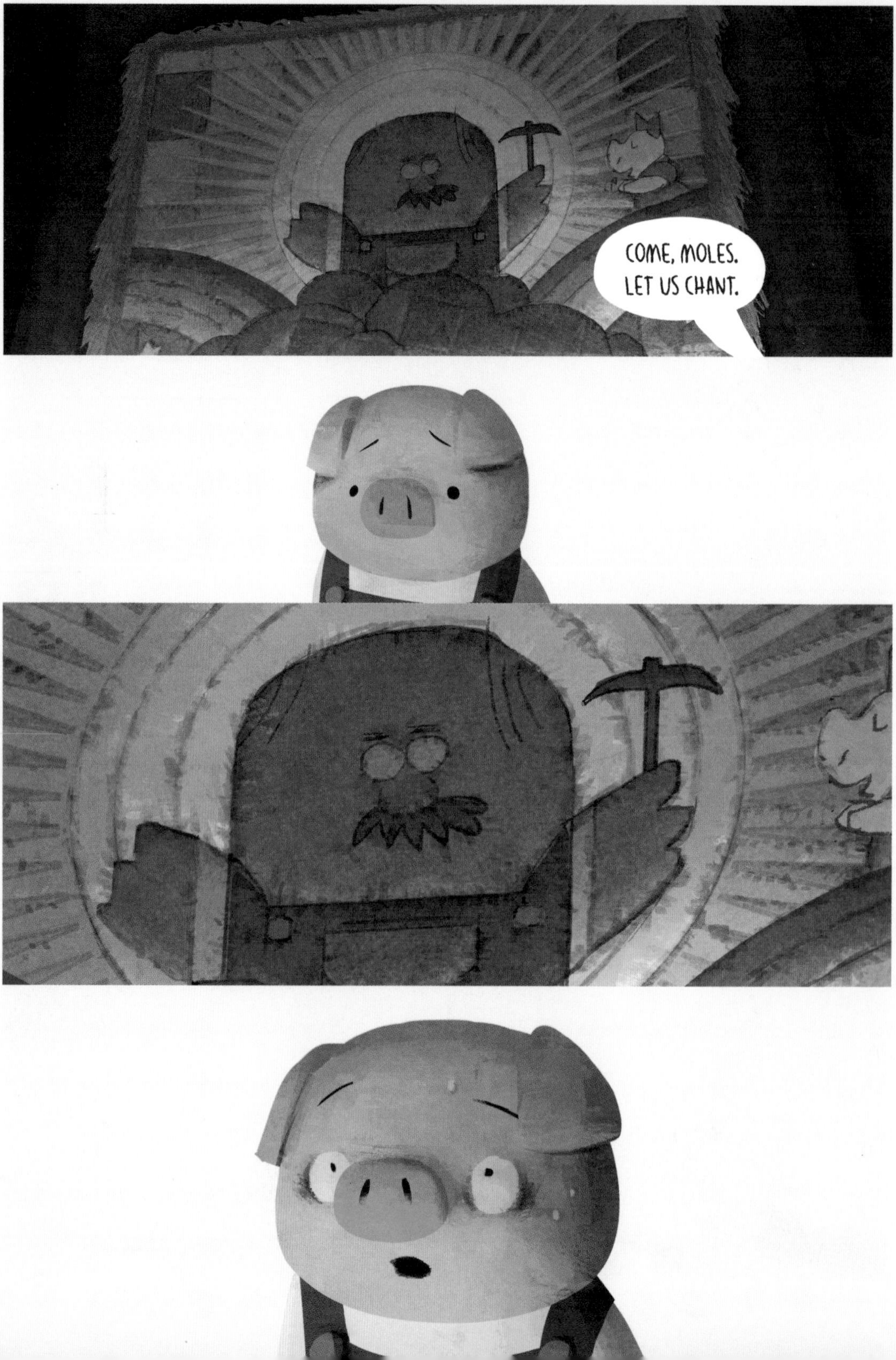
COME, MOLES.
LET US CHANT.

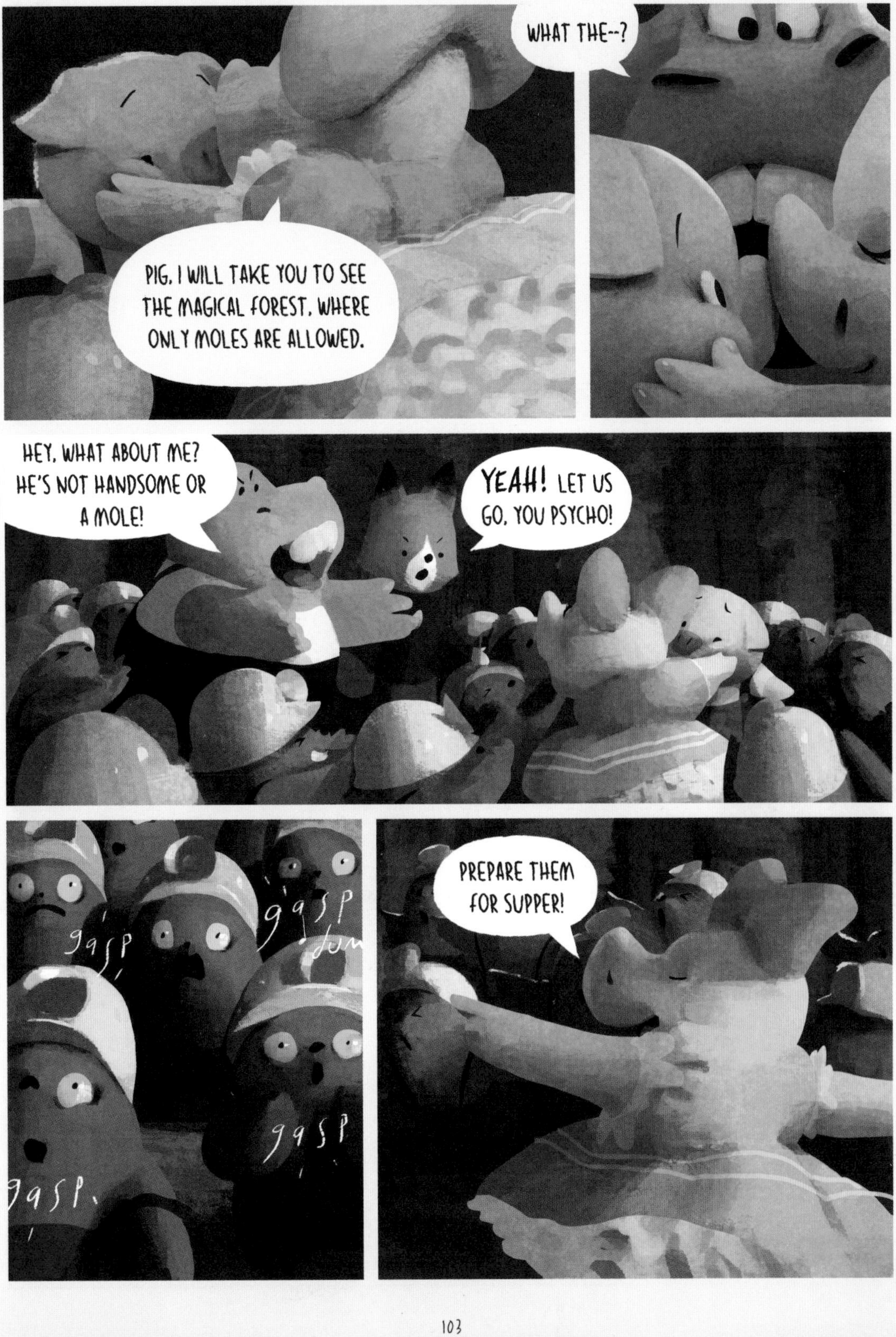
PIG, I WILL TAKE YOU TO SEE THE MAGICAL FOREST, WHERE ONLY MOLES ARE ALLOWED.
WHAT THE--?
HEY, WHAT ABOUT ME? HE'S NOT HANDSOME OR A MOLE!
YEAH! LET US GO, YOU PSYCHO!
gasp
gasp
gasp
gasp
PREPARE THEM FOR SUPPER!

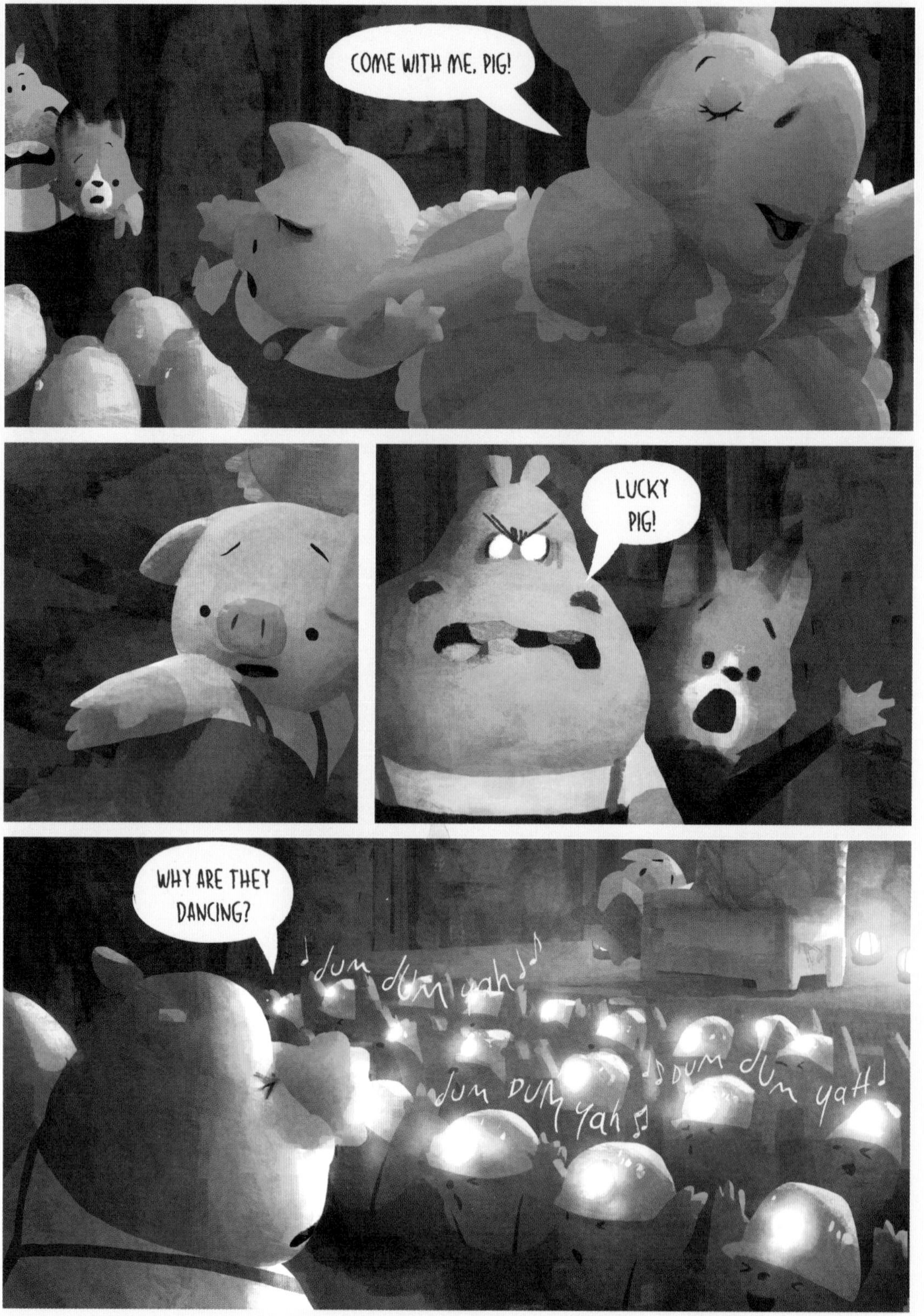
COME WITH ME, PIG!
LUCKY PIG!
WHY ARE THEY DANCING?
♪ dum dUm yah ♪♪
dum DUM yah ♫
♪♪ DUM dUm yaH ♪

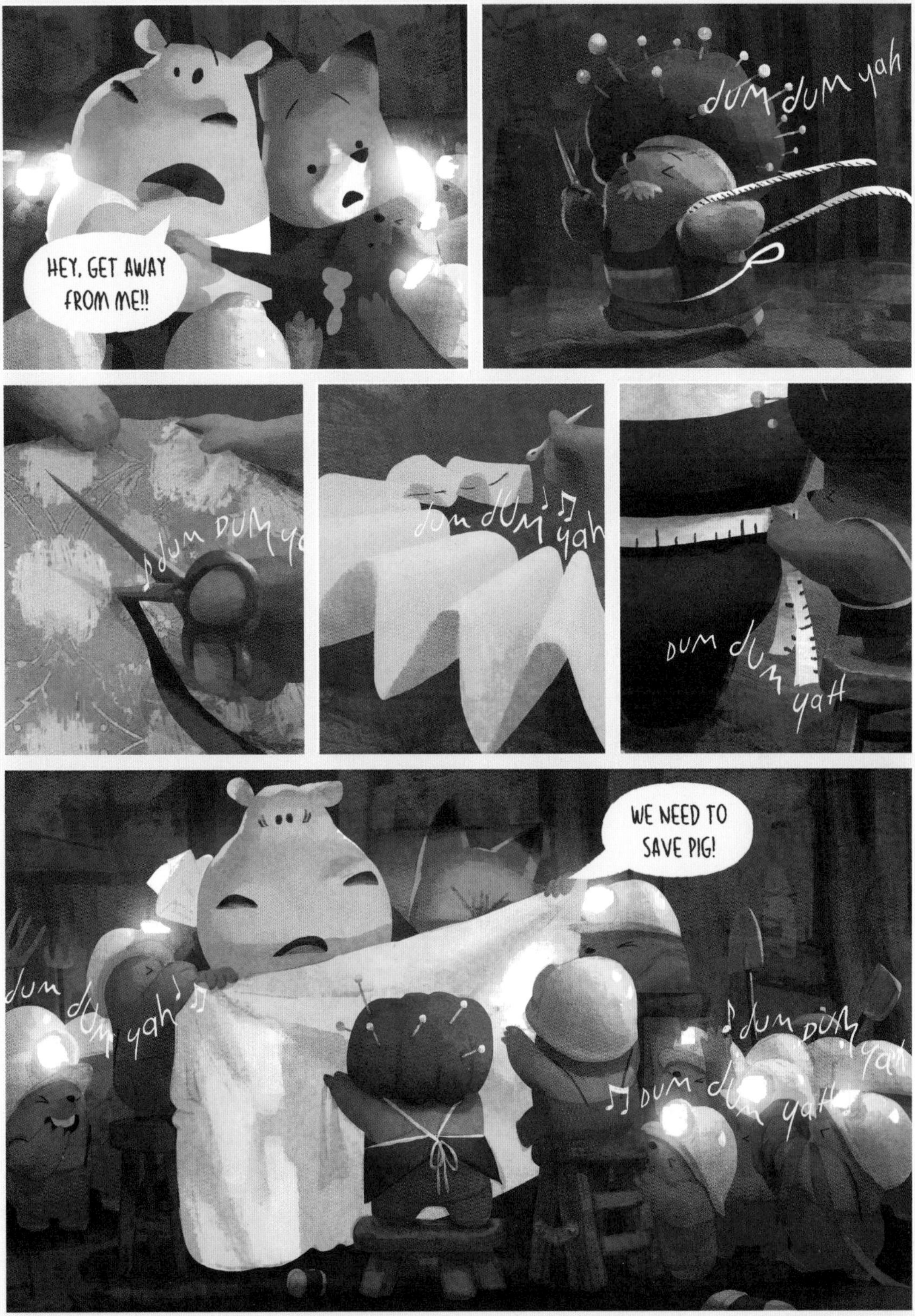
HEY, GET AWAY FROM ME!!
DUM DUM YAH
DUM DUM YA
DUM DUM YAH
DUM DUM YAH
WE NEED TO SAVE PIG!
DUM DUM YAH
DUM DUM YAH
DUM DUM YAH

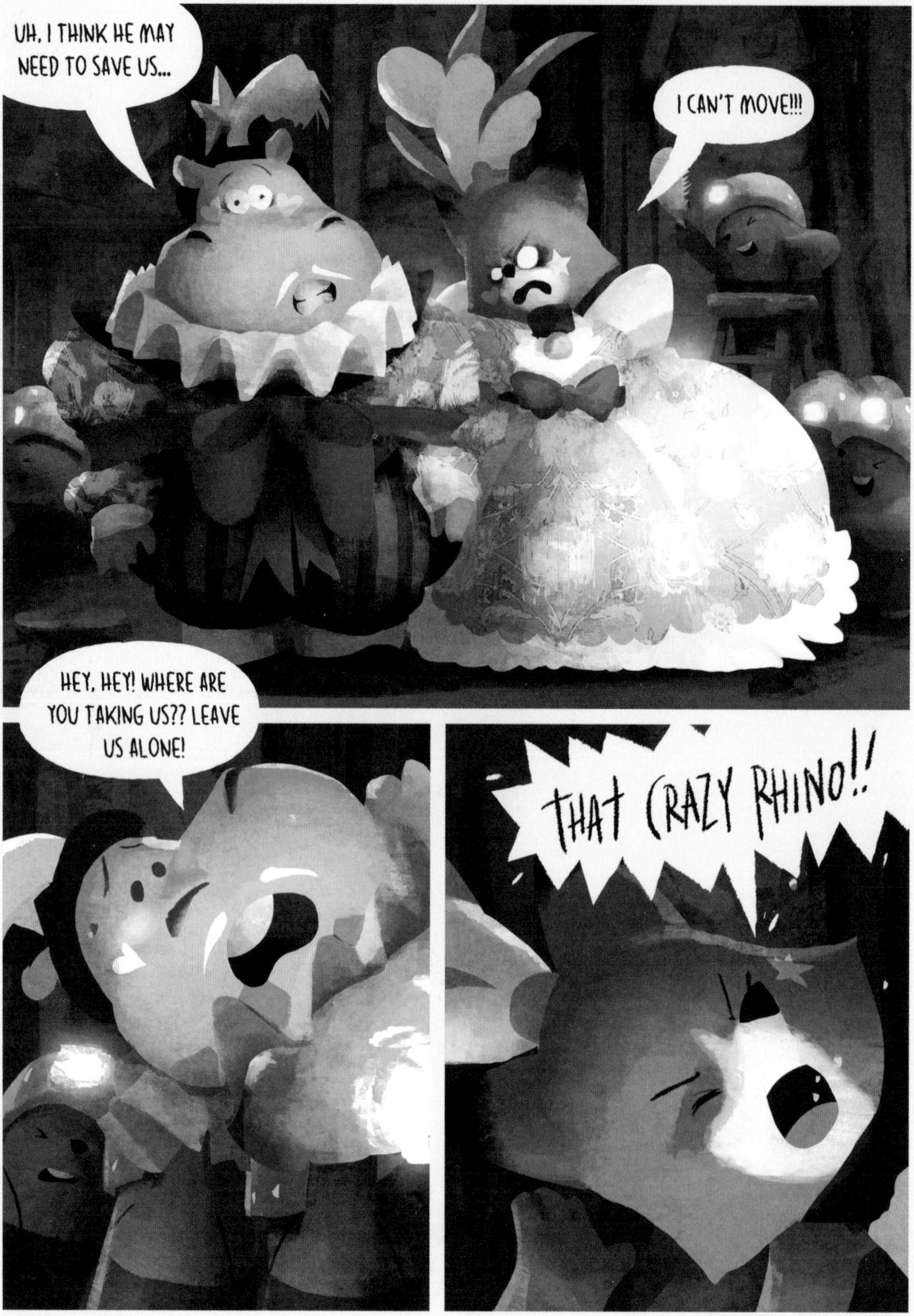
UH, I THINK HE MAY NEED TO SAVE US...
I CAN'T MOVE!!!
HEY, HEY! WHERE ARE YOU TAKING US?? LEAVE US ALONE!
THAT CRAZY RHINO!!

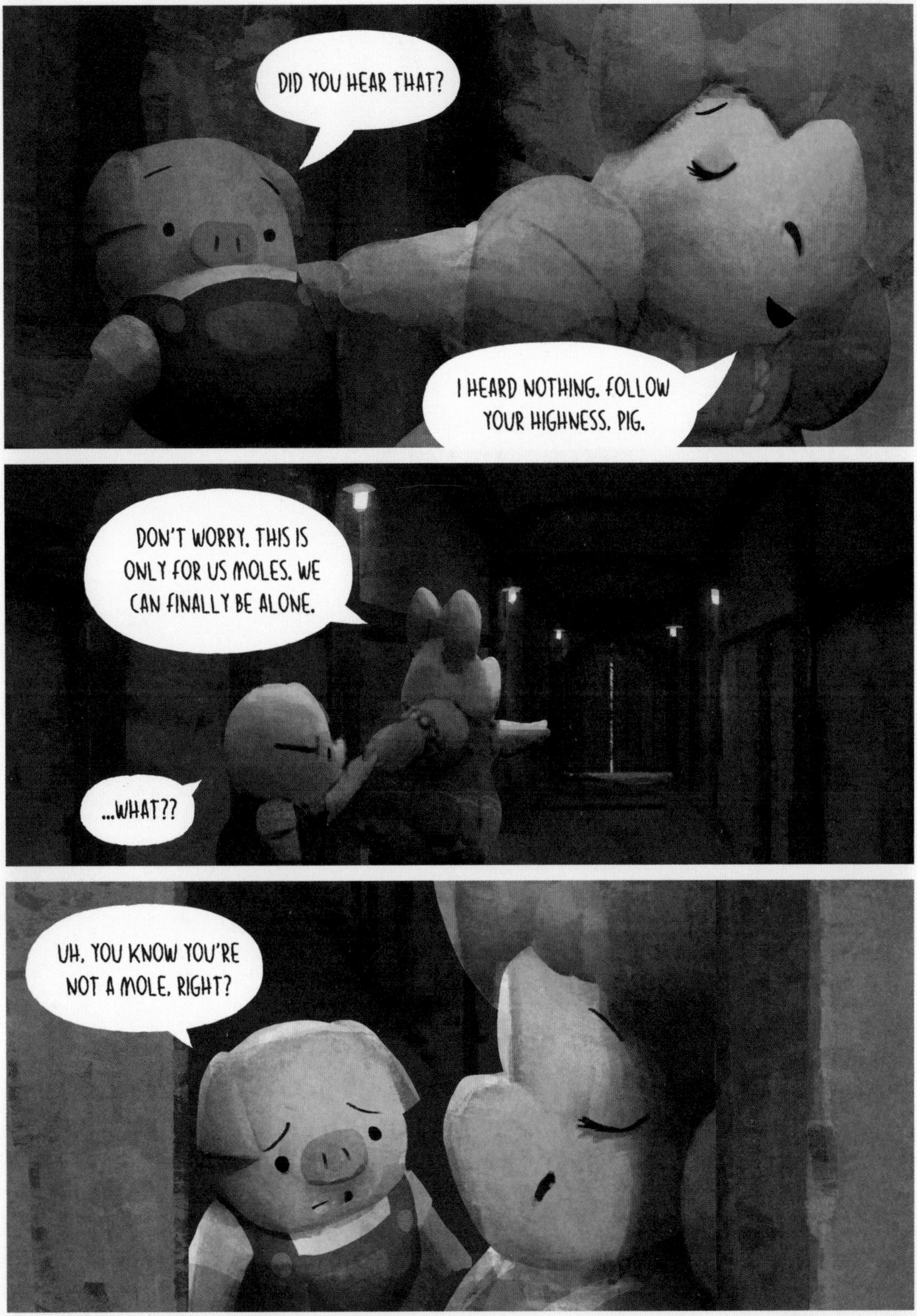
DID YOU HEAR THAT?
I HEARD NOTHING. FOLLOW YOUR HIGHNESS, PIG.
DON'T WORRY. THIS IS ONLY FOR US MOLES. WE CAN FINALLY BE ALONE.
...WHAT??
UH, YOU KNOW YOU'RE NOT A MOLE, RIGHT?

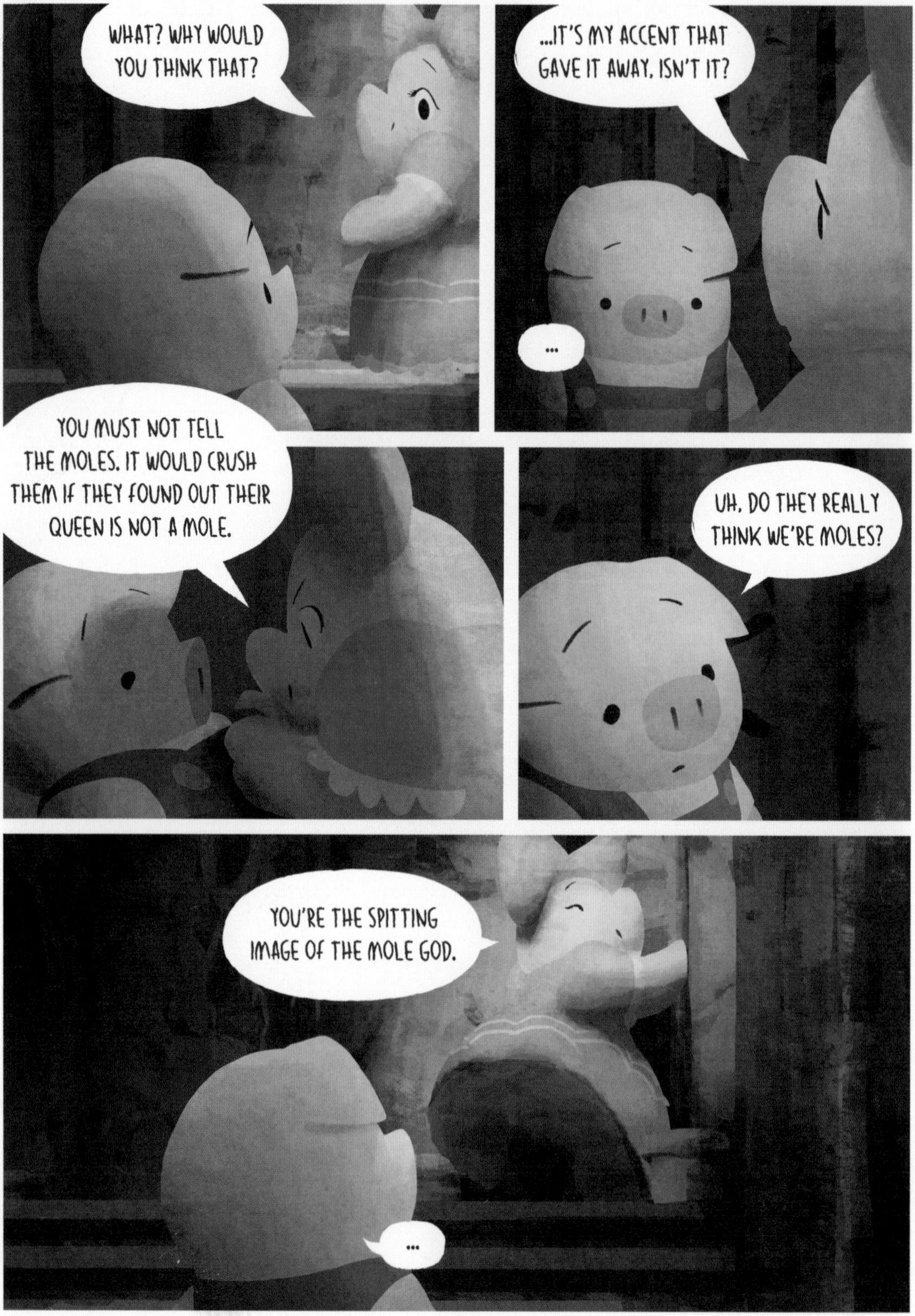
WHAT? WHY WOULD YOU THINK THAT?
...IT'S MY ACCENT THAT GAVE IT AWAY, ISN'T IT?
...
YOU MUST NOT TELL THE MOLES. IT WOULD CRUSH THEM IF THEY FOUND OUT THEIR QUEEN IS NOT A MOLE.
UH, DO THEY REALLY THINK WE'RE MOLES?
YOU'RE THE SPITTING IMAGE OF THE MOLE GOD.
...

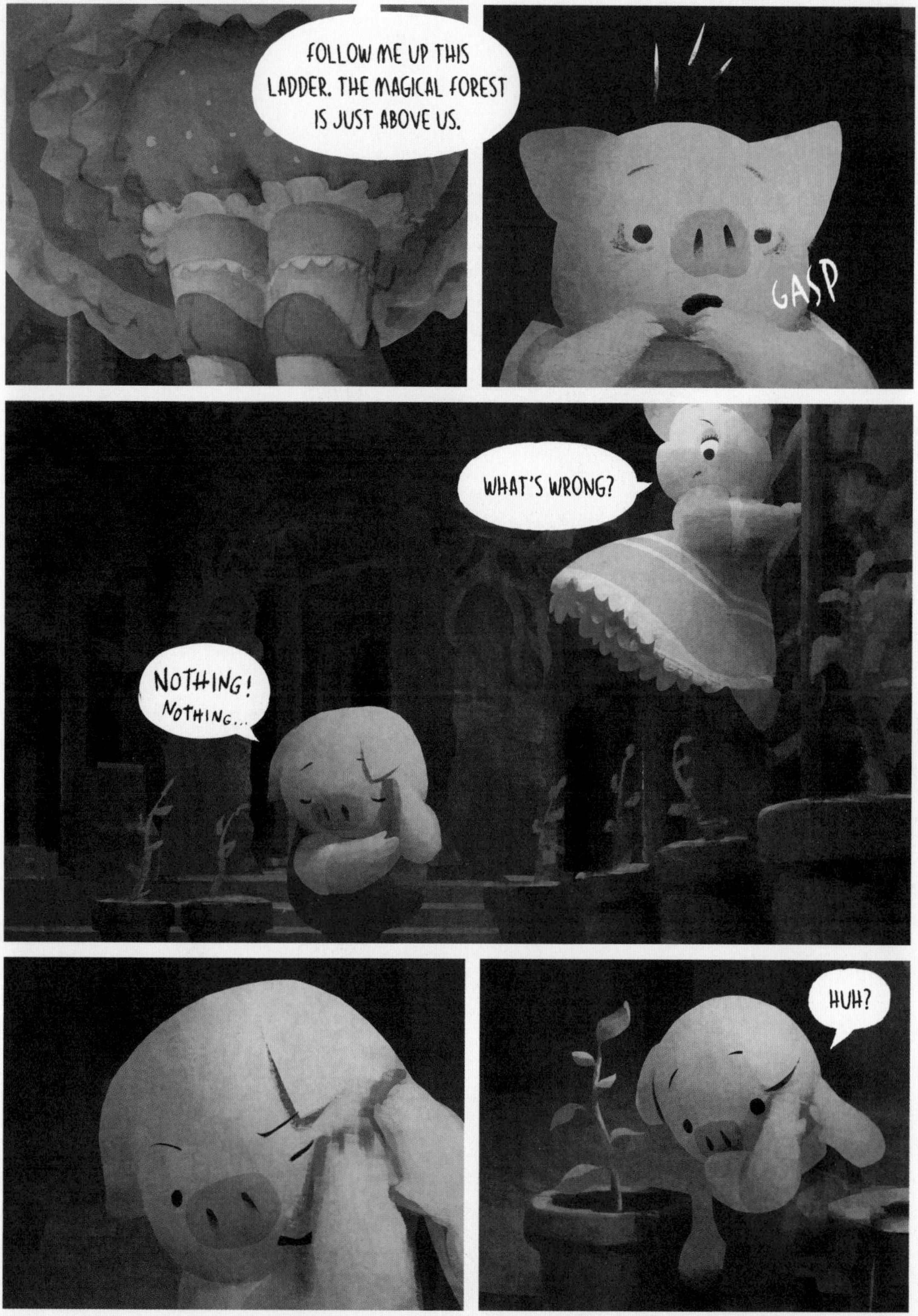
FOLLOW ME UP THIS LADDER. THE MAGICAL FOREST IS JUST ABOVE US.
GASP
WHAT'S WRONG?
NOTHING! NOTHING...
HUH?

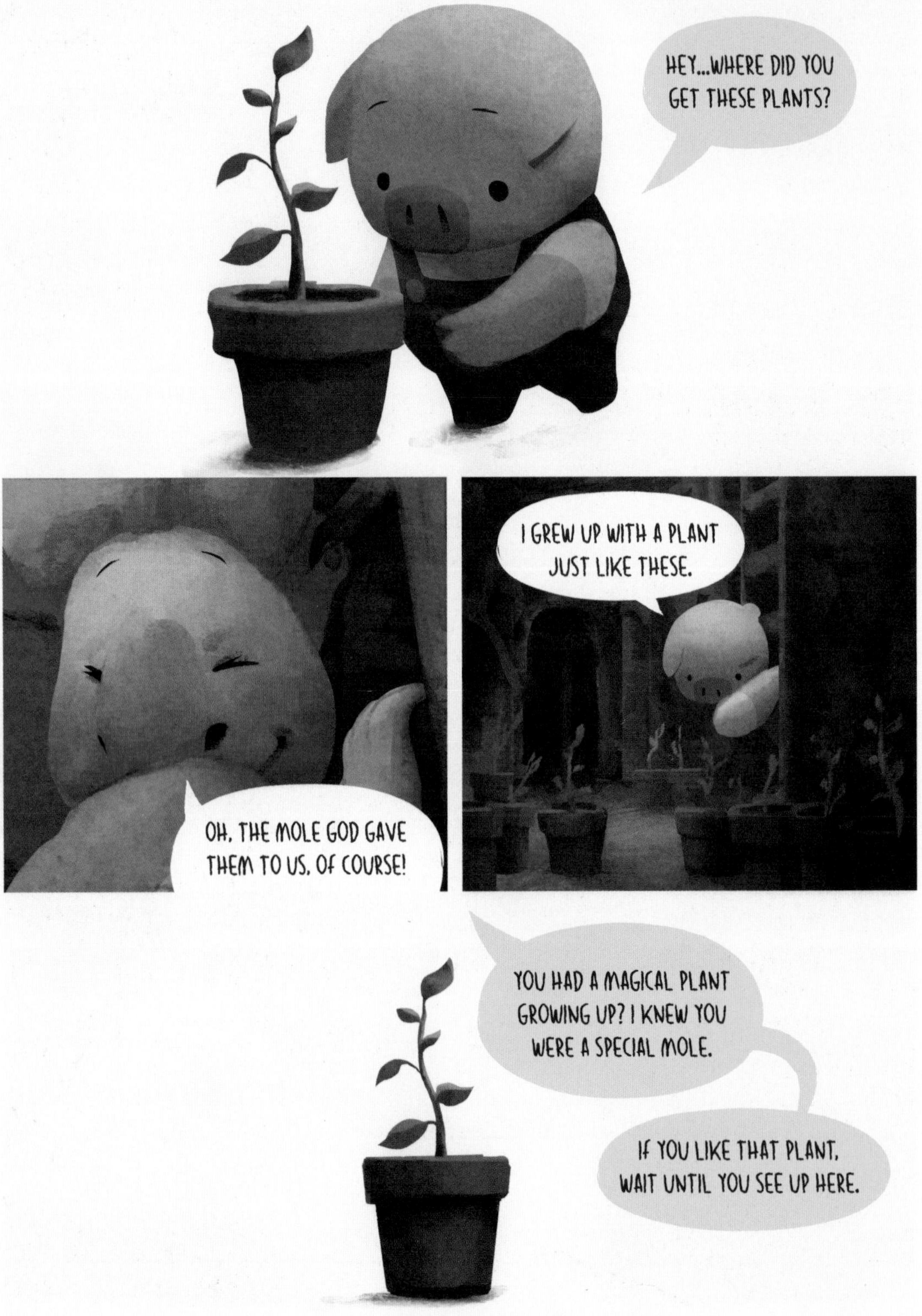
HEY...WHERE DID YOU GET THESE PLANTS?
OH, THE MOLE GOD GAVE THEM TO US, OF COURSE!
I GREW UP WITH A PLANT JUST LIKE THESE.
YOU HAD A MAGICAL PLANT GROWING UP? I KNEW YOU WERE A SPECIAL MOLE.
IF YOU LIKE THAT PLANT, WAIT UNTIL YOU SEE UP HERE.

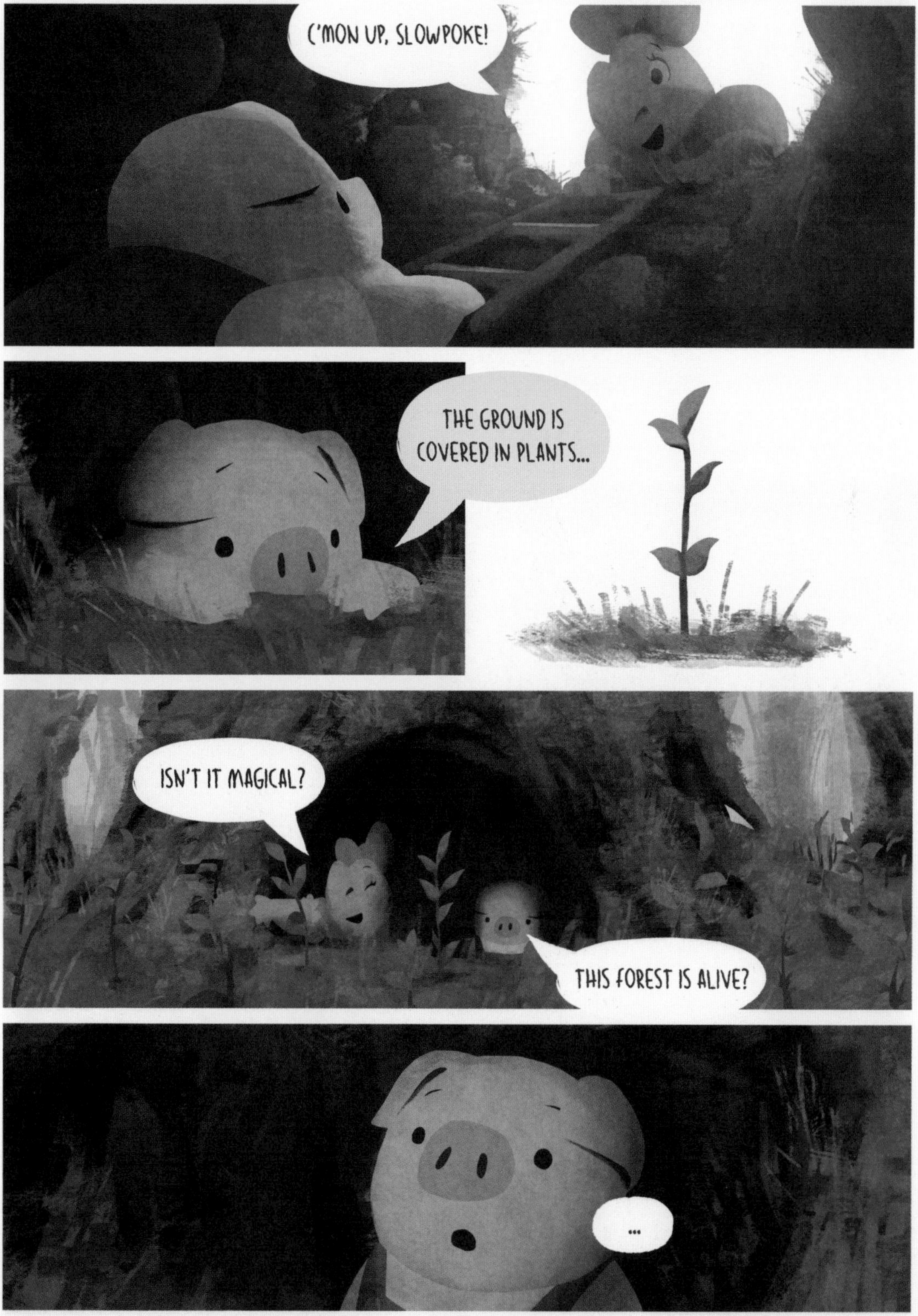

C'MON UP, SLOWPOKE!
THE GROUND IS COVERED IN PLANTS...
ISN'T IT MAGICAL?
THIS FOREST IS ALIVE?
...

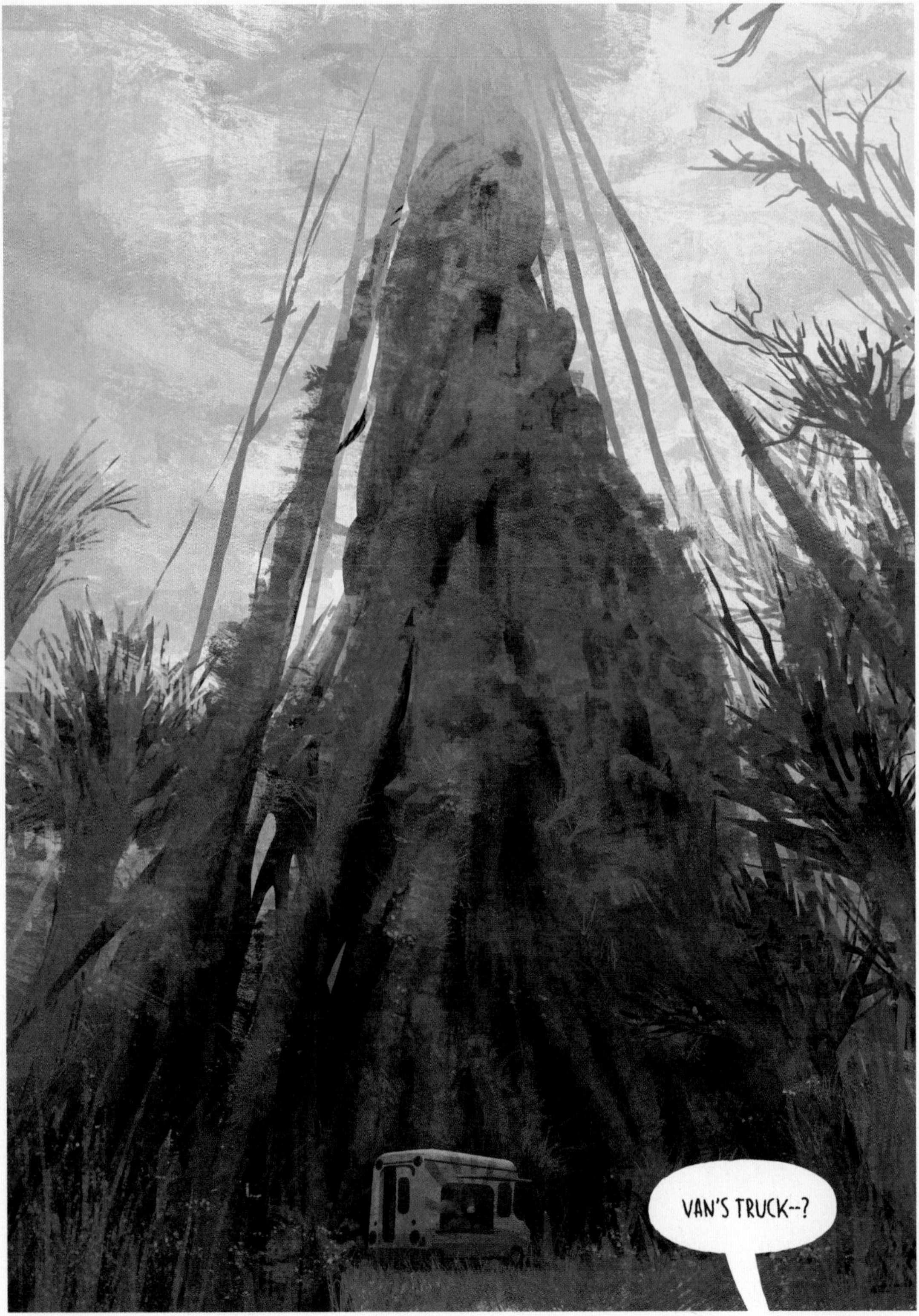
VAN'S TRUCK--?

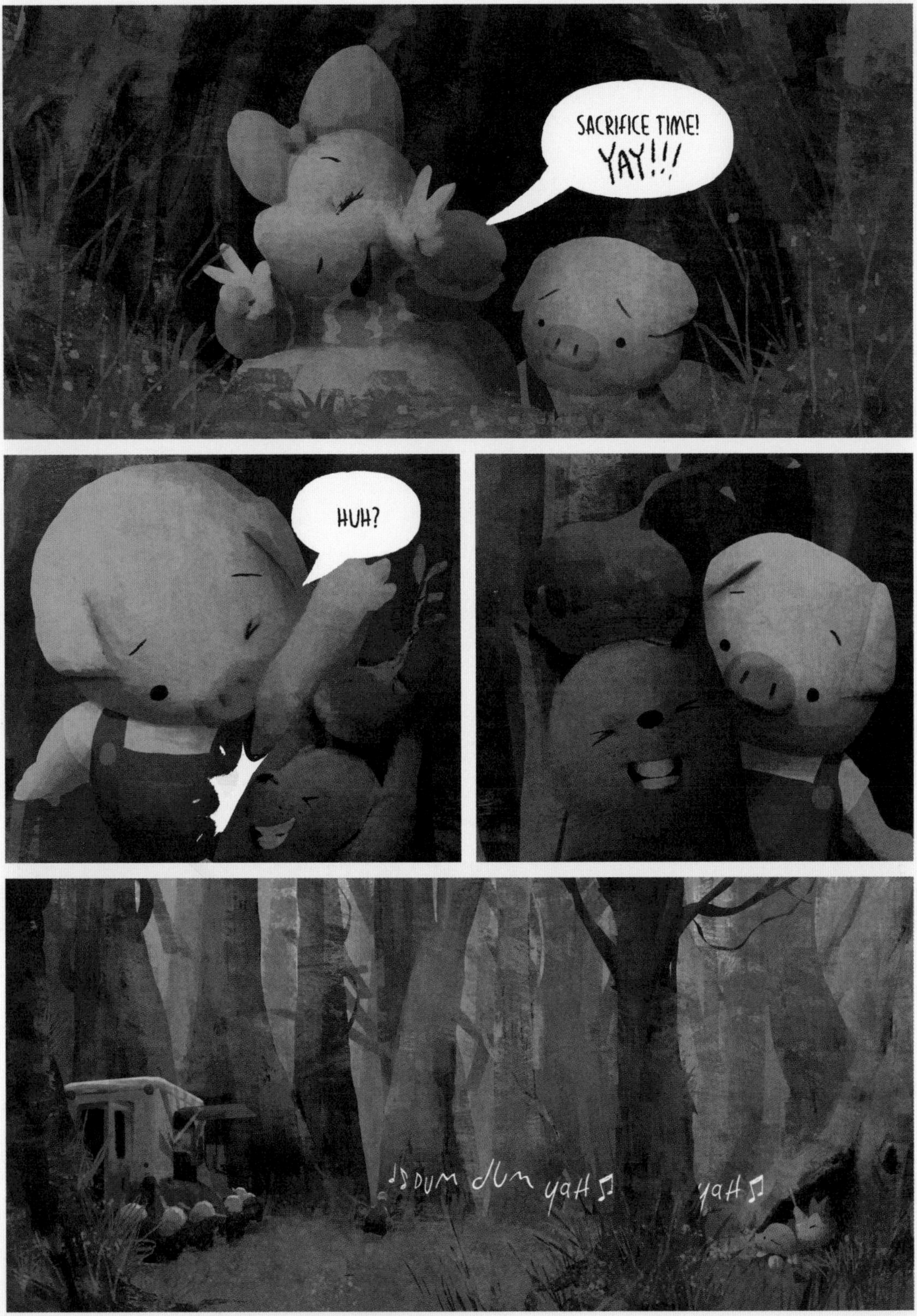
SACRIFICE TIME!
YAY!!!
HUH?
♪DUM DUM YAH♫
YAH♫

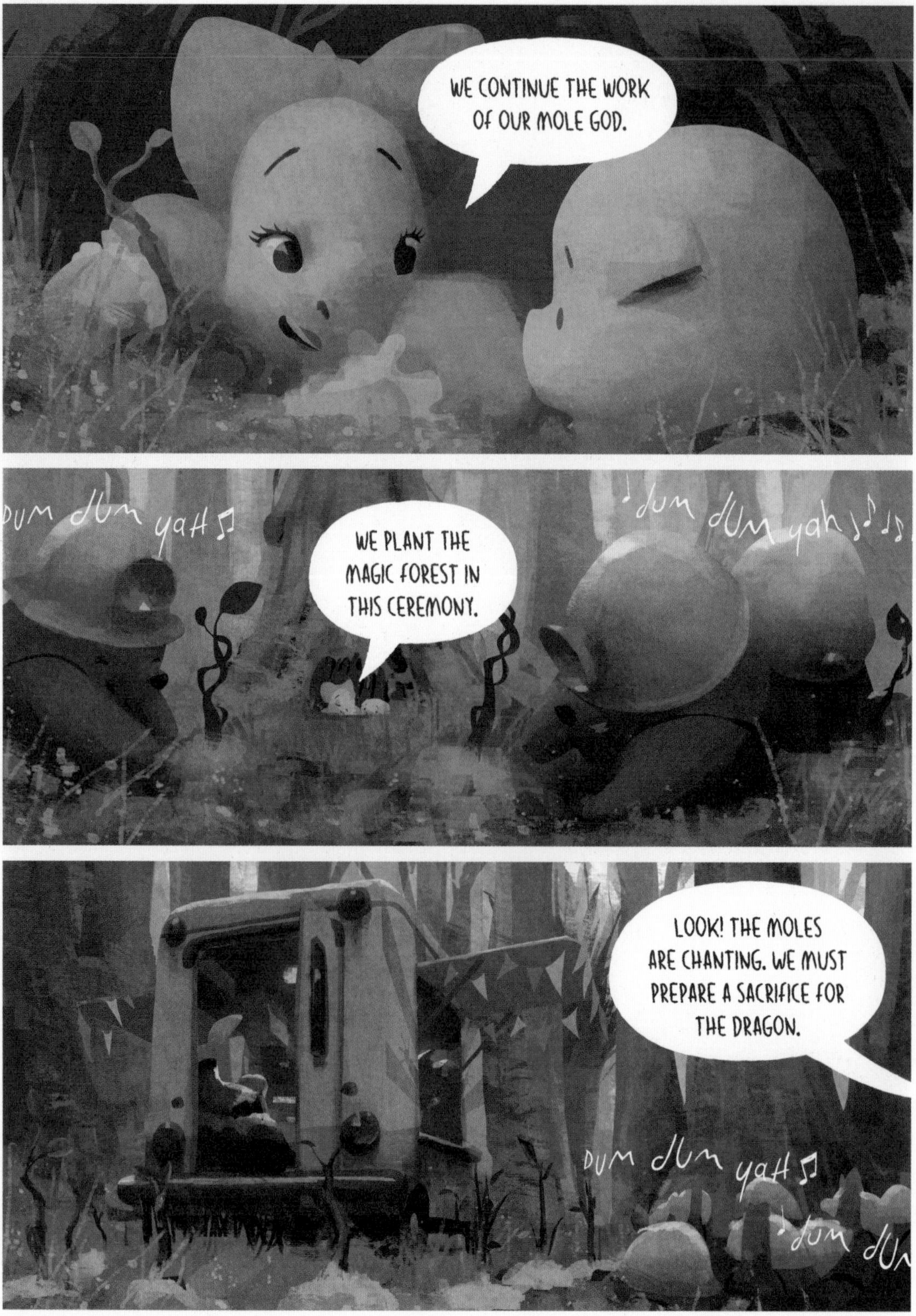
WE CONTINUE THE WORK OF OUR MOLE GOD.
DUM dUM yaH ♫
♪ dum dUM yah ♪♪♫
WE PLANT THE MAGIC FOREST IN THIS CEREMONY.
LOOK! THE MOLES ARE CHANTING. WE MUST PREPARE A SACRIFICE FOR THE DRAGON.
DUM dUM yaH ♫
♪ dum dU

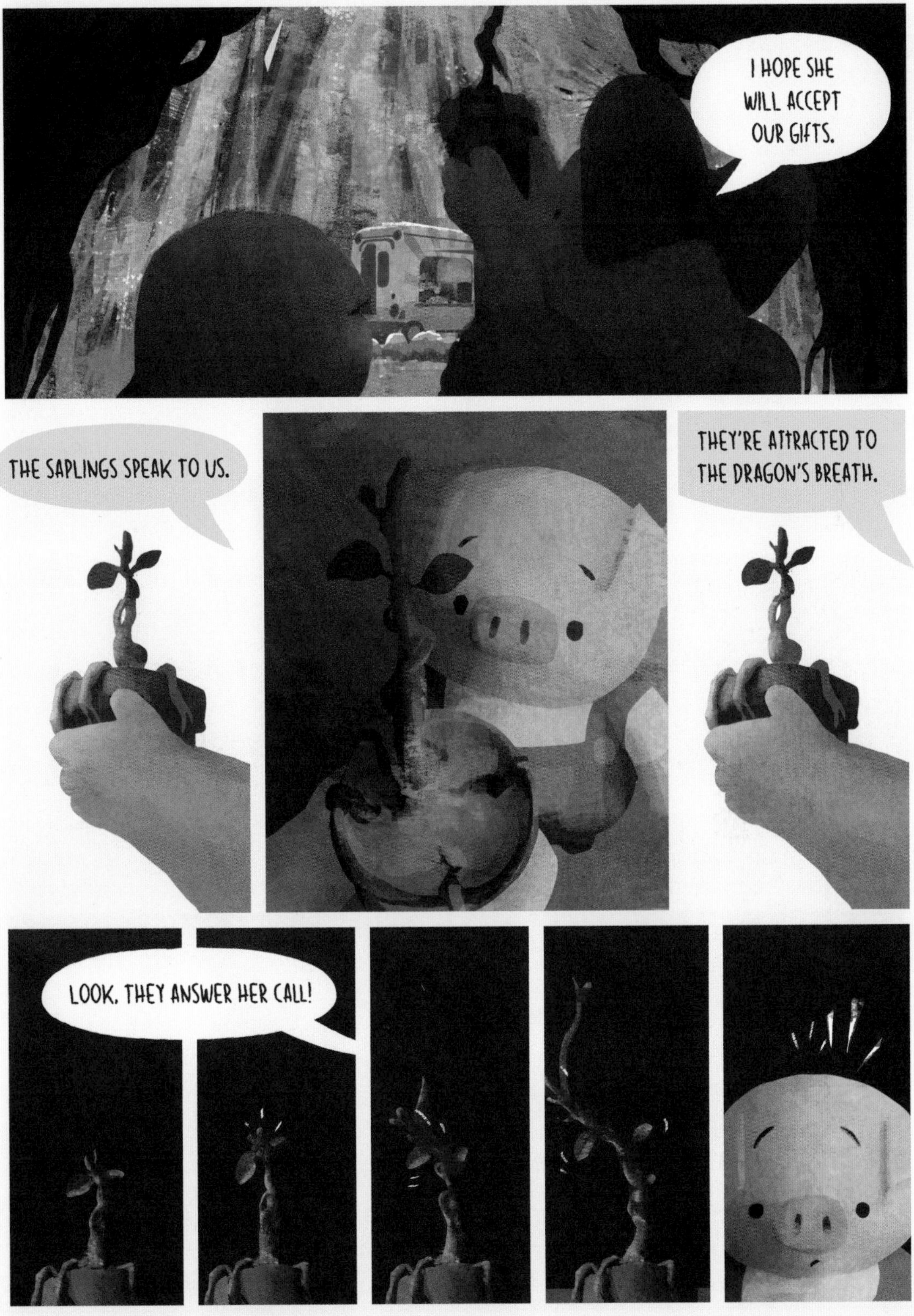
I HOPE SHE WILL ACCEPT OUR GIFTS.
THE SAPLINGS SPEAK TO US.
THEY'RE ATTRACTED TO THE DRAGON'S BREATH.
LOOK, THEY ANSWER HER CALL!

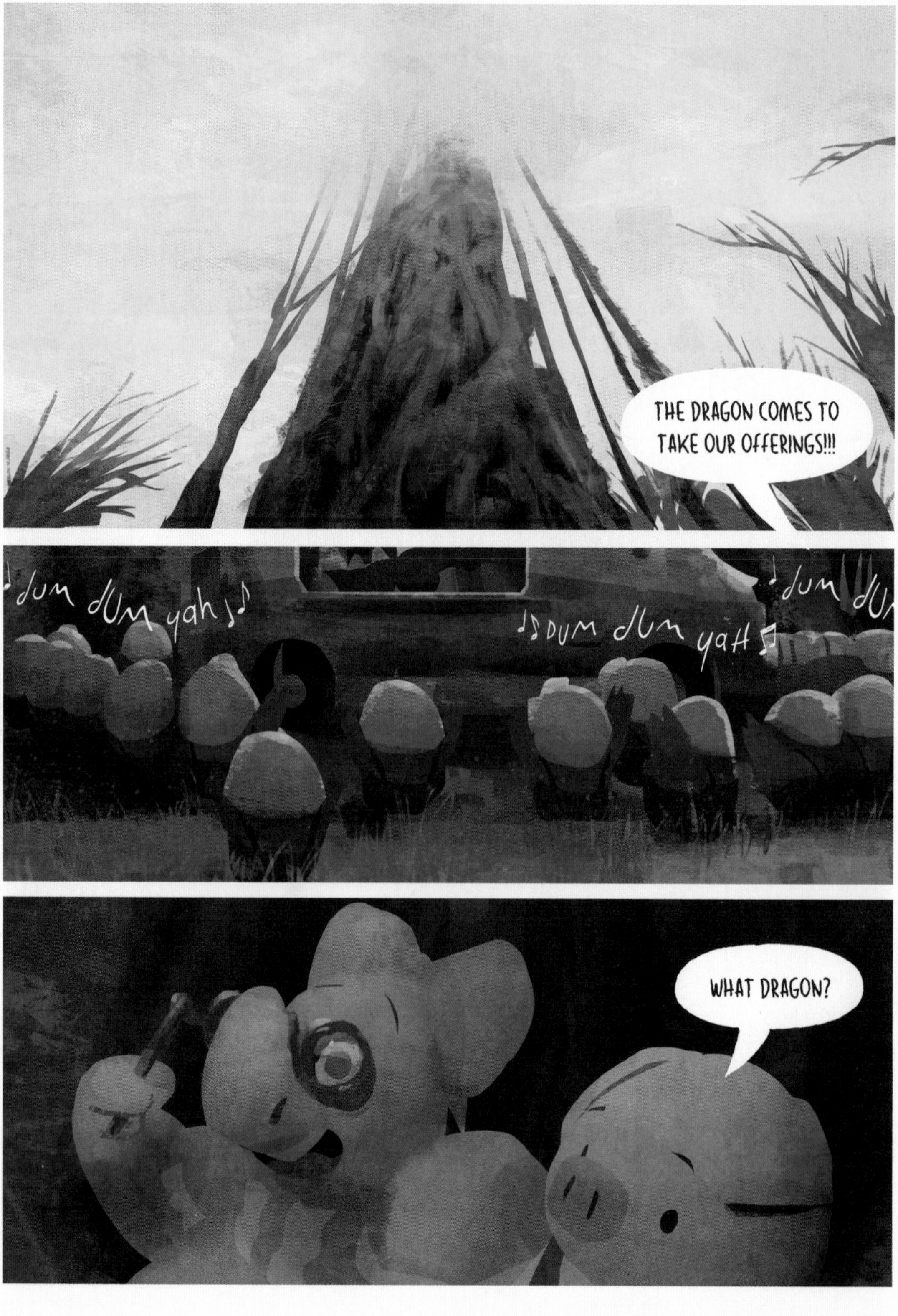
THE DRAGON COMES TO TAKE OUR OFFERINGS!!!
dum dUm yah
DUM dUm yaH
dum dU
WHAT DRAGON?

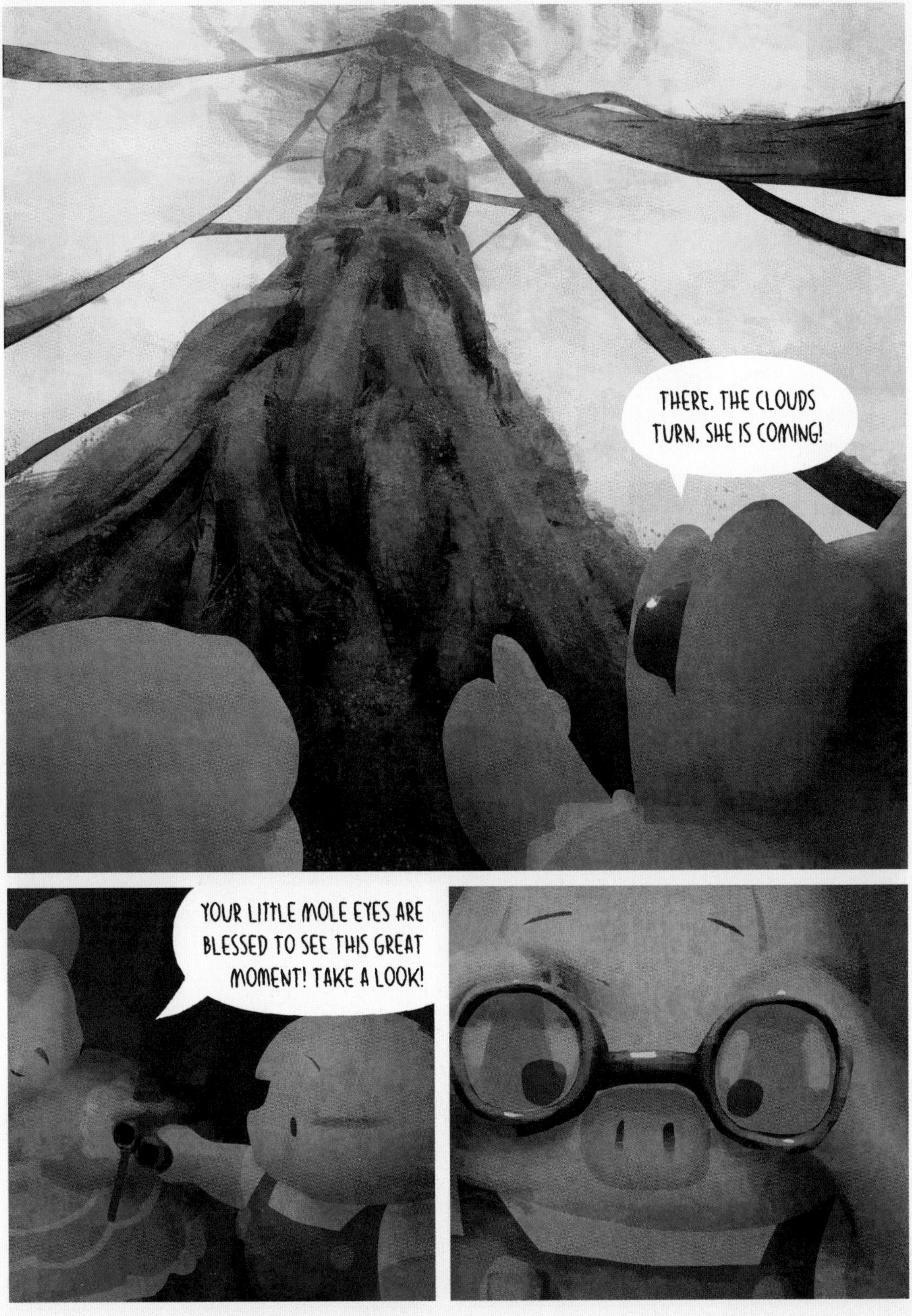
THERE, THE CLOUDS TURN, SHE IS COMING!
YOUR LITTLE MOLE EYES ARE BLESSED TO SEE THIS GREAT MOMENT! TAKE A LOOK!

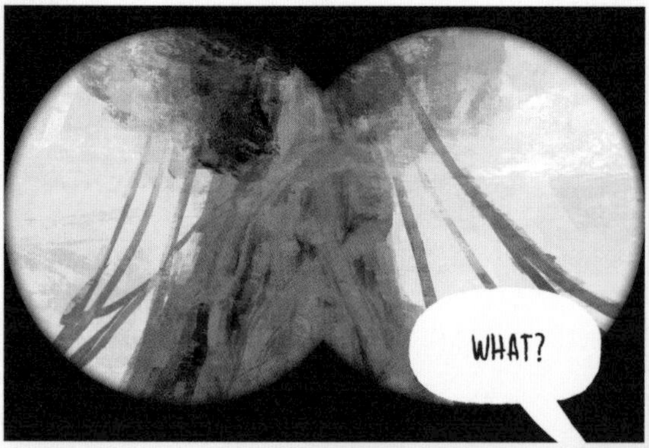
WHAT?
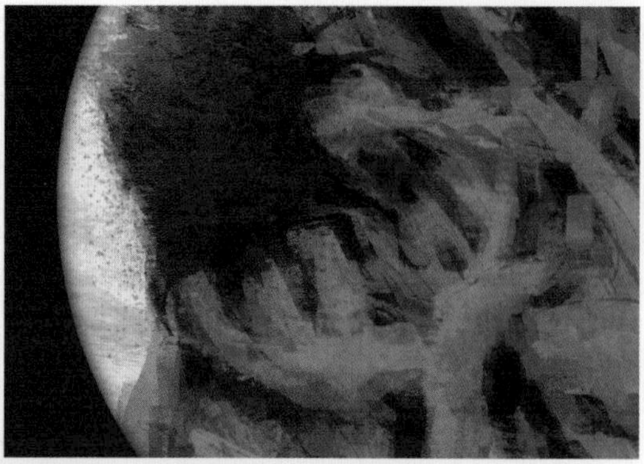
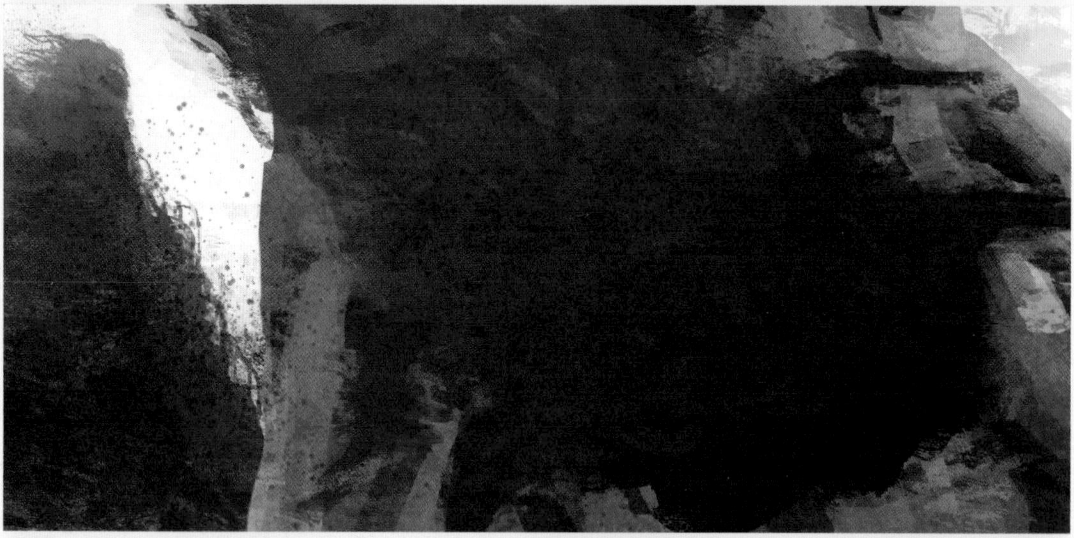
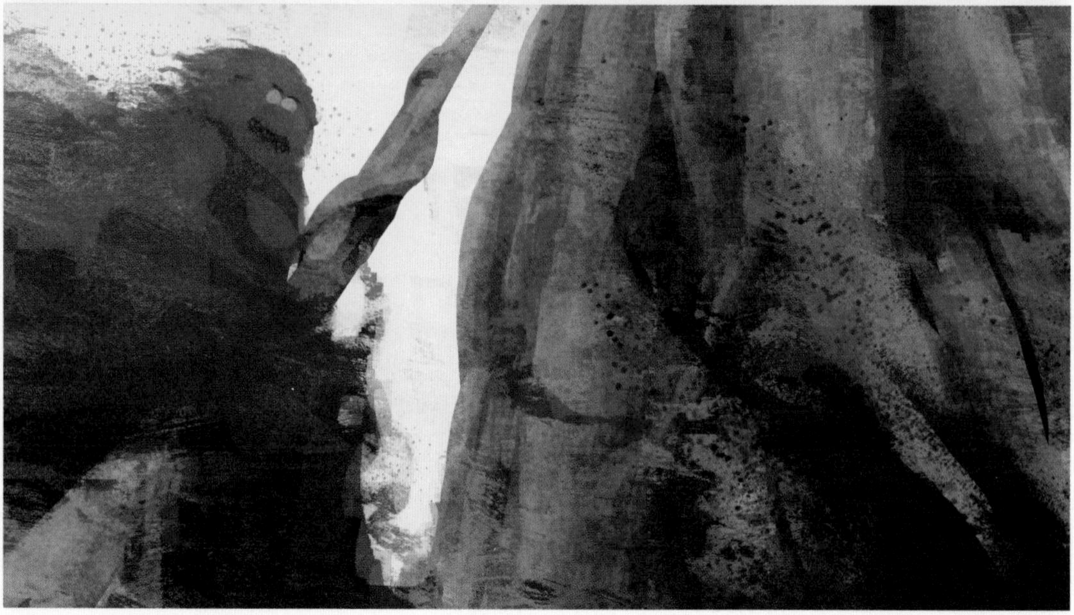

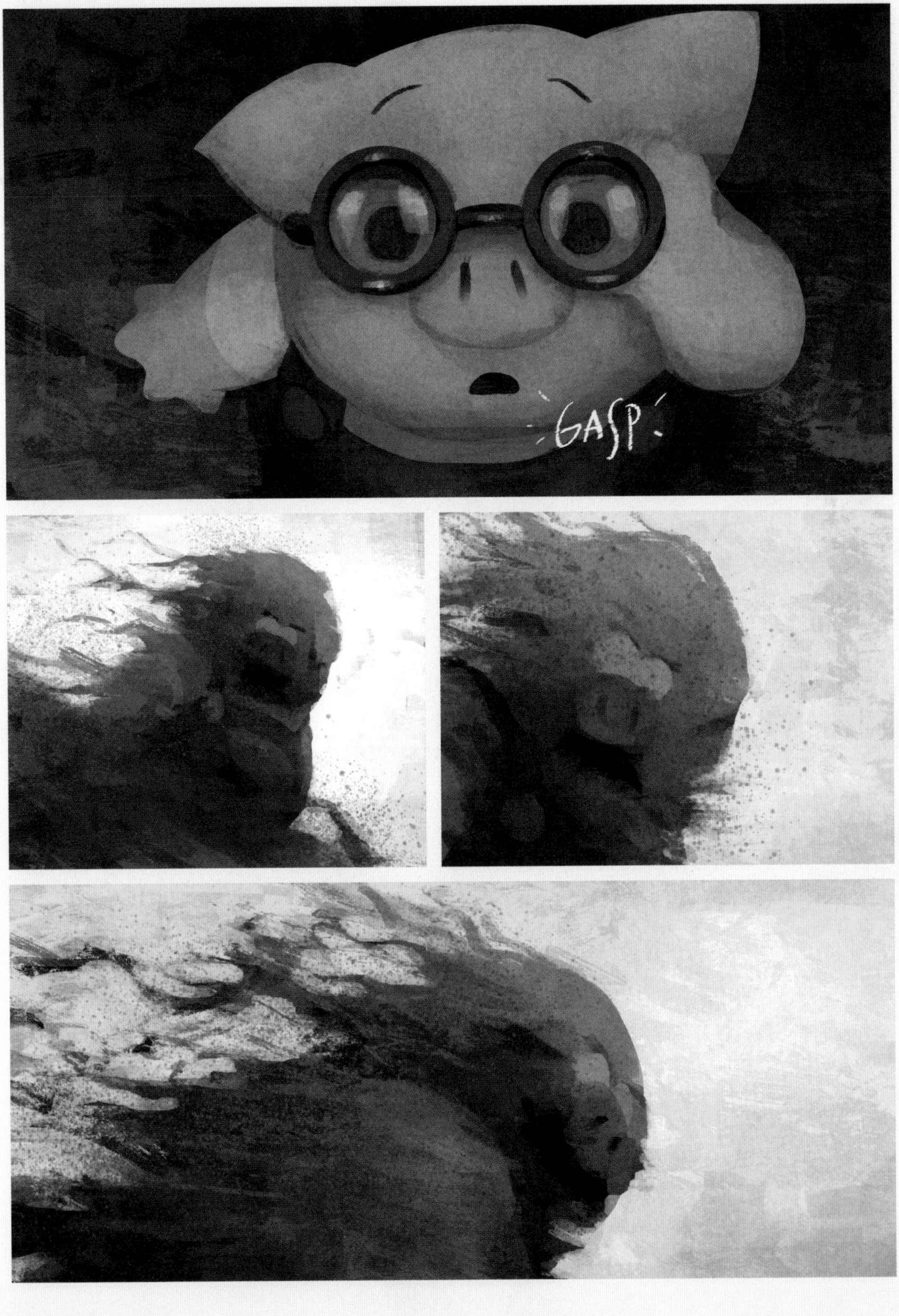
GASP

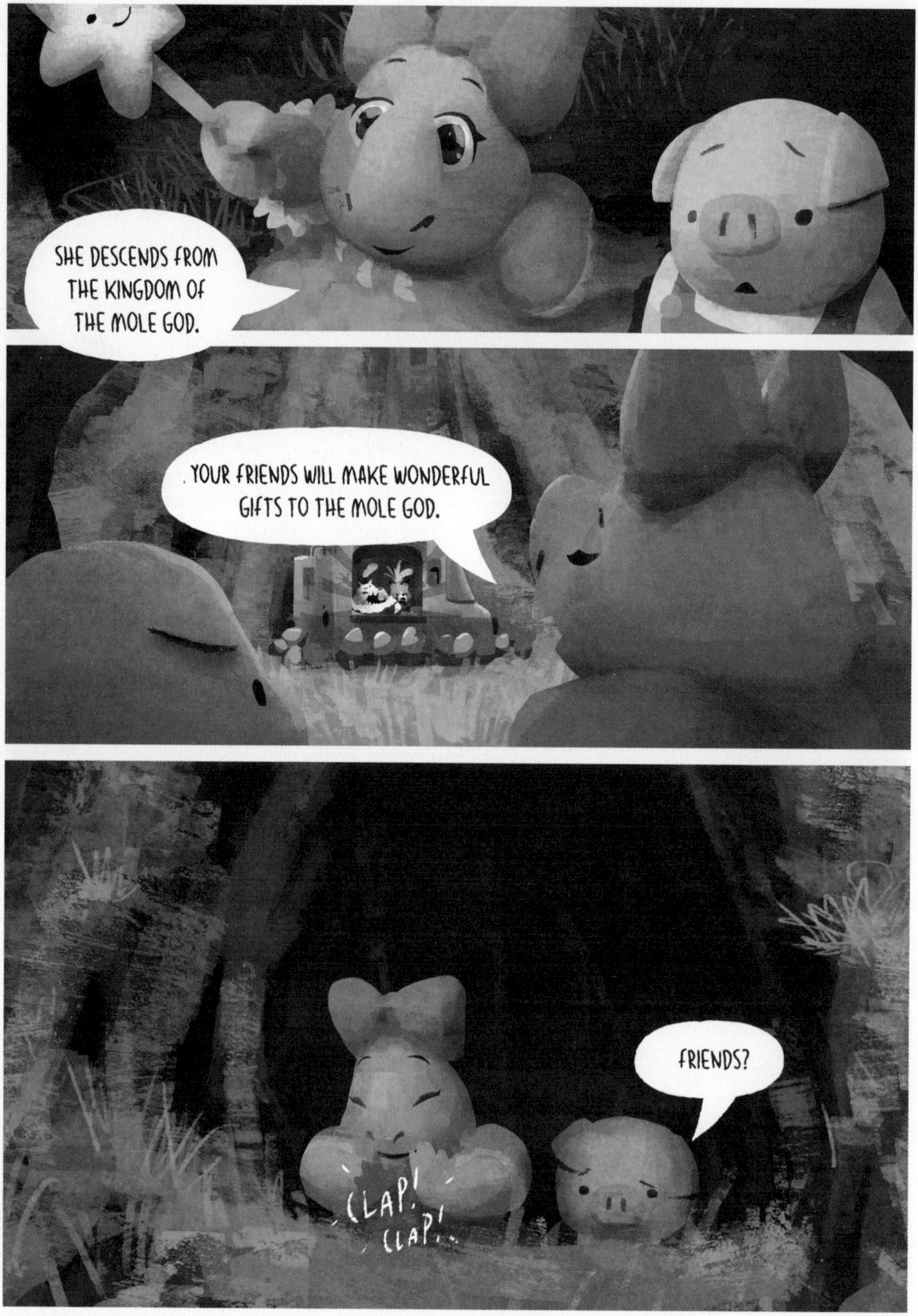
SHE DESCENDS FROM THE KINGDOM OF THE MOLE GOD.
. YOUR FRIENDS WILL MAKE WONDERFUL GIFTS TO THE MOLE GOD.
FRIENDS?
CLAP!
CLAP!

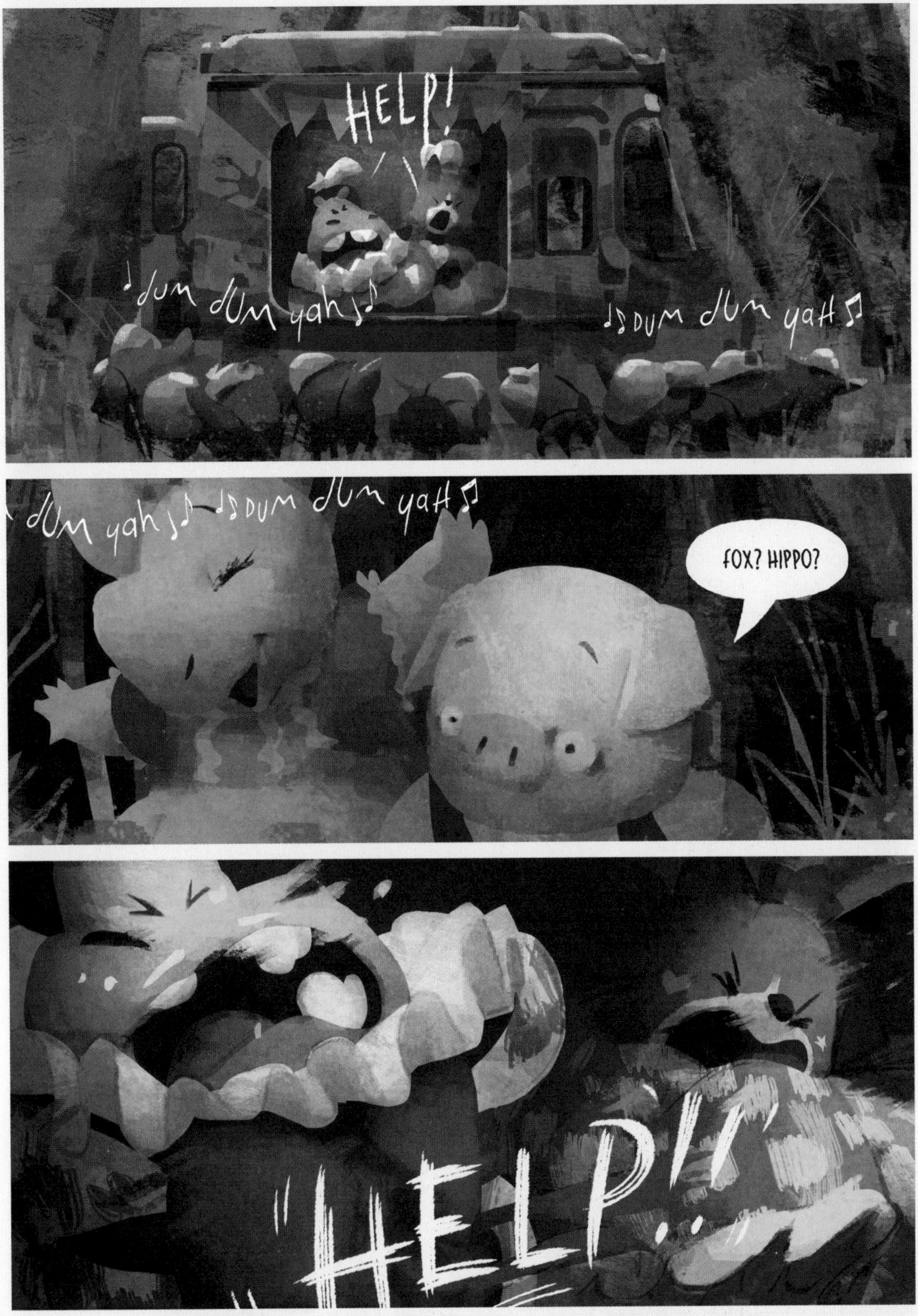
HELP!
dum dum yah
DUM dUm yaH
dUm yah
DUM dUm yaH
FOX? HIPPO?
HELP!!

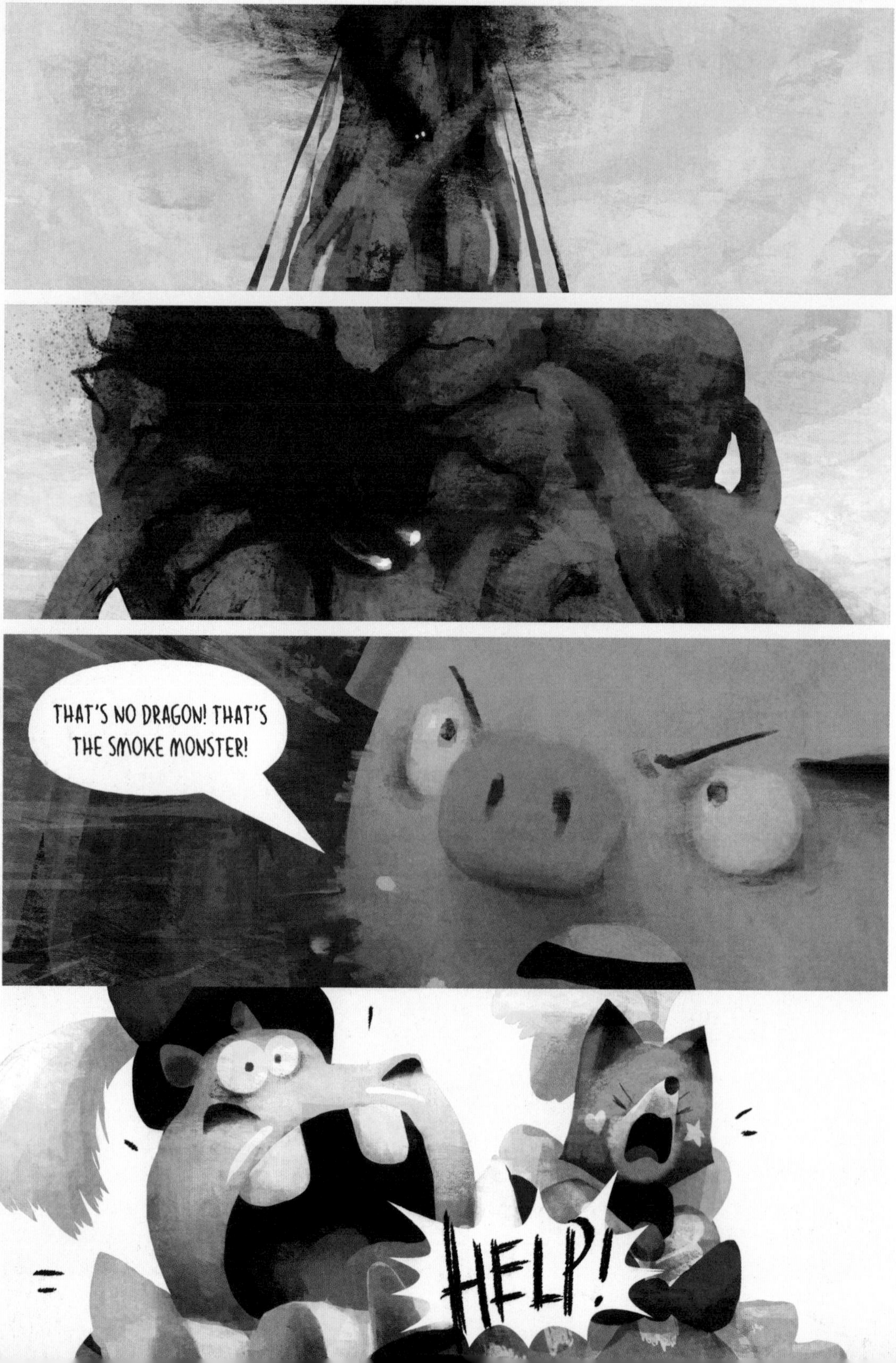
THAT'S NO DRAGON! THAT'S THE SMOKE MONSTER!
HELP!

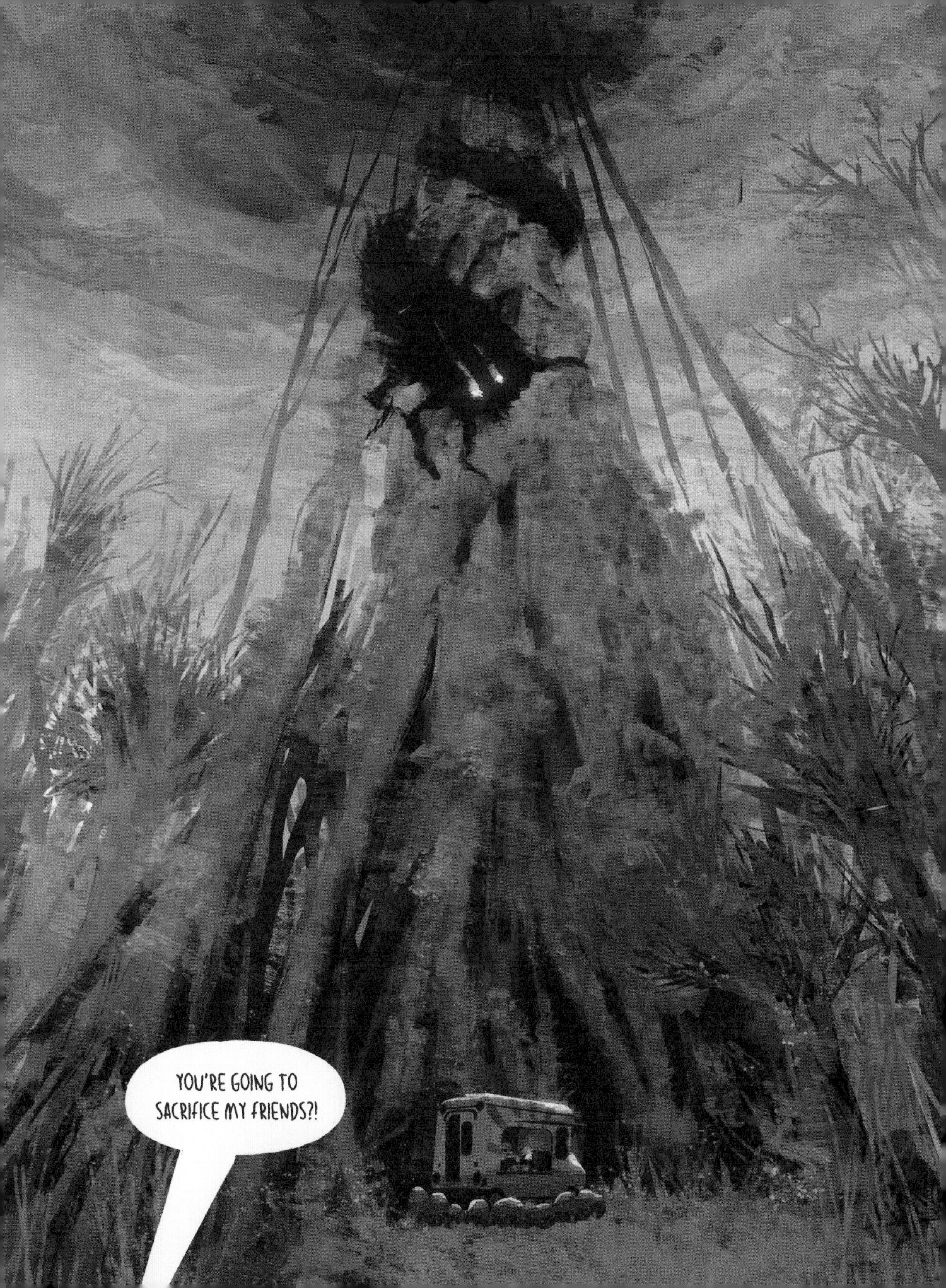
YOU'RE GOING TO SACRIFICE MY FRIENDS?!

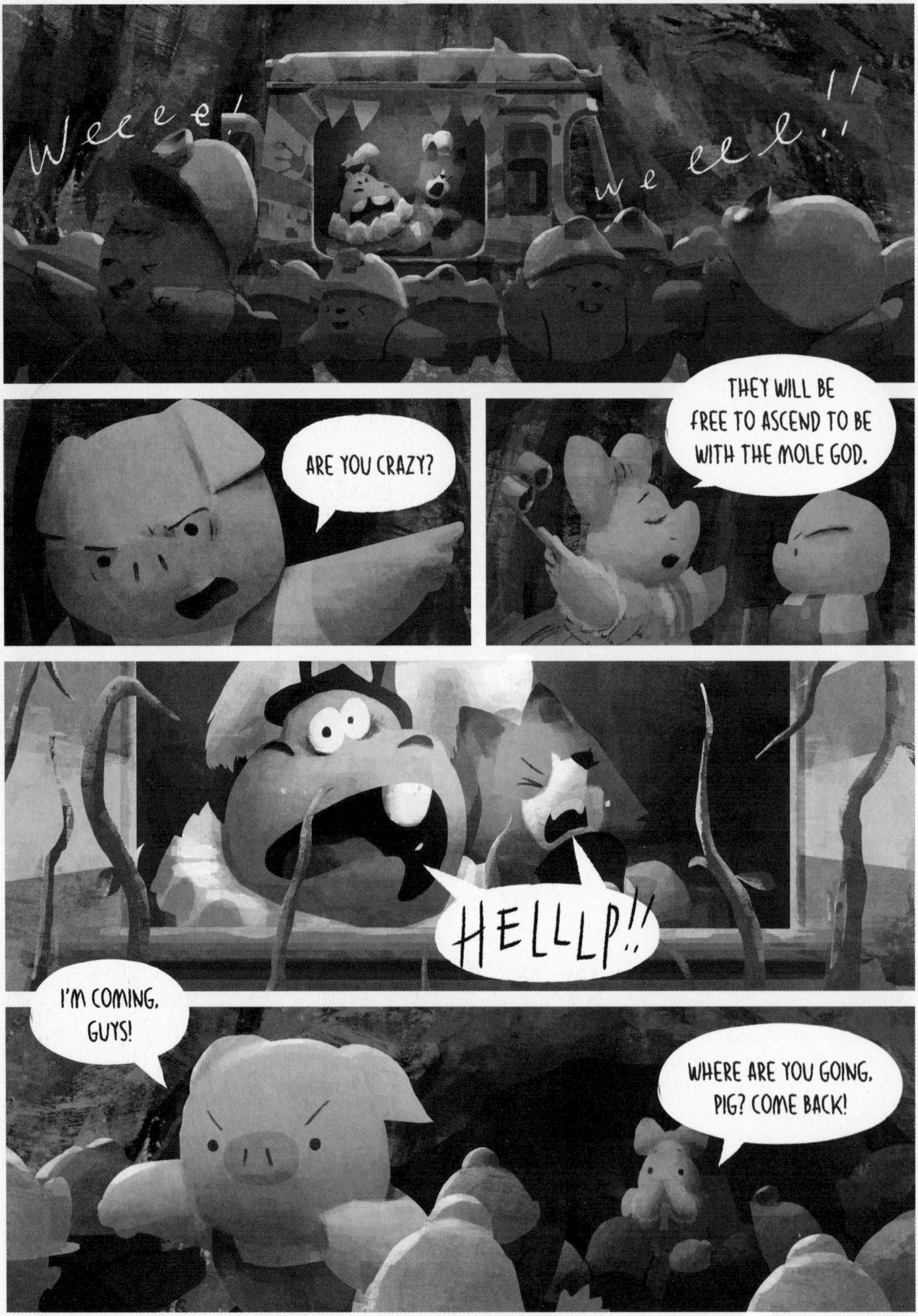
Weeee!
weeeel!!
ARE YOU CRAZY?
THEY WILL BE FREE TO ASCEND TO BE WITH THE MOLE GOD.
HELLLP!!
I'M COMING, GUYS!
WHERE ARE YOU GOING, PIG? COME BACK!

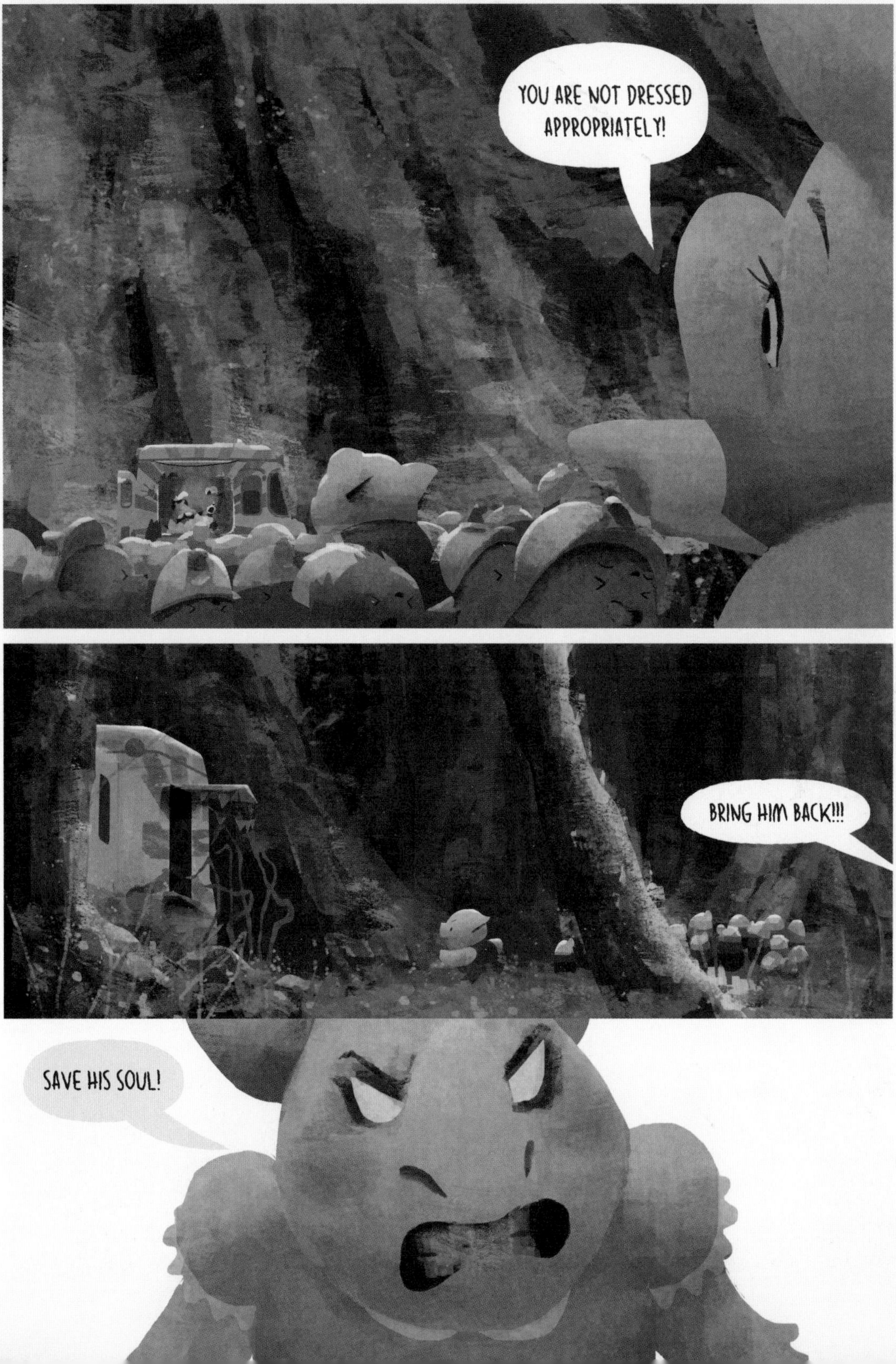
YOU ARE NOT DRESSED APPROPRIATELY!
BRING HIM BACK!!!
SAVE HIS SOUL!

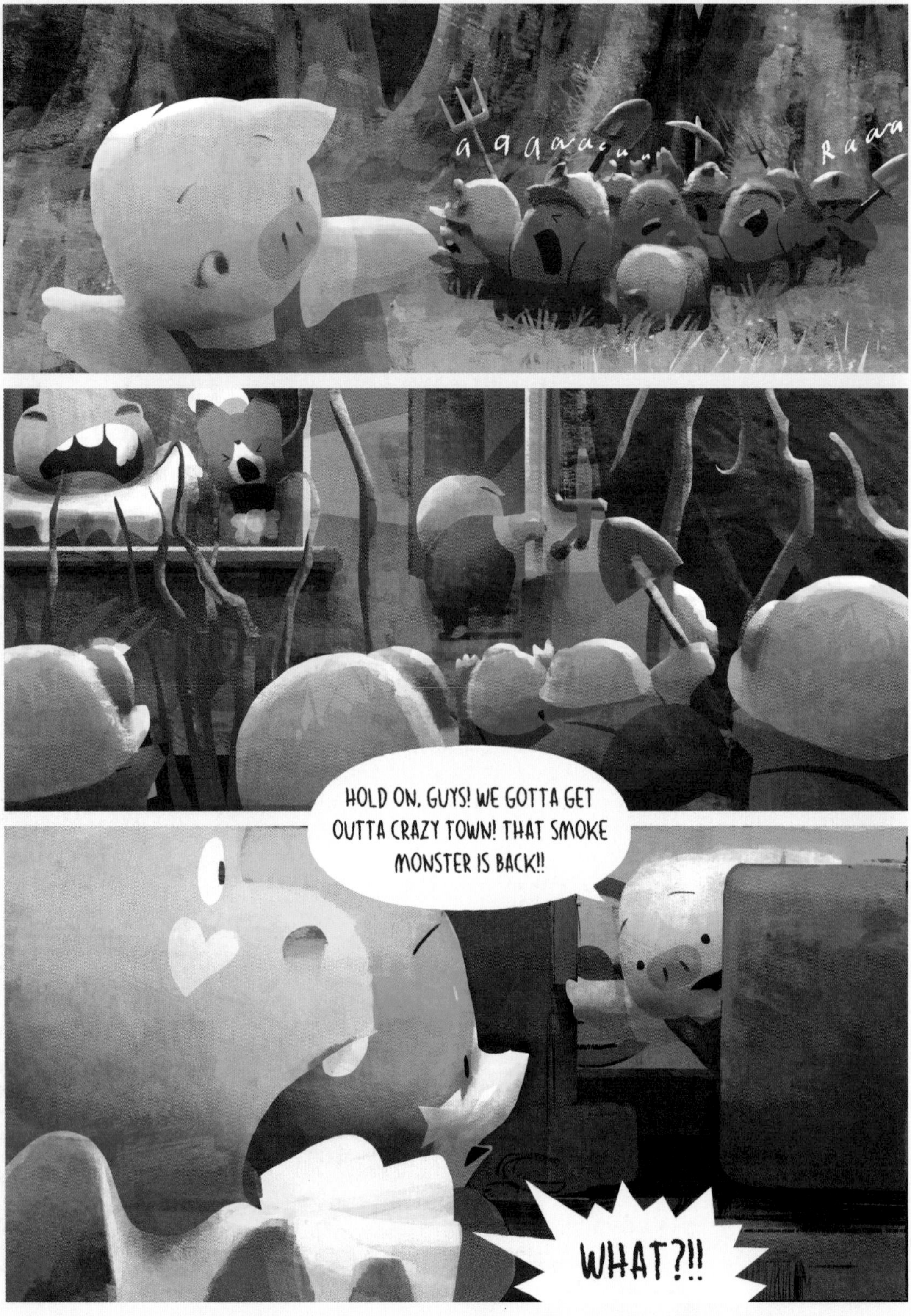
HOLD ON, GUYS! WE GOTTA GET OUTTA CRAZY TOWN! THAT SMOKE MONSTER IS BACK!!
WHAT?!!

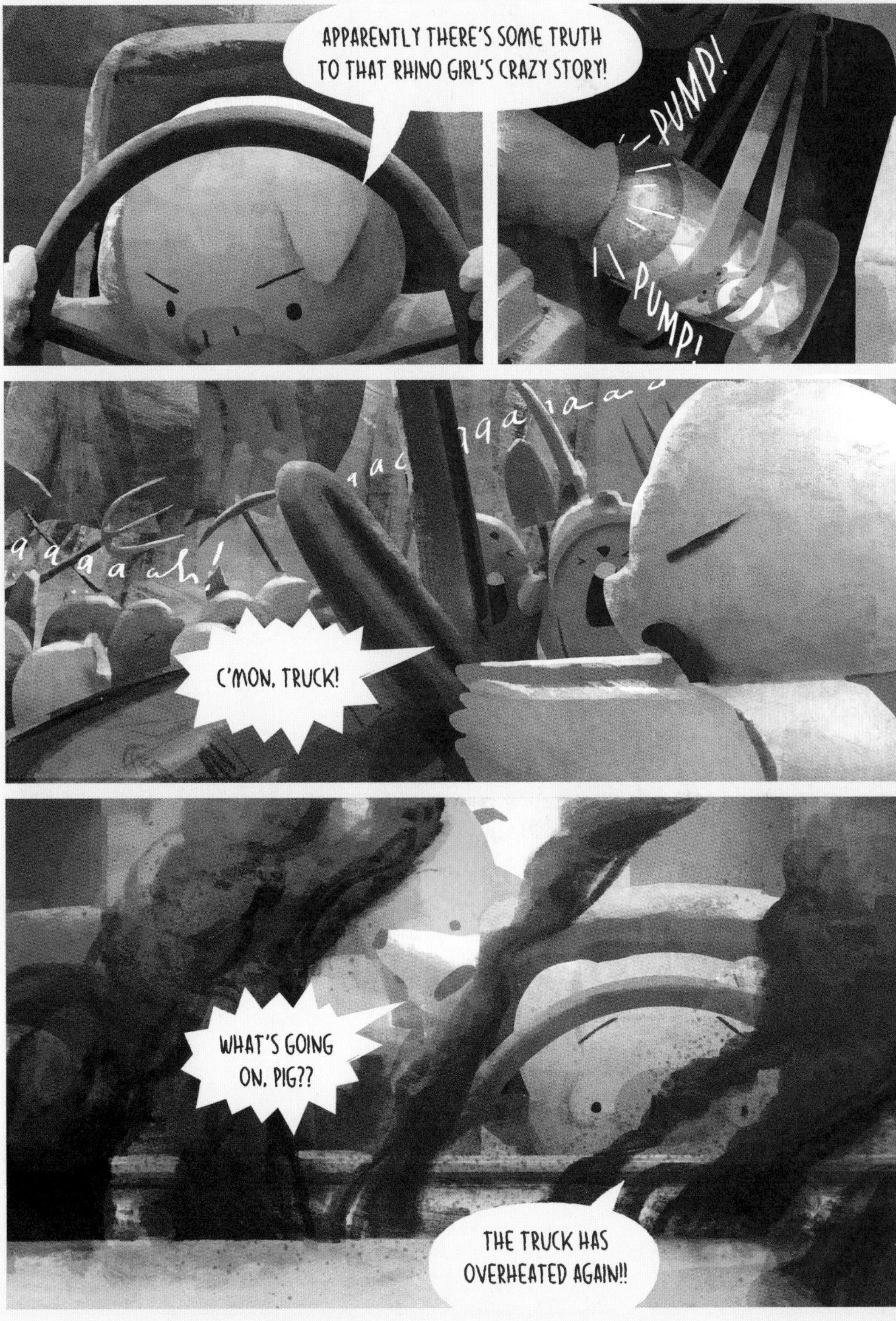
APPARENTLY THERE'S SOME TRUTH TO THAT RHINO GIRL'S CRAZY STORY!
PUMP!
PUMP!
aaaaaah!
aaaaaaa
C'MON, TRUCK!
WHAT'S GOING ON, PIG??
THE TRUCK HAS OVERHEATED AGAIN!!

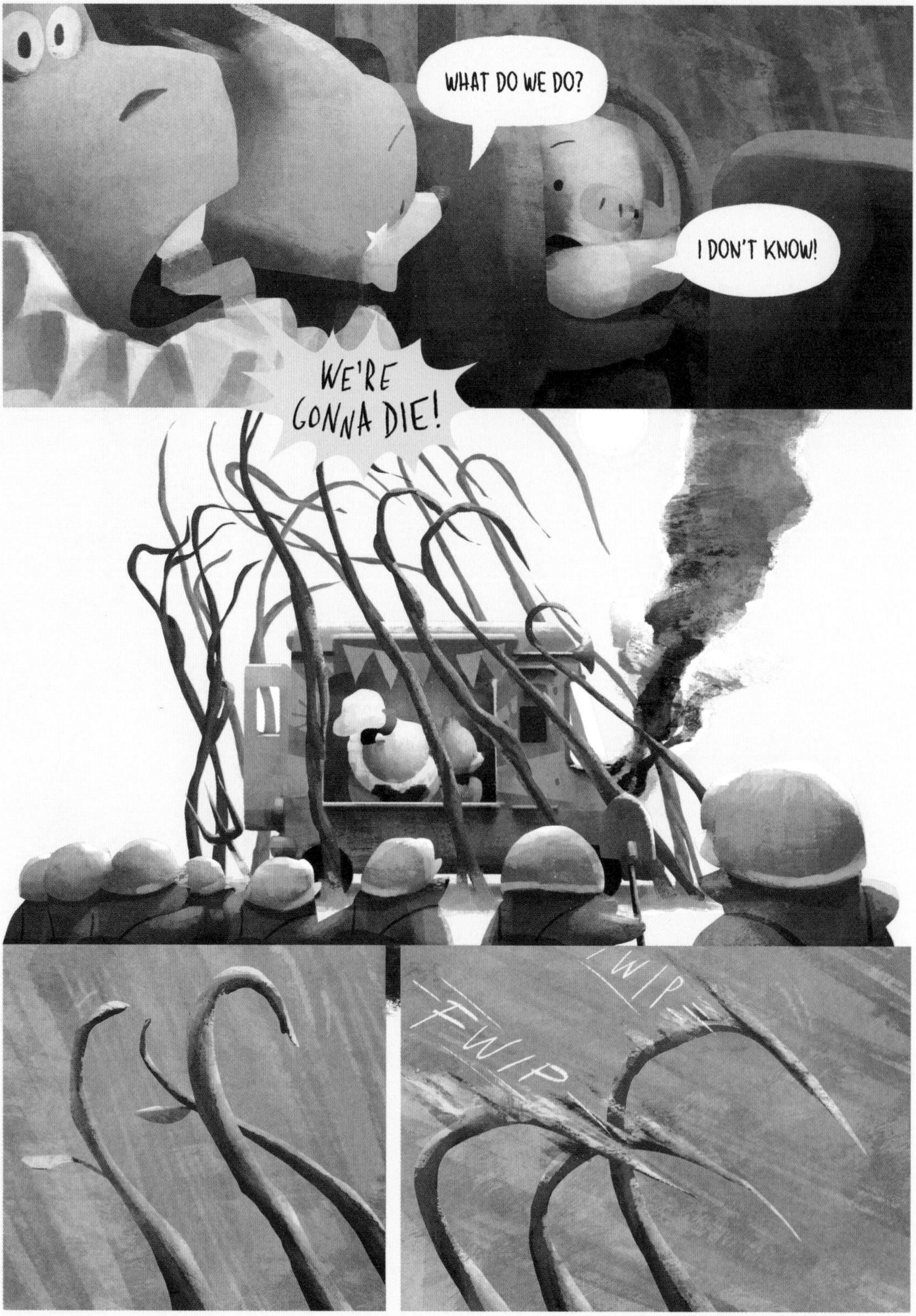
WHAT DO WE DO?
I DON'T KNOW!
WE'RE GONNA DIE!
FWIP
FWIP

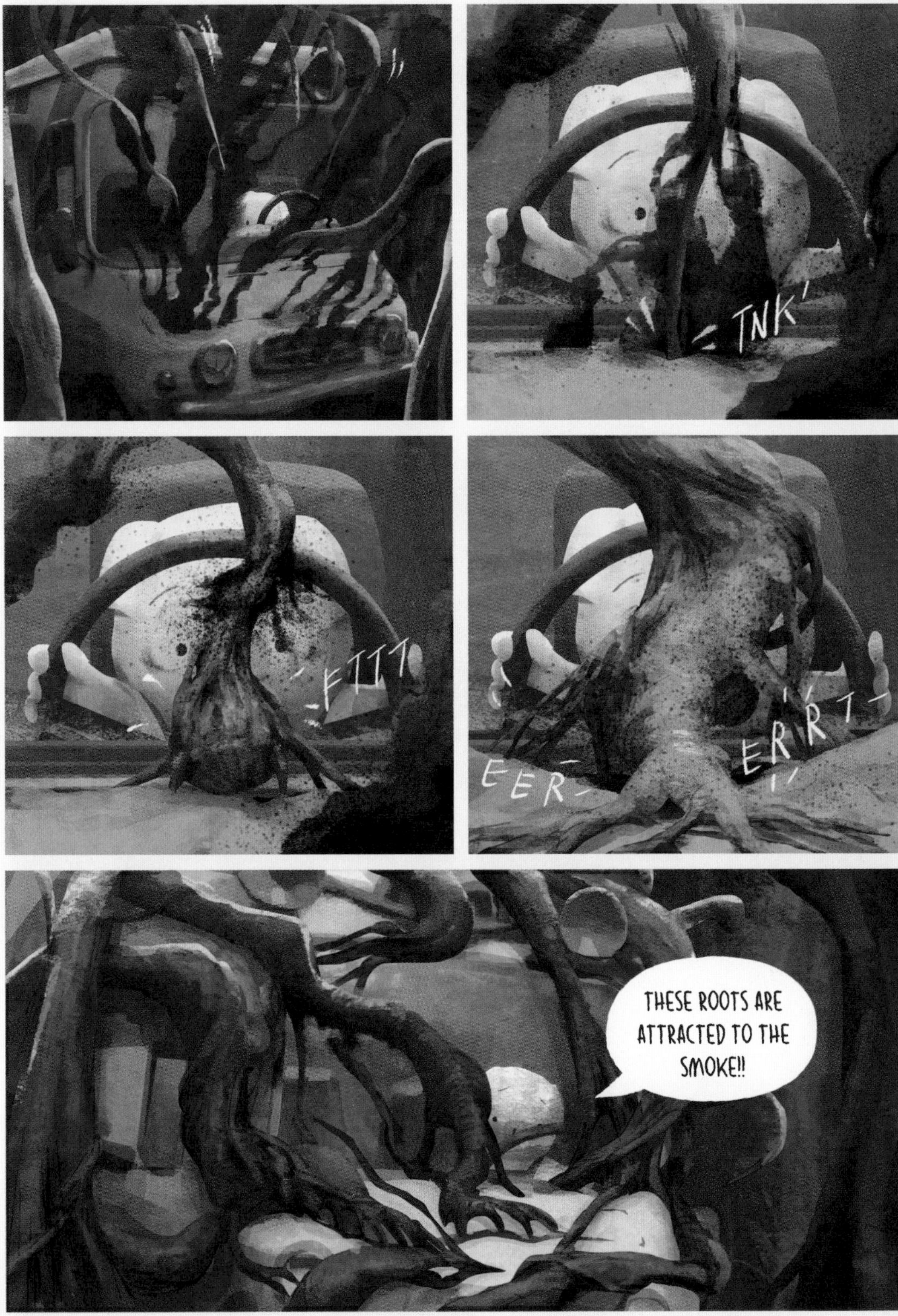
TNK
FTTT
EER-
ERRT-
THESE ROOTS ARE ATTRACTED TO THE SMOKE!!

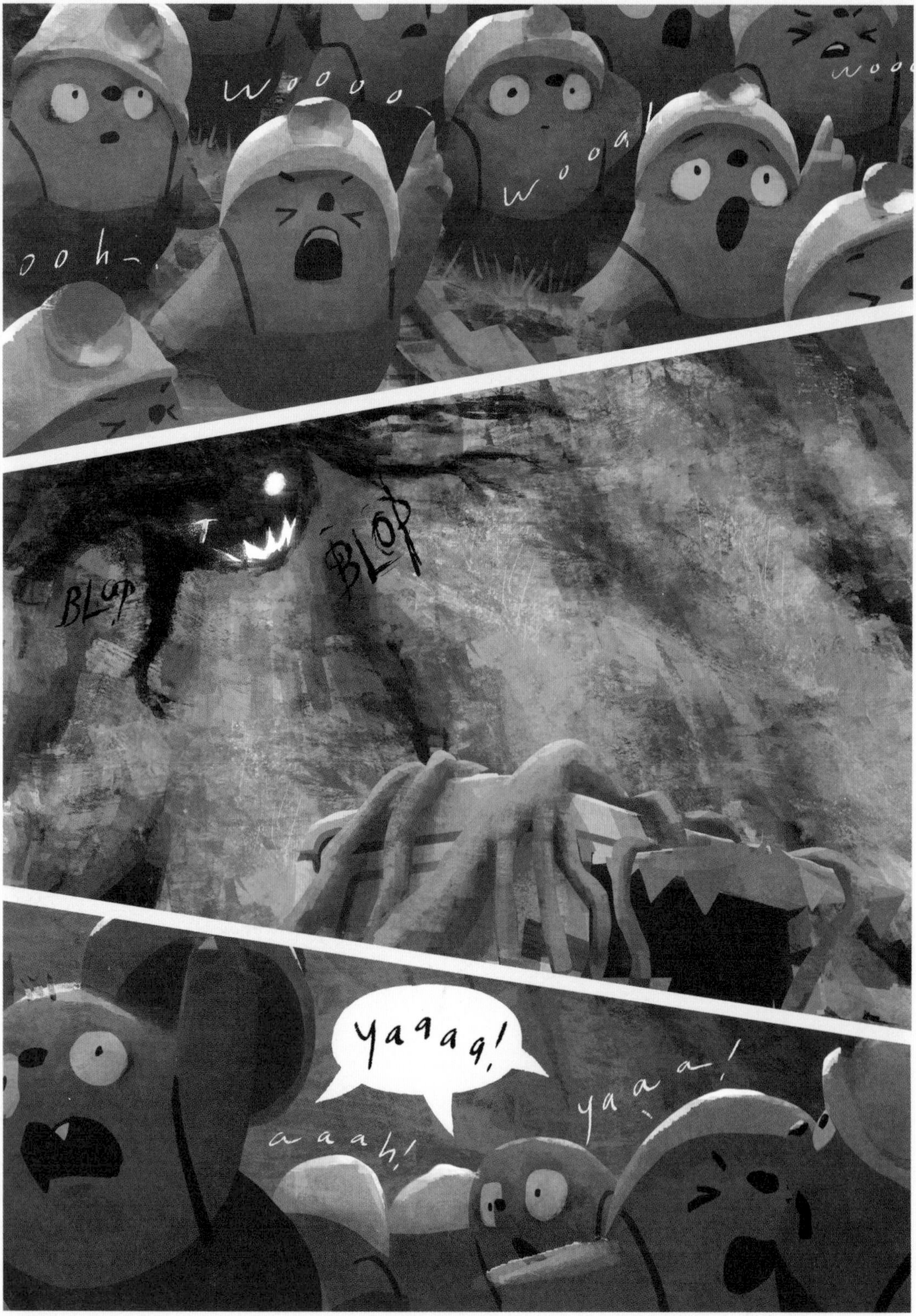
woooo
wooo
ooh
wooah
BLOP
BLOP
Yaaaa!
aaah!
yaaa!

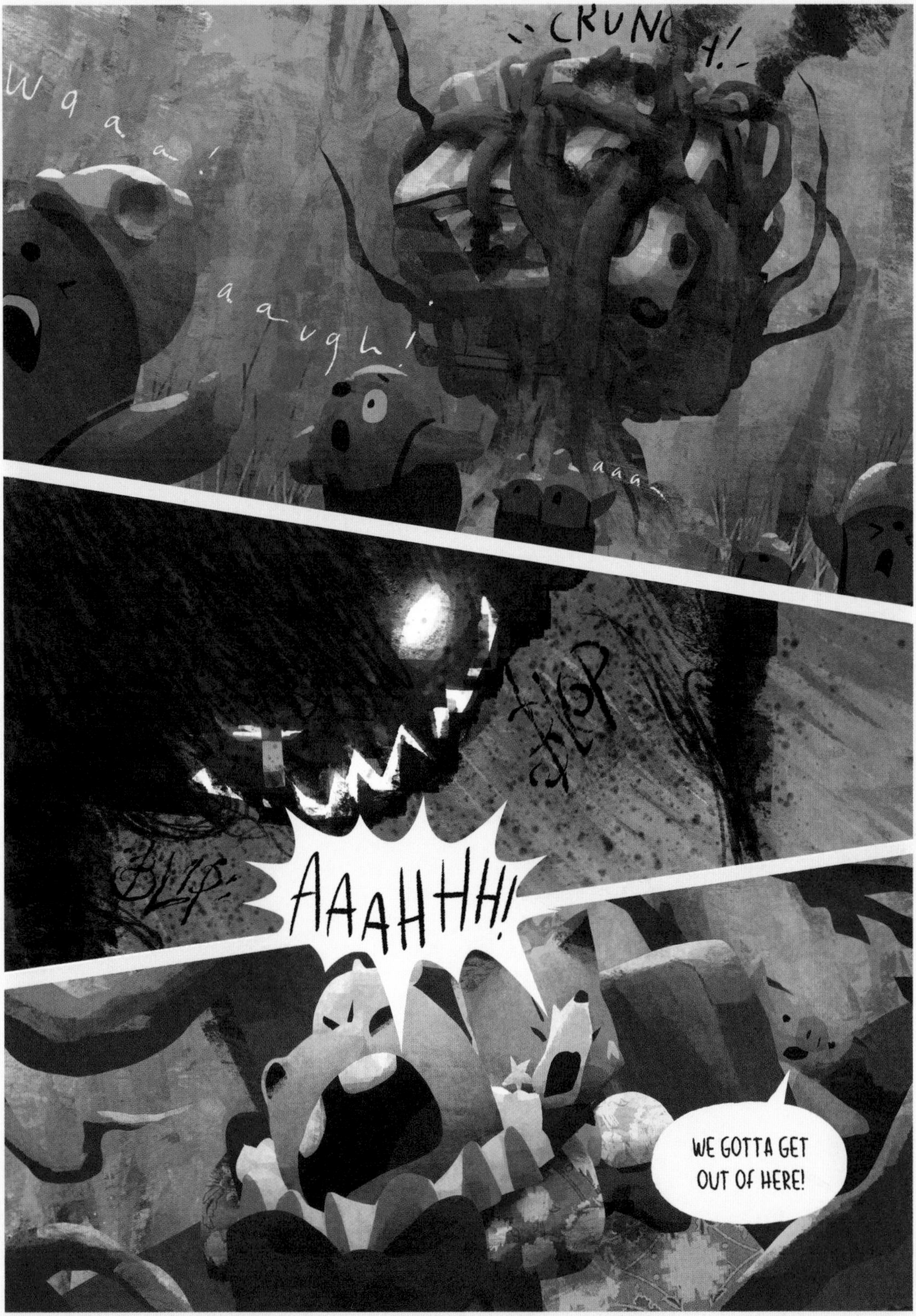
Waaaa!
CRUNCH!
aaaugh!
aaa
BLOP
BLIP
AAAHHH!
WE GOTTA GET OUT OF HERE!

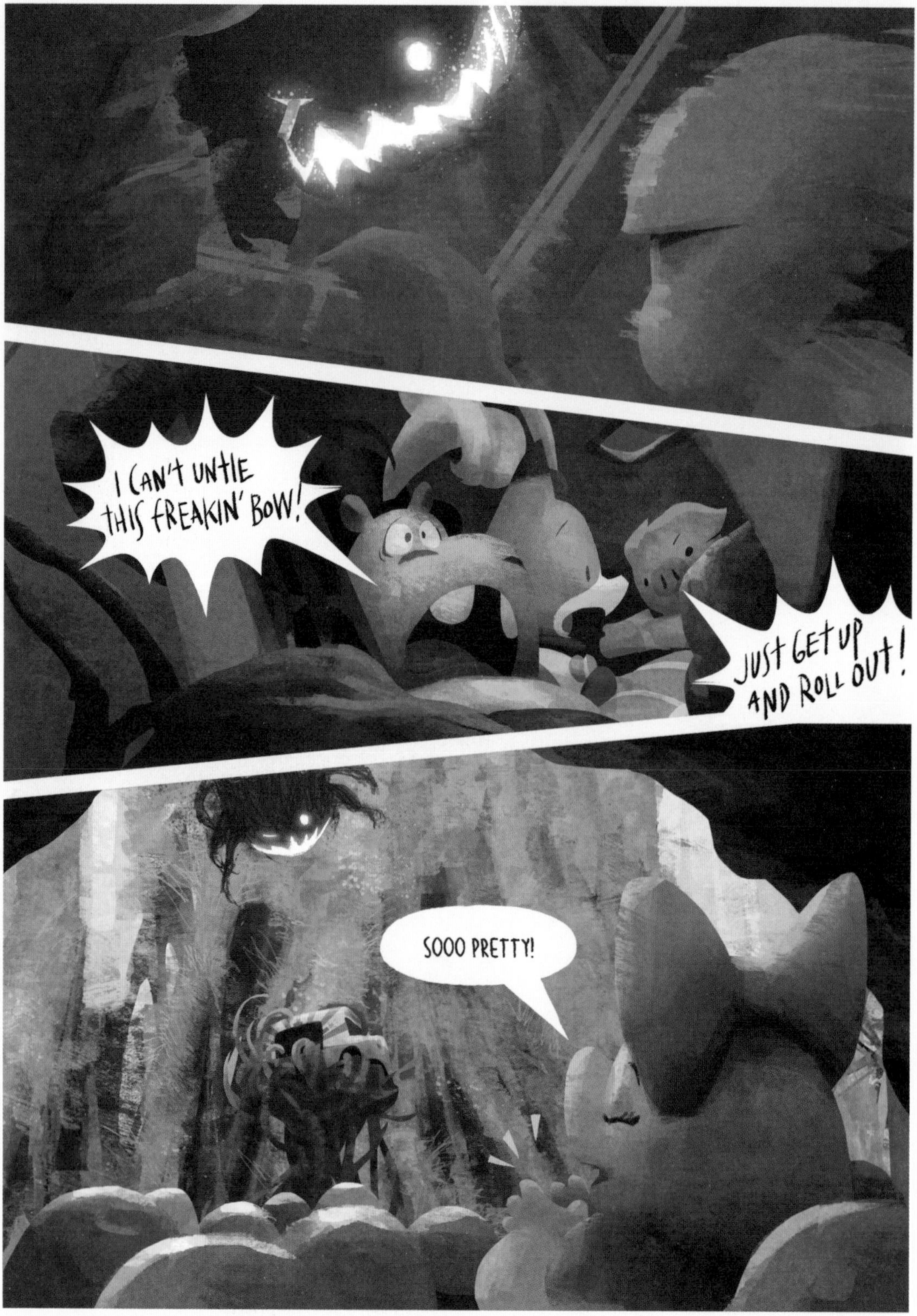
I CAN'T UNTIE THIS FREAKIN' BOW!
JUST GET UP AND ROLL OUT!
SOOO PRETTY!

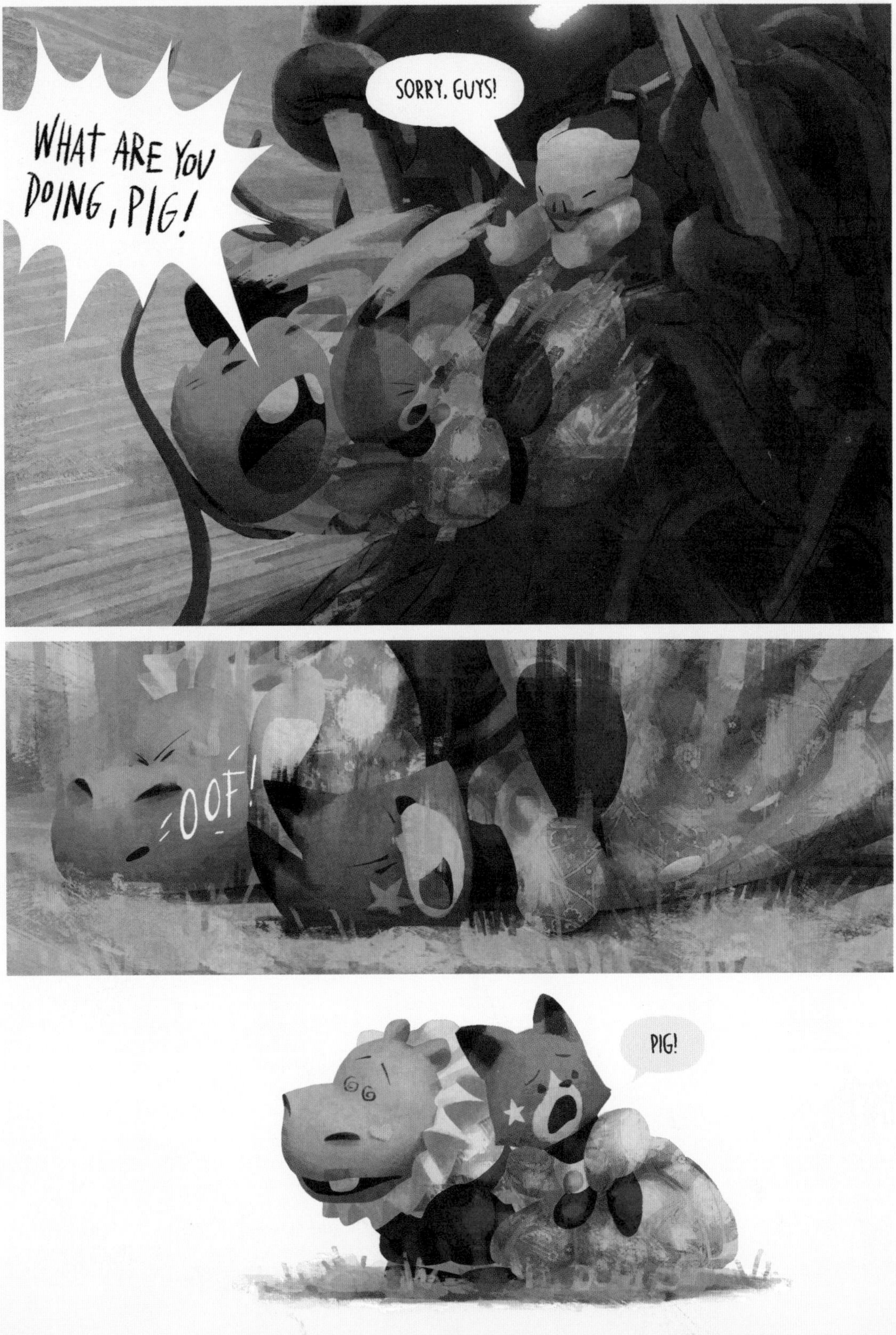
WHAT ARE YOU DOING, PIG!
SORRY, GUYS!
OOF!
PIG!

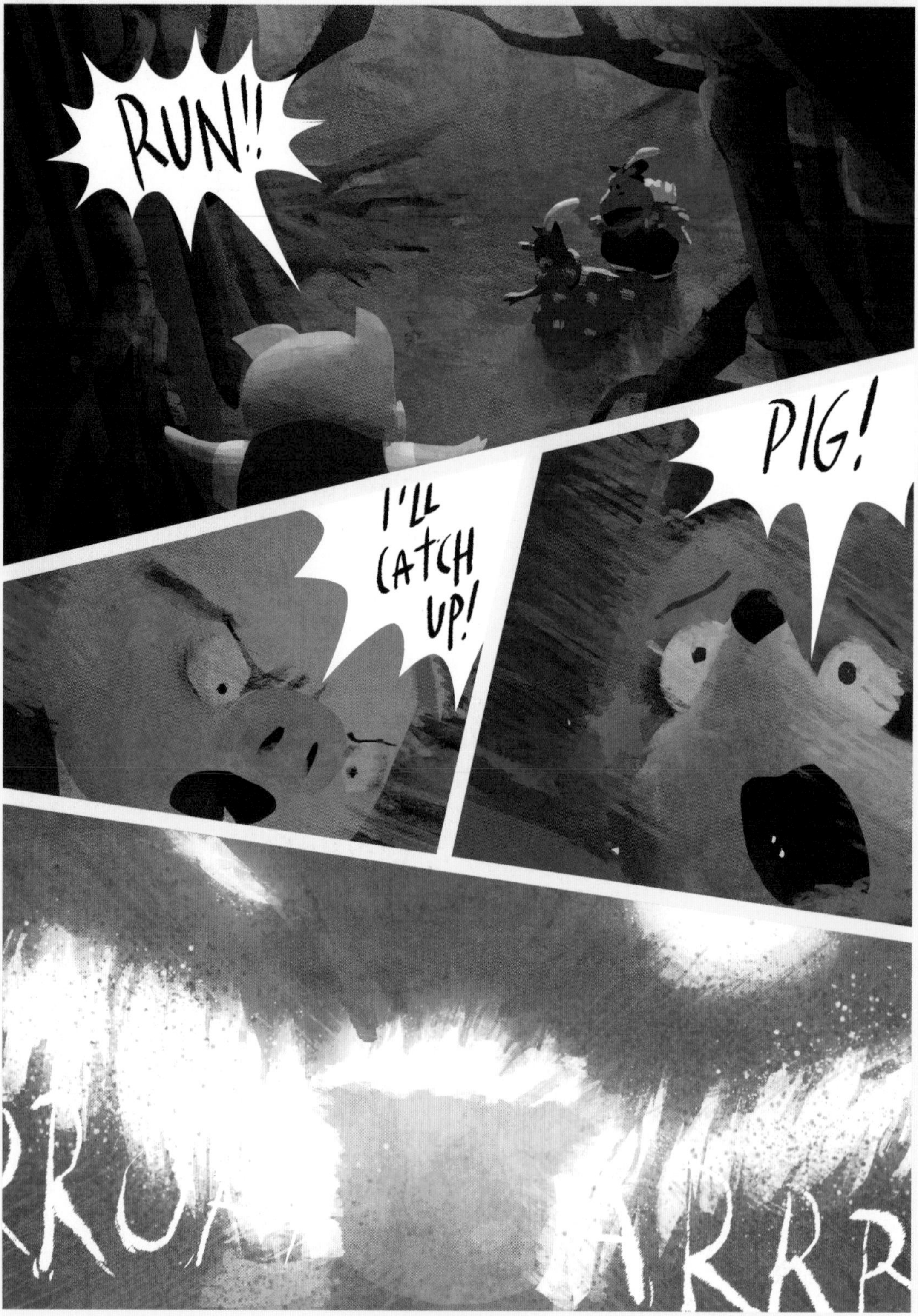
RUN!!
I'LL CATCH UP!
PIG!
RROAARRR

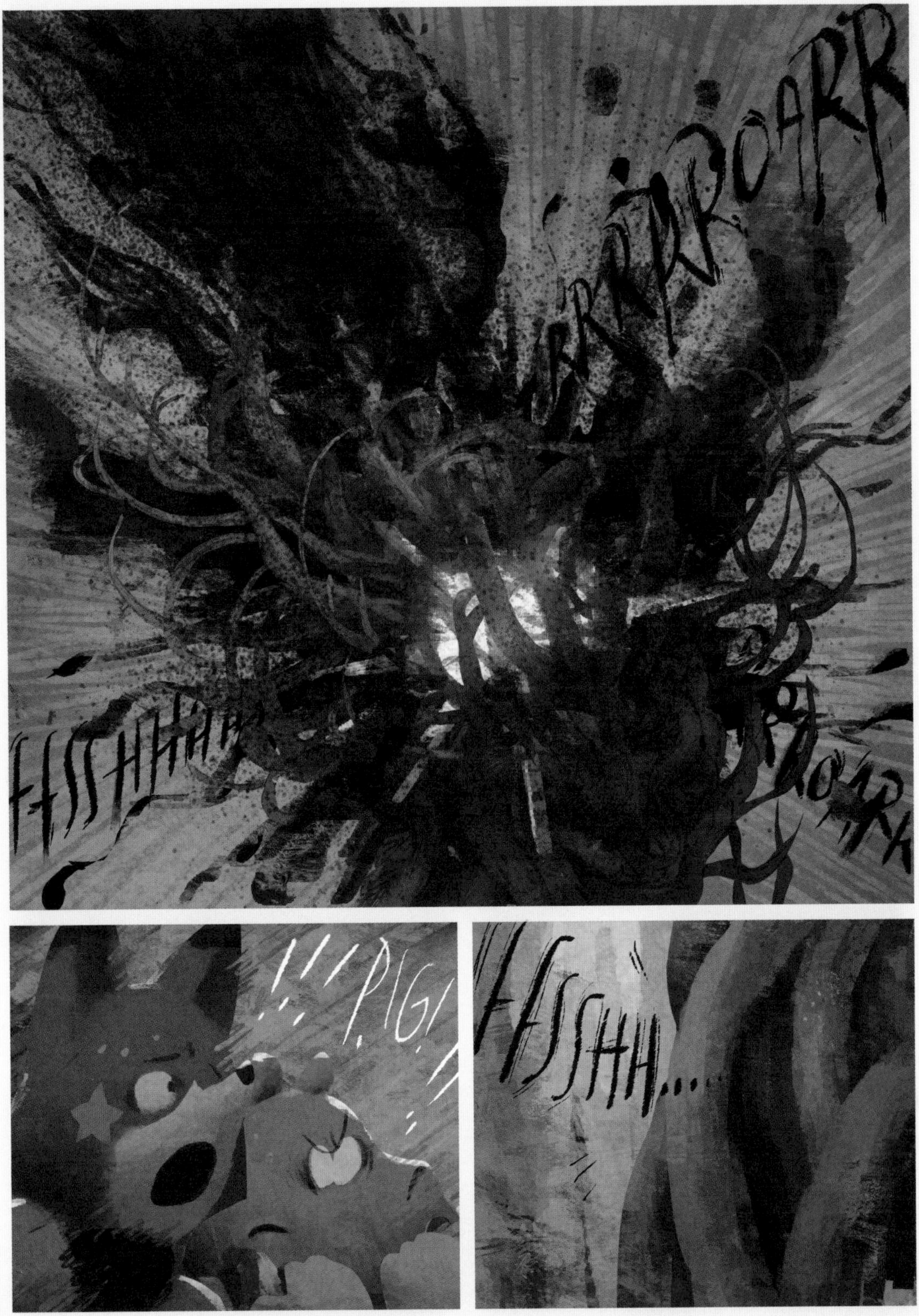
RRRROARR
FSSHHHH
PIG!!!
FSSHH....

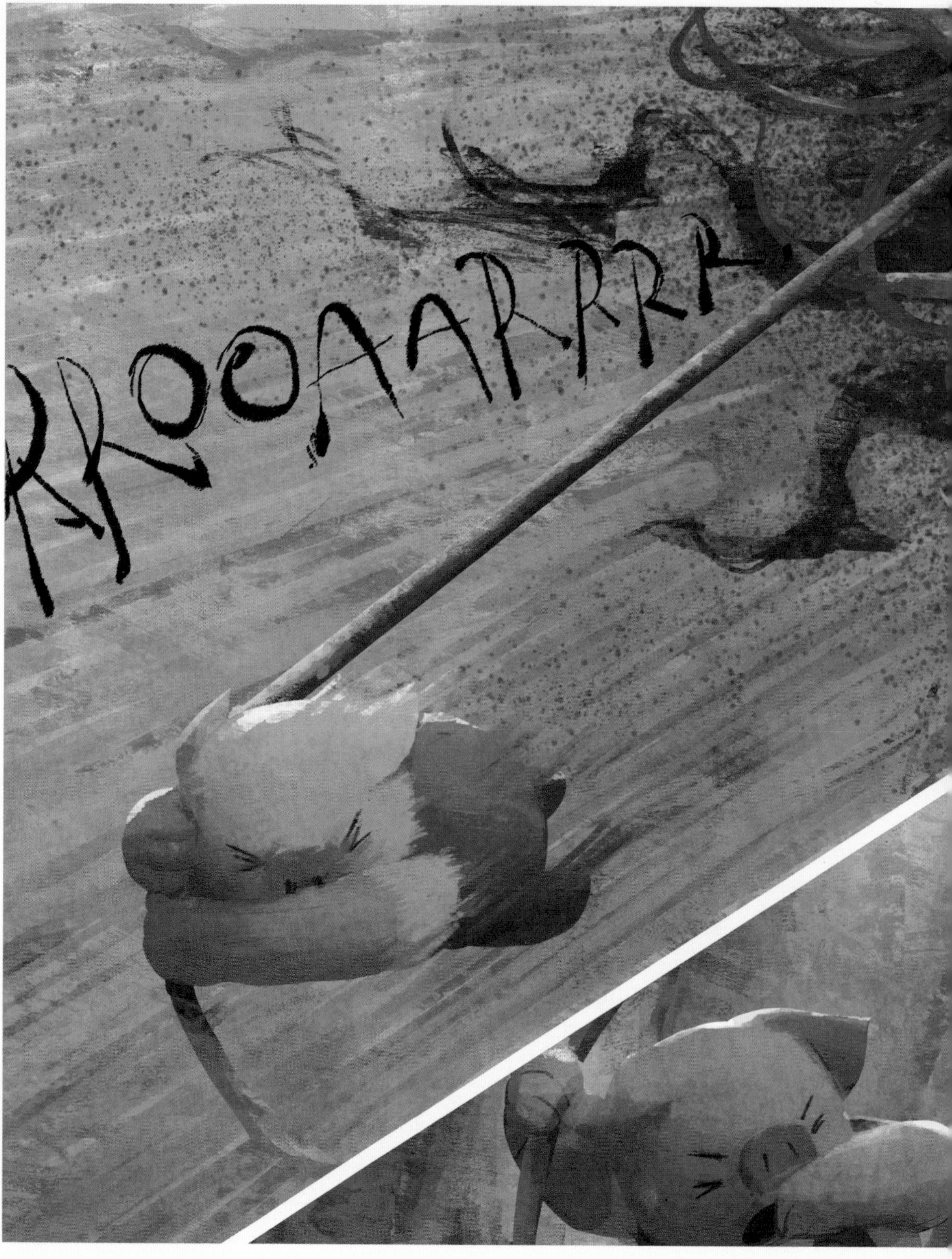
RROOAARRRR

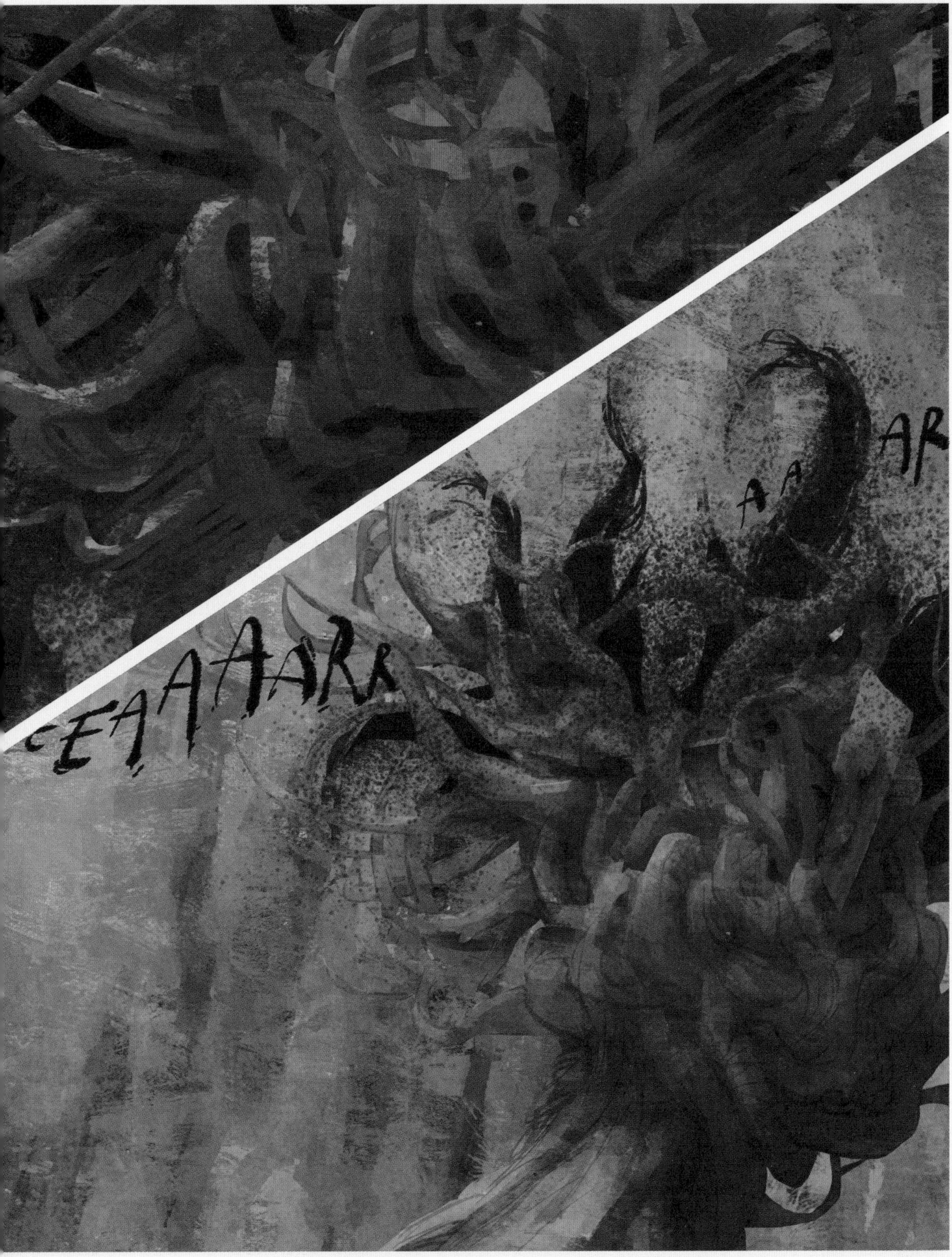
EAAAARR
AA
AR

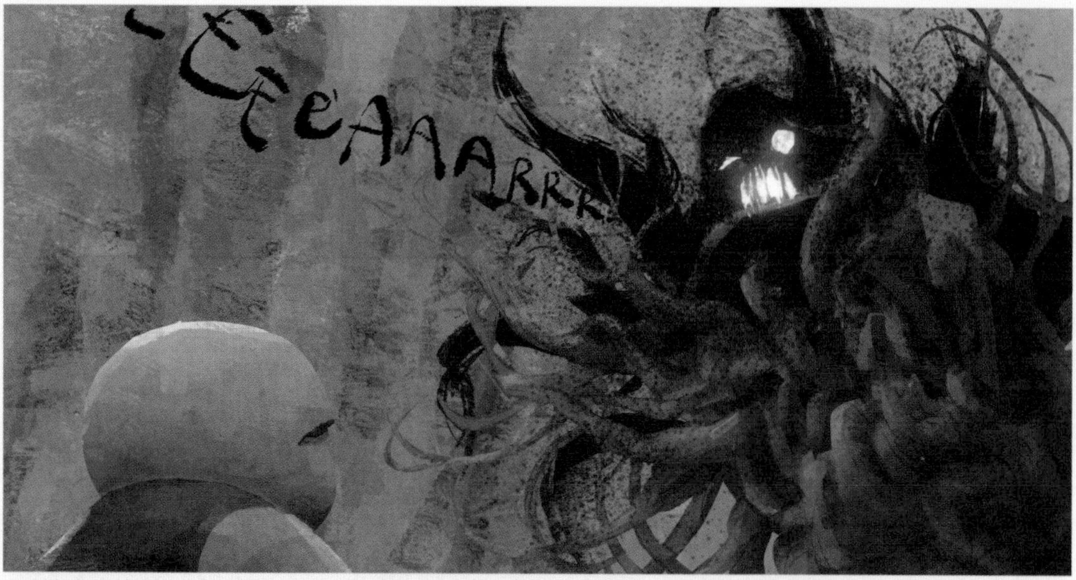
EEeAAARRR

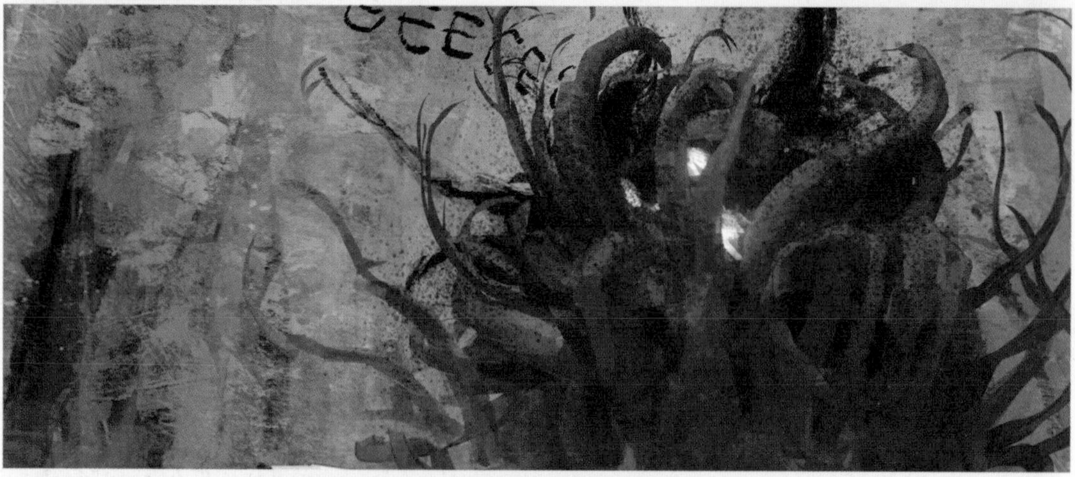
GEEE

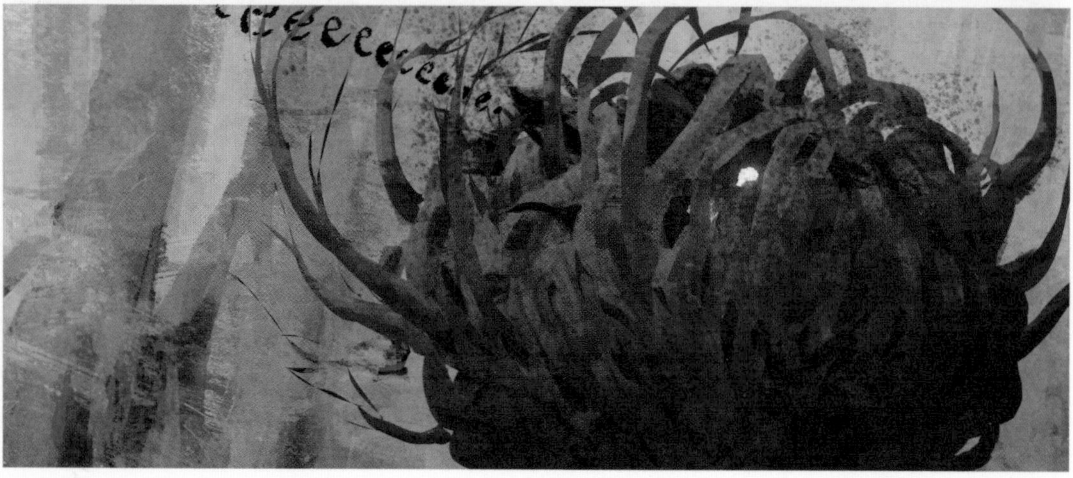
eeeeeeeee

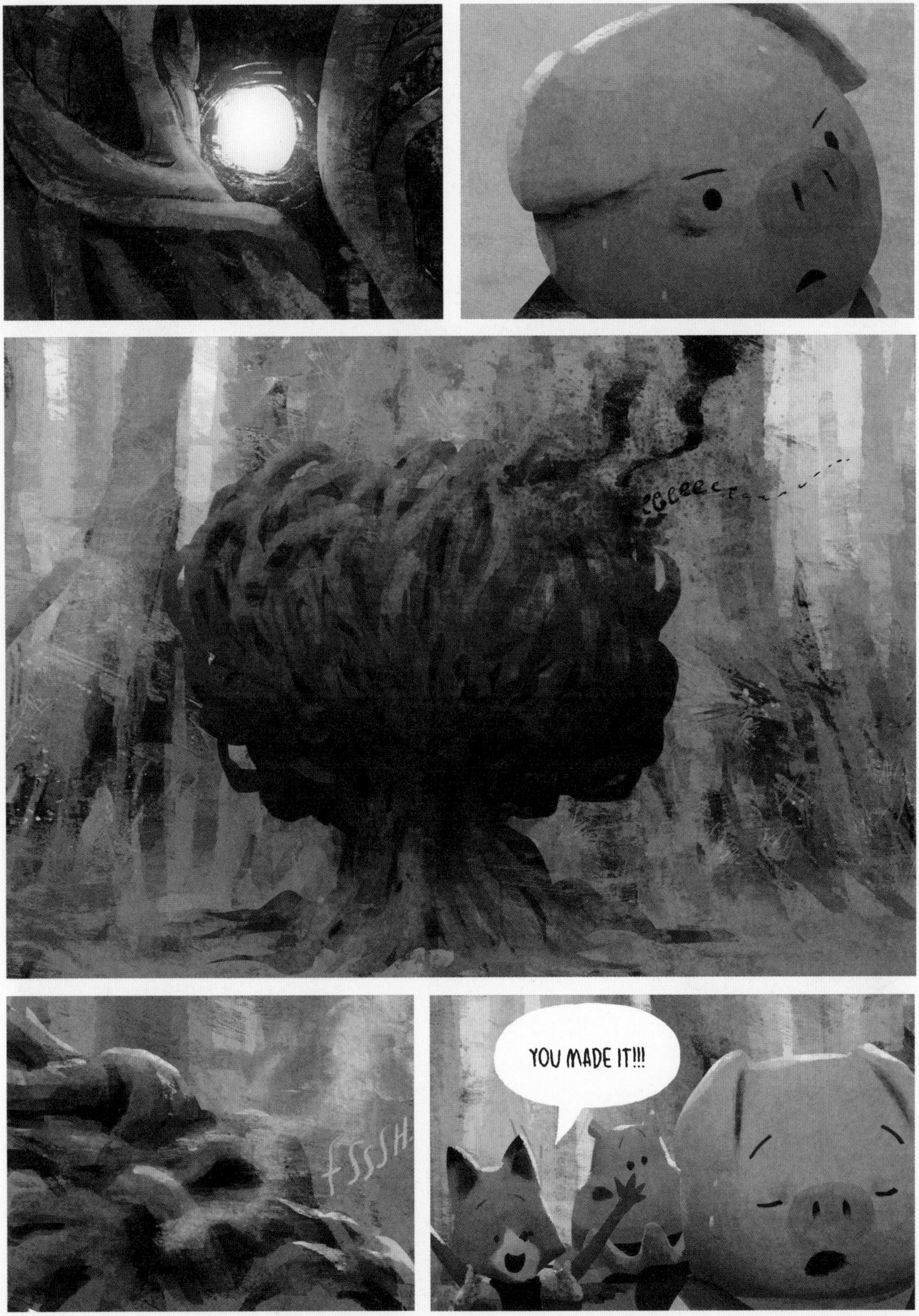
eeeeee
FSSSH
YOU MADE IT!!!

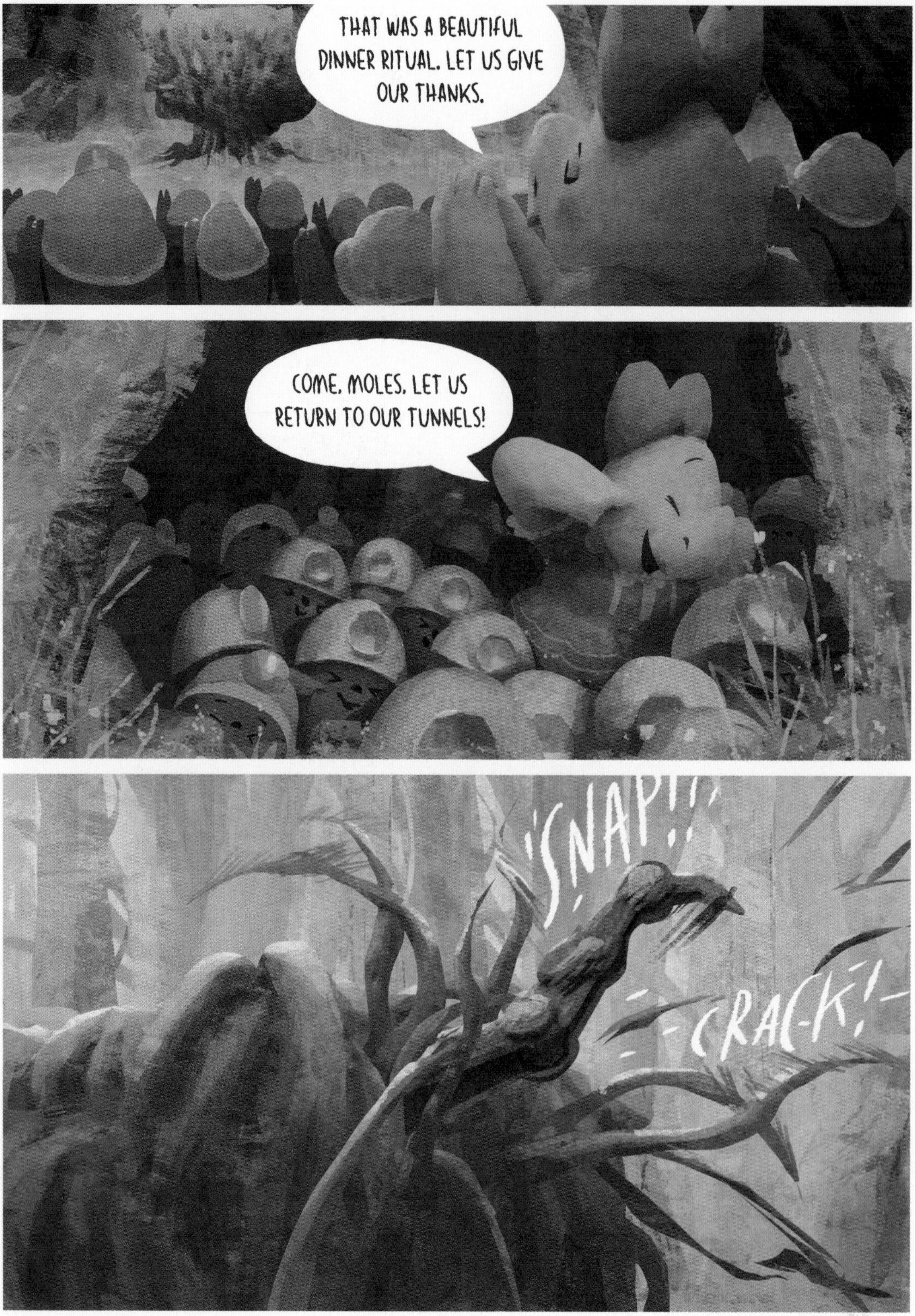
THAT WAS A BEAUTIFUL DINNER RITUAL. LET US GIVE OUR THANKS.
COME, MOLES, LET US RETURN TO OUR TUNNELS!
SNAP!
CRACK!

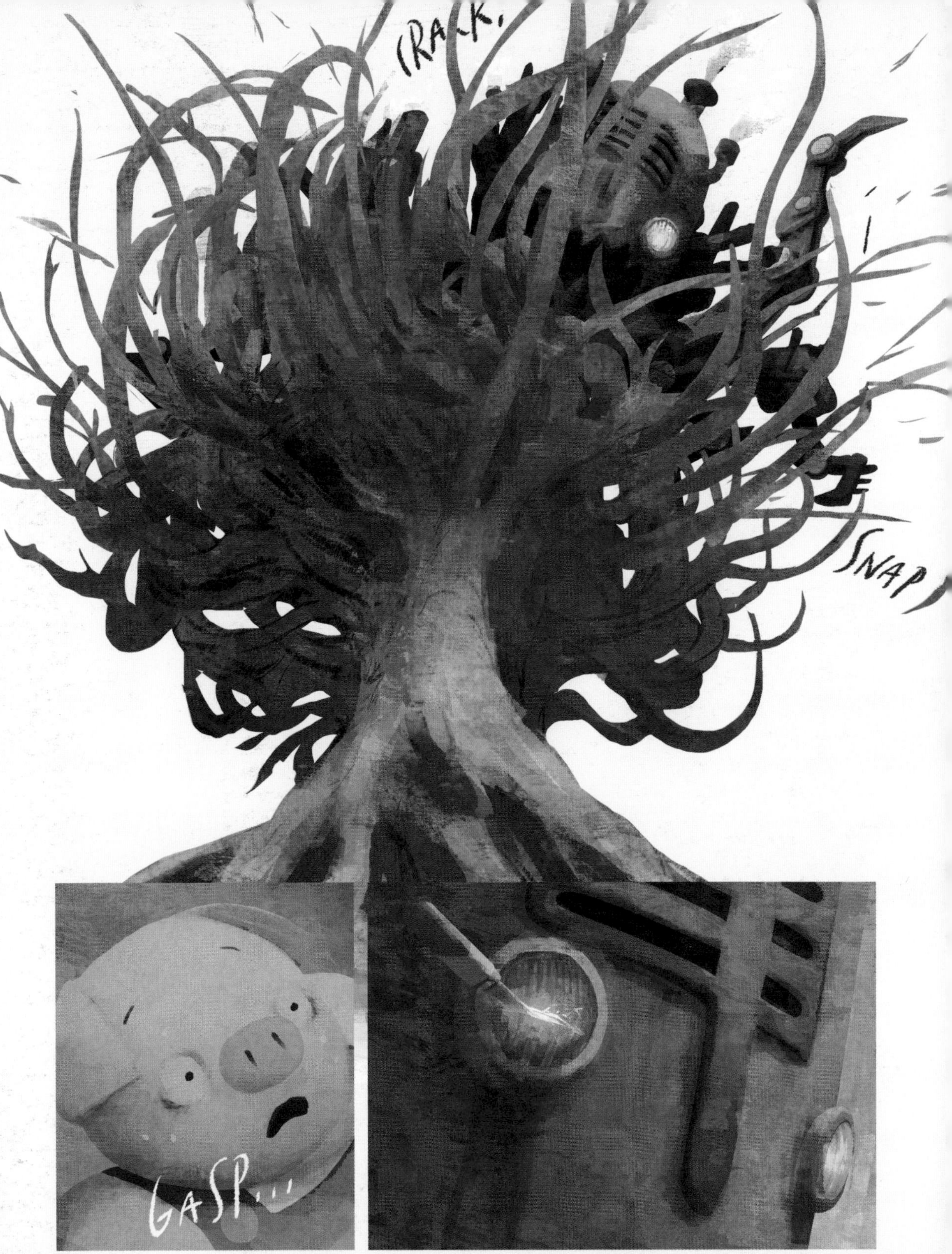
CRACK,
SNAP
GASP...

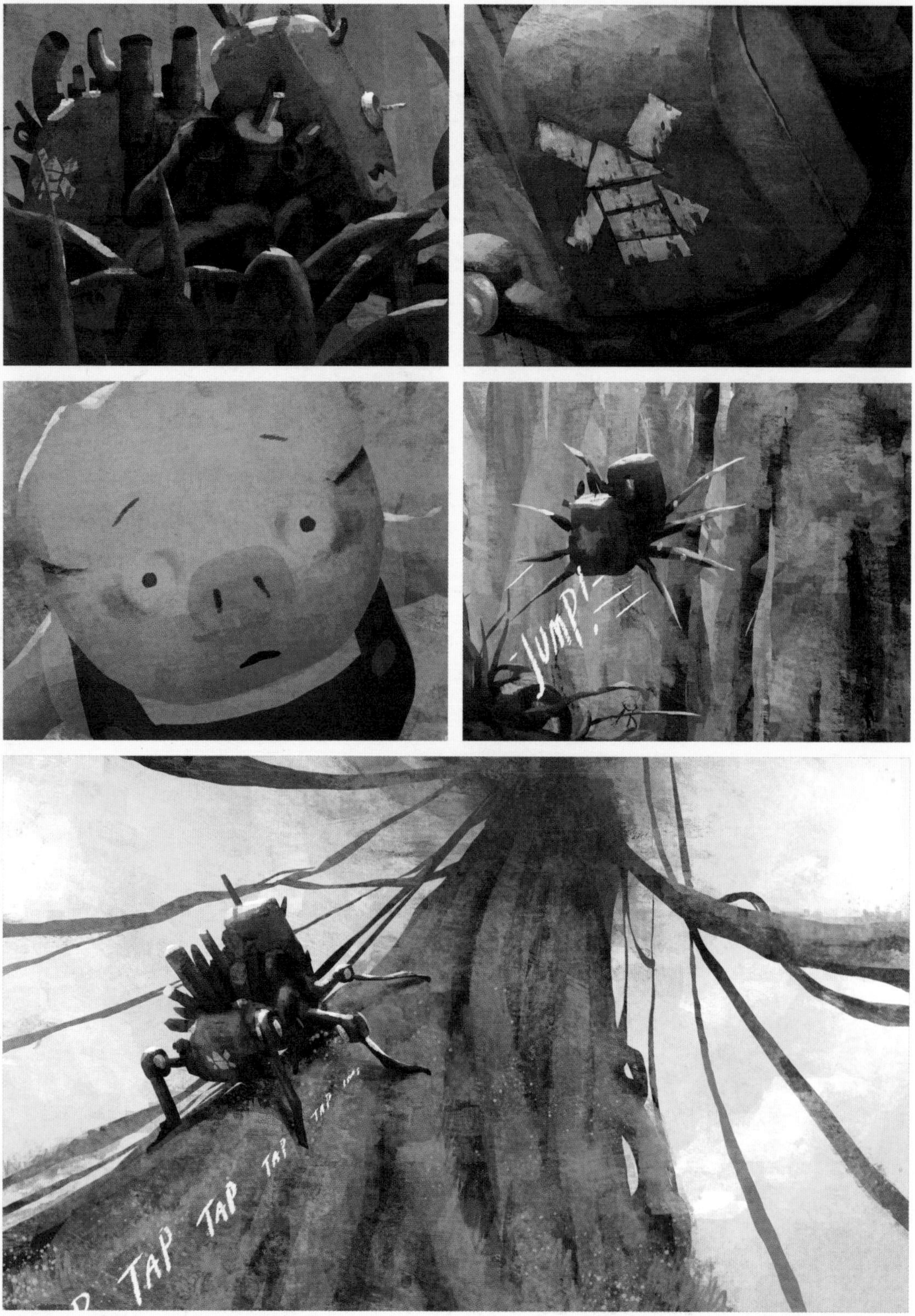
JUMP!
TAP TAP TAP TAP TAP

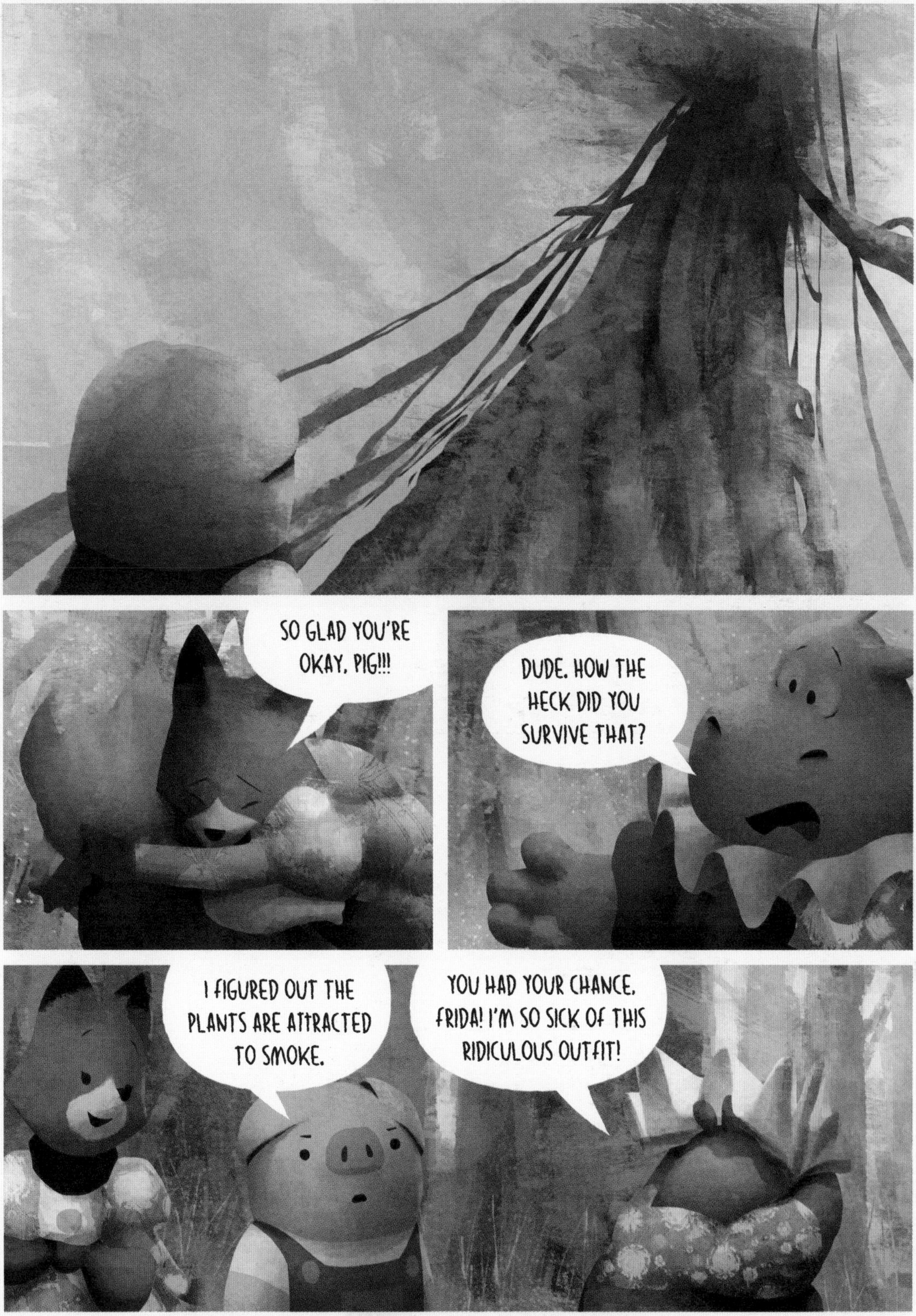
SO GLAD YOU'RE OKAY, PIG!!!
DUDE. HOW THE HECK DID YOU SURVIVE THAT?
I FIGURED OUT THE PLANTS ARE ATTRACTED TO SMOKE.
YOU HAD YOUR CHANCE, FRIDA! I'M SO SICK OF THIS RIDICULOUS OUTFIT!

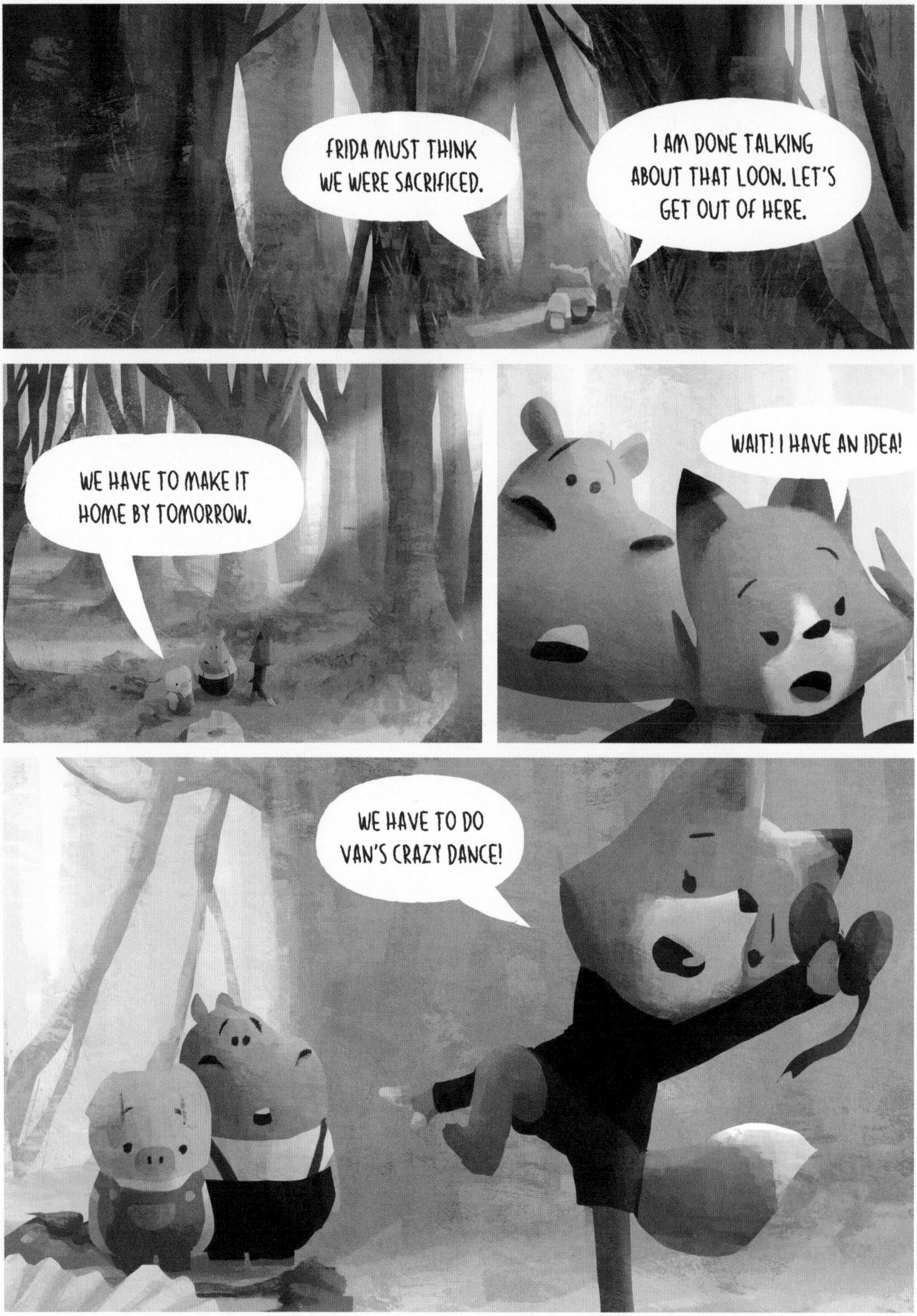
FRIDA MUST THINK WE WERE SACRIFICED.
I AM DONE TALKING ABOUT THAT LOON. LET'S GET OUT OF HERE.
WE HAVE TO MAKE IT HOME BY TOMORROW.
WAIT! I HAVE AN IDEA!
WE HAVE TO DO VAN'S CRAZY DANCE!

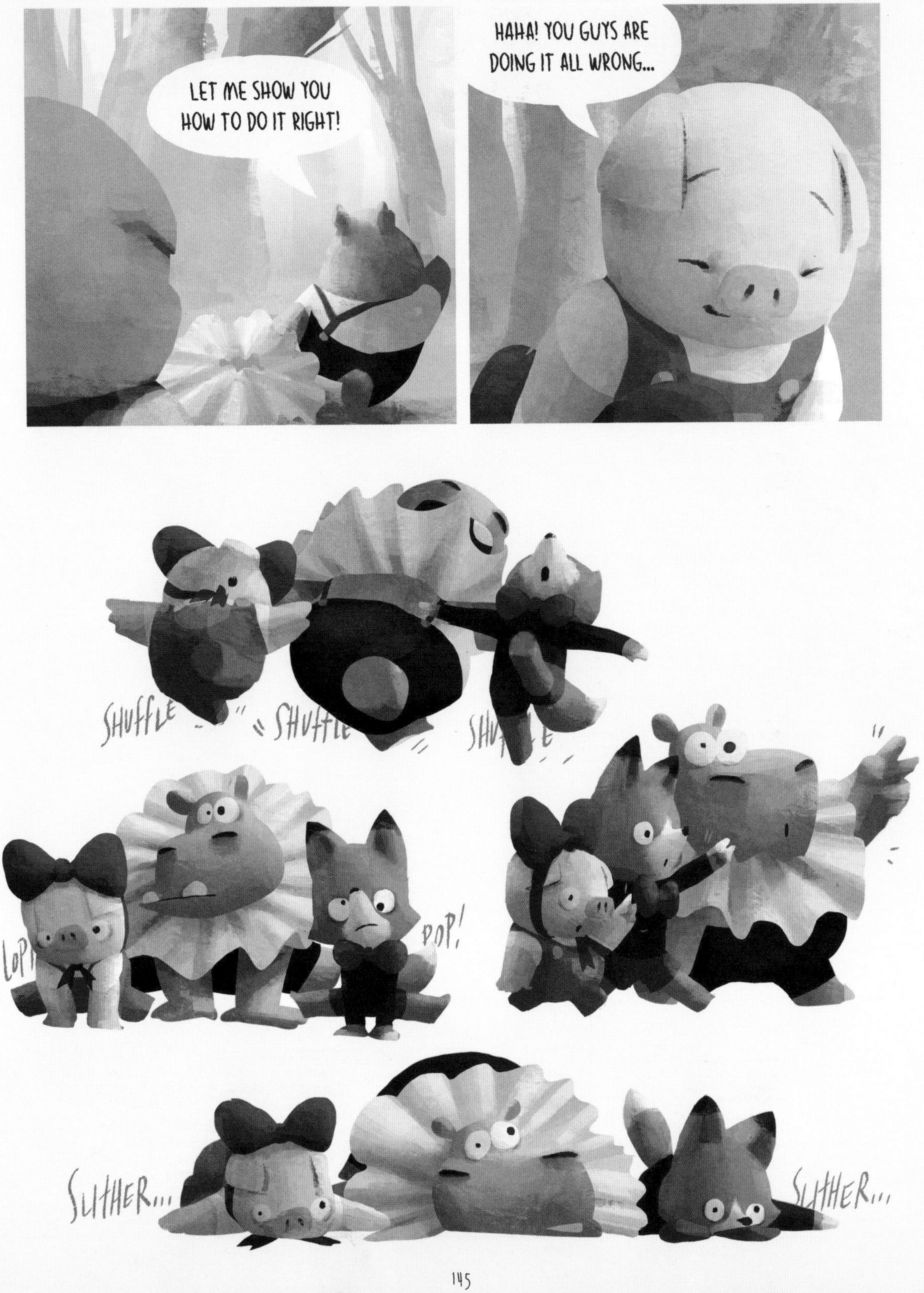
LET ME SHOW YOU HOW TO DO IT RIGHT!
HAHA! YOU GUYS ARE DOING IT ALL WRONG...
SHUFFLE
SHUFFLE
PLOP!
POP!
SLITHER...
SLITHER...

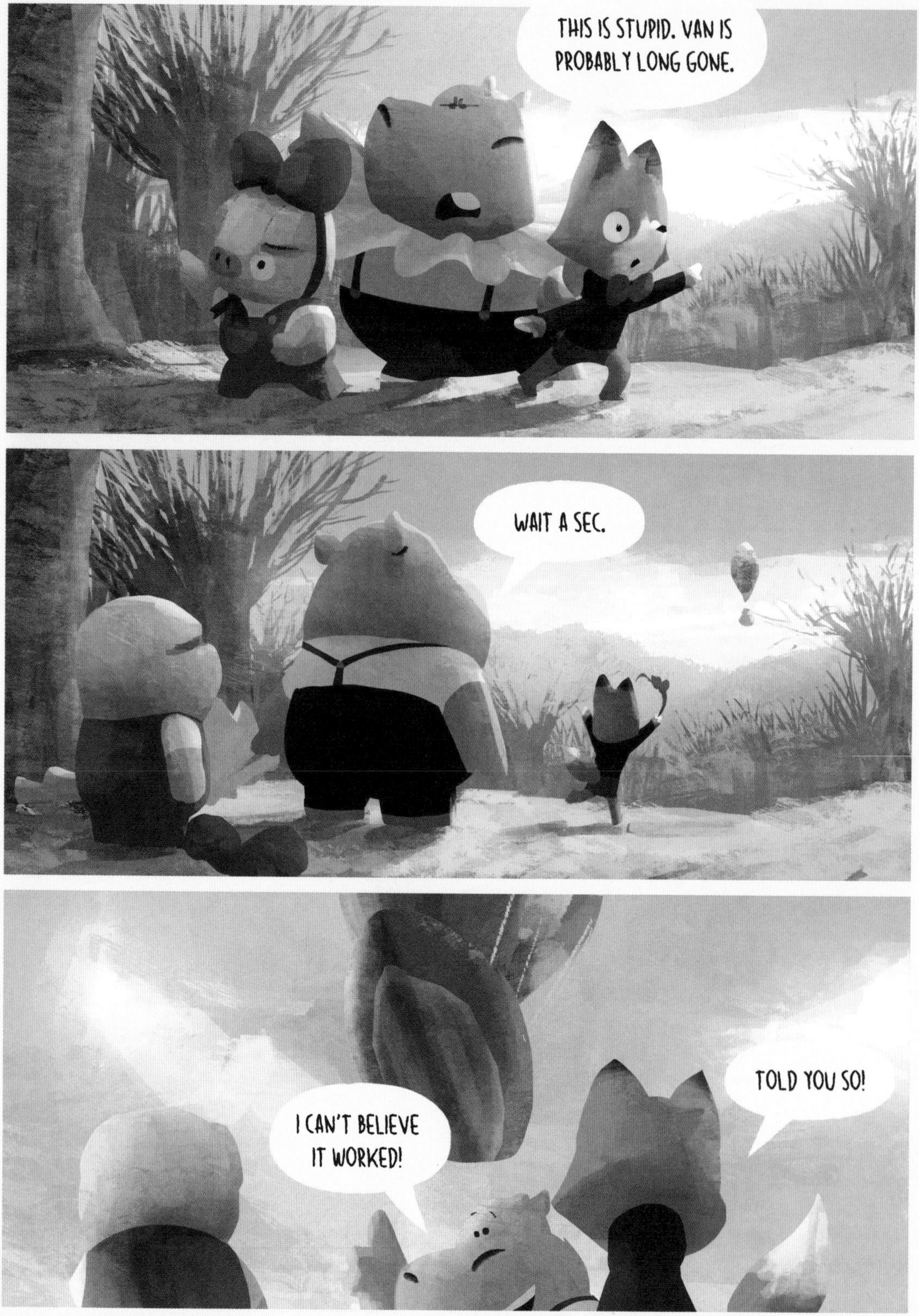
THIS IS STUPID. VAN IS PROBABLY LONG GONE.
WAIT A SEC.
I CAN'T BELIEVE IT WORKED!
TOLD YOU SO!

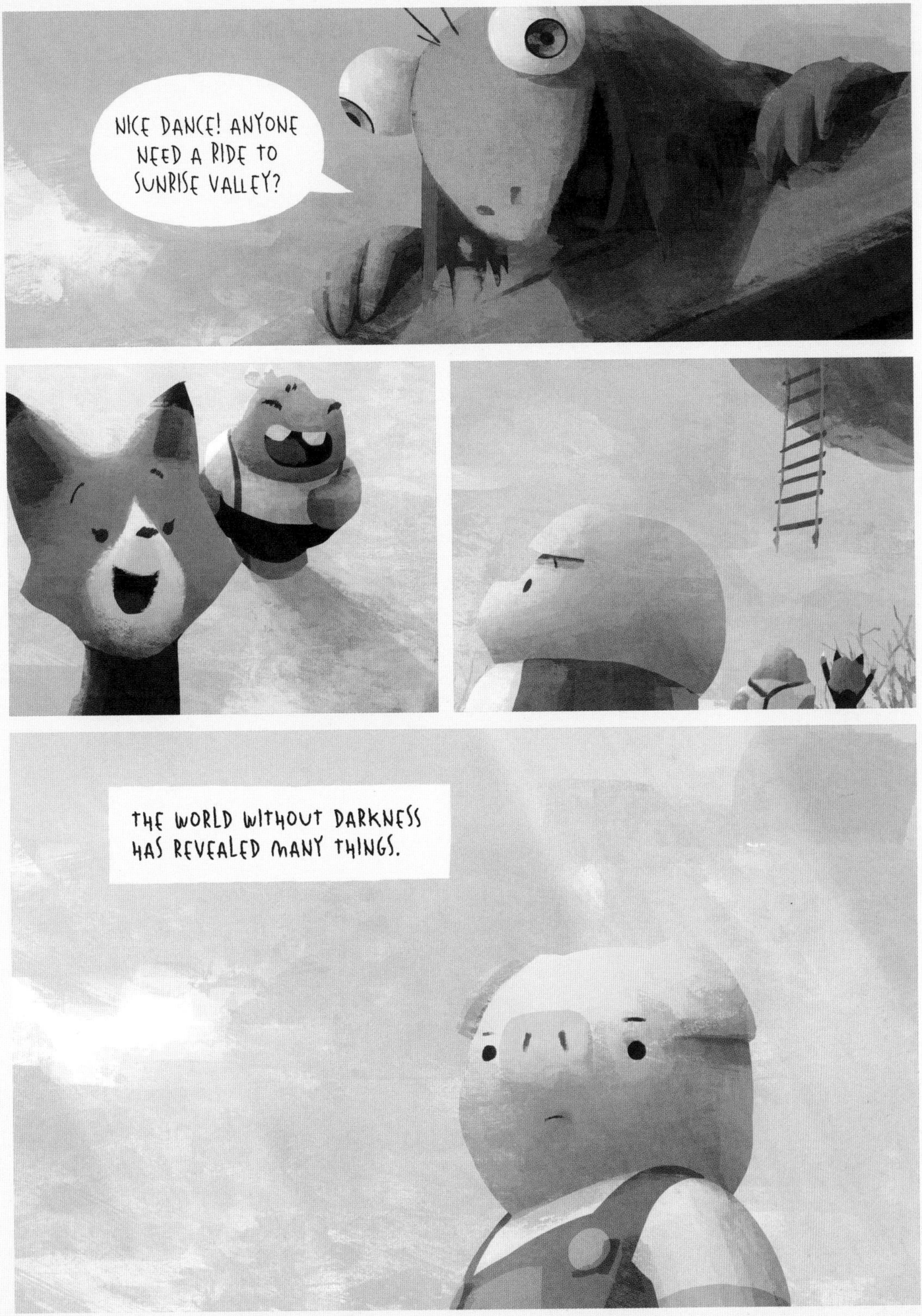
NICE DANCE! ANYONE NEED A RIDE TO SUNRISE VALLEY?
THE WORLD WITHOUT DARKNESS HAS REVEALED MANY THINGS.

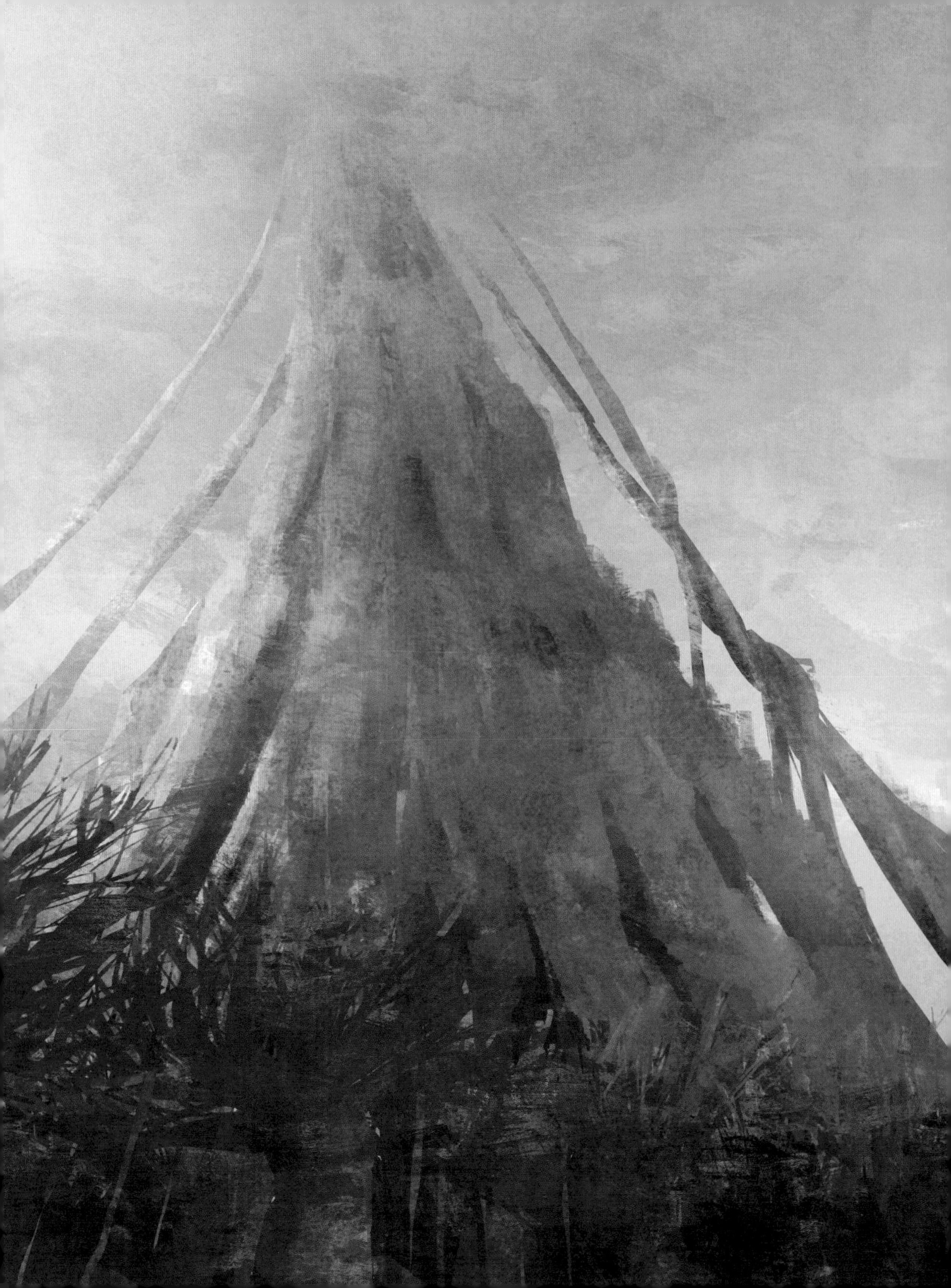

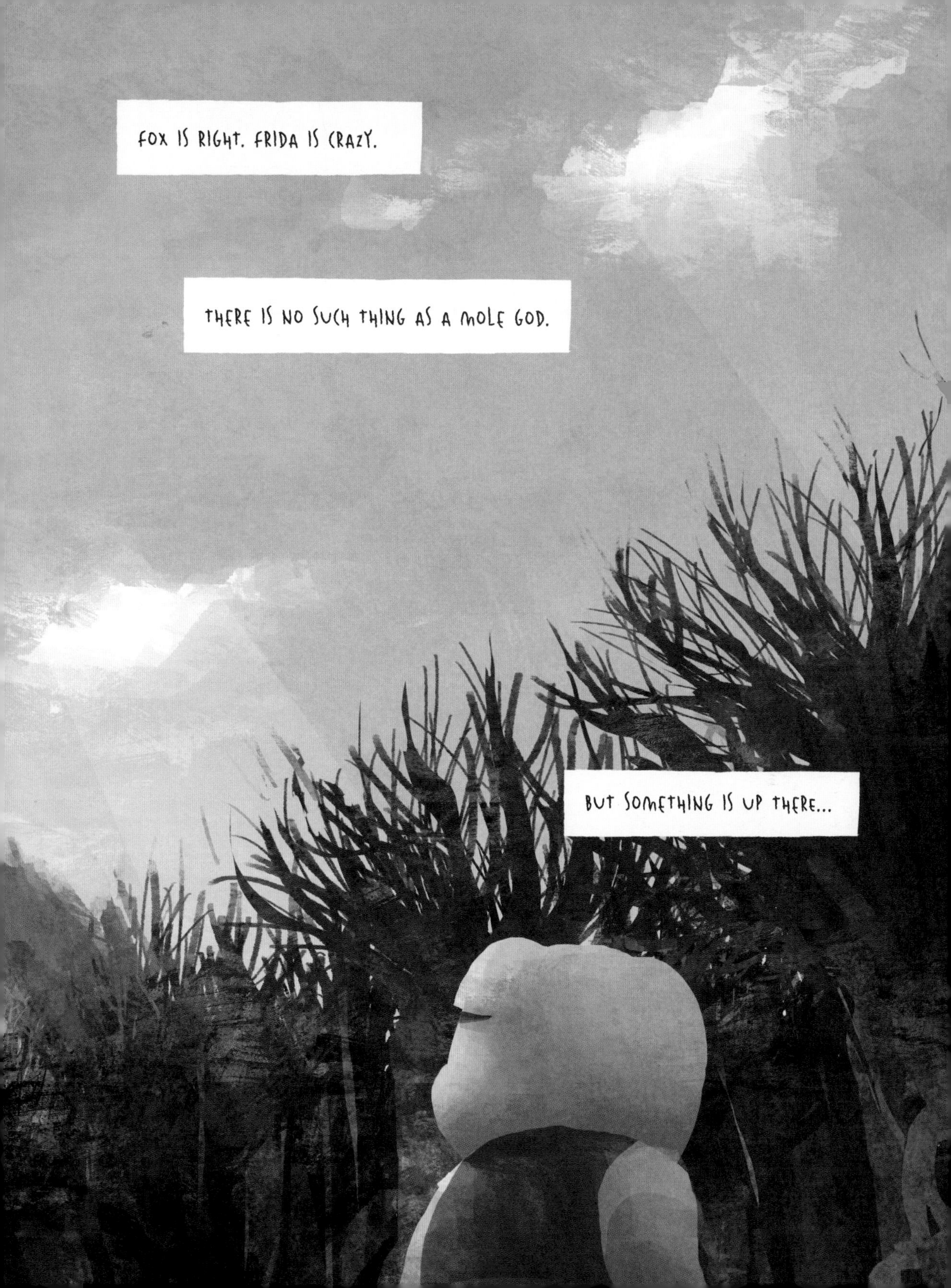
FOX IS RIGHT. FRIDA IS CRAZY.
THERE IS NO SUCH THING AS A MOLE GOD.
BUT SOMETHING IS UP THERE...

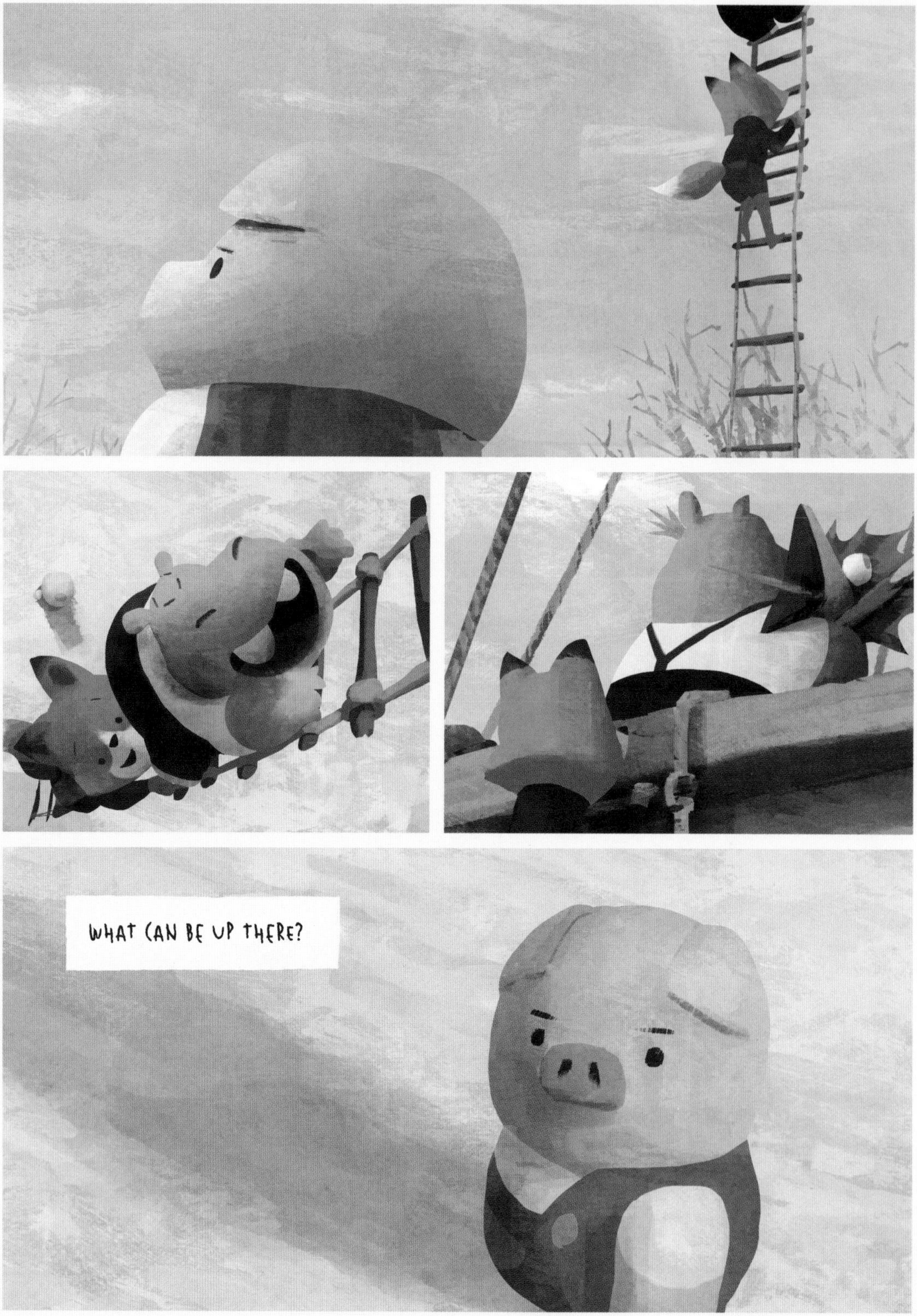
WHAT CAN BE UP THERE?

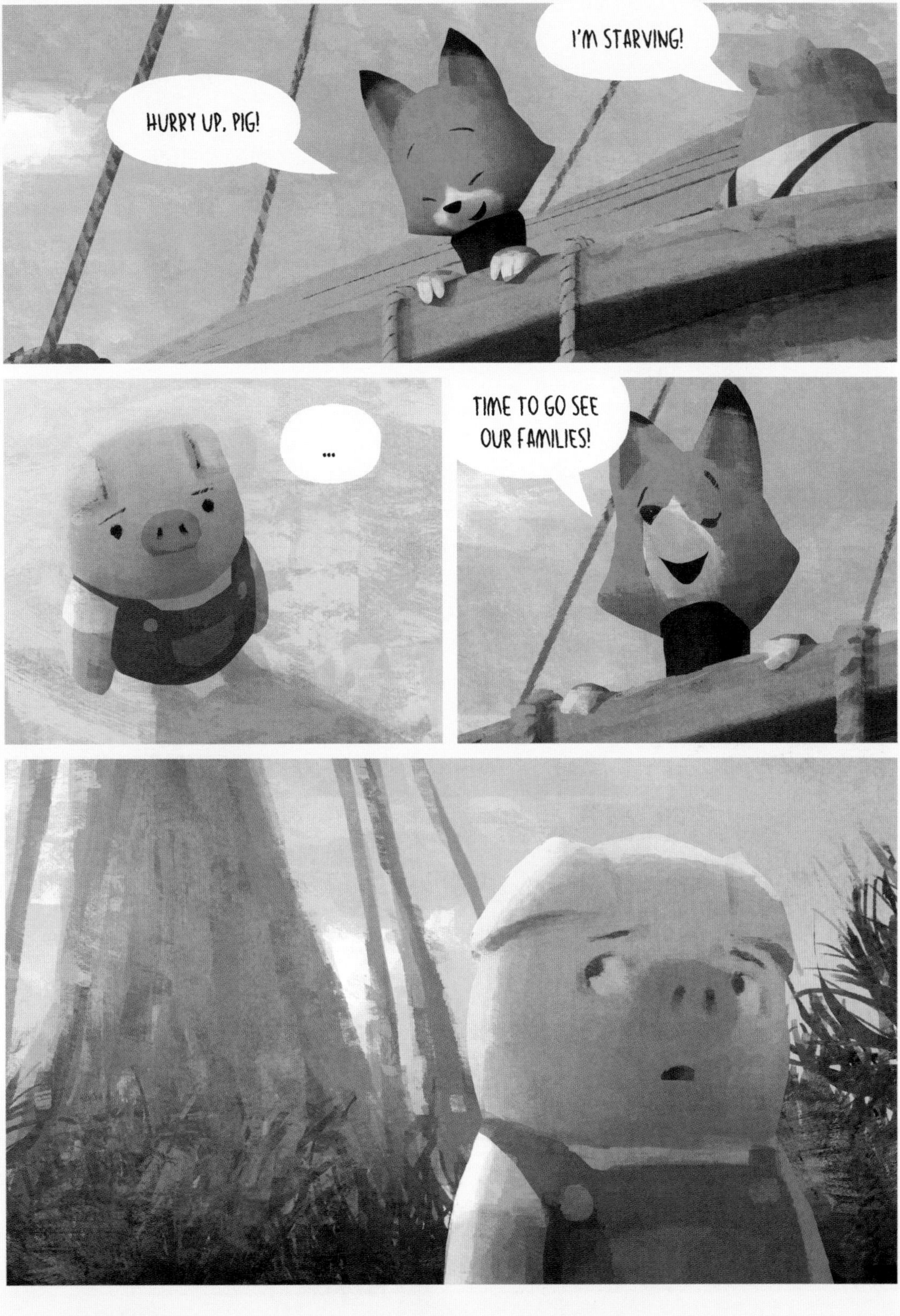
HURRY UP, PIG!
I'M STARVING!
...
TIME TO GO SEE OUR FAMILIES!

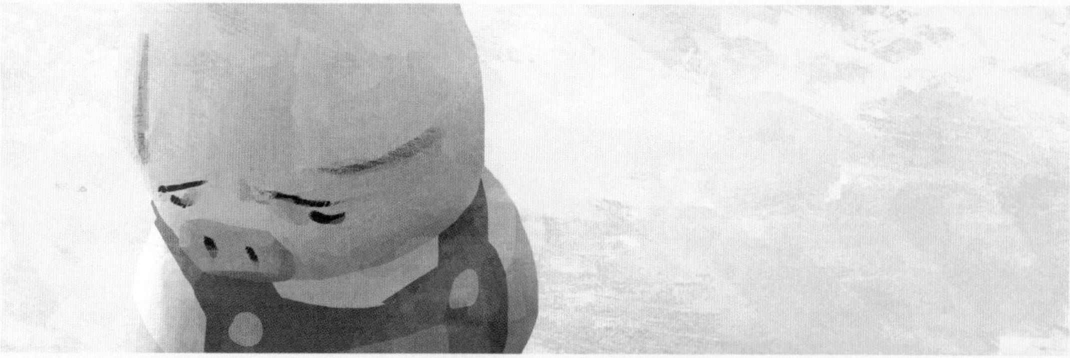

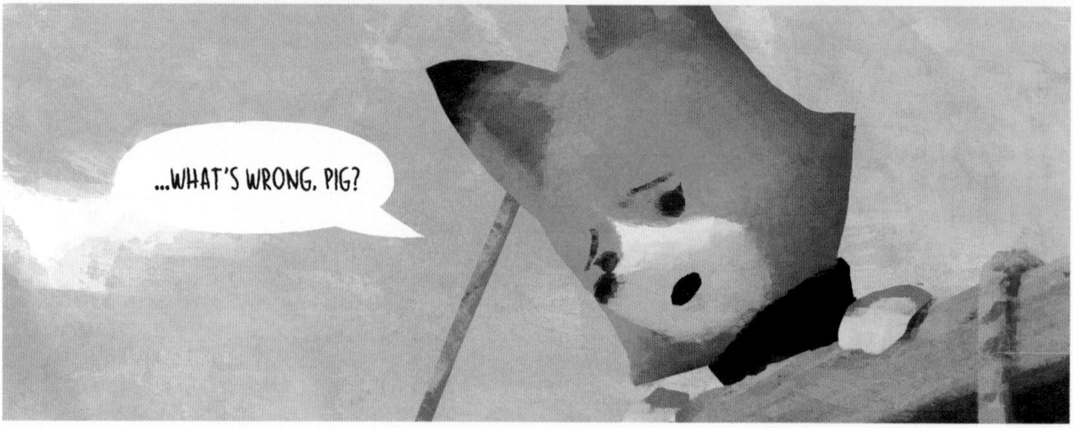
...WHAT'S WRONG, PIG?

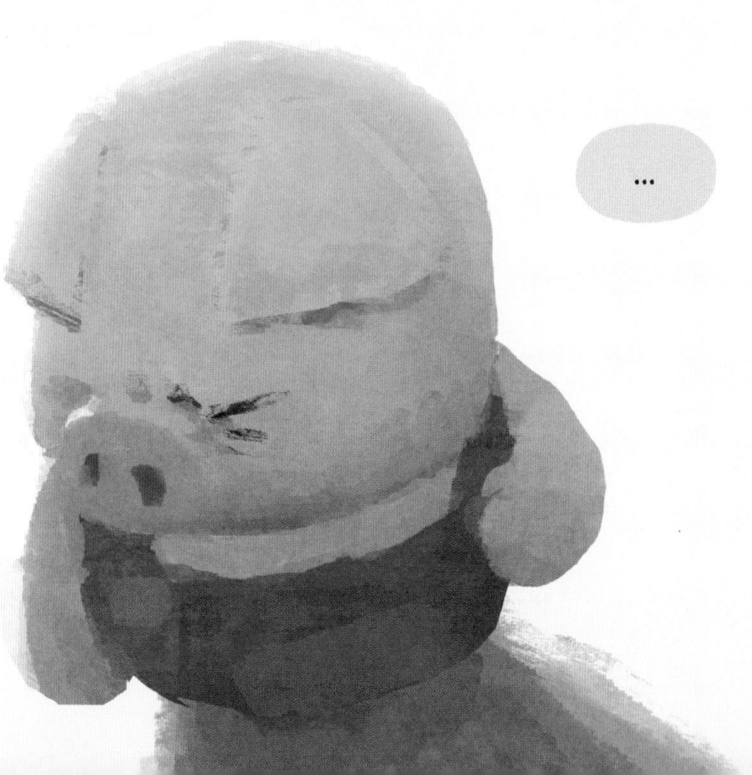
...

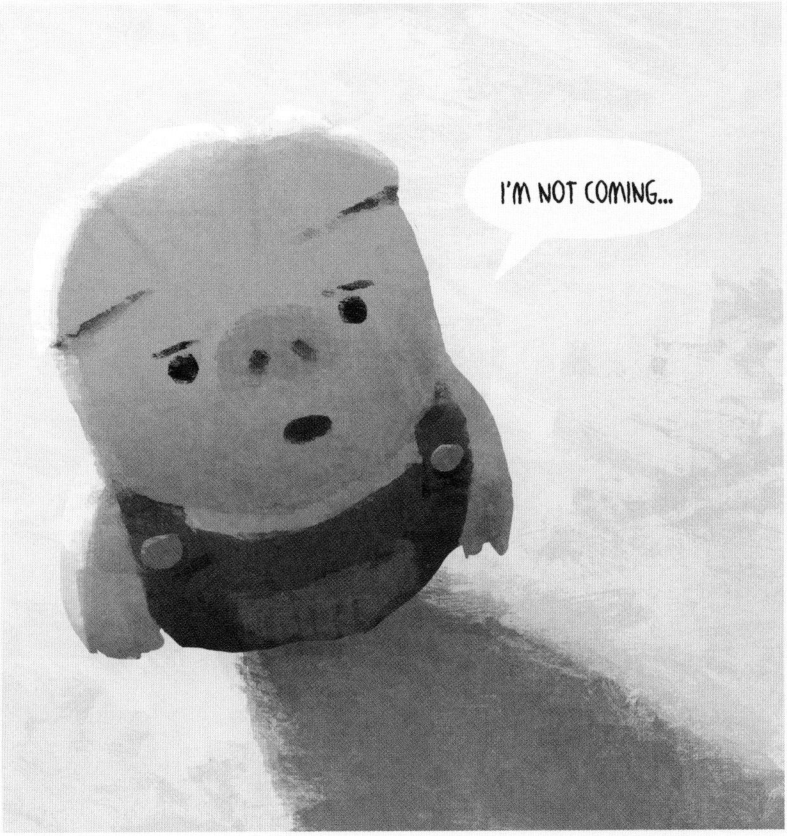
I'M NOT COMING...

THE ADVENTURE CONTINUES IN...

ROBERT KONDO and DICE TSUTSUMI
the
DAM KEEPER
RETURN FROM THE SHADOWS

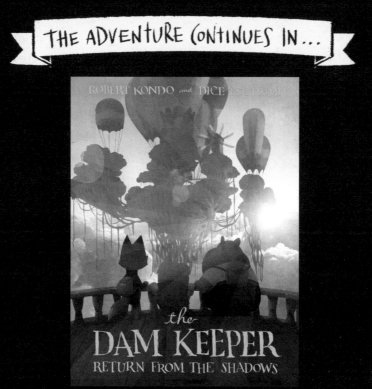

Special thanks to John Henry Hinkel, Asami Kanzaki, Namiko Yodono, Mark Siegel, Robyn Chapman, Gina Gagliano, Andrew Arnold, Kristin Dulaney, and the entire team at First Second and Macmillan Publishers.

First Second

Published by First Second
First Second is an imprint of Roaring Brook Press,
a division of Holtzbrinck Publishing Holdings Limited Partnership
175 Fifth Avenue, New York, NY 10010
All rights reserved

Library of Congress Control Number: 2017946149

ISBN: 978-1-62672-427-3

Our books may be purchased in bulk for promotional, educational, or business use.
Please contact your local bookseller or the Macmillan Corporate and Premium Sales Department
at (800) 221-7945 ext. 5442 or by e-mail atMacmillanSpecialMarkets@macmillan.com.

FIRST

EDITION

First edition, 2018
Book design by John Green

Printed in China by RR Donnelley Asia Printing Solutions Ltd., Dongguan City, Guangdong Province

Penciled with Shiyoon Kim's Wet Ink brush and painted with
Tonko House's custom paintbrush in Adobe Photoshop.

1 3 5 7 9 10 8 6 4 2

BY ART
WE LIVE